William C. Church

The Life of John Ericsson

William C. Church

The Life of John Ericsson

ISBN/EAN: 9783337332556

Printed in Europe, USA, Canada, Australia, Japan

Cover: Foto ©Andreas Hilbeck / pixelio.de

More available books at **www.hansebooks.com**

THE LIFE

OF

JOHN ERICSSON

BY

WILLIAM CONANT CHURCH
EDITOR OF THE ARMY AND NAVY JOURNAL

ILLUSTRATED

VOLUME I

NEW YORK
CHARLES SCRIBNER'S SONS
1906

PREFACE.

It was the declared wish of John Ericsson that I should tell the story of his life. The executors of his estate, Messrs. George H. Robinson and Cornelius S. Bushnell, have accordingly placed in my hands all of his letters and papers. His life-long friend, Mr. John O. Sargent, has freely opened to me the letters received from Captain Ericsson during fifty years of intimate intercourse and has given me the benefit of his recollections of the great engineer. The associates of Captain Ericsson in his office work, Mr. Samuel W. Taylor and Mr. Valdemar F. Lassöe, have also rendered me valuable assistance. To all of these gentlemen my thanks are due. While the task of sifting the voluminous correspondence and collecting the necessary facts has not been a light one, it has brought full compensation in the study of a great intellect and a generous heart.

W. C. C.

CONTENTS OF VOLUME I.

CHAPTER I.

EARLY YEARS IN SWEDEN.

CHAPTER II.

EXPERIENCE IN THE SWEDISH ARMY.

CHAPTER III.

ERICSSON IN ENGLAND.

CHAPTER VIII.

THE SCREW IN WAR VESSELS.

CHAPTER IX.

STOCKTON'S TREATMENT OF ERICSSON.

CHAPTER X.

SUCCESSES AND FAILURES.

CHAPTER XV.

INCEPTION OF THE MONITOR.

CHAPTER XVI.

BUILDING THE FIRST MONITOR.

CHAPTER XVII.

BATTLE BETWEEN THE MONITOR AND MERRIMAC.

CHAPTER XVIII.

THE SUCCESS OF THE MONITOR.

LIST OF ILLUSTRATIONS.

THE LIFE

OF

JOHN ERICSSON

"L'homme vertueux qui remplit fidèlement ses devoirs envers le pays qui l'a vu naître, a des droits à la reconnaissance de sa patrie. Le philanthrope qui voue ses lumières et ses veilles au bien-être de l'humanité entière, a droit de citoyen chez tous les peuples."—*Charles-Jean (Bernadotte), King of Sweden.*

LIFE OF JOHN ERICSSON.

CHAPTER I.

EARLY YEARS IN SWEDEN.

Birth.—Ancestry.—Parental Influences.—Youthful Home.—Early Education and Associations.—The Gnome Prophecy.—First Inventions.—The Göta Canal.

THE story of the development of special faculties under favoring conditions is always interesting, always instructive; and this is the story of John Ericsson. In him Nature and Opportunity combined their forces to produce the great engineer. The good seed falling upon good ground brought forth abundantly.

He was born at the opening of this century of mechanical achievement, on July 31, 1803, and was a native of Vermland, a division of Swedish territory nearly equivalent in size to British Wales or the American State of New Jersey. Vermland is one of the seven "läns" into which Central Sweden is divided, and follows the "län" of Stockholm in the order of importance. On its easterly boundary lies the mining district of Nordmark, and here, at the time of John's birth, resided his father, Olof Ericsson, Inspector of Mines at Långbanshyttan.

Whether or not we accept the theory that the physical and intellectual vigor to which Greater Britain owes its glory is of Scandinavian origin, it is beyond question that the Norseland has been, for more than two thousand years, the home of one of the most intelligent and energetic of peoples; a sturdy race which has never yielded to a foreign conqueror since Odin, with his Scythians from the Black Sea, colonized the Scandinavian peninsula. No kingdom of equal extent occupies a higher place in modern history than Sweden. In territory she is exceeded by California, and is scarcely more than one-half the size of Texas. In population she is outnumbered by the States of New York and Pennsylvania, and nearly equalled by the single city of London. Even when under Gustavus Adolphus she held chief place among the great powers of the world, her people did not exceed two millions and a half—a population

John Ericsson's Birthplace and Monument.

less than that of any one of half a dozen States of the American Union.

John Ericsson was a Swede of Swedes. Explaining his use of the signature of "Thule" on one occasion, he states that "Ultima Thule" was the home of his "remote ancestry;" not a very definite designation, for some locate Thule in Southern Norway, others in Iceland; and Procopius, the secretary of Belisarius, who described Scandinavia thirteen centuries ago, gave to it the name of "Thule." The family name suggests nothing, as Eric is simply the equivalent of the Italian Enrico, the Spanish Enrique, the German Heinrich, the English Henry, and the French Henri. The sons of Eric have always been numerous in Scandinavia, and they have been equally at home in the palaces of kings and the huts of the peasantry. Gustavus Vasa, before he was crowned, bore this name, as the son of Eric Johansson, the Swedish senator.

As far back certainly as the seventeenth century John Ericsson's ancestors were miners in the district where he was born. Sir John Sinclair,* who visited Sweden shortly before John's birth, describes this class of Swedes as tall, robust, active, and good-looking; loyal to the death, brave beyond question, and so honest that they could be trusted with anything. Robbery was almost unknown among them. They were civil, obedient, contented, and ardent lovers of their country; possessing, in short, the characteristics of those who have cultivated for generations unnumbered the virtues of a free people.

The first of this Ericsson family of whom we have any account was Magnus Stadig, a miner, who died in 1739. Magnus had a son Eric, born in 1724. He died in 1755, leaving a son Nils, born in 1747. Nils Ericsson advanced the family one step beyond their ancestral employment as laborers in the Nordmark mines. He was a mining proprietor and accumulated some property. This property was transmitted to his son Olof, the father of John, but Olof's inability to keep it returned the family to its original condition of poverty; so that among John's earliest recollections was that of the appearance of the sheriff selling the family furniture to satisfy the demands of importunate creditors.

A better inheritance than ancestral wealth was the education Olof received. To it were due the early influences that shaped the career of his sons. He was a graduate of the gymnasium, or college, of Karlstad, the principal town of Vermland. As Latin and Hebrew were part of the compulsory course, Olof was well educated, after the standards of his time. He was a clever mathematician and possessed an excellent mechanical judgment. He does not appear to have been a man of very

* Correspondence of the Right Hon. Sir John Sinclair, Bart., with Reminiscences of Distinguished Characters. Two vols. London, 1831.

vigorous personality, nor did he inherit a strong constitution, if we may judge from the record that he died at the age of forty, his father at forty-three, and his grandfather at thirty-one. Olof Ericsson is described as having been a man notable for his good looks, his amiability of disposition, and his devotion as a father. In 1799 he married Brita Sophia Yngström, of the same age as himself, twenty-one. Her family was of Flemish origin, and the marriage of her grandfather with a woman of Scottish descent introduced a strain of Caledonian blood into the veins of John.

Sir John Sinclair * reported a century ago that more than sixty of the noblest and most powerful families in Sweden were of Scotch extraction and proud of their origin. The Caledonian Swedes are descended from officers of the Scottish regiments who served with great distinction under Gustavus Adolphus in his German war and afterward settled in Sweden. Tradition does not tell us to what family of Scotch Swedes John Ericsson's great grandmother belonged, but the strains of blood that came to him through his mother must have been strong and rich in quality. Her family was originally named Horn, her father, John Ericsson's grandfather, having been compelled, while serving in his youth in the Swedish army, to change his name, to satisfy the susceptibilities of his commanding officer, a Count Horn of the illustrious Flemish line of that name. Jan Horn, or Yngström, seems to have been a man of a sturdy nature, for he refused to accept from Count Horn the money offered him in compensation for his patronymic. He would change his name he said, but would not be paid for doing so. Two generations later, his descendant, John Ericsson's brother Nils, was created a baron, and had the satisfaction of hanging his escutcheon in company with that of the proud Horns on the walls of the Swedish House of Knights.

If to his father he was indebted for his mechanical bent, it was from his mother, apparently, that John Ericsson derived some of his most distinguishing characteristics. She came of a longer-lived race, and lived to be seventy-five. She is described

* Correspondence of the Right Hon. Sir John Sinclair, Bart., with Reminiscences of Distinguished Characters. Two vols. London, 1831.

by a relative as a "warm-hearted, intellectual, high-spirited woman of great firmness of character, a cheerful disposition, and active habits; very handsome, tall and slender in figure, with magnificent light blue eyes that deepened in color, sparkling and flashing most brilliantly, when she was animated. Love of reading is a Swedish characteristic, and Sophie Ericsson studied ardently works of a philosophical, social, religious, and political character. She was fond of fiction and poetry as well, and if we are to judge by a little library she left, Walter Scott was among her favorite authors."

The family of Mrs. Ericsson had been mining proprietors and landowners in Vermland for several generations. "The bounty of God," said Duke Charles of Sweden three centuries ago, "has replenished the mountains of Vermland with all sorts of ores." The mining district where the Ericssons and Yngströms had so long lived has yielded its treasures for more than five hundred years, and during that time has developed a people of a striking individuality. The Vermlander is a mountaineer, and he exhibits in marked degree the sturdy independence and passionate local attachment distinguishing the highlander. He is moreover by nature cheerful, intelligent, industrious, persevering, frank, and hospitable.

Vermland lies among the chief watercourses and lakes of Sweden, within six degrees of the arctic circle, two degrees north of Sitka, Alaska, and in the latitude of southernmost Greenland. It is on the borders of Norway, on the direct line of travel between Stockholm and Christiania. During the Middle Ages it was the home of Swedish Robin Hoods, who levied toll upon the caravans carrying tribute to the Norwegian King from the subject province of Sweden, and it was long a debatable ground between the two Scandinavian kingdoms. In Ericsson's youth dense forests still covered portions of its territory, and in their hidden depths were to be found forgotten villages, depopulated by the "black death" of the fourteenth century.

Vermland is a region of legend, song, and romance, and here the old Norse spirit has been least influenced by modern change. It was the birthplace of Geijer, the historian and poet of Sweden. In its imposing scenery and primitive Scandinavian spirit he found inspiration for those Swedish folksongs

which were so powerfully influencing national sentiment at
the time John Ericsson's mind was receiving its strongest
impressions.   Here too was born Esias Tegner, the author of
" Frithiof Saga," and chief of those to whom Sweden owes the
Gothic revival that marked the opening of the present century.
It was in Vermland forests that Almquist sought in 1823 to
establish a colony which was to return to the old Norse principle of natural living, and to the old Norse paganism likewise.
To be a Vermlander, in short, is to be a Swede of the inten-
sest and most distinctive type.

In its natural features Vermland is a confusion of mountains, streams, and lakes.   Across it extend spurs from a range
of snow-clad hills whose northern limit is within the arctic
circle.   These mountains are the spine of the Scandinavian
peninsula, and the dividing line between Sweden and Norway.
From their eastern slopes flow across Swedish territory the
streams emptying into the Gulf of Bothnia, and from the west
come the rivers whose waters pour into the Atlantic through
the Norwegian fiords whence Harold the Fairhaired and Rolf
the Ganger set forth a thousand years ago upon those conquests " momentous at this day, not to England alone, but to all
speakers of the English tongue, now spread from side to side
of the world in a wonderful degree."

Through the narrow rifts or valleys separating the mountain
ridges of Vermland flow southward numerous swift streams, of
which the river Klar is chief.   These streams empty at the
south into Lake Venern, the boundary of the district, and
chief of European lakes, Lake Ladoga in Russia alone excepted.   East of Elfdale, as the central valley of the Klar is
called, rise numerous hills, none exceeding twelve or thirteen
hundred feet in height.   Here are found those ores of iron
famed the world over, from which is wrought the steel used in
the best cutlery.   The soil in Vermland is scanty and yields
meagre returns, though the Vermland plough is famous throughout Sweden.

The scenes and circumstances of John Ericsson's early life
in this glorious mountain region, and among these primitive
people, were sure to powerfully influence a nature so intense as
his.   After he left Sweden his affections seem never to have

rooted themselves elsewhere, and he turned toward the home of his youth with always ardent devotion. "I am so entirely Swedish," he wrote in the midst of his triumphs, "that I cannot bear the thought that I am believed to have forgotten, or set aside in preference for some other, our beautiful mother tongue, 'the language of glory and heroes!'"

Belief in the utterance of Volvas or Sibyls is one of the ancient superstitions of Scandinavia. So the ancient Swede who announced to the family of the Yngströms that there should be born to them two sons who would be famous the world over found sufficient credence to secure a place in the family annals.

In the middle of the seventeenth century, when Brita Sophia's father was a young man, he had in his service a poor cripple, who, during the summer, drove his cattle into the depths of the forest in search of pasture. In a measure his deformity shut "lame Eric" out from his kind, and he was more at home with the birds and the brooks, his friendly herds and the wild animals who had grown accustomed to his harmless presence. Alone with them and his own meditations he had abundant opportunity to cultivate the spirits of the wood and had unquestioning faith in their existence. On one occasion Eric failed of his customary weekly visit to Långbanshyttan, and when search was made he was found lying sick in a lonely barn. With illness added to his solitude, strange fancies had come to him, and he reported the visit of a friendly gnome who brought report that a house was soon to be built at a certain point on the Yngström property, and that there should be born two boys "whose names would be known the world over."

This story became a tradition in the Yngström family, and when Brita Sophia went to housekeeping with her young husband in a little one-story cottage with a turfed roof, inherited from her father, and standing on the very spot the gnome had indicated, she was sufficiently impressed with the prophecy to remember it when the time for its application came.

After her marriage to Olof Ericsson in 1799 she bore to him three children, Caroline in 1800, Nils in 1802, and John in 1803. The young husband was part owner of a mine and also superintendent of the works at Långbanshyttan, a region noted for the beauty of its scenery. Mountains covered with

fir enclosed narrow valleys where lay hidden tiny lakes, their
shores bordered by leafy woods, showing here and there among
the clearings clusters of cottages, the homes of an industrious
people; prosperous and contented after their fashion, for Swedish country life was at that time of the most frugal sort.

Shut out from the great world by the inaccessibility of their
position, they were a primitive folk, simple in their habits and
wholly removed from the French influences and ideas controlling at the capital; for France and Sweden were at this period
united by a common dislike of Russia, and every effort was
made by the French to maintain intimate relations with their
ally. So powerful was the influence of the French in Sweden
toward the end of the last century and the beginning of this,
that they were accustomed to say that they kept the Swedes,
as they kept the Turks, "like wild beasts in their dens, to be
let loose for fighting whenever they desired."

The Ericsson family would have commanded attention anywhere. The daughter was a child of unusual beauty and the
boys were handsome, intelligent, and spirited. John was the
wonder of the neighborhood. From the very first he exhibited
the qualities distinguishing him in later life. He was ceaseless
in his industry; busied from morning to night drawing, planning, and constructing. The machinery at the mines was to
him an endless source of wonder and delight. In the early
morning he hastened to the works, carrying with him a draw-
ing-pencil, bits of paper, pieces of wood, and his few rude tools.
There he would remain the day through, seeking to discover
the principles of motion in the machines, and striving to copy
their forms.

When it came to learning his letters, the precocious John
had opinions of his own as to how they should be formed. He
quickly perceived that the characters set before him were symbols, and he was discovered one day on the shore of the little
lake "Hytt," bordering the homestead, drawing in the sand
characters that suited his fancy better than those of the Swedish alphabet. There was born with this sturdy spirit an uncon-
querable disposition to rebel against routine. Usually the boy
was too much occupied with his studying and contriving to
join in the pastimes of other children. When the family left

home, on some one of those excursions that furnish the mild excitements of rural life, he would run down to open the gate for them and then return to his drawing-board and his work-box, delighted to find himself alone and free to follow his own devices. Among his treasures was found a collection of drawings —circles, lines, squares, and curves in great variety; not the meaningless pencillings of a child at play, but complete mechanical sketches representing the machinery of the mines and saw-mills of the district.

The elder brother, Nils, was more fond of pleasure, but his subsequent career as an engineer shows also the influence of early training, for Olof Ericsson sought in every way to encourage the mechanical occupations of his sons; and John remembered his father with special affection as the one who had first stimulated into activity the faculties in whose exercise he was to find the joy of his life.

Olof Ericsson made no name for himself, but the world owes him honor for what he did for his children. The Chinese ennoble the ancestors and not the descendants of those who do the state service, and the custom has its foundation in reason; great men, good men, useful men are the product of the high thought and noble aspiration, the useful labors, and the self-discipline of their ancestors. In the curious kaleidoscopic changes of character produced by the admixture of bloods, almost every pattern may appear, but none the material for which could not be found in ancestral inheritance.

The years from 1811 to 1814 were trying ones for the Swedes; the war with Russia, depriving them of Finland, was in progress, and the freaks of the insane Gustavus IV. kept the little kingdom in constant turmoil. Business did not thrive; many were ruined, and among them Olof Ericsson. The happy life at Långsbanshyttan was ended, the home there broken up, and the Ericsson family were for the first time brought face to face with the rude realities of life. The father had been educated for prosperity; he was a man of sensitive and refined rather than of robust nature; his son tells us that "he could not bear the smell of a peasant," and to a peasant's condition he had now come. The blow was a cruel one, and Olof Ericsson would have sunk under it had he not been sustained by the courage

and vigor of his wife. A hard winter followed and the misery
of the distressed family was great.   But the old life was ended
that a new and better one might open before them, and their
opportunity soon came, as the hopeful mother had insisted that
it would.

The project of the Göta Canal, with which the fortunes of
the Ericssons were to be identified, was revived at this time.

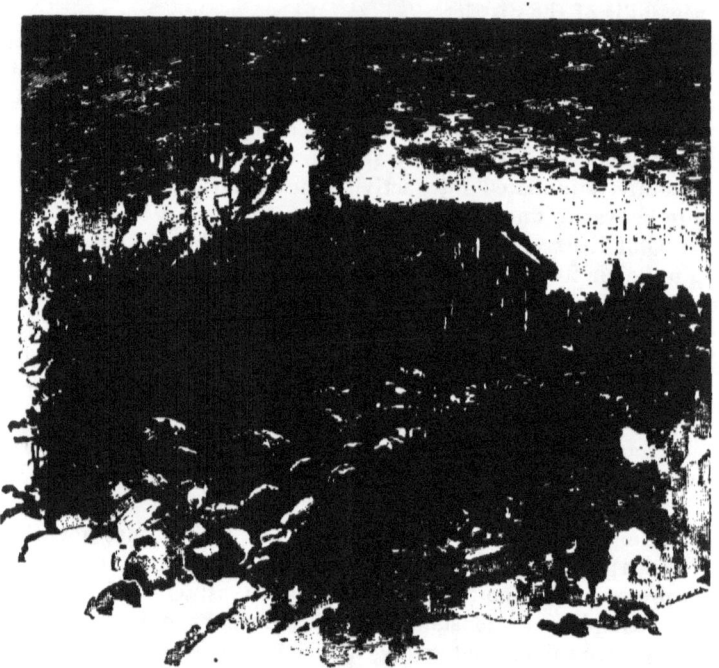

Ericsson's Home after his Father's Failure.

Olof Ericsson secured the position of engineer or foreman in
charge of a gang of men engaged in blasting rock on the line
of the canal, his station being at Forsvik, near Lake Vettern,
one hundred miles from his old home among the mountains of
Vermland. The purpose of this canal was to establish ship
navigation across the Swedish peninsula by a series of short

canals connecting a chain of navigable waters stretching across the country, and improving the navigation of the Göta River, which carries the waters of Lake Venern into the North Sea. The first suggestion of this improvement is traced to a Swedish bishop, Brock, who proposed it in 1526, during the reign of King Gustavus Vasa. For nearly two hundred years the proposition slumbered, until, in 1716, the attention of Emanuel Swedenborg was called to it by his brother-in-law, Eric Benzelius, at that time librarian of Upsala, afterward archbishop, and always a tireless delver after forgotten facts.

Swedenborg, whose scientific and engineering reputation has been discredited by his later claims to seership, was then in the service of Charles XII. as "Assessor Extraordinary of the College of Mines." To the King he went, full of the plan thus suggested to him. His proposal that the project of the time of the Great Gustavus should be revived was received with eagerness by Charles, for the possession by Denmark of the "Sound" had closed the natural exit for Swedish vessels from the Baltic. During the succeeding year Swedenborg was surveying the route for the canal, and in February, 1718, he was ordered to undertake the work at the King's expense. The death of Charles, on December 11, 1718, put an end to the project for a time.

Swedenborg declared that the Göta Canal "would have been the wonder of the world if it had been completed," and a recent traveller tells us that having been completed it justly ranks as one of the engineering triumphs of the age. From the sea level to the summit is one hundred and fifty feet, and yet vessels of large size have no trouble in ascending or descending. "It is curious to see steamships half way up a hill, as helpless as turtles turned on their backs. To stand on the deck and serenely contemplate the watery steps before you, or shudderingly look at the slippery staircase behind, is very novel and well worth a trial. All this happens at Akersvass, where there are eleven locks now in use, and several others half ruined—the remnants of philosopher Swedenborg's plans." *

In Swedenborg's time the canal does not appear to have pro-

* Aalesund to Tetuan, a Journey. By Charles R. Corning. Cupples & Hurd.

gressed farther than the partial completion of an enormous sluice, sixty feet deep. Remains of this are still shown. This sluice and two others were completed by Viman, whose work succeeded that of Swedenborg, or rather of Polheim, Councillor of Commerce, and Swedenborg's superior officer in the direction of this undertaking. In 1755 the malicious discharge of an enormous quantity of timber over the Trolhetta Falls destroyed the locks and the labor thus far expended was lost.

For more than half a century the canal waited upon fate until it was once more taken in hand, this time by Count von Platen. Meanwhile the science of canal building had made great progress in Holland and England. Thomas Telford, chief of canal builders at that day, had completed the Elsmere Canal, joining the Mersey to the Dee and the Severn, and was busied with the grander project of the Caledonian Canal, opening a water-way across the highlands of Scotland from the Atlantic to the North Sea. In 1808 Telford was invited to Sweden by Count Platen and made a careful survey for the Göta Canal, which presented precisely the same difficulties as those he was contending with in Scotland.

After working for two months, with a corps of assistants, Telford sent to Platen an elaborate report with detailed plans and sectional drawings. These were accepted and excavation began. In 1810 Telford again visited Sweden to inspect the work, leaving this time drawings for the locks and bridges. The relations of England to Sweden were so friendly that he was permitted to furnish the Swedish contractors with patterns of the tools he used in canal making and to provide them with experienced lock-makers and navvies from England for the purpose of instructing the native workmen.

Thus were the latest results of English engineering experience carried into the wilds of Sweden, and brought to the very door of the Ericssons, where the busy brain of the boy John was already occupied with the study of such mechanical contrivances and engineering undertakings as were within his reach.

A new career was opening to Sweden. Internal dissensions were ended by a grant of the constitution now in force, the termination of the royal line by the abdication of the insane King Gustavus IV., in 1809, and the death of his uncle and

successor, Charles XIII., in the year following. A vigorous
soldier, Bernadotte, a Marshal of Napoleon, had assumed authority over Sweden as elected Crown Prince. The enterprise,
originated in the time of the first of the great soldiers controlling Scandinavia, Gustavus I., and commenced by that other
great military sovereign, Charles XII., appealed at once to the
instinct of Bernadotte. Its nature was military no less than
commercial, for it was essential to the defence of a kingdom
whose vessels were shut into the narrow Baltic by foreign control of the only passage out. The enterprise henceforth proceeded with as much vigor as the circumstances of the times
would permit, under the direction of the Mechanical Corps of
the Swedish Navy.

CHAPTER II.

Autobiographical Account of Ericsson's Early Life.—Finds a Friend in
Count von Platen.—Training on the Göta Canal.—Death of Erics-
son's Father.—Becomes a Soldier.—Military Life in Jemtland.—
Wonderful Gymnastic Skill and Physical Strength.—Promoted to
a Lieutenantcy and Appointed Government Surveyor.—Birth of a
Son.—His Flame Engine.

WHEN Olof Ericsson, in 1811, removed from Långbanshyttan to Forsvik, in the län of Skaraborg or Mariestad, his eldest son, Nils, was nine years old, and John was
eight. Up to this time the boys appear to have been dependent
largely upon home instruction for their education. Indeed, in a
fragment of autobiography left by Nils, he relates that he had
no other education previous to 1814. This did not agree with
the recollection of the younger brother, and John's eagerness
for knowledge in his youth makes him much the more reliable
witness. A letter in Swedish, addressed in 1879 to a relative
in Stockholm, gives some interesting particulars of his early
education. In this John says:

MY DEAR HJALMAR: Thanks for your letter of the 26th of April,
enclosing a copy of Nils Ericsson's autobiography. It was with the
greatest surprise I read this incomplete and very erroneous account.
I have also received the biography of the deceased engineer, written by
Major Adelskold at the request of the Royal Academy of Science. I
have read with great sorrow and indignation the biography reflecting on
my father's character and representing him as neglecting the education
of his sons No reproach could be more unjust. Olof Ericsson made
all possible sacrifices to give us a good education.

To begin with, he had in his house as a governess during the years
1811 and 1812, Mrs. Malmborg from Vermland, and I remember thank-
fully all she taught me. At the same time he gave free board to the
talented controller who was then employed at the station of Forsvik,

that he might teach us drawing and the modern English style, which he executed in a manner rivalling that of the most skilful engravers. Our father also secured for us permission from the chief, Captain Forsell, to draw in the office of the draughtsmen of the canal company. Thus I secured the opportunity in the year 1811 to make my first drawing to the scale. I was also enabled to learn the art of drawing maps, and by the end of the year 1812 could make a pretty accurate drawing, had an excellent knowledge of drawing instruments and was well skilled in their use.

In the year 1813 my father succeeded in persuading the renowned director of instruction, Pohl, to give me lessons in architectural drawing. During the winter of 1813-14, while we were living at the saw-mills of Edet, where my father was commissioned to select the timber for the lock gates of the west line of the canal, he kept in his house, as a tutor for his sons, Dr. Azelius, a near relative of the celebrated chemist.

Of course he plagued us with lessons in the Latin grammar, etc., but I learned from him many other things of use to me; for instance, how to make and mix, out of materials obtained at the druggist's for a few cents, the colors required for my drawings. In the summer of 1814 we were living in the parish of Fredsberg, on the beautiful Lefsäng, near Hajstorp station, where my father held a position next to that of the chief of the work. Then he got permission from the Court Chaplain to employ the curate at Lefsäng to teach his boys French.

During the same period our indefatigable father succeeded in persuading the greatest mechanical draughtsman at that time in Sweden, Lieutenant Brandenburg, of the Mechanical Corps of the Navy, to teach us the modern art of shading or finishing off of mechanical drawings. The great draughtsman was also good enough to make for us drawings to serve as models for our guidance. These I afterward used as patterns until I was able in some measure to emulate the master's skill.

On one of his visits to Lefsäng, Lieutenant Brandenburg was accompanied by the skilful Captain J. Edstrom, just returned from England. This warm-hearted man took such a liking to Brandenburg's pupils that he advised our father to take us, without loss of time, to Count Platen and show him our little works. The great man, who was then living at Halmatorp, encouraged us with many kind words, and in a few months the boys Nils and John Ericsson were appointed cadets in the Mechanical Corps of the Swedish Navy. Its uniform we had the honor of wearing until the authorities of the company resolved to receive 'Canal Pupils.' It was not long after I entered the draughtsman's office of the Canal Company at Tåtorp before I was able to make, under Captain Edstrom's friendly and useful direction, profiles, maps, and working drawings required in the construction of the canal.

As early as the summer of 1815, Captain Edstrom commissioned me to make drawings for the archives of the Canal Company, and in the year 1816, at the age of thirteen, I was assistant leveller at the station of

Riddarhagen. In the year 1817 I was the only leveller at Rottkilms station, on the west line of the canal. In 1818, at the age of fourteen and three-quarter years, I secured the position of leveller on the east line of the canal at the station of Norsholm, under the command of Lieutenant Ryding, chief of the works. My salary was then thirty crowns a month with quarters and travelling expenses.

This extraordinarily quick promotion, the ability to fulfil the duties of an officer required to make the plans and calculations needed for the work of the canal, after comparatively little practice, does not bear witness to a neglected education. The want of learning of which

Headquarters Göta Canal Company.

my brother complains I never felt, probably because I devoted all my leisure hours to study, while he was occupied with society. It is certain that when I entered the Swedish Army in 1820, at the age of seventeen, I would not have exchanged my knowledge for that possessed by any of the youth who had passed their time at the university. When I arrived in England, at the age of twenty-two and three-quarter years, I was not only equal, but superior to the English engineers in acquired skill. This brief account should be sufficient to refute the accusation that Olof Ericsson neglected the education of his sons.

At another time I will give you a fuller account of what his youngest son did in Sweden from the time when, in 1809, seventy years ago, he dug his first mine, twelve inches in depth, and made for it with his little hands, a ladder and windlass, until the day when, in Jemtland, he made his final experiment in raising water by means of a vacuum created by condensing flame.

My father wrote a beautiful hand and was an excellent bookkeeper and accountant. He possessed keen discernment in mechanical matters and was a great admirer of Polhem. Before I was eleven years old, the "mining laborer" had, among other things, taught me to construct an ellipse, and how to overcome the difficulty connected with the rotary motion of the angles by the use of a ball-and-socket joint. The "mining laborer" also taught me at the same time how to create a vacuum and raise water by the condensation of flame. I shall never forget the joy I experienced when my father extinguished the confined flame and I for the first time saw the water rising in the glass cylinder.

Nor is it true that my mother "assisted in providing for her family by keeping a restaurant for the laborers." My father's salary was sufficient for the support of his family, but she was persuaded to take as boarders the civil and military officers located at Forsvik station during the years 1811–12. This charge she fulfilled rather as a hostess than as the keeper of a boarding-house, and the result was most unfortunate for my father. At the end of the two years he was deeply in debt to the tradesmen at Mariestad, who provided groceries for the too liberal table. In 1818, after the death of my father, and when her sons were officers upon the canal, my mother again undertook to board the officers belonging to the different stations. As everybody saw that she set too generous a table and was always losing money, she was given permission to brew a liquor to sell to the troops. This enabled her to make good her losses and to pay the debts she had contracted against her husband. I recollect so well the pride with which the sensitive wife told me that she had sent the last payment to her husband's creditors. "Nobody," she said, "can now insult me by reminding me that they have suffered loss of money through my husband." After my father left his position at Hajstorp station he was employed at the quarantine station of Kanso, where he died, in the summer of 1818, after a long illness, during which he was nursed by my mother.

The statements of the two brothers can be reconciled by assigning that of Nils, concerning his dependence upon his mother for his education, to the period preceding his father's transfer to work upon the Göta Canal. The Captain Edstrom referred to in the letter quoted was "Chief of the Central Canal District," and one of the two Swedish engineers, Lagerheim being the other, sent by Count Platen to England,

2

at the expense of the Canal Company, for the purpose of obtaining exact information concerning the details of canal construction. These two officers returned in 1815, thoroughly informed as to the best engineering work of that time, and proceeded to instruct a number of pupils, cadets of the Swedish Corps of Mechanical Engineers. The Ericsson brothers were among these cadets; John being then eleven years old and Nils twelve. During the winter of 1816–17 John received lessons in chemistry and algebra from Professor Rasl, of local reputation, who was engaged upon the canal. He was also taught field-drawing and geometry by a German engineer officer, Captain Pentz, who was building the fortification of Wanas at the mouth of the Göta Canal, on Lake Vettern. He learned English from the English controller of the works at Hajstorp station, and had the opportunity to practise it with Englishmen employed on the canal.

The particulars I have given of John Ericsson's early education are important in their bearing upon his future career. While his eagerness for instruction was extraordinary, and his capacity for absorbing knowledge unusual, his opportunity for acquirement was also a rare one for that time and place—indeed for any time and place—combining, as his instruction did, the practical and the theoretical. He learned thoroughly the art of presenting his ideas through the medium of mechanical drawings and made himself independent of models. To a friend who once said to him, "It is a pity you did not graduate from a technological institute," Ericsson replied, "No, it was very fortunate. Had I taken a course at such an institution I should have acquired such a belief in authorities that I should never have been able to develop originality and make my own way in physics and mechanics, as I now propose to do." "The end," writes his friend, Count Rosen, in the letter quoted from, "has proved your words true."

Except for the advantageous circumstances of John Ericsson's youth his faculties could not have received the early development which made possible his subsequent achievements; for continually occasions arose when his facility in handling the tools of his profession was an important element in his success. His extraordinary natural ability having been thus developed by early training, he was able to do as much at the drawing-board in a given time as two ordinary men. Not only did nature endow Ericsson with an aptitude for his chosen profession amounting to genius, but fortune also favored him with exceptional opportunities for early training in its mysteries.

The encouragement he received from Platen had also a deciding influence in determining Ericsson's future career. "Continue as you have begun," he said to John, "and you will one day produce something extraordinary." The lad was not one to forget such a greeting. When nearly seventy years old, writing of another who in his youth had shown him similar kindness, he said, "I always held him in the greatest esteem; he often encouraged me, and I have not yet forgotten his words. What he said to the warm-hearted boy were not empty words, and the grain he sowed has borne fruit." Even at the time he was introduced to Count Platen the future engineer had astonished the local gossips with a saw-mill, pumping-engine, and a set of drawing instruments which he had made, "all out of his own head." Certainly he had no other tools than a gimlet and a jack-knife. The saw-mill and pump were not childish attempts at imitation; they were practical working models, needing only to be repeated upon a larger scale to be useful machines. The boy was then only nine years old, and we may imagine the delight that transported this youthful inventor when he saw the water actually turning the wheel he had attached to this mill and setting its miniature machinery in motion.

Half a century later, when John Ericsson was asked to prepare a list of his most noteworthy mechanical achievements, the construction of this saw-mill headed the list of inventions, the pumping-engine and the drawing instruments coming next. The mill was neat and tasteful in design and in every way a remarkable piece of work for one so young. In a square wooden frame was set a watch-spring, transformed into a saw by the aid of a file borrowed from a neighboring blacksmith. This saw was moved by a crank cast from a broken tin spoon. The rest of the machinery was of wood, and everything was complete—the bed carrying the log and moved by a cord wound on a drum; the ratchet-wheel and lever to turn the drum; the crank-shaft and the handle for turning it.

Encouraged by the success of this venture, the next year this lad of ten undertook to design a pump for draining the mines of water. The motive power was to be obtained by the use of a windmill. Such a contrivance the youthful inventor had never seen, yet he succeeded in drawing designs for his mill after the most approved fashion of skilled engineers by following a verbal description given by his father of a mill he had just visited. But alas, he could conceive of no way of adjusting it to the changes of the wind! Again the father visited a neighboring mill and in describing it referred to a " ball-and-socket joint." The boy seized the idea at once and with his pencil joined the connecting-rod for the driving-crank to the pump-lever with a ball-and-socket joint.

John's visits to the office of the draughtsmen engaged upon the plans of the grand ship canal had familiarized him with drawing instruments and he imitated them as well as he could. His home was in the depths of a pine forest, where his father was superintending the selection of timber for the lock-gates of the canal; nothing was to be bought and he had nothing to buy with. But the boy was as independent of outside assistance as the much-contriving Crusoe on his island. Compasses were made of birch-wood with needles inserted at the ends of the legs; steel tweezers borrowed from his mother's dressing-case and ground to a point furnished a drawing pen, the thickness of the lines being effectually regulated by a thread slipped up and down the prongs.

At that time coloring was deemed essential to the completeness of mechanical drawings. Gamboge and indigo were at hand but no drawing brushes. After many refusals the young draughtsman at length secured permission to rob his mother's sable cloak of the hairs required for two small brushes, taking care that these should be abstracted with such skill that their absence would not be revealed. Thus equipped he was able to complete his drawing with the wood and iron distinguished by appropriate colors.

It was this plan, conceived and executed under such circumstances by a mere child, that attracted the attention of Count

Platen and opened to young Ericsson the career he was to follow with such brilliant results. He was not precocious, nor was he the victim of any process of forcing, but with him the comprehension of the science of motion was as intuitive as the perception of the harmonies of color with Raphael or those of musical expression with Beethoven.

Seeing his two sons raised to the dignity of cadets in the Mechanical Corps of the Navy, and wearing the uniform of his Majesty's service, Olof Ericsson was a proud and happy father. His sacrifices for his children were rewarded, and their future, under the patronage of the powerful Count Platen, then one of the most influential of Swedish subjects, seemed assured. At this time John also executed a drawing of the Sunderland iron bridge, and this Count Platen, years after, was accustomed to show to visitors, when recounting his experience with his youthful prodigy.

The canal opened a new world of mechanical interest to John and he was not content to limit himself to the labor and study required by his duties as one of the corps of construction. After his work for the day was done he would employ himself during the long winter evenings with copying the plans of the canal and the designs of the machinery and implements used in its construction. Of these he had a complete portfolio by the time he was fifteen years of age. Still this healthy lad found time for the sports peculiar to the Swedish country life, and many years after a friend of his youth wrote to remind him of the occasion when he saved from drowning one of his fellow-pupils on the Göta Canal while they were skating on the ice at Motala.

Upon Europe had just dawned an era of peace destined to last for a generation, but its results were not yet apparent and Sweden was one of the poorest of European states. It was a constant struggle to woo from the sandy soil of the stony peninsula even a scanty harvest of red rye, and the minerals wrested from the still more reluctant rock barely sufficed to make good the lack of daily food. Accumulation was almost impossible and enterprise was paralyzed by the lack of capital to set the wheels of industry in motion. "That canal," the people in its vicinity were accustomed to say, "is sure to get water in the end, for the tears of the stockholders will supply it." The changes in the working force were frequent, because of the lack of money, but these changes did not disturb the Ericsson boys.

Though Nils was the elder by a year his position did not equal that of John, for he tells us that he was occupied for four summers, or until he was seventeen years old, in making mortar and in carpenter-work. John, on the contrary, was kept at this menial work less than six weeks. In the winter the brothers were busied in the draughtsmen's office established by Edström for the instruction of his canal pupils. During the long summer days of that high latitude they were occupied with out-door work, and John gained such skill that before he was fourteen years old six hundred Swedish troops labored upon the canal under his direction, though he was still too small to reach the eye-piece of his levelling instrument without the aid of a stool carried by his attendant. Thus was John Ericsson identified almost from his cradle with great engineering works, for the Göta Canal was one of the most formidable undertakings of its kind. There could be no better school for professional training, and for seven years he enjoyed its advantages.

While the prospects of the sons were daily improving the fortunes of the father were on the ebb. His capacity to spend was beyond his ability to earn, and the generous-hearted and liberal Olof Ericsson was again in pecuniary difficulties. Failing health added to his troubles, and the burden of life grew too heavy for him. By favor of Count Platen he secured a situation in the Quarantine Office at Kanso, a little island in the Kattegat, near Göteborg, and immediately opposite the northern extremity of Denmark. Hither he removed, leaving the mother with her two boys, who were still employed upon the canal. Soon Mrs. Ericsson was called from the care of her sons to attend upon her husband, and, in the summer of 1818, death ended his unavailing struggle with adverse fortune.

The death of the father seems to have made but little change in the fortunes of the Ericssons. The energetic mother was able not only to maintain her family, but, as her son has shown, to pay the debts left by her husband. Her sacrifices for her children were rewarded by their love and reverence, and neither time nor absence could change their feeling toward her. Mrs.

Ericsson lived until her sons were past middle life, dying in 1853, at the age of seventy-five. When her eldest son, Nils, married in 1833, she removed to his home, and afterward to that of her daughter Caroline, who had married the Rev. J. Odner. She was a welcome addition to the household, where she occupied herself with the education of her grandchildren, and in domestic duties, such as the care of the garden and poultry-yard, for, like her son John, she was always busy. Her passion for reading novels does not appear to have been transmitted to him, though he did inherit her marked tendency to liberality in religious opinions. In spite of this peculiarity, Mrs. Ericsson lived pleasantly with her orthodox son-in-law, Pastor Odner, whose lines seem to have fallen in pleasant places, for his Rectory of Kinnekuna was charmingly situated at the base of a mountain of that name, rising from the shores of Lake Venern. Here Sophie Ericsson enjoyed a tranquil old age, telling her grandchildren, as stories of her sons' achievements reached her, of the prophecy that preceded their birth.

Nils, who most resembled his father, was the mother's favorite. He was more fond of pleasure and society than his younger brother, less original and aggressive, and more disposed to follow the beaten track of conservatism than his brother John, who was from the beginning searching for some new way of doing things, for some novel application of the mechanical powers to add new forces to the world's wealth. Commenting on a photograph, John once said: "The form of the forehead indicates that the man will see things as they are, and not as they ought to be, a circumstance that will remove obstacles from his path through life." This prophetic instinct toward things as they should be was destined to keep him at war, so much of the time, with received opinions on engineering subjects.

In 1820, when Ericsson was seventeen years old, he reached a point in his career where two ways parted. With the first suggestion of manly independence dawning in his mind he began to rebel against the career laid out for him by friends and guardians, though before he had been more than content with it. To the home of his widowed mother had come as boarders officers, civil and military, at work upon the canal, and her house was the rendezvous for the troops under their direction. Her son was brought into association with those who entertained him with stories of the great world; the world in which the Corsican cadet of Brienne had won an empire with his sword, and the lawyer's apprentice, Bernadotte, a marshal's baton and a crown. Military ambition began to stir in the breast of the youth. Although he had worn the king's uniform, and had directed the king's troops, it was not as a soldier. He aspired to martial deeds, to break away from the bonds of routine, and to lead the life of romance and adventure which, to the imagination of the young man, always lies just beyond. So he resolved to enter the army.

Knowing well that his military ambition would receive no encouragement from his good friend Platen, boy-like he concealed his purpose from the Count. When it was made known to Platen he was greatly disturbed and urged upon his young protégé the importance of continuing a career which opened with such promise before him. By every possible argument he sought to turn him from his purpose, but in vain. Finally, out of all patience with the perverse youth, the Count left him with the parting admonition, to "go to the devil."

The organization of the Swedish army is peculiar. In addition to a small body of troops of the line, there is a larger force, composed of a sort of peasant yeomanry attached to the soil and supported by it, an institution dating from the distribution in 1697 of crown lands, subject to an obligation of military service. When not in active service these troops cultivate their lands, or they are employed by the government in constructing roads and fortifications, in draining marshes, digging canals, or in other public works. It was to one of these regiments, then known as the Twenty-third Regiment Rifle Corps, and now as the Royal Fält Zägar, or Field Chasseurs of Jemtland, that John Ericsson was assigned with the rank of Ensign. The headquarters of the regiment were at Frösön, near Ostersund, the capital of Jemtland, the *län* of Sweden now governed by the second Baron Ericsson, the nephew and namesake of John, and eldest son of Nils. The regiment was a famous body of riflemen and Ensign Ericsson was soon numbered among its most expert marksmen.

Just at this period Henrik Ling was introducing into Sweden his scientific system of gymnastics, based upon a study of anatomy, and was endeavoring to restore the invigorating customs of ancient Scandinavia, where grew such men as Olaf Tryggveson, the first Christian king of Norway, who, as Carlyle tells us, "could keep five daggers in the air, always catching the proper fifth by its handle, and sending it aloft again; could shoot supremely, throw a javelin with either hand; excelling also in swimming, climbing, leaping, the then admirable Fine Arts of the North; in all which Tryggveson appears to have been the Raphael and the Michael Angelo at once."

If Ensign Ericsson could not equal this "magnificent far-shining man," the Hercules of Scandinavian history, he certainly was a worthy successor. With characteristic enthusiasm and energy he entered into the sports of his fellows and was soon the champion in wrestling, leaping, lifting, and the like. He had the bodily strength of two ordinary men. At first his zeal outran his discretion and in leaping bars he was again and again thrown, hurting himself badly; but difficulties never discouraged him. On one occasion while in garrison at Fröson, across the river from Ostersund, he lifted a cannon weighing six hundred pounds, a feat making such an impression on his comrades that one of them wrote to remind him of it half a century afterward. He was only eighteen years old when he performed this exploit. The effort was too great, and he suffered in after life at intervals from the injury to his back resulting from this supreme effort of strength. On the whole, however, he gained greatly from this thorough physical training and was noted through life for his vigor and endurance.

Not in physical feats alone did the young officer excel. He devoted himself with ardor to the study of his new profession and, with his previous training to assist, became known almost immediately as an expert artillery draughtsman. He studied the science of artillery, too, and familiarized himself with the manipulation of the eighty-pounders employed on the Baltic gunboats when nothing larger than a forty-pounder was known in the American navy. He never lost the interest in military and naval subjects then acquired and it was in part the secret of his later successes in a field wherein he was supposed to be a novice.

Lieutenant John Ericsson, Jemtland Field Chasseurs.

In a letter to his mother, written at this period, Ericsson thus describes his early experiences as a soldier:

OSTERSUND AND STORVIKEN, August 15, 1821.

MY DEAR MAMMA: We have now finished our Annual Military Manœuvres, which lasted for seven weeks. During that time I have learned tolerably well what it means to be a soldier, and am inspired with an unchanging love for the military profession. Our colonel has just left for Stockholm. As we parted I reminded him of his promise. "I will keep my promise to you," he said, "and the drawing you gave me I shall present to the King at the first audience. He certainly will appoint you an officer; at any rate, you are sure to be promoted." He also told me he wished me to pass my examination in the art of land surveying; for this reason I shall be obliged to spend the winter in Stockholm, whatever my means may be. The expenses will, I fear, be heavy enough, as I must buy geodetical instruments; besides, the pattern of our new uniform is now fixed, and in consequence I must get a green coat with epaulettes, new uniform trousers, epaulettes for the dress-coat, scales for the shako, a new sword of the special pattern of our regiment, a scarf and other small military ornaments. I must also pay for my commission. Now, I don't mention all this to cause you anxiety, dearest mother, only to show you that I really have necessary expenses and do not spend my money carelessly and to no purpose.

I think I can defray most of the charges myself, but if you could spare fifty rixdollars early in the winter without inconvenience, I should be glad to have them. However, if you are short of money, I should consider myself unworthy to be called your son if I ever thought of such a thing. I know your business is getting along well now; still I feel almost ashamed of my request and I am really grieved to think that, old as I am, I have many times been forced to solicit the assistance of a mother who has to work for every farthing without aid. I know, however, the kindness of my mother's heart! "No sacrifice is too great when the happiness of my child is concerned," you think. What a blessing to have a mother with such sentiments! I have about one hundred and seventy-five rixdollars left out of the money you gave me, and I expect some more from Captain Edström. By careful economy I can manage to get on until I receive my salary, when I shall be quite comfortable, for with eleven hundred and twenty-five a year I shall be able to save money for a lieutenant's commission and pay my debts to you.

With God's help, I hope to be appointed a lieutenant within two years' time, for there are only four second lieutenants in advance of me, and many vacancies just now. I am the oldest staff ensign of those who are to be officers at the same time as I.

With the heartiest wishes for your happiness, and kindest regards for my brother and sister, I remain,

Your obedient and loving son,

J. ERICSSON.

P. S.—At present I board in a farm-house very cheaply. I am studying Euclid. Later on I am going to practise plotting under the Surveying General, as it requires a certificate to show that I can measure and map before I am allowed to pass my examination. My kind regards to Halström ; I long impatiently for a letter from him.

Jemtland, where young Ericsson's regiment was stationed, and with which the fortunes of his family have now been associated for two generations, is a mountain district, lying two hundred miles further north than Vermland, and it is even more striking in natural scenery, being the location of the highest mountains of Sweden. From the hills of "beautiful Frösön," a little town divided from Ericsson's station by a narrow channel spanned by a wooden bridge, a splendid view of the greater part of the northern portion of Sweden is to be obtained. In the foreground is the picturesque lake, or rather net-

work of lakes, called " Storsjön," numerous wooded islands dot-
ting its surface, and beyond, to the west, the " dark Oviks " furnish a sombre background, until they blend in the distant ho-
rizon with the mountains whose huge peaks seem to stand like
a wall of separation between the two kingdoms of Sweden and
Norway.   To the north stretches an immense wilderness where,
in Ericsson's day, roamed the Laplanders with their herds of
reindeer.   To the south lies a charming landscape of hill and
dale, intersected by numerous watercourses, lakes smiling in
the sun, and foaming brooks plunging down the steep hill-
sides to disappear in the green-clad valleys beyond.

In other sections of Sweden the valleys near the high mountains are uncultivated and almost uninhabited ; here they support a thrifty population.   The general character of Jemtland
is that of a highland nearly a thousand feet above the sea level.
It is as far north as Hudson Straits, or Southern Greenland
and Iceland, and nowhere else is there to be found in a corresponding latitude, with an equal elevation, a section so highly
cultivated as this has been from time immemorial.   Rich
meadows furnish pastures for the herds that constitute the chief
wealth of the people.   The eighteen churches which can be
counted from a mountain on the southern shores of Lake Storsjön testify to the extent and character of the population now
under the government of Ericsson's nephew.

The recommendation for Ensign Ericsson's promotion went
to Stockholm in due course, but unfortunately his colonel, Baron
Koskull, was in disgrace at court, and the recommendation was
not heeded.   The young Duke of Upland, Bernadotte's son, in-
terceded with the king, winning his interest in Ericsson by
showing his soldier-father a military map made by the ensign.
This not only secured the desired commission of a second lieutenant, but it also directed the attention of Bernadotte to the
great skill of Ericsson in this work.   As a result, later on he
was summoned to the royal palace to draw maps to illustrate
the campaigns of the Marshal of the Empire.

A comrade of this period, Major Hjarne, who survived Ericsson, describes the young officer as " a noble lad, frank, faithful,
and honest."   He was never given to promiscuous acquaintance,
but with his little circle of intimates he was a special favorite.

His temper was hasty, but his disposition was lively, cheerful, and amiable. Major Hjarne recalls the picture of him as he lay extended on the floor of his quarters, "eating sugar and enjoying himself like a merry school-boy, for he was very fond of sweets." Not a strictly personal characteristic, for he was at that time a lad not yet out of his teens. Still, it was a taste that he never outgrew, and three score and ten years later, there was found in his room, after his death, the little store of the sweetmeats which he always kept by him. "He was exceedingly active," we are further told, "always inventing, designing, constructing."

Young Ericsson had made such excellent use of the instruction in topographical drawing received from the German engineer officer Pentz, that when he entered the Swedish army he found no one to excel him, with the exception of one officer, Major Södermark, who was renowned in this department. Soon after he joined the service orders were given to survey the district of Jemtland in which he was stationed. Officers to perform this work were selected by a competitive examination at Stockholm, and in this contest Ericsson easily won a prize. The pay in his new employment was determined by the amount accomplished, and the young surveyor from the Göta Canal was so indefatigable in his industry and so rapid in execution, that he performed double duty and was carried on the pay-roll as two persons in order to avoid criticism and charges of favoritism. The results of his labors were maps of fifty square miles of territory, still preserved in the archives at Stockholm.

Even this double duty was not sufficient to satisfy the restless energy and activity of the young chasseur, for in this high northern latitude he could protract his work at the drawing-board through the entire night, and this he frequently did, without resort to artificial light, except for a few hours. As occupation for his "leisure" he bethought himself of the sketches and mechanical drawings he had accumulated during his service under Count Platen. He decided to use them in a work he proposed to prepare for publication, containing a full description of the machinery and methods used in canal work, the locks, and the various appliances for transportation. He enlisted in this enterprise Major Pentz, late pro-

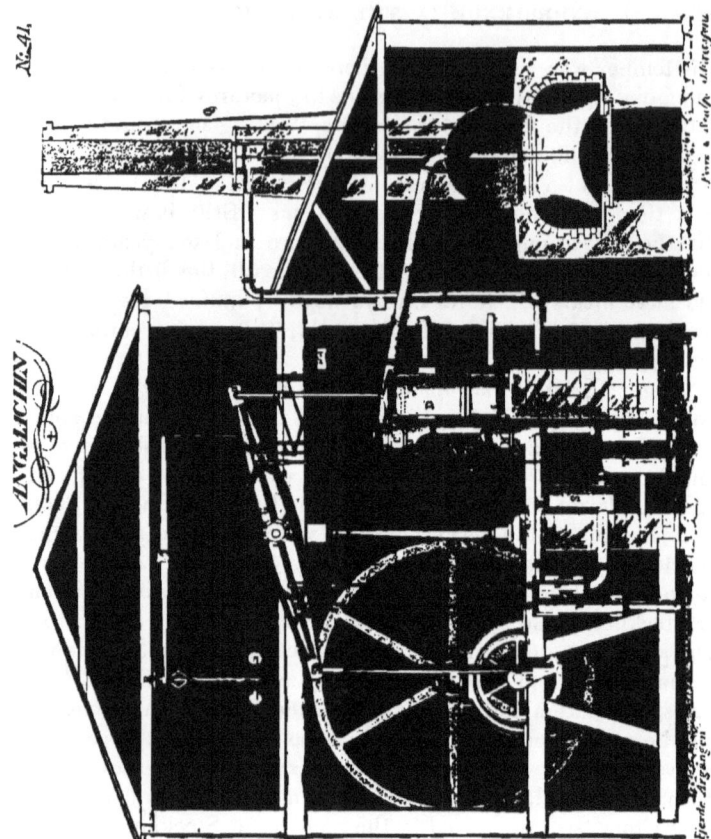

Second Engraving made by Ericsson, 1821, aged eighteen.

fessor at Rostock, Germany, and probably the officer of the same name from whom his lessons in topographical drawing had been received. Pentz was to translate the work into German to give it foreign currency.

It was necessary to engrave the drawings selected to illustrate the book, and Lieutenant Ericsson determined to do this work himself. So he obtained leave of absence and hastened to Stockholm where he applied to one of the best engravers for permission to inspect his tools, and was laughed at for his simplicity in supposing that he was to be thus permitted to learn the mysteries of the craft. Nothing daunted he hastened to his room and set busily to work devising a machine for engraving. This he was soon able to show in triumph to the disobliging craftsman. Back to his station he went with his new machine and commenced work upon the sixty-five plates of copper carried with him. Within a year he had completed eighteen plates, averaging in size fifteen by twenty inches. One of these plates, the second one completed, was reproduced in a Swedish illustrated magazine and is given here. In acknowledging the receipt of a copy of this Ericsson said: "I remember very well the surprise of certain engravers at the sharp white edges of the pump-rods against the dark ground. The plan of rubbing these parts with a fine varnish before the plates were prepared for the aqua fortis, which suggested itself to the beginner, enabled him to surpass the work of experienced artists."

Other occupations delayed the book, and before it had gone farther it became apparent that the swift changes in the applications of machinery and the use of new methods were rendering the knowledge acquired at Göta out of date. So this undertaking was abandoned. Major Pentz never got farther than the preface with his part of the work, but as he had advanced some money to purchase the copper plates, the completed engravings were all turned over to him in settlement of this account. Busy as he was, the ardent young Swede found time for sentiment, for this was the romantic period in the young man's life. During it Ericsson established friendships and developed enthusiasms which continued with him to the end. More than fifty years after, when his knowledge of Swedish had grown somewhat rusty from disuse, he wrote home to Sweden:

"Overwhelmed with work, I have not had the time to write the description you ask for in my native tongue. I can think in English four times faster than I can write in Swedish, and write four times faster than I can think. As, now, $4 \times 4 = 16$ you will find my excuses sufficient. But this is only the case in mechanical matters, because when the language of the heart is to be used I prefer to express myself in my native tongue. Although ignorant of all that properly belongs to mechanical philosophy when I left Sweden, I was by no means inexperienced in the language of feeling. I sometimes wrote poetry to the wonderful and enchanting midnight light of Norrland. Connoisseurs often doubted that it came from the second lieutenant and surveyor up among the mountains." Norrland is within less than three degrees of the Arctic circle, and there the phenomenon of the midnight sun is to be seen in perfection.

Human nature is the same under the Arctic circle as in the torrid zone; indeed, as Ericsson was fond of arguing, the conditions of life in high latitudes are even more exciting. He was a man of ardent temperament, and his veins, through life, were always swollen to bursting with the swift-flowing current of healthy masculine vitality. The glories of the midnight sun could inspire him with poetry, but the sparkling eyes of the Jemtland maidens moved him still more profoundly. To one of these the young lieutenant became deeply attached. She was of an ancient and noble family, and her father was an officer of high rank. To her Ericsson was betrothed, with those formalities which, in Swedish opinion at that time, imposed the obligations of marriage, and were not infrequently extended to include its sanctions as well. Indeed, under early Scandinavian law, a betrothal without marriage secured rights of inheritance to a child born of such a connection that did not belong to the child of a marriage not preceded by betrothal.

The laws of Sweden regulating the marriage of army officers were exacting, and made impossible a legal union between a poor lieutenant and a maiden whose womanly charms and her excellent birth were her only dower. Precisely how the pair stood related to one another from our point of view cannot, at this distance of time, be determined. The connection was subsequently dissolved, and being free, the young woman married

Ericsson at the Age of Twenty-one.

another Swede of distinguished reputation, and lived to old age as his wife. One son, Hjalmar, was born at this time, and was left in charge of Ericsson's mother in Sweden when he removed to England. This child was well educated, and became a man highly respected and holding a prominent position in government employ. Ericsson at the age of twenty-one is described as a handsome, dashing youth, with a cluster of thick, brown, glossy curls encircling his white, massive forehead. His mouth was delicate but firm, nose straight, eyes light blue, clear and bright, with a slight expression of sadness, his complexion brilliant with the freshness and glow of healthy youth. The broad shoulders carried most splendidly the proud, erect head. He presented, in short, the very picture of vigorous manhood. A portrait of him at this age, painted upon ivory for his mother by an English artist named Way, has been preserved and is reproduced here.

Recalling his father's experiments, Ericsson at this time conceived the idea that flame might be used in a receiver corresponding to the cylinder of a steam engine. Thus he hoped to obtain power equal to that of steam with less expenditure of time and fuel. Devoting to this project such leisure as he had, he finally succeeded in constructing a machine to illustrate his principle. He set it in motion, and to his delight discovered that it worked perfectly and produced several horse-power. Dreams of a coming revolution in the mechanical world occupied his waking thoughts. He prepared a paper, a translation of which now lies before me, entitled, "A Description of a New Method of Employing the Combustion of Fuel as a Moving Power." This was written in Swedish, and sent, in 1825 or 1826, to the newly-organized "Institution of Civil Engineers," London, where a translation of it is still filed among the archives, "No. 119."

CHAPTER III.

Removes to London.—His Promotion and Resignation as a Swedish
Officer.—Becomes a Partner of John Braithwaite.—First Use of
Compressed Air and Artificial Draught.—His Novel Applications of
Steam-power.—Invents Surface Condensation.—Quarrels with Sir
John Ross.—Invents the Steam Fire-engine.—Prejudices of the
London Firemen against it.

WITH the invention of the Flame Engine a new era opened
before John Ericsson. If the dreams suggested by this
first appeal to the judgment of the great world were not destined to literal fulfilment they were at least prophetic of his
future. Military life lost its zest, and he turned from it, as he
had turned to it, with characteristic impatience of control.
King Charles John, when shown his drawings, had advised
him to go abroad, as his own country could not reward him as
he deserved. This advice was given now with more effect by
one of Ericsson's brother officers, who, in a letter written forty-
seven years afterward, said : "I remember the ensign, by whom
I was so struck that I asked my brother officers to accept him
as a comrade, and urged the colonel to secure his promotion.
I could not bear the thought of his genius burying itself in
Jemtland, and when I heard of his attachment for a poor girl
I considered him lost to the world if he should settle there.
I advised him to go to England. He at once replied that I
ought not to have awakened a thought that had long slumbered
within him when I knew that his want of means made it impossible for him to realize his ambition. 'How much do you
need to start out with ?' I asked. He answered, 'I could go
in a fortnight if I had a thousand crowns.' I asked him to
draw a note for this sum ; this I endorsed and took to the bank,
and a fortnight later he had the money."

Leave of absence was obtained, and the bright young lieutenant, who had been the pride of the Royal Chasseurs, turned his face toward England, carrying with him the hearty good wishes of his comrades and their honest regrets at parting. On his way through Stockholm he spent a week in the capital, participating in the festivities attending the birth, on May 3, 1826, of the heir to the throne, afterward Charles XV. of Sweden and Norway.

The snow was melting from the mountains and the birches were budding in the valleys when John Ericsson left the native land he never ceased to love, to seek elsewhere the opportunities she was too poor to offer him. What possibilities were too great in the wider field that opened before this vigorous young genius, with a thousand crowns in his pocket and a substitute for the steam-engine among his luggage? Arriving in England on Friday, May 18, 1826, Ericsson proceeded as soon as possible to exhibit his wonderful Flame Engine in operation. It worked satisfactorily under the conditions intended, but unexpected difficulties arose when he was compelled to use coal instead of the resinous woods, so abundant in his native forests. Coal burned too slowly, and in place of the gentle flame gave out a fierce heat that speedily destroyed the working parts of the engine.

This was no light misfortune for the young man whose hopes were centred in the venture. Even a thousand crowns will not last forever, especially where the money is borrowed, and to the expenses of travel were added the cost of setting up and exhibiting his machine. Cynical criticism succeeded to the friendly admiration he had received at home, and the necessity of securing an income speedily convinced him that it was useless to give further attention to the Flame Engine; so he turned his back for a time upon his ambitious scheme of superseding steam. He was compelled to seek employment, and almost before he knew it, was committed to remain in England. Apparently, he had obtained leave of absence with the intention of resigning from the Swedish service. For some reason he seems to have overstayed his leave, and was technically in the position of a deserter. Through the intervention of his friend, the Crown Prince, he was honorably restored to the service by the issue to him on October 3, 1827, of a commission as captain in the Swedish Army. This commission he resigned on the same day. The peculiar circumstances under which it was received appear to have given the title of Captain special value in his eyes, and he used it until the end of his life.

If the immediate purpose of Ericsson's transfer to England was not accomplished, his introduction to another field of activity was timely. A new era was opening to English engineers, and for this the young Swede's peculiar abilities and special training exactly fitted him. It was the characteristic of his mind, as I have said, to see things as they ought to be, and not as they are. His spirit of adventure into new regions was as indomitable as that of the Norse rovers from whom he inherited his mental constitution. All things in the engineering world were to be made new, and there was need of men able to discard the teachings of precedent without substituting the conceit of ignorance. To England Ericsson carried his wonderful physique, his magnificent brain, an unusual training in the technique of his profession, and a capacity for work which was in itself genius. The Flame Engine had not realized the expectations of the Norrland garrison, but in it were the germs of ideas destined to grow and produce fruit.

There was something about the young man that inspired confidence in those brought into personal contact with him. To the ingenuousness of youth he added the experience of manhood, and the lieutenant of twenty-three was too obviously a master in his profession to be kept long in waiting. He was fortunate enough to establish himself almost immediately in intimate relations with the machine manufacturing house of John Braithwaite, and soon after he became the junior partner in the firm of "Braithwaite & Ericsson." "It was my good fortune," he tells us, "to meet with Mr. Braithwaite's approbation and friendship. In the various mechanical operations we carried out together I gained experience which, but for the confidence and liberality of Mr. B., I probably never should have acquired. I am happy to acknowledge having, during our labors, benefited much by his exquisite taste in the arts." *

Ericsson was not idle during the eighteen months interven-

* Letter to the editor of the London Builder, April 23, 1863.

ing between his arrival in England and the acceptance of his resignation as an officer of the Swedish army. Turning from his Flame Engine, he attempted to combine steam with the gases arising from the combustion of coal, and patented an engine constructed on this plan. This patent was assigned to a fellow-countryman, Count Adolph E. Von Rosen.

Next he took a step farther in the direction of the future engine, and attached a fire-place underneath a piston so as to actuate it by the expansion of the air and communicate suction to a working piston. An engine on this plan was patented and a model erected at Limehouse, 1827. A motive engine of the same general character was also put in operation at Limehouse in the same year. In this the fire-place was fixed, at the bottom of an eighteen-inch cylinder, and through the fire air was forced so as to expand by heat and at the same time combine with the gases from combustion. A loosely fitting piston moved up and down in this cylinder and set in motion a sixteen-inch working cylinder.

A difficult problem of mine draining presented itself. To solve it Ericsson invented and patented a pumping-engine consisting of a series of cisterns rising one above the other. By exhausting the air from these in succession the water was lifted to the desired height. The patent for this was taken out in the name of, and assigned to Charles Seidler, who introduced the first steamer on the Rhine and into whose family Ericsson afterward married. In 1828 Ericsson constructed and put into successful operation at the tin mines near Truro, in Cornwall, an air compressor having an air-cylinder of twenty inches diameter and five feet stroke. This operated a machine for raising water from a mine shaft situated off shore at a considerable distance from the point on the land where the actuating steam-engine and compressing cylinder were placed.*

Upon this invention Ericsson founded his claim to priority in the use of compressed air for transmitting power. His friend, Count Von Rosen, showed his unbounded confidence in the abilities of his young countryman, by investing £10,000 in this last invention, in the days when fifty thousand dollars was no small sum.

* Letter of Ericsson to Horace Day, October 13, 1873.

Ericsson accepted in the beginning the conclusion, now universal, that a substitute must be found for the wasteful steam-engine. His studies by day and his dreams by night were occupied with the problem as to how he might bestow upon his race the priceless boon of a new work-compelling force. Still, the improvement and adaptation of the steam-engine was the business immediately in hand, and this was not neglected. In the month signalized by the birth of Ericsson in Vermland Robert Fulton completed at Paris the trial of his first experimental steamboat. In 1819, while the young Swede was at work on the Göta Canal, the Atlantic was crossed for the first time by a steam vessel, the *Savannah*, which made a flying visit to Stockholm, where he may have seen it. By the time he reached England the steam fleet of Great Britain had increased to two hundred vessels, and the promising field of engineering enterprise offered by steam navigation opened before him. He was quick to perceive the deficiencies of the existing machinery and prompt in suggesting remedies. To hasten the sluggish fires under the boilers was a prime necessity. On this speed depended. A boiler was invented with an attachment of bellows or centrifugal blowers to produce artificial draughts. This principle of artificial draught was patented in England, in 1828, a year before Stephenson made his reputation by the application of the same principle to the *Rocket* in connection with Booth's tubular boiler. The tubular principle Ericsson also anticipated, for his boiler contained twenty copper tubes and an internal furnace. It economized fuel, and was so much smaller and lighter than other boilers that new applications of steam-power were made possible. Patents were also taken out for this in England, France, Sweden, and other countries.

An opportunity to test the new boiler soon offered itself. In 1827 Captain John Ross, who had made one unsuccessful attempt to discover a Northwest passage, endeavored to induce the British Government to equip another expedition to the Arctic seas under his command. Failing in this, he finally persuaded a liberal London distiller, Mr. Felix Booth, to furnish eighteen thousand pounds to equip an expedition. Mr. Booth was subsequently made a baronet for his liberality, served a term as Sheriff of London, and had the honor of giving his name to the arctic region known as "Boothia Felix."

An important part of the business of Braithwaite & Ericsson at this time was that of constructing refrigerators and coolers for the mammoth London breweries and distilleries. This brought them in contact with Mr. Booth, and through him they made the acquaintance of Captain Ross, who was fitting up with new machinery an old side-wheel steamer he had purchased for his expedition and named the *Victory*. Ross fell in love with the new boiler and ordered one for his vessel, to accompany a marine engine of eighty horse-power. To this was applied a "surface condenser" of Ericsson's invention. The success attending Ericsson's efforts to condense steam, in connection with his brewery and distillery experiences, suggested the idea of adapting the same machinery to steam vessels, as a substitute for the plan then in vogue for cooling the steam by discharging into it jets of cold water. In his new condenser the steam was passed through a series of horizontal copper tubes, collected in a boiler or evaporator into which sea water was driven by a force-pump. This condenser was operated upon the well-known principle that steam of somewhat less than one-half atmospheric pressure will cause water to boil rapidly in a vacuum.

It was almost impossible to keep the condensers then in use clear of water and preserve a vacuum in a marine engine, when it was moving slowly in heavy weather, and it was then, if ever, that perfect action was needed. As the ratio of condensing surface increased in Ericsson's condenser in proportion as the steam diminished, it was the most efficient when the engine slowed down. In reference to this invention he said, May 16, 1868, in a private letter to John Bourne, the author of a work upon the "Steam Engine," who applied to him for information: "I claim to be practically the inventor of surface condensation applied to steam navigation." Various methods of condensing the steam had been tried, but nothing had been found to supersede the plan of bringing the steam into contact with jets of water. Watt, Cartwright, Napier, Trevithick, Symington, Mills, and many others in England failed in the attempt to apply the plan of condensing by the application of cold water to

the outside of the vessel containing steam. Mr. Hale, of Bas-
ford, did finally succeed, and claimed priority for his invention,
in ignorance of Ericsson's successful application of the principle a dozen years before. "The high-pressure boilers of
the *Victory*, said Ericsson, "would have been destroyed in a
single day but for the application of the surface condenser."
"The condenser," says John Scott Russell, "is the most wonderful part of the marine engine, as indeed of the ordinary steam-
engine. It is here that the whole process carried on in the
boiler in so great bulk, and at so much expense, is instantly
reversed, and all its laborious effects are at once annihilated.
Without a condenser of some form the development of the
steam-engine would have been impossible." Ericsson's condenser made it possible, also, to use in steam navigation tubular
boilers, on which so much depends.

Into the *Victory* Ericsson also introduced the plan, afterward universally adopted in war vessels, of putting the machinery below the water-line to protect it from shot. Fearful of
being anticipated, Ross concealed his intention of making another voyage to the Arctic zone. Ericsson supposed he was fitting out a vessel of war for experimental purposes, and "in
experimenting," as he was accustomed to say, "complication is
not regarded, since the intention generally is to ascertain facts
and effects never known, for guidance in future practice."
For the purpose intended the machinery of the *Victory* was
wholly unsuited, as its designer well knew. Ross concluded
that its room was better than its company and tumbled it into
the depths of the Arctic waters, where it may, in some post-
glacial age, furnish proof that the Esquimaux had advanced
ideas upon the subject of steam navigation.

Eighteen months after his return to England, in September,
1833, and six years after the *Victory* sailed, Sir John published
a narrative of his voyage, and then Ericsson for the first time
learned that he was most unfairly held responsible for the failure of Ross's second attempt to discover a Northwest passage.
He called his detractor to account in a vigorous letter, and Mr.
Booth was compelled to interfere to prevent a duel that threatened, for Ericsson charged Ross with an "utter forgetfulness of
justice and candor" in dealing with him and Mr. Braithwaite.

To steam machinery wholly unsuited to the purpose intended Captain Ross added further complications in the shape of gearing and paddle-boxes, described by Ericsson as "a perfect specimen of ignorance of the laws which should be consulted in the construction of bodies intended to move through water." A specific contract had been entered into as to the amount of power the engines were to furnish, but when the vessel was put into the water from the dry-dock, she drew three feet more than was intended. Captain Ross was unfair enough to ascribe the consequent diminution of speed to want of sufficient engine power, in spite of the fact, obvious to every one, that his paddle-wheels were half immersed in water, besides being boxed in such a way as to prevent a free current to and from the wheels, which were themselves constructed on a false principle. Undoubtedly a great mistake was made in fitting out the *Victory* with new and untried machinery, but this was in accordance with Captain Ross's own orders, and he, and not Ericsson, was responsible for the result.

The letter setting forth these facts appears to have been signed by Braithwaite, but the rough draft of it in Ericsson's hand-writing is found among his papers, with erasures and changes showing it to be the original document. Ericsson was accustomed to state his opinions with sufficient frankness, especially in his hot youth, and he was by no means reserved in his characterization of what he declared to be deceit practised by Captain Ross. After describing one of his misrepresentations, Ericsson said: "The deception had been so well kept up that there was no occasion for this fresh lie to mislead us." This is not the kind of language that captains in the royal navy were accustomed to receive with equanimity, in the days when Wellington fought with Winchelsea, and Benjamin Disraeli challenged O'Connell, and the other party to the contention having a military reputation to sustain it is not strange that this dispute should have threatened to end in bloodshed.

As soon as Messrs. Braithwaite & Ericsson learned the purpose to which the *Victory* was to be applied, and thus for the first time realized the mistake they had been led into, they exerted themselves to the utmost to correct her deficiencies, spending night after night personally upon the vessel, "to make good," as Ericsson said, "as far as lay in our power, the baneful effect of the wanton deception practised upon us." They also kept their men at work night and day at a heavy expense. Hence they were naturally impatient of the charges of "gross neglect so freely brought against them by Captain Ross."

Whatever the deficiencies of the *Victory* as a vessel for Arctic voyaging, she marks a stage in the development of the modern war vessel, and the ideas introduced into her, with the intention of fitting her for naval service, have since become common in the construction of machinery for war ships. The engines of the *Victory* were at the bottom of a frozen sea, but the experience of the young engineer acquired in adapting them to their supposed use was of great value to him in his subsequent career as a naval constructor.

The year 1828, noted for the advancement made in naval construction, was signalled by another revolutionary invention by Ericsson. This was the steam fire-engine which is now in universal use, substituting machinery for the workers at the polls who for so many years made the streets of our principal cities hideous with their noisy rivalry and oftentimes bloody contentions. The "fire laddies" had certain prescriptive rights, for they were an ancient, if not a time-honored institution; even Rome was disturbed in the time of Pliny by the rivalry of her various companies of *matricularii*. Fights were common among the London firemen previous to the year 1830, and the methods of extinguishing fires showed no great advance upon the use of the early "divers squirts and petty engines to be drawn upon wheels, from place to place, for to quench fire among buildings." The chief advances had been in the introduction of the air-chamber in fire-engines by the German, Leupold, about 1720, the adoption of the system of arranging two sets of men on a hand-engine, one above the other, by Richard Newsham in 1725, and the use of flexible delivery hose so that the engines could be removed far enough from the fire to prevent their being burned up, as they frequently were before.

Some of the fire-engines and implements brought from Holland by King William III., when he landed in Torbay in 1688, were in 1828 still to be found in the public buildings of London.

The engines of Ericsson's time required some sort of a reservoir from which to suck the water, and it was the custom of the London firemen to supply this by tearing a great hole in the street to gather water, with the necessary result of filling the suction hose with stones and dirt.

Thrice had London been nearly destroyed by fire, Astley's Theatre had been three times burnt, Drury Lane, Covent Garden, and the Surrey, each twice, and the Lyceum and Italian Opera once each. As these conflagrations were largely the re-

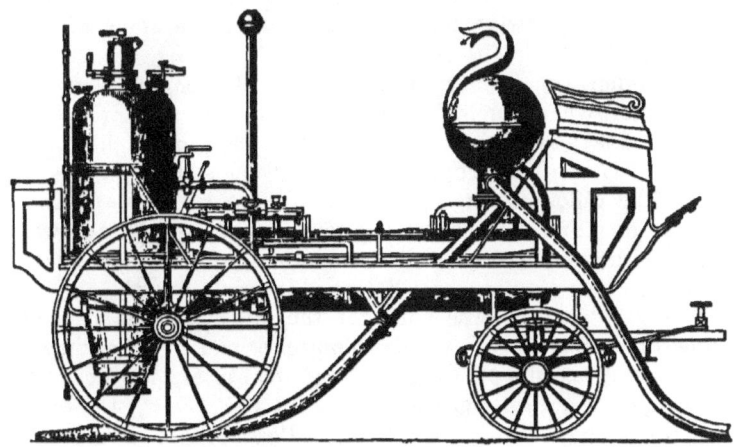

The First Steam Fire Engine, 1829.

sult of insufficient fire service, it seemed obvious to young Ericsson's enthusiastic mind that a steam fire-engine was certain of immediate adoption. He first designed one in 1828, for experimental purposes, and it proved entirely successful, throwing jets of water, varying from one inch to one and one-quarter inch in diameter, to the tops of the highest chimneys of breweries. Into this engine was introduced the artificial draught boiler, supplying the air for combustion by the reciprocating blowing machine worked by the engine when in operation.

The experimental engine was followed by another, mounted on a light frame and suspended on springs, so that it could be run over the pavements without jar. This too proved a perfect success on its first trial, and shortly after its completion the memorable conflagration at the Argyle Rooms gave opportunity for proving in actual practice its great superiority over the engines then in use. The service of the engine was offered gratuitously, and the insurance companies showed their appreciation of the courtesy by presenting Mr. Braithwaite's men with the magnificent testimonial of *one sovereign*. The night was cold and the hand-engines became quickly frozen up and useless, but the steamer worked incessantly for five hours without a hitch, throwing its stream clear over the dome of the building.

Another opportunity for testing the fire-engine occurred soon after, when Barclay's brewery was burned and Ericsson's engine was borrowed and kept at work day and night for a month, without interruption, pumping and starting the beer from the different vats in the establishment. It was afterward taken on a sort of starring tour to France, where it was used with great success in several towns, and from there to Russia, where similar results followed its trial.

A third engine was built for the Liverpool Docks, and used for many years in extinguishing fires and in other operations requiring the pumping of large quantities of water. A fourth, of beautiful construction, called the *Comet*, was built for the King of Prussia in 1832, and Berlin was the first continental city to supply this means of extinguishing fires.

The fire-engine made by Braithwaite & Ericsson, with its substitution of steam for hand power, was the first distinct departure in principle from the engines in use, in one form and another, at various periods since the beginning. The oldest fire-engine of which we have any account is described by Hero in his "Spiritalia," B.C. 150, and the description answers very well for the ordinary form of hand-engine displaced by the steam-engine. This early engine had the air-chambers and two single acting pumps, worked by a beam moved by brakes and uniting their two streams in a common discharge, connected with a nozzle capable of being turned in any direction.

When an American hand-engine was first taken to Constantinople, many years ago, the Pasha viewed its performance with admiration, but exclaimed at the end, "Mashallah! very good, but it will require a sea to supply it with water. It won't do for us, for there is no sea in the middle of the city." So he decided to continue the use of his squirts, and to follow the received method of letting the fire spread until the wind changed or it could find nothing more to destroy. A similar objection was raised to Ericsson's invention, known from the manufacturer as "Braithwaite's engine." Speaking of it, an authority says: "The engine of Mr. Braithwaite, although most successful in its working and adaptability to the purpose to which it was designed, met with the usual opposition which all really useful or important introductions seem destined to encounter, and his proposals for bringing them into general use in London met with the most determined hostility. First, it was urged that to be good for anything it must constantly have a fire alight or the steam kept up, as it would otherwise take too long to bring it into operation; then it was 'too powerful for common use, too heavy for rapid travelling, and required larger supplies of water than could be obtained in London streets.' This in spite of the fact that Ericsson's engine had worked for five hours at the Argyle fire when the other engines were frozen up. Even if the steam fire-engines 'could get water,' it would not be desirable to use them, as the quantity of water thrown by them might be injuriously applied and cause mischief. In short, the managers of the fire brigade declined to entertain Mr. Braithwaite's proposals, and their servants perpetrated every possible annoyance toward Mr. Braithwaite when they met him with his engine at fires, which he for a long time attended gratuitously, so that ultimately he withdrew in disgust from the new field in which he had hoped to have both profitably and usefully employed his talents and resources." *

Steam-power for extinguishing fires was in use in manufacturing establishments before it was employed in portable machines, every factory of any pretensions having its steam-driven pump with hose and other attachments.

A floating steam fire-engine, having the speed of nine miles an hour, was designed in 1835 for the London Fire-engine Es-

* Young: Fires, Fire-engines, and Fire Brigades. (The author acknowledges his indebtedness to this work for many of the facts given here.)

·tablishment, but a land steam fire-engine was used by them for the first time in July, 1860, in one of the back streets of Doctors Commons. "In point of ' efficiency, simplicity, durability of parts, weight, and cost,' it was in no respects superior to Mr. Braithwaite's [Ericsson's] steam fire-engine of 1829, while in some respects it was inferior to it. In a report to the committee, the superintendent of the brigade admitted that this engine required delicate handling; and so unsatisfactory upon the whole was its performance that at the end of ten months' trial it was withdrawn and replaced by one of a different construction, bearing a close resemblance to that of Mr. Braithwaite."

This claim for Ericsson of the invention of what has been extensively known as Braithwaite's steam fire-engine is made upon Captain Ericsson's distinct declaration that it was built from his designs, as well as upon other authority. In a statement appearing in the London *Engineer*, December 31, 1875, he said: "Having originated, elaborated, and perfected a new system, I claim to be the father of steam fire-engines; cheerfully admitting that but for the confidence and liberality of my friend and patron, John Braithwaite, it would not have been in my power to carry my plans into practice." This refers to the experimental engine and the one first built from its design. Continuing, Ericsson says further: "I designed two other steam fire-engines ordered from Braithwaite's establishment about the same time; one for the Liverpool Docks and one for the Prussian Government."

In his contest with the London Fire Brigade Ericsson appears to have had his first introduction to the official inertia and prejudice he was destined to become further acquainted with during his long career of invention. "Prejudice was never reasoned into a man, and for that reason can never be reasoned out of him."

CHAPTER IV.

OPENING OF THE ERA OF LOCOMOTIVE ENGINEERING.

Aristocratic Prejudice against Railroads.—Stephenson's Contest with Philistine England.—The Liverpool & Manchester Railroad offers a Prize.—The Argument for and against the Locomotive Engine.— The Rainhill Trial of 1829.—Stephenson's *Rocket* and Ericsson's *Novelty.*—The *Novelty* shoots by the *Rocket* like a Projectile.—A Mile in Fifty-six Seconds. — Steam Power Supersedes Muscle.— Public Excitement.—A New Era Inaugurated.

IN 1798, when Lord Campbell went up to London to seek his fortune, he was the subject of anxious apprehension on the part of his relatives because of the speed with which he was to travel by stage. The distance of three hundred miles between Edinburgh and the capital was made in sixty hours, and stories were rife of deaths by apoplexy, as the result of travelling at this alarming rate of five or six miles an hour. During the quarter of a century following Lord Campbell's journey there was some increase on even this remarkable rate of speed. Twenty thousand miles of turnpike had been constructed in England previous to the date of Ericsson's transfer there in 1826 and £2,200,000 had been expended upon them to increase the possibilities of land carriage.

Advance in this direction had reached its limit. Light vehicles, mounted on springs and speeding over the perfect highways of Macadam had gradually replaced the pack-horses and rude carriages of a hundred years before. Great attention had been paid to improving the breed of carriage-horses, and seven, eight, and even ten miles per hour were common with passenger coaches. The Quicksilver Mail to Falmouth made eleven miles an hour, including stoppages, and even seventeen miles an hour were obtained for a short stage with the Shrewsbury coaches over the exceptional route between Cheltenham and Tewksbury.

The three thousand miles of canal in England had relieved

4

to some extent the demand for heavy carriage, and suggestions
of a coming revolution were found in the development of the
system of tramways employed in the coal districts of Newcastle
where George Stephenson served his apprenticeship and
gained experience in engine construction. These had been in
use for a century and a half, or since the time when Master
Beaumont, a gentleman of "great ingenuity and rare parts,"
had expended his fortune of £30,000 in substituting for the
ancient "waynes" "waggons" running on these parallel ways of
timber. But no one dreamed of the great changes involved in
the use of steam as a means of traction. As to the general
public, it ridiculed in its wisdom the idea of exceeding the speed
of the quick passenger coaches. Philistine England combined
its strength to defeat the projects of the engine-driver from
Killingworth colliery, with his wild plans for carrying freight
at the rate of twelve or fifteen miles an hour. His idea of a
tramway laid to a uniform grade over hill and valley, instead
of following the sinuosities of the ground, was bitterly opposed,
and the most alarming prophecies were in vogue concerning
the danger attending his plans.

As early as 1749 Watt had suggested the idea of applying
steam power to passenger coaches travelling over the common
roads, and various attempts had been made to realize this conception. Experience at the collieries had shown the possibilities of moving heavy wagons on tramways with stationary
engines, but a great contention had arisen over the suggestion
that it was feasible to use locomotives on such roads, while the
best engineers in England, Ericsson included, were seeking
some means of overcoming the supposed want of adhesion between the wheels and the rails. A learned advocate expended
his eloquence before a committee of Parliament ridiculing the
idea of going "at the rate of twelve miles an hour with the
aid of the devil in the form of a locomotive, sitting as postil-
ion on the fore horse." To his own satisfaction this man of
law proved that a gale of wind "would render it impossible to
set off a locomotive engine either by poking the fire or keeping
up of the steam until the boiler was ready to burst."

It is difficult now to realize the extent of the prejudice then
existing in England against railroads, especially among the

classes whose interests fortified their prejudices. Aristocratic sentiment was long arrayed against a mode of conveyance bringing noble and peasant to a common level; even after success was assured English fashion clung to its earlier and less convenient mode of locomotion simply because its abandonment by the vulgar made it more exclusive, as it still clings to its wax-candles to the exclusion of gas.

The Duke of Wellington refused to trust himself upon a railroad until the year 1843, and went then only because he was in attendance upon the Queen, who the year before followed the example of Prince Albert in making use of this conveyance between London and Windsor. The favored of fortune always have a keen appreciation of the menace to their privileges involved in radical changes of any sort in existing conditions. In this case they appear to have had a particularly lively premonition of the revolution to follow the success of the Yorkshire engineer. The peers of England as landowners, and the classes they represented or influenced, were among the chief opponents of the railroad projects. "Journeys at that time," says James John Garth Wilkinson, "were restricted to a small portion of the community. The more the coaches were perfected, and the better horsed, the more expensive and select they became. How shall we popularize travelling? By a viler expedient of canals, carts, and the like? This, too, existed, but it was used merely for necessity, and did not attract, or make all men into travellers. To effect the better result an invention grander and cheaper than had then traversed space was required. To move the rich needed only a four-horse coach, running in an agony of ten miles an hour; but to move the poor required cars before which those of the triumphing Cæsars must pale their ineffectual competition. Thus, though the problem was the enfranchisement of the meaner classes from the fetters of pedestrianism, yet the only solution of it lay in the increased convenience of all ranks, from the noble to the peasant, and not in the degradation but in the elevation of the locomotive art." *

The early projectors of railroads intended them for goods transport; especially for carrying ore a short distance from the mines. They did not realize the possibilities of passenger traffic;

* Wilkinson's Human Body and its Connection with Man, pp. 12, 13.

these revealed themselves only when rapid motion was assured and in this revelation it was the fortune of John Ericsson to play a most conspicuous part. He was at work on his marine boiler, and fighting adverse public sentiment with his steam fire engine, while the Stephensons were bringing to a successful issue the great scheme of a railroad between Liverpool and Manchester. The appearance of the prospectus of this railroad in a volume labelled "Some of the Bubbles of 1825," and found in one of the public libraries, shows how this project was then regarded.

The elder Stephenson, who was the engineer of the railroad, was an earnest advocate of locomotives, and argued strenuously against the project of using stationary engines to draw the cars from station to station. The possibilities of such engines were limited to the carrying of forty tons of coal at the rate of six miles an hour. Stephenson urged that ten miles could be obtained with the locomotive, and in the hidden recesses of his own mind cherished the thought of twenty miles. He did not dare express it, for fear of still further increasing the prejudice against his plans.

Upon the decision of this question of power turned the whole future of railroad development, as the result has shown. After much painstaking investigation the railroad officials yielded to Stephenson's solicitations, and resolved to make a trial of the locomotive engine in spite of the baleful prophecies concerning it. An advertisement was issued offering a prize of five hundred pounds for the best locomotive adapted to a road of 5 feet 8½ inch gauge, capable of drawing a gross weight of twenty tons at the rate of ten miles an hour, and conforming to certain stipulations. It must consume its own smoke, according to the provisions of the railway act, and its limit of weight was fixed at six tons. The learned Government Inspector of the Post Office Steam Packets pronounced the men who prescribed this impossible condition of ten miles an hour "a set of charlatans," and offered a breakfast on a stewed engine-wheel in case their requirements were met.* Not a single eminent pro-

* For many of the facts given thus far in this chapter I am indebted to Smiles's Life of George and Robert Stephenson, which is, however, truthfully described by Knight's American Mechanical Dictionary as "ignor-

fessional man sided with Stephenson in his preference for locomotives, and public opinion was greatly excited over the dangers
supposed to attend this novel system. When Parliament had
been applied to for a charter for the Liverpool & Manchester
road, great care had been taken to avoid the suggestion of locomotives, and the discussion before the committee was as to
the possibilities of traction on a railroad by horse-power. The
biographer of C. B. Vignoles, who was principal resident engineer of the road from 1825 to 1827, says: "There can be no
doubt it would have risked the success of the bill if the pro-
moters had laid any stress on the possibility of steam becoming the traction agent." *

Five months were allowed for completing the engines, yet
it was only by a bare chance that Ericsson was able to enter
the contest, for only seven weeks of the twenty-two remained
when he learned of the competition and commenced work on
his engine. He had never built a locomotive; Stephenson had
been for five years at the head of an establishment for the manufacture of such locomotives as were then in use on the colliery
tramways; he had made a special study of this form of engine,
and he enjoyed the further advantage of controlling the road
ordering the trial and had the sympathy and support of its officials. He was thoroughly equipped for the contest, and before
Ericsson began work had substantially completed his trial engine with the assistance of his son Robert, a young engineer of
Ericsson's own age, twenty-six. The Stephensons were able to
test their engine in actual practice on the Killingworth Railroad, and to correct defects that would have been fatal to success on the day of the trial.

Describing the occasion, Mr. Booth says: †

The intense interest excited by the offer of this premium was almost
unparalleled. The friends of Locomotive Engines hailed it as an era

---

ing facts and pettifogging the whole case; about as one-sided an affair as
Abbott's Life of Saint Napoleon." This is certainly true, so far as concerns
Smiles's meagre reference to Ericsson's part in the Rainhill contest.

* Life of Charles Blacker Vignoles, by his son, p. 111. Longmans, Green
& Co. 1889.

† Account of Liverpool & Manchester Railway, by Henry Booth, Treasurer
to the Company, p. 101. Philadelphia, 1831.

which was to create one of the greatest changes in the internal commu-
nications of the kingdom that had ever yet taken place.   The canal proprietors dreaded lest the issue of these trials should prove that a more
economical mode of conveyance might be established; and the projectors of the Railway viewed the experiment as one calculated to make
that grand work profitable to themselves and beneficial to the country,
or show to them what an immense expenditure had been incurred which
might otherwise have been avoided.

The public were not idle spectators; they considered that the successful termination would not only confer individual benefits and local
advantages, but a great national good, by introducing a system of conveyance throughout the country which is at once easy, safe, expeditious,

" Rocket " Locomotive.

and economical, affording to the poor a luxury hitherto denied to them,
and to the opulent a despatch which hitherto no sum could purchase.

The conditions required a run of seventy miles, but when
the day for the contest came, the only portion of the railroad
completed was a level stretch of about two miles at a little place
called Rainhill.   The competing locomotives were compelled,
therefore, to cover their distance by making twenty trips back
and forth over one and three-quarter miles of track.   Five engines entered for the trial at Rainhill.   Three were of little account.   The only one which disputed for the supremacy with
Stephenson's *Rocket*, was Ericsson's *Novelty*.   Minor defects
in its workmanship, such as Stephenson had every opportunity
to detect and correct, prevented the *Novelty* from completing

the required distance. So Stephenson was the only one who strictly conformed to the conditions, and the prize was awarded to him.

According to contemporary accounts, however, the *succès d'estime* was with Ericsson. His singularly quick comprehension of the problem before him, and his masterly control of its conditions were shown in his ability to enter such a contest with so little time for preparation, and no time for experiment. Previous experience with the *Victory*, and with his steam fire-engine no doubt led up to this result. In both of these he used artificial draught, which is the essential factor in the production of high speed, increasing heat in the furnace as the blacksmith does in his forge with his bellows. Without this the modern locomotive would be an impossibility.

To whom belongs the credit of first inventing what is known as the steam-blast does not appear. It is certain that its value, indeed its absolute necessity, in locomotives constructed for speed, was never understood until the Rainhill contest made it clear. Ericsson's previous use of this means of creating power with the least expenditure of grate surface, and corresponding compactness of construction, shows his thorough appreciation of its importance.

In an article on the "Civil Engineers of Britain," in *Blackwood's Magazine* for October, 1879, we are told that: "There are various claimants for the honor of the invention, which proved to be the very vital breath of the locomotive, the steamblast, and the actual discovery, not of the method itself, but of its prodigious efficacy, seems to have taken Stephenson as much as anyone else by surprise at the experiments at Rainhill, in 1829. On the first day of her trial the *Rocket* derived but little benefit from the discharge of the exhaust steam up the chimney, and, indeed, made steam nearly as freely when standing as when running. The mean speed kept up by the engine was under 14, and the maximum 24 miles an hour. Without any load a velocity of $29\frac{1}{2}$ miles an hour was attained. Ericsson's engine, the *Novelty*, shot by the *Rocket* like a projectile; but the workmanship was not equal to that of the stout Northumbrian, though the scientific condition of the *Novelty* was probably of a more advanced order. Had the workmanship been as strong as the design was original, the prize would have been won by the *Novelty*, and the early history of railways would have assumed a different complexion. After the trials, the two exhaust orifices of the *Rocket* were thrown into one, and so contracted that the exhaust steam produced a powerful blast in the chimney. The results were such as to indicate the full value of this mode of developing heat."

Edward Alfred Cowper, a member of the Institution of Civil Engineers, said in 1884,[*] of the *Novelty:* "It was a very light engine, and would not draw a heavy load, and the flue gave way several times, but I think it due to the memory of my old master, John Braithwaite, to state that it was the first engine that ever ran really fast, as it did a mile in fifty-six seconds."

Sir Charles Fox, afterward the engineer of the London Crystal Palace, was at that time a young man in the employ of Ericsson, to whom he was indebted for his first start in life. He was on the *Novelty* when it shot by the *Rocket*, and never, he was wont to say, could he forget the expression on the face of Robert Stephenson at the moment.[†]

Speaking of this trial, *Frazer's Magazine* said, in 1881: "For the first time the shrill whistle of the locomotive was heard in Middlesex. Few were the spectators, for the trial was essentially a practical experiment; but the faces of wonder and dismay with which they beheld the advancing, the self-moving machine were not to be forgotten. As the engine gained her breath, and with the sharp sigh, or rather snort, now so familiar to our ears, rapidly attained the speed of thirty miles an hour, the anxious lines on the face of the great engineer relaxed. By the time of the return to Kilburn it was clear that the engines designed for the London & Birmingham traffic would answer the expectations of the engineer."

The defects of Ericsson's engine were such as might be expected in a construction put at once to the test without previous experiment. These defects were all easy of correction had opportunity offered. But time did not allow, and Ericsson was even obliged to ask for a delay, to adjust the wheels

---

[*] Heat and its Mechanical Applications, p. 73.
[†] Blackwood's Magazine, p. 37. July, 1889.

of his engine to the track, for it had never been on the rails before. He always claimed the credit of being the first to demonstrate the error of the then received opinion that extensive surface must be exposed to the fire to secure the necessary amount of steam. His little *Novelty*, with its compact machinery, was a revelation as to the possibilities of steam, yet neither for Stephenson nor for Ericsson is to be claimed the exclusive credit for that memorable day at Rainhill. As Stephen-

The Novelty Locomotive, built by Ericsson to compete with Stephenson's Rocket, 1829.

son has himself said: "The locomotive is not the product of any single man, but of a nation of engineers."

If he spoke critically of Stephenson's engine Ericsson always refrained from attacking Stephenson personally, contenting himself with defending his own invention when unfair comparisons were made. "As to George Stephenson," he once instructed his secretary to say in reply to a letter, "the Captain refrains from doing anything calculated to tarnish the fame of that truly great engineer."

Neither Ericsson nor his friends were satisfied with the justice of the decision against him at Rainhill, so far as it assumed to decide as to the merits of the rival engines. This decision was in part due to the hasty action of the hot-blooded young Swede, in withdrawing the *Novelty* from the contest. In a manuscript left by Ericsson, he says :

It is very surprising that the several writers on railway locomotion have overlooked the fact that the *Novelty* contained the essential properties indispensable to success, while the *Rocket*, which took the premium, lacked those very properties. A glance at these locomotive machines as first placed on the Liverpool & Manchester Railway shows that the constructor of the former had grasped the subject and that the constructor of the latter had not.

Ericsson, duly appreciating the necessity of protecting the mechanism from shaking and jar on the rail, suspended the entire framework, boilers and engines, on springs of the most perfect elasticity ; but in doing this he did not, like Stephenson, overlook the fact that unless the power of the engines be applied to cranks on the axle of the driving-wheels in a *horizontal* direction, the action of the springs would be interrupted and counteracted. Consequently the *Novelty*, actuated by horizontal connecting-rods, moved along the road with perfect steadiness while the *Rocket*, with her diagonal connecting-rods had a violent racking motion from side to side. Mr. Hackworth's *Sans Pareil*, with her vertical connecting-rods, proved worse even than the *Rocket*, in fact did not admit of springs of sufficient elasticity to be of any utility.

But a far more important feature in the construction of the *Novelty* claims attention. Ericsson, duly estimating the insufficiency of chimney-draught, provided his engine with artificial means for supporting the combustion in the boiler furnace. A blowing machine was applied, moved directly by the engine, so that the supply of air was greatest when the engine worked at maximum speed. Stephenson, on the other hand, depended on the chimney-draught. True, a discovery was made by Mr. Hackworth, during the trials at Rainhill, that the admission of steam into the chimney in a peculiar way produced a powerful draught. But this principle of artificial draught did not enter into the original construction of the *Rocket*, while the plan of the *Novelty* was wholly based on that principle. In fact, no chimney at all was applied.

Ericsson has been justly censured for withdrawing the *Novelty* from the contest in the absence of his friend John Braithwaite, to whose liberality, keen mechanical perceptions and enterprise the directors of the Liverpool & Manchester Railway were indebted for the benefit conferred on their great undertaking at the time by the performance of the *Novelty*. It is difficult to see how, if the contest had not been abandoned, the judges could have refused awarding the prize to the *Novelty*, in view of her greater speed than the other competing engines, and in view of her superior principle of construction compared with the *Rocket*.

In reply to an inquiry from Mr. C. H. Haswell, Ericsson said (February 2, 1875):

My DEAR HASWELL : As far as I know the boiler of the *Novelty*, as well as the boilers which I designed for the steamship *Victory*, 1828, were the first in which the furnace with its surrounding water space was placed below the horizontal part of the boiler which contained the flues. The present locomotive boiler, as well as the boilers of Stephenson's engines built 1830, are, with reference to the point mentioned, copies of my originals of 1828. The boiler of Stephenson's *Rocket*, 1829, it should be observed, had a *separate fire-box* secured to the horizontal part or flue boiler, the water surrounding the furnace circulating through pipes connected with the said flue boiler. Yours truly,

J. ERICSSON.

Stephenson ran the whole distance without the carriage containing his water-tank, an essential part of his outfit, and with the water in the boiler raised to the maximum temperature. This offended Ericsson's sense of fair play, as his engine, owing to its construction, was compelled to run handicapped with the load of a water-tank. The contemporary accounts certainly awarded the palm of victory to him, and those who read the newspapers of that day will suppose that the prize was surely his. The account of the performance of the *Novelty* given in the London *Times* (October 8, 1829) was very full and most enthusiastic. Aside from its commendation of Ericsson's *Novelty*, it is interesting as a contemporary account of an historical contest. The *Times* said :

The directors of the Liverpool & Manchester Railroad having offered, in the month of April last, a prize of £500 for the best locomotive engine, the trial of the carriages which had been constructed to contend for the prize commenced to-day. The running ground was on the Manchester side of the Rainhill bridge, at a place called Kenrick's Cross, about nine miles from Liverpool. At this place the railroad runs on a dead level, and formed, of course, a fine spot for trying the comparative speed of the carriages. The directors had made suitable preparations for this important as well as interesting experiment of the powers of locomotive carriages. For the accommodation of the ladies who might visit the course (to use the language of the turf) a booth was erected on the south side of the railroad, equidistant from the extremities of the trial ground. Here a band of music was stationed and amused the company during the day by playing pleasing and favorite airs.

The directors, each of whom wore a white riband in his button-hole, arrived on the course shortly after 10 o'clock in the forenoon, having come from Huyton on cars drawn by Mr. R. Stephenson's locomotive steam carriage, which moved up the inclined plane from thence with considerable velocity. Meanwhile ladies and gentlemen in great numbers arrived from Liverpool and Warrington, St. Helens and Manchester, as well as from the surrounding country, in vehicles of every description. Indeed, all the roads presented on this occasion scenes similar to those which roads leading to race-courses usually present during days of sport. The pedestrians were extremely numerous, and crowded all the roads which conducted to the race-ground.

The spectators lined both sides of the road for the distance of a mile and a half; and although the men employed on the line, amounting to nearly three hundred, acted as special constables, with orders to keep the crowd off the course, all their efforts to carry their orders into effect were rendered nugatory by the people persisting in walking on the course. It is difficult to form an estimate of the number of individuals who had congregated to behold the experiment, but there could not, at a moderate calculation, be less than ten thousand. Some gentlemen even went so far as to compute them at fifteen thousand. Never, perhaps, on any occasion were so many scientific gentlemen and practical engineers collected together on one spot. The interesting and important nature of the experiments to be tried had drawn from all parts of the kingdom to be present at this contest of locomotive carriages, as well as to witness the amazing utility of railways in expediting the communication between distant places. The attendance of the members of the Society of Friends was extremely numerous also, and their appearance on a race-course gave rise to some amusing *badinage* during the day.

There were only one or two public-houses or taverns in the vicinity of the trial ground. These were, of course, crowded with company as the day advanced, particularly the railroad tavern at Kenrick's Cross, which was literally crammed. The locomotive carriages attracted, of course, the attention of every individual on the road. They ran up and down during the afternoon more for amusement than experiment, surprising and even startling the unscientific beholders by the amazing velocity with which they moved along the rails. Mr. Robert Stephenson's carriage attracted the most attention during the early part of the afternoon. It ran without any weight being attached to it, at the rate of twenty-four miles in the hour, shooting past the spectators with amazing velocity, emitting very little smoke but dropping its red-hot cinders as it proceeded. Cars containing stones were then attached to it, weighing, together with its own weight, upward of seventeen tons, preparatory to the trial of its speed being made. This trial occupied, with stoppages, seventy-one minutes, and proved that the carriage can, drawing three times its own weight, run at the rate of more than ten miles an hour.

But the speed of all the other locomotive steam carriages on the course was far exceeded by that of Messrs. Braithwaite & Ericsson's beautiful engine from London. It was the lightest and most elegant carriage on the road yesterday, and the velocity with which it moved surprised and amazed every beholder. It shot along the line at the amazing rate of thirty miles an hour ! It seemed, indeed, to fly, presenting one of the most sublime spectacles of human ingenuity and human daring the world ever beheld.

Of the second day's trial the *Times* of October 12, 1829, said :

Messrs. Braithwaite & Ericsson's engine (the *Novelty*) proved itself to-day to be as good (proportionally) at drawing a load as running without one. It drew, in one hour, three times its weight a distance of 20¼ miles !

In its issue of October 16, 1829, the *Times* said :

The definite trial of Messrs. Braithwaite & Ericsson's locomotive carriage (the *Novelty*) was fixed for this day. The load having been attached, the engine started on its journey shortly after one o'clock. It performed two trips with great celerity ; but when running down the course for the third time the pressure of the steam was too great for the boiler, which unfortunately burst.* This accident put an end to the trial and the *Novelty* was taken from the course.

The trials which have taken place have satisfactorily proved the superiority of the principle on which the *Novelty* is constructed. The machine was, however, too hastily and slightly fabricated—defects which Messrs. Braithwaite & Ericsson can easily remedy in any future engines which they may construct for railroads.

To John Bourne Ericsson wrote (January 19, 1875) saying :

The *Novelty* was provided with a *blowing* machine operated by a short lever attached to the extension of the axle of one of the bell-cranks. The air was forced into a close ash-pit, the fuel, coke, being supplied from the top by means of a hopper having two slide valves. The bottom of the ash-pit, as well as the grate, moved on hinges in

* This is a mistake. The escape of steam from the yielding of green joints misled the reporter.

order to admit of cleaning. The furnace was upright, resembling an inverted truncated cone. The flue, made of copper, was a descending one, leading out of the top of the furnace and returning three times, with the exit at the extreme end of the horizontal part of the boiler. Several boilers built on this plan all proved very satisfactory. In my steam fire engine of 1840, however, though the blowing machine was retained, the fire-box was square and the tubes straight, as in Booth's boiler—I persist in *not* calling it a Stephenson boiler.

As to *straight* tubes, Braithwaite and myself built a boiler with twenty straight copper tubes and an internal furnace in 1828, the operation of which was witnessed by Captain Ross and other persons. We abandoned this mode of construction because it was difficult to make steam-tight joints and not so economical as the descending flue, or the helical flue coiled round the furnace. Ill-natured people in Liverpool, during the Rainhill trials, insisted that Booth borrowed his idea from London.* Unfortunately my drawings of these boilers were destroyed many years ago.

The *Novelty* was planned and built ready for transportation to Liverpool in *seven* weeks. But for a letter received from a friend in that town, at the end of July, 1829, informing me, merely as news, that a " steam race " was expected, the *Novelty* would never have been constructed.

After the Rainhill trials, I used the *Novelty* as an experimental engine to test the efficiency of exhaust draught and independent power for operating the blowing machine, etc., etc. At the end of those experiments, the *Novelty* could hardly be recognized as the *Novelty*. I afterward designed another form of locomotive engine of very elegant appearance, two of which were built by Braithwaite, intending to astonish the world at the opening of the Liverpool & Manchester Railway. They proved utter failures for want of steam ; my opponents' outcry against a close ash-pit having induced me to abandon the blowing machine and resort to exhaust draught, produced by a small fan-wheel turning within a magnificent polished copper vase placed on the top of the boiler ; very classical but miserably inefficient.

The two locomotives here referred to were called the ' *King William* ' and ' *Queen Adelaide*.'† To them was for the first time applied in 1830, the link motion for reversing steam-

---

* That is to say, from Ericsson's previous use of it in London.

† Speaking of the opening of the Liverpool & Manchester Railway, September 15, 1830, Rev. Olinthus J. Vignoles, in his life of Charles Blacker Vignoles, says: " New engines made by Ericsson & Co. for this occasion, viz., *Queen Adelaide* and *William the Fourth*, had been contracted for by the Liverpool & Manchester directors, but they had not reached Liverpool in time to be ' proved ' before the day of opening."

engines. The so-called Stephenson link is a modification of Ericsson's original link motion.

The several statements made by Ericsson concerning the Rainhill trial, and here quoted, were all of them sent in answer to requests for information coming from authorities on steam engineering and the authors of works of professional reputation. The final paragraph of the letter last quoted shows how ready he was to admit his mistakes when once thoroughly convinced that he was wrong.

Among those present at Rainhill was a young man named John Scott Russell, who has since become so widely known as one of the most eminent of English engineers. To the seventh edition of the "Encyclopædia Britannica," published three years after the contest, Mr. Russell contributed an article in which he said : "The *Novelty* had to be withdrawn, through a series of unfortunate accidents which had no reference to the character or capabilities of the engine; and we well recollect that it made a powerful impression on the public mind at the time. On the first day of the trial, Thursday, October 6, 1829, it went twenty-eight miles an hour (without any attached load) and did one mile in seven seconds under two minutes. This performance will now appear trifling; but at the time the sensation it produced was immense."

The directors asked for ten miles an hour and Ericsson gave them nearly thirty-two miles (31.9). It is true it was with an unloaded engine, but this immense step forward was enough to prove the possibilities of locomotion. "It is far from my wish," Mr. Nicholas Wood, one of the judges, had said before the trial, "to promulgate to the world that the individual expectation, or rather profession of the enthusiastic specialist will be realized and that we shall see engines travelling at the rate of twelve, sixteen, eighteen, or twenty miles an hour. Nothing could do more harm toward their adoption or general improvement than the promulgation of such nonsense."

What was to be said, then, of this Swedish youth of twenty-six, fresh from his Norrland forest, who gave them more than thirty miles an hour? Stephenson, too, exceeded his expectations, for Mr. Russell credits his locomotive with twenty-four miles an hour, drawing three times its own weight, and thirty miles without a load.   "Had the seventy miles been one length," says Mr. Russell, " the *Rocket* would have maintained an average velocity of fifteen miles an hour."

Ericsson, while vastly increasing the speed of locomotives, at the same time reduced the weight eighty-five per cent., as compared with those then in use.   The *Rocket*, though it weighed four times as much as the *Novelty*, was also a great improvement in this respect upon the engines preceding it.

Charles Blacker Vignoles, F.R.S., rode with Ericsson that day, and forty-one years after (January 11, 1870), in his address upon taking the chair as president of the English Institution of Civil Engineers, Mr. Vignoles said : " The *Novelty* was long remembered as the beau ideal of a locomotive, which, if it did not command success, deserved it."

" To most men," says another authority, John Bourne, " the

View of the Novelty with a Train of Engine and Coaches in 1829.
(From pen-and-ink drawing by C. B. Vignoles.)

production of such an engine would have constituted an adequate claim to celebrity.   In the case of Ericsson, it is only a single star of the brilliant galaxy with which his shield is spangled."

Ericsson's engine leaped at once to the very front of locomotive performance thus far, if we are to accept the statement of Mr. Cowper, confirmed by the excellent authority of Ericsson and Vignoles, who declared that the *Novelty* ran, on one occasion, with them on board, at the rate of fifty miles an hour. The Great Western Railway of England had distanced all competitors when it made this speed on a continuous journey, excluding stops from the calculation.   The average speed of all the express trains in England is now $44\frac{1}{2}$ miles an hour, excluding stops, and in the United States $41\frac{2}{3}$ miles.   The maximum speed is 47 miles, and the highest speed beyond the bounds of

Anglo-Saxon civilization is 37 miles an hour. This is the speed of the trains that skirt the base of the Pyramids. France follows next with an average of $36\frac{1}{4}$ miles and a maximum of 43 miles from Paris to Calais. The great advance is in the increasing number of the trains run at these high speeds.[*]

We may imagine the excitement following the announcement in the *Times* concerning the performance of the *Novelty*, for to this engine, as we have seen, England's great daily devoted chief attention. Railroad shares leaped at once to a premium, and excited groups gathered on 'change to discuss the wonderful event which British opinion had led everyone not to expect. The pessimists were silenced; the art of modern railway travel was inaugurated, miles divided where leagues separated before; men were called upon to adjust themselves to new conditions created by the possibilities of freer intercourse, and the era of great cities and mighty states extending their sway over continents was opened.

To the young engineer who played his part so well that day was accorded the rare privilege of living long enough to witness the development of the new age he had helped to usher in. In the closing years of his life he could look back upon " a change in the physical relations of man to the planet on which he dwells greater than any that can be distinctly measured in any known period of historic time:" a change he had a most memorable part in creating, and all of which had come within the period covered by his professional labors.

In 1841, when the railroad had fairly established itself as a popular means of transit, eighteen hundred miles of track had been built and three hundred thousand passengers were carried weekly. When Ericsson died, nearly half a century later, the annual receipts of English railroads were more than the capital outlay in 1841 and the number of passengers had increased more than forty-fold.

The trial on the Liverpool & Manchester road not only attracted the attention of all England, but it brought together, as the reports show, a great gathering of the engineers of that day. Coming together and dining together are in England re-

[*] Express Trains, English and Foreign. By E. Foxwell and T. C. Farrer. London, 1889.

5

lated as cause to effect. A grand banquet was given in Liverpool to the directors and officers of the railway and to the competing locomotive builders. Toasts and speeches followed, and if Ericsson did not carry home with him the £500 offered as a prize, he at least made himself known to all England as one of the rising men of his profession.

If slow to realize the possibilities of railroad locomotion in advance, the capitalists were prompt to take advantage of the change when it came. A powerful combination was formed to open communication with the French capital by railroad and steamboat, and Vignoles was sent over to secure the necessary concession from the French Government. Thiers, then Minister of Public Works, visited England with his under-secretary to inquire into this method of locomotion. But he did not propose to trust himself to it, for he carried with him for private use a lumbering coach of the time of Louis Quatorze. M. Thiers examined, listened, responded politely to those who sought to instruct him, and went back to report that railroads were not suited to France, and to violently oppose them from his place in the Corps Législatif. Thus the introduction of railroads into France was postponed for eight years, and an illustration given of the enormous difficulties against which such men as Ericsson contend. Naturally, Ericsson did not share the reverence for official utterance entertained by " Sir Joseph Porter, K.C.B.," and if he on occasion spoke evil of dignitaries, his experience through life gave him ample justification.

CHAPTER V.

THE HOT-AIR ENGINE.

A Spendthrift in Invention.—Associations with William Laird.—The Caloric Engine the Sensation of London.—Faraday's Lecture upon it.—Ericsson Anticipates Sir William Thomson's Sounding Apparatus.—Applies Steam to Canal Navigation.

JOHN ERICSSON was now fairly entered upon his engineering career. Fortune, as well as fame would have been within his reach had he possessed what is called "the nose for money." But the Swede has been described as "one born to own a million and to spend two." And if this description does not apply to the race, it certainly does apply to this particular representative of it. He was accustomed to say he cared not who drew at the spigot, so long as he controlled the bung, and the spigot was always open. Nor was Ericsson in any active sense anxious for fame. He wished to accomplish, not to proclaim his accomplishment; though he was quick enough to defend his reputation when assailed, or to assert himself when he detected a disposition to set him aside. His one consuming passion was to bring forth some new thing, or to transform the old in the alembic of his creative imagination. For this he would sacrifice his own means and, so far as they would let him, the means of his friends. Not otherwise extravagant, in realizing his engineering conceptions he was a spendthrift. For this reason, the partnership with Braithwaite, so valuable in practical experience, was not a commercial success. The steam fire-engine was a mechanical triumph, but it did not bring orders to the workshop. It was a generation in advance of the demand. Though the experiments with the *Victory* laid the foundation for future triumphs in naval construction their immediate result was most unfortunate.

In the field of locomotive construction Ericsson was distanced by the more steady-going, if less brilliant, Stephenson, whose labors, concentrated upon the work of improving and adapting, were not disturbed by the constant buzzing of inventive conceits. Ericsson's energies, on the contrary, were divided among the numerous schemes constantly born of a prolific brain, and such of these adventures as were profitable were, like the "good ears " of Pharaoh's dream, " devoured by the thin ears blasted by the east wind." Invention followed invention at the average rate of three or four a year for a long period, limiting the term to devices put in actual operation, and excluding the numerous modifications introduced into existing patents.

Ericsson shared the experience common to inventors, and discovered at times that he was forbidden to use his own ideas because they were vaguely suggested in some previous patent or had been monopolized by some later discoverer, more enterprising than he in availing himself of the protection of the Government. He never invented anything, he was accustomed to say, without finding it claimed by some one, as soon as attention was called to its value by its introduction into use.

Following his abandonment of the field of locomotive construction, he designed a steam-engine formed of a hollow drum of metal with inclined planes set on the inner surface. The steam was admitted at the centre and striking these planes set the globe in motion, at the rate of over six hundred miles an hour, or nine hundred feet in a second. This steam wheel was a beautiful piece of work, so true a circle and so highly polished that it continued to rotate for several hours after the steam was shut off. It was set up at Birkenhead, England, in 1831, and connected to a centrifugal pump by band wheels to reduce the speed. The pump, another of Ericsson's inventions, raised a standard column of water thirty-two feet high, and two feet in diameter. The enormous speed of the prime motor rapidly destroyed the belts, but the action of the pump was perfect. A patent for this rotary engine was obtained February 8, 1832, and one-half interest in it assigned to William Laird, of Liverpool, who advanced the money to pay for the patent and conduct experiments. The title of the engine was " an improved engine for communicating mechanical power." One-half interest in another rotary engine, bearing the same title, was also assigned to Mr. Laird. This, as we are informed by a memorandum found among Ericsson's effects, "proved a complete failure when put to trial."

Rotary engines have been the dream of inventors for generations; indeed, since the time of Hero of Alexandria, B.C. 130. They are practicable, and have been to a certain extent successful. Other engines convert reciprocating into rotary motion; in a rotary engine the steam is applied directly in the line of motion, and thus follows the movement of the earth upon its

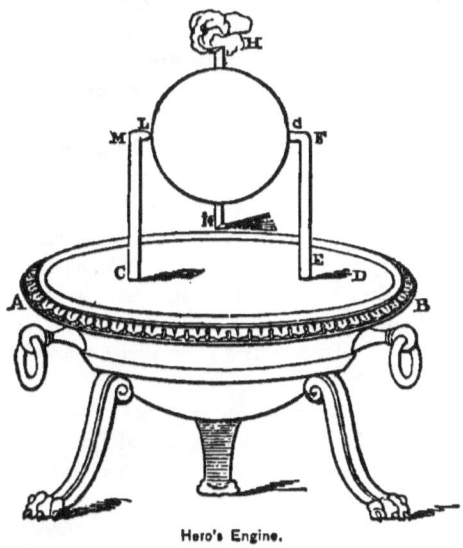

Hero's Engine.

axis. The enormous speed of nine hundred feet a second, obtained by Ericsson's engine, was almost exactly equal to that of Liverpool around the axis of the globe.

William Laird, with whom Ericsson became associated at this time, was one of the founders of Birkenhead, opposite Liverpool. As late as 1818 this place was nothing more than a fishing village, with less than fifty inhabitants, and the first shipbuilding docks were not erected there until 1824. The friendship established by Ericsson with the heads of the great shipbuilding house of Laird & Son extended to the third generation. On the death of the father of the present Mr. Will-iam Laird in 1874, his son wrote to Ericsson, saying : "I re-member very well that in the earlier days of Birkenhead you were intimate with my father and grandfather, and it is pleas-ant to know that the lapse of so many years has not altered your feelings of friendship and esteem for them."

On February 27, 1830, Ericsson patented, in the name of John Braithwaite, an apparatus for making salt from brine. The fluid was first heated in closed boilers, placed underground, and next turned into large open cisterns, there agitated by centrifugal fan-wheels, and then allowed to settle and de-posit the salt. It worked perfectly, and proved to be economi-cal. The crystals were of unusual size but much discolored, and numerous experiments failed to discover any method of overcoming this fatal defect. Messrs. Cropper, Benson & Co., of Liverpool, advanced £5,000 for obtaining the patents for this invention and erecting experimental works at Liverpool and Winsford in Cheshire. To them the patent for this "im-proved method of manufacturing salt" was assigned, and they were given control of it as general agents. Twenty years later the Siemens Brothers wasted a still larger sum in the unsuc-cessful attempt to improve the process of manufacturing salt by their "Regenerative Evaporator."

To the steamer *Corsair*, plying between Liverpool and Belfast, was applied in 1832 a centrifugal fan-blower, operated by a separate small engine, and intended to increase the draft in the furnace by creating an artificial current of air. This was the first employment, for marine purposes, of a device subsequently brought into general use on American steamers. "I claim," said Ericsson in a letter to John Bourne, "to be the father of the independent power fan-blower system for steam vessels, now universally adopted in American river navigation. So far no one has disputed my claim."

On February 8, 1832, a novel device for a rotary engine made its appearance from the busy workshop of the inventor's brain, and a modification of it followed during the succeeding year. These engines were patented, and experimented with, at the expense of Mr. William Laird, who received a one-half interest in the patents. One was applied to a vessel on the

Mersey and the other was set up for trial at the establishment of Messrs. Maudsley. They worked well, but consumed more steam than ordinary reciprocating engines, having the piston moving backward and forward in the steam cylinder, as in Watt's engine.

These failures to introduce more economical methods in the use of steam seem to have intensified Ericsson's determination to find a substitute for it. He had never laid aside the expectations connected with his earliest invention of a flame-engine; indeed, their influence may be traced through all the experiences of his long and busy life. They at one time led him very near to the danger-line of speculation as to the possibility of perpetual motion. He knew of no engineer, he said, who had not at some time been fascinated with this conceit. In the mechanical operations of nature there seemed to be, with continual waste, some law of compensation at work, and Ericsson was led to the conclusion that there exists in nature a principle of absolute reproduction of mechanical force. For this he sought as for the pearl of great price. The dynamical theory of heat was not accepted when his studies began, and his experiments led him to believe that heat was an agent exerting mechanical force without itself undergoing change. In this opinion he was supported by the declaration of his countryman, Professor Harvefeldt, a famous mathematician, that there was nothing in the accepted theory of heat to prove that a common spirit-lamp might not be sufficient to drive an engine of one hundred horse-power. Ericsson hoped at least to so lessen the consumption of fuel in the production of mechanical power as to extend the range of manufacturing industries into regions not furnished with fuel, as well as to remove farther into the future the inevitable period when the world's coal supply will be exhausted.

The smoke-jack, setting figures in motion by the action of the rarefied air rising from a hot stove, is the simplest expression of the mechanical force Ericsson sought to control in his "caloric engine." As early as 1699, the Frenchman, Amouton, had applied this principle to a wheel moved by a column of heated air. A century later, in 1797, an Englishman, Glazebrook, patented the idea of transferring the heat in an air-engine from the hot air going out after doing its work to the cool air coming in to take its place and continue the circuit. The same idea is found in Lilley's English patent of 1819, and in the hot-air engines of Rev. Dr. Robert Stirling, to whom the credit for its conception is usually given.

Stirling, who was a clergyman of Ayrshire, in the year Ericsson arrived in England, 1826, applied for a patent for an air-engine representing what is known as the regenerative principle. The fact that Ericsson opposed this application shows what he thought of Stirling's claim to originality. His opposition was unavailing, for a patent is on record as having been granted in the following year.* The reverend gentleman describes his apparatus for receiving and transferring the heat as similar in principle to "Jeffrey's Respirator," then used by consumptive patients to transfer the heat contained in the air exhaled from the lungs, to the cool air inhaled to take its place. Stirling's device was imperfect, and his engine, as Chambers states, was crude and incomplete. Nevertheless, it greatly annoyed Ericsson by its claims to priority. His own application of a "regenerator" was first made in 1833, when he invented and patented in England, France, the United States, and other countries a "caloric engine" with an "organ-pipe regenerator" consisting of a faggot of small copper tubes. Through these tubes the heated air passed on its way out of the working cylinder to the "cooler," and on the outside of the tubes the cold air from the cooler passed in an opposite direction on its way into the cylinders. Thus, there was a transfer of heat from the air going out, after doing its work, to the cold air coming in to take its place over the furnace. This transmission of heat from the outgoing to the incoming air reduced to the minimum the waste of heat, and consequently of power. This "regenerator" was the result of many years of study and careful experiment to determine the most effective means of preventing the loss of heat, for Ericsson had discovered that it was necessary to maintain the air in his working cylinder at a high temperature until the end of the piston's stroke. The cylinder for compressing the air was surrounded by a water-jacket, to keep down the temperature and protect the leather fastenings from the high heat.

* See Volume 6, Third Series, Repertory of Patents, 1828.

An experimental caloric engine of five horse-power, and with a working piston fourteen inches in diameter, was set in motion at London, in 1833, and at once excited extraordinary interest. Sir Richard Phillips has recorded, in his "Dictionary of the Arts of Life and of Civilization," the "inexpressible delight" with which he witnessed the workings of this machine. "With a handful of fuel applied to the very sensible medium of atmospheric air and a most ingenious disposition of its differential powers, he beheld a resulting action in narrow compass, capable of extension to as great forces as ever can be wielded or used by man."

"The principle of the new engine," Sir Richard tells us, "consists in this, that the heat that is required to give motion to the engine at the commencement, is retained by a peculiar process of transfer, and thereby made to act over and over again, instead of being, as in the steam-engine, thrown into a condenser, or into the atmosphere as so much waste fuel. And the well-known phenomenon that temperature, or quality of heat, is always equalized between substances, however unequal they may be in density, forms the basis of the new application of heat." *

Dr. Alexander Ure, author of the technical dictionary bearing his name, was another believer in the caloric engine, asserting that this invention would throw the name of James Watt into the shade. The little engine was in its day the sensation of London in scientific and mechanical circles. It was visited by a large number of men of reputation, as well as by curious crowds of sightseers, and for many years after was a theme of discussion in engineering circles. Among those who called to visit this new motor was Lord Althorp, afterward Earl Spencer, then Chancellor of the Exchequer and Ministerial leader in the House of Commons. He was accompanied by Mr. Brunel, the distinguished engineer and citizen of two worlds, whose name is associated in London with the Thames Tunnel, and in New York with the Bowery Theatre of his designing. Mr. Brunel was not favorably impressed. Believing that his judgment was founded on an erroneous impression of the new pow-

* Dictionary of the Arts of Life and Civilization. By Sir Richard Phillips. London, 1833.

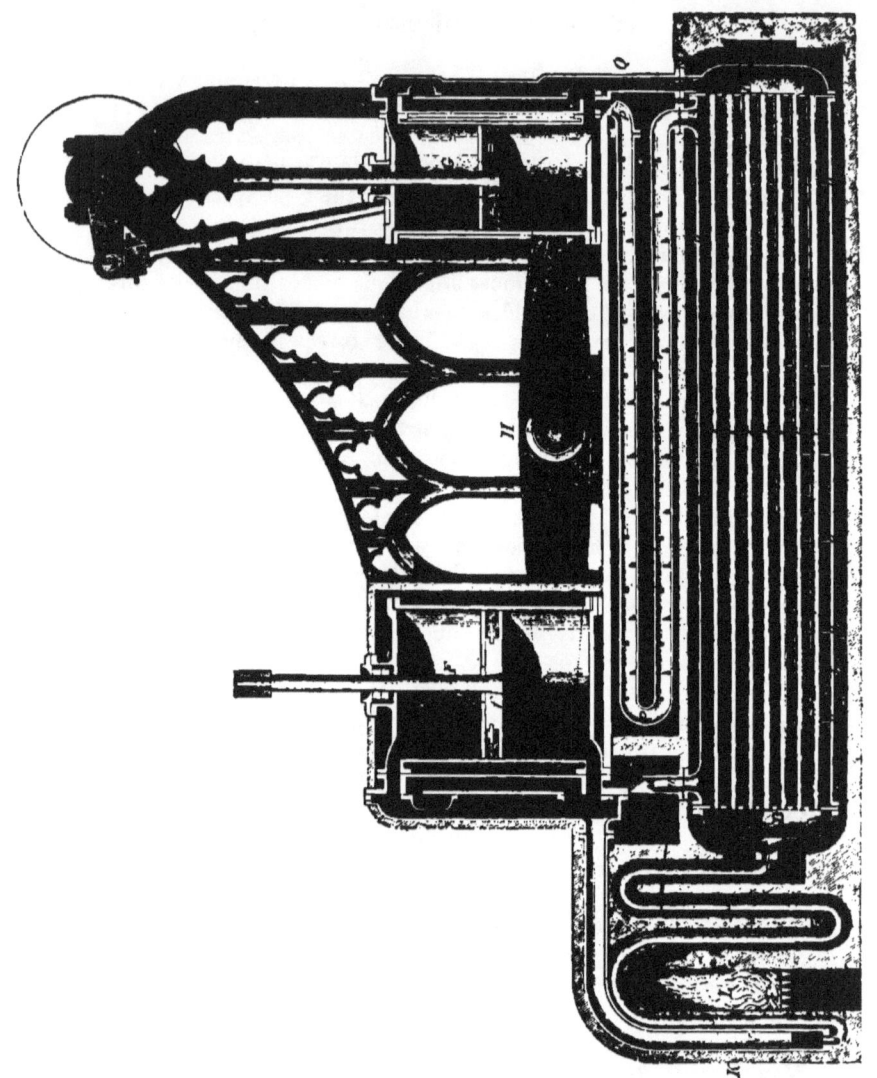

Ericsson's Caloric Engine.

er, Ericsson entered into a lively discussion with him. This was continued by correspondence, with the usual result of establishing each party to the controversy more firmly in his own opinion.

Professor Michael Faraday, however, declared by John Tyndall to be "the greatest experimental philosopher that the world has ever seen," was prepared to give a hospitable welcome to Ericsson's theories and studied his new engine with the greatest attention and interest. He refused to accept the condemnation passed upon it by nearly all the leading scientific men of that day, and denied that the principle on which it was based was unsound. Ericsson counted with great confidence upon the results expected to follow Faraday's advocacy of his invention, for the distinguished investigator announced his intention of delivering a lecture upon it at the theatre of the Royal Institution, London. A large audience was attracted by this announcement, including many gentlemen of distinguished scientific reputation. Just as Faraday was preparing to appear upon the platform he came to the conclusion that he had made a mistake as to the principle of the expansion of air upon which the action of the machine was dependent. He accordingly commenced his lecture, greatly to the disappointment of Ericsson, by the announcement that he was unable to explain why the engine worked at all. He confined himself, therefore, to an explanation of the regenerative apparatus, for using the heat over and over again in the production of force. "To this part of the invention he rendered ample justice, and explained it in that felicitous style to which he is indebted for the reputation he deservedly enjoys, as the most agreeable and successful lecturer in England." *

The caloric engine of 1833 was a sore puzzle to the savans of that day. They were unwilling to accept Ericsson's theories and claims concerning it, but their own opinions as to the nature of heat were not sufficiently settled to enable them to explain clearly their skepticism. Aristotle had told them that the first principle in nature, through all of its manifestations, was

---

* A Lecture on the Late Improvements in Steam Navigation and the Arts of Naval Warfare, with a brief Notice of Ericsson's Caloric Engine, delivered before the Boston Lyceum, by John O. Sargent. New York, 1844.

unity, and that these manifestations were always reducible to
motion as their foundation, and Bacon had declared that " the
very essence of heat or the substantial self of heat is motion,"
but the science of thermo-dynamics was not yet established on
the present basis of theory and experiment. It was not until
sixteen years later, in 1849, that Joule, in his paper before the
Royal Society, presented his final conclusion as to the mechanical equivalent of heat, and established the existence of an exact
relation between heat and force.   .

The regenerator was correct in theory, as subsequent experience has shown, but its advantages were to some extent
neutralized by the obstruction it offered to the free passage
of air.   Other practical difficulties presented themselves in an
engine that required 450° F. of heat instead of the temperature
of 212° at which water is turned into steam.   Oxidation soon
destroyed the pistons, valves, and other working parts.

Ericsson's use of high temperature in an air engine seems
to have suggested the use of a similar apparatus to increase
the temperature of steam.   Accordingly his next invention was
a super-heating condensing steam-engine.   It consisted of two
sixteen-inch cylinders and had a stroke of eighteen inches.   The
power was communicated through cog-wheels to a double-acting
pump, thirty inches in diameter and thirty inches stroke.   Steam
was generated at only eight pounds above the atmosphere.   In
Watt's time five to ten pounds was the ordinary pressure and
it has since risen as high as seventy-five or even one hundred
pounds.   With this low pressure the engine proved to be economical.   But here again arose the difficulty attending the use of
high temperatures.   The lubricants were carbonized, and the
pistons, left without protection from friction, were rapidly destroyed.

In the intervals of his study of new motors, Ericsson found
time to perfect a variety of minor inventions.   Most of these
appear to have been more ingenious than profitable.   There
was at least one exception.   This was a sounding instrument
constructed upon the principle of measuring depths by the
compression of air, and anticipating by many years the similar
device for which credit has been given to Sir William Thomson.   It was patented in England and the United States, sub-

sequently improved, and under the name of "Ericsson's Sea
Lead" came into extensive use. Thousands were sold and the
instrument stood the test of many years' trial in the British and
American mercantile and naval marine, and was especially approved of by the hydrographic bureaus of the two governments. By means of tallow, held in the usual manner by a cav-
ity in the base, it was determined whether the lead had touched
bottom or not, and a dial registered the depth in fathoms. Sir
William Thomson's instrument, like that of Ericsson before it,
is based upon the theory that the pressure of the sea for each
succeeding fathom of descent increases in a definite and practically direct ratio. The difference in the two instruments is
in the method of registering the pressure. In Ericsson's instrument this is done by noting on the dial the height to
which the column of water ascends against the pressure of the
air; in Sir William Thomson's, by the change the rising water
effects in the color of tubes lined with chromate of silver.

The anxiety to make quick passages, and the temptation to
avoid the delay occasioned by the old method of taking soundings, resulted in the loss of many fine ships. As soundings
could be taken by the new lead without stopping the vessel, it
was welcomed with enthusiasm by those who tested it. The
British Admiralty referred it for trial to Lieutenant Philip
Bisson, R. N. After testing it for nine days, at depths varying
from five hundred to six hundred fathoms, he reported, saying:
" Respecting the accuracy of the instrument, I found it perfect;
and as to simplicity I need only say that all my crew soon understood its use. And on these grounds I can strongly recommend this instrument as being of great practical utility. I took
accurate soundings in sixty fathoms from a vessel going at the
rate of six knots." Sir William Thomson's machine has since
taken soundings in one hundred and twenty fathoms from a
vessel moving sixteen knots an hour, and this could have been
done with Ericsson's. Captain Ogden, U. S. S. *Decatur*, reported that it never failed to give correct soundings, and that it
was of great use in running in the night along shoals and reefs
in the Indian Ocean. "No commander who has ever used
one of them," he said, "would be willing to be without it."
Speaking of this instrument, Ericsson says: "It was contrived

in conjunction with Francis B. Ogden, Esq., U. S. Consul at
Liverpool, a gentleman practically skilled as a sailor and known
for his scientific attainments. The writer has great pleasure
in according to Mr. Ogden the principal merit of this very useful instrument." Doubtless the idea was Ogden's, and the development of the mechanical details Ericsson's. As finally
completed it was known as "Ericsson's Improved Sounding Instrument," and a patent for improvements on it was taken out
as late as September 23, 1863.

When Ericsson arrived in England there were some 2,500
miles of canals in operation in the United Kingdom, and by the
time the railroads appeared as a rival to check their growth,
the mileage had increased to 4,000 miles. The traffic upon
these artificial water-ways, connecting the natural watercourses,
was an important factor in commercial enterprise. The result
of the Rainhill trial of locomotives had greatly alarmed the
canal proprietors as to the future of their property. Ericsson
sought with others to find some means of enlarging the capacity
of the canals. In connection with C. B. Vignoles he patented
a plan for propelling canal-boats by placing on board a steam-
engine and using it to set in motion two rollers, pinching between them a flat bar of iron fastened to a wooden rail running
along the bank. This was simply the application of a device
previously invented by Ericsson, and designed primarily to enable locomotives to ascend heavy grades. It was originally
supposed that it would be impossible for a locomotive to draw
trains of cars even up ordinary grades without some such device, and among those suggested was the one appearing in the
illustration. The railroad on Mount Cenis was constructed
over thirty years later on Ericsson's plan.*

In 1834 Ericsson tested on the Regent's Canal a system of
propulsion by movable shutters resembling Venetian blinds.
These shutters projected beyond the stern post of the boat and
were set in motion by a steam cylinder placed in the bottom of
the vessel parallel with the keel. The speed obtained was
satisfactory, but the movement of the shutters jarred the
mechanism so much that it could not be made to work continuously. In a modification of this system, patented in 1834, the

* See New York Times, March 18, 1866.

propelling blades were operated by the engine and the jarring
motion was thus avoided. This was applied to a canal-boat in
France with economical results.

A hydrostatic weighing machine was another of Ericsson's
inventions during his residence in England. For this a prize
was awarded by the Society of Arts. Its inventor had given
much attention to hydrostatics and had noted, without reasoning concerning it, this remarkable peculiarity of fluids : " with

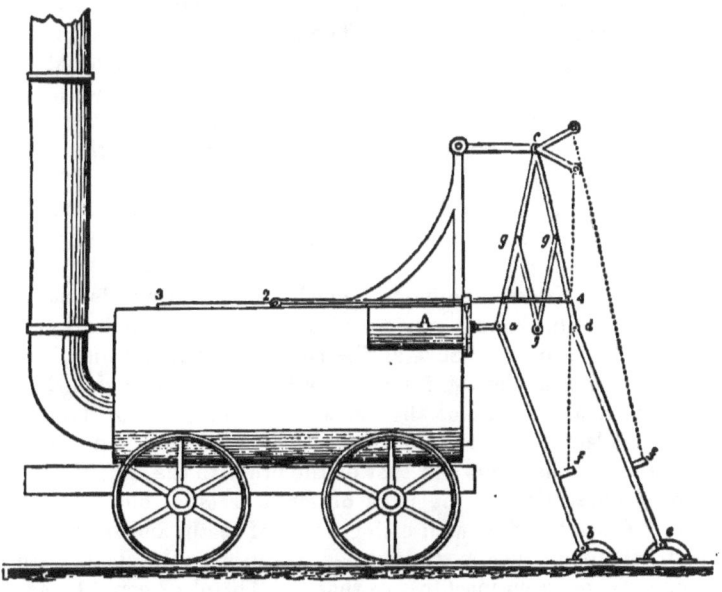

a specific gravity only one-twentieth part that of gold, water
holds, bulk for bulk, a greater quantity of heat, and while so
light that no substance once immersed in it can ever rise from
its surface, except in an aëriform state, it resists pressure to a
degree nearly equal to that of the metals themselves." " Who
can prove," asks Ericsson, " that the waters on the surface of
the globe would not ages ago have become crusted over with
solid matter, and the world converted into a parched desert,

but for its remarkable property of submerging and retaining every solid inanimate substance, permitting only a partial escape in the aëriform state?" Believing that a fuller knowledge should be acquired of the mechanical laws governing this mysterious combination of matter, he invented an apparatus for testing the compressibility of water. This he called the "hydrostatic gauge." The measurement was effected by means of mercury brought into contact with distilled water at sixty degrees, this water being subjected to hydrostatic pressure. A compression of $\frac{1}{1000000}$ was thus readily detected in a column of water only a few feet high. The possibilities of this instrument were of course limited to the strength of the material of which it was composed. This, Ericsson estimated at two hundred thousand pounds per square inch of section. As he had no time to experiment with this device, to determine the precise relations of force and compression characterizing a fluid, he placed it in the London Crystal Palace Exposition of 1851, with a hydraulic machine constructed for the purpose of testing it.

In 1836 Ericsson patented a machine for cutting files automatically. One model was put into operation at Sheffield and another in Belgium. Several files could be cut at one time, and in cutting taper files the force of the blow was proportioned to the width and depth of the cut at different parts of the file. For double-cut files two machines were used, the bed of one inclining to the right and that of the other to the left, to give proper inclination to the rows of teeth crossing one another. For "floats," or files with a single row of teeth, and for round and half-round files a straight bed was used. Two beds were employed on each machine, so that the "blanks" could be adjusted upon one while the other was cutting. The machine made two hundred and forty strokes in a minute; three times the rate of handwork. As these blows were of uniform strength, steel of uniform hardness was required, and with this excellent files could be made.

Another steam-engine was added to the list of inventions about this time and applied to a canal-boat in France, a patent being taken out there, as well as in England and the United States. It was a "semi-rotary engine," the steam cylinder containing a piston projecting like the spoke of a wheel from a central axis. This piston was moved back and forth by the action of the steam through an arc of three hundred degrees: and imparted a continuous rotation to the driving-shaft by the means of a peculiar application of "friction disks." It was ingenious but not economical. A semi-rotary engine was among the ideas patented by John Watt in 1782. If equal power could be thus obtained, rotary engines would have the great advantage of compactness of construction. There are two difficulties: first in securing a satisfactory packing of the piston, without excessive friction, and next in the loss of effective pressure in consequence of the resistance of the steam behind the piston.

Ericsson had now been ten years in England, and during this time he had patented thirty inventions, considered by him of sufficient importance to claim a place in a list I have before me in his handwriting. It was prepared in 1863 and includes just one hundred inventions, after the precedent of "The Century of Invention," written in 1655 by Edward Somerset, Marquis of Worcester, who in his turn may have derived his idea from the "Centuria di Secreti Politici, Cimichi, e Naturali," by Francesco Scarioni of Parma (Venice, 1626).

Very little is to be learned concerning the details of Ericsson's life in London. We find him recorded on his patents as an engineer, located, October 10, 1834, at "Union Wharf, Albany Street, Regents Park;" July 13, 1836, at "Brook Street, New Road," and on July 6, 1839, at "Cambridge Terrace, Hyde Park." He was an agreeable companion, and by no means unsocial in his nature, but constant occupation gave him small opportunity for the ordinary intercourse of society. Still, he was an admirer of ladies in his own way and did not scorn to trim his plumage accordingly. In matters of dress he was at that time very particular and maintained an extensive wardrobe. His friendships were usually the result of professional association, and through them he secured a circle of acquaintance sufficiently large for the limited need of social intercourse, since he was less dependent than most men on human friendship.

Among his earliest acquaintances in England was Mr.

G

Charles Seidler. The wife of Mr. Seidler had a half-sister, Amelia Byam. When Ericsson first knew her brother-in-law, Amelia was a child of ten years. She grew into a lovely woman, the most fascinating he had ever seen, as he was accustomed to say, intelligent, generous in disposition, cultivated, and a fine musician, as well as very handsome. Her father, Edward Byam, was the second son of Sir Charles Byam, at one time British Commissioner for Antigua, and her uncle, Rev. Richard Burke Byam, was for forty years rector of Kew and Petersham, where he confirmed several members of the royal family.

When Amelia Byam was nineteen years old, and John Ericsson thirty-three, they were married by license, on October 15, 1836, by the incumbent of St. John's Church, Paddington. The witnesses signing their names to the register of the church were Mr. and Mrs. Seidler and their daughter; Mrs. Seidler's sister, Louisa Browning; John Braithwaite, Ericsson's partner; and "John Milner." Referring to this occasion thirty years after, the bridegroom said: "I have not been in a church since March, 1826, except once in London, when on a certain morning I committed the indiscretion of not only going inside the holy room, but of also appearing before the altar and there giving a promise difficult to keep."

Speaking of one of his rivals, he said: "That the beautiful and musical Miss Byam preferred the foreign engineer hurt the proud banker's vanity exceedingly, as he was one of the handsomest men in London."

A niece of Mrs. Ericsson married, in 1868, Colonel, afterward Lieutenant-General, Sir Trevor Chute, K.C.B., of the British army, and one of the Chutes of "Chute Hall," England. She appears frequently in Ericsson's domestic correspondence as "the magnificent Lady Chute," descriptive in this case, no doubt, but not necessarily so, for he was accustomed to relieve the strain of exactitude required in his daily pursuits by indulging in hyperbole when he found occasion to deal with ladies. His native Swedish is said to lend itself to this form of expression more readily than any other European language, except the Spanish. Lady Chute lived in New Zealand, and of Ericsson it must be said that his admiration for women was in in-

verse ratio to their social demands upon him. He was willing
enough to be entertained by them when the humor pleased
him, but quite unwilling to assume any responsibility for them
necessitating the occupation of his valuable time. He was himself accustomed to say that he was not fitted for domestic
life.

CHAPTER VI.

THE SCREW PROPELLER.

Fortunate Result of the Rainhill Contest.—Ericsson's Viking Blood.—Studies in Naval Engineering and Gunnery.—Relations to Captain Robert F. Stockton.—The Screw Propeller.—The First Steam Tug.—Early Experiments with the Screw.

NEITHER the comments of the critics nor the failure of his plans could discourage Ericsson's belief in the principle of his hot-air engine. In it he proposed to substitute air for water, as a medium for transferring heat into power, and thus escape the danger attending the explosive properties of steam. But what particularly fascinated his imagination was the idea that he could, by the use of his " regenerator," or respirator, as it should more properly be called, save the waste of heat attending its use in the steam-engine. Brande describes the respirator as " an instrument covering the mouth with a net-work of fine wire, through which persons of weak lungs can breathe without injury. The wire being warmed by the breath, tempers the cold air from without." *

A similar net-work of wire was used in a second caloric engine contrived by Ericsson in 1838, the " orifice through which the air to be expanded by heat into working force passed in and out being covered by a metal box wherein sheets of wire gauze were closely packed, their meshes receiving heat from the warm air passing out and transferring it to the cold air coming in.

Theoretically, this " regenerator " would prevent all waste of heat, except such as was lost by radiation from the machine itself ; practically this result was only partially accomplished. The name given to the engine indicated that Ericsson was at this date possessed by the idea which, as Professor Rankine tells us,

* Brande's Dictionary of Science. Literature, and Art.

"has been the chief impediment to the progress of the accurate knowledge of the laws of the relations between heat and motive power"—the idea that the phenomena of heat are caused by the presence, in greater or less quantity, of a substance called "caloric." * Heat was not then recognized as a mere form of activity, and no account was taken of the large amount of heat necessarily transformed into work. No sufficient provision was made in the furnaces for this loss of power, and unexpected difficulties were met with in heating at all a substance so little affected by radiant heat as air. Hence, the inventor did not at this time go beyond the construction of a model engine for the purposes of experiment.

In the interval of five years between this experiment and the preceding one, with the first caloric engine, in 1833, Ericsson had made good use of his studies into the conservation of heat by improving the steam-engine, so as to lessen the loss of heat attending the process of condensing the waste steam into water. With these labors he found time for others, destined to produce even more important results.

Reviewing his life toward its close, he was accustomed to say that his failure to secure the much-coveted prize in the Rainhill locomotive contest was most fortunate for him. With success would have come immediate prosperity and corresponding temptation; as it was, his struggle with adverse fortune continued until his blood was cooler, and the heat and passion of youth had in a measure abated. He was naturally an intense man in every way, and when the full tide of life poured through his veins they were fairly bursting under the constant strain of a vigorous vitality that must find relief in some form of activity. With his great mental power and intense nervous force were combined enormous muscular strength and corresponding physical passion. He was, in short, in every respect, a high-pressure engine.

The taste for strong drink is a Swedish characteristic, and in his younger years Ericsson shared it, though he never permitted it to master him; still, until he changed his habit, when he was about fifty years old, he was accustomed to take his brandy and his heavy sherry, if not immoderately or imprudently, at least

* Rankine's Manual of the Steam Engine and other Prime Movers. 1861.

with studious regularity. With his ardent temperament he felt that idleness, or the temptation of leisurely social intercourse, would have put a lion in his path, for it was the time of high living and hard drinking in England. From this possible danger, as well as from other temptations, he was saved by the strain of constant occupation.

Naturally amiable and generous, Ericsson was, at the same time, a man of ungovernable temper. Like the Scandinavian hero, Odin, "he looked so fair and noble when he sat with his friends that every mind was delighted, but when he was in a heat then he looked fierce to his foes." He was controlled by a strong sense of justice, but he did not readily brook opposition, and he had his experiences of the "Berserk fury," such as compelled the Norse warriors of old to bite their shields, and to wrestle with the stones and trees, lest they slay their friends in their rage. "There was no king who would not give them what they wanted rather than suffer their overbearing;"* and they were few who cared to encounter John Ericsson when the Berserk fury was on him.

At the time when Ericsson was first busied with his caloric experiments steam navigation upon the ocean was opening the way to new conquests over space. In 1807, on August 7th, the *Katherine of Clermont*, nicknamed by the derisive "*Fulton's Folly*," left her wharf at New York, followed by taunting shouts of "God help you, Bobby!" "Bring us back a chip off the North Pole," "A fool and his money," etc., and steamed up the North River to set the farmers on its banks fleeing home with the tidings that the devil was sailing up the Hudson "on a saw-mill."

In 1832, the year before the caloric engine appeared, came the first wild suggestion of the possibility of establishing a regular line of steamers between England and America. In 1838, when the improved caloric engine was finished, the pioneer of the ocean line, the *Great Western*, crossed the Atlantic in fifteen days; just equalling the time of the sailing ship *Pennsylvania*, which three months before had made "the shortest passage as yet."

To Ericsson seems to have been apparent ten years earlier

* Vide Du Chaillu's Viking Age.

what did not become clear to others until this experiment in ocean navigation, that steamers could not compete in a fair contest with sailing vessels until there was a radical revolution in the means of applying power. Especially did he see that the objections taken by the old salts to the use of steam for naval vessels were well founded, so long as the imprisoned steam was in danger of being let loose by exploding shell, and the clumsy paddle-wheels, with the machinery coupled to them, to be torn to pieces when most needed in order to escape the perils of battle. Some time previous to 1833 he was called upon by a carrying company in London to conduct numerous trials with submerged propellers on the London & Birmingham Canal, and we find evidence that he was certainly conducting such experiments as early as 1833. Describing his subsequent progress, he said, in a letter to John Bourne, published in the London *Engineer*, December 31, 1875:

1835. Designed a rotary propeller to be actuated by steam power, consisting of a series of segments of a screw, attached to a thin broad hoop supported by arms so twisted as also to form part of a screw. The propeller subsequently applied to the steamship *Princeton* was identical with my said design of 1835. Even the mode adopted to determine, by geometrical construction, the twist of the blades and arms of the *Princeton's* and other propellers was identical with my design of the year last mentioned.

1836. Constructed a small propeller boat, operated by steam power, in a large circular cistern, for the satisfaction of certain parties intending to take an interest in my invention, and to furnish means for securing letters patent for the same.

1837. Designed an engine for imparting motion directly to the screw propeller shaft, consisting of two steam cylinders placed diagonally at right angles to each other, the connecting-rods of which were coupled to a common crank-pin. This engine was applied, in the year 1838, to the iron screw steamer *Robert F. Stockton*, which crossed the Atlantic, under canvas, 1839, and was afterward employed as a tug-boat on the river Delaware for upward of a quarter of a century.

This last was the first direct-acting screw propeller engine ever built.

The large circular cistern here referred to was one of the public baths in London. A steam boiler was placed over this and steam from it conducted through a pipe to a small engine

set in the little boat. The accuracy of the inventor's theoretical calculation was shown by the complete success of the experiments. On the first trial the toy boat, less than two feet
in length, as soon as the steam was turned on started on a
voyage around the basin at the rate of more than three miles
an hour. This was an instance of the nice application of theory
to practice for which Ericsson's career was remarkable. If he
could not always control the conditions of economical success,
he never proposed mechanical absurdities or impossibilities.

His chief rival for the honor of introducing the screw,
Francis Pettit Smith, was at this time striving to work out the
problem of using the old device of an Archimedean screw by
"rule of thumb," for he was a farmer and not an engineer or
mechanic. Only by the accidental breaking of the long screw
he was using did he discover that he was on the wrong track.
His labors undoubtedly did much to smooth the way for the
early introduction of the propeller, and up to the time that
Smith and Ericsson appeared no permanent or practical progress had been made in screw propulsion. In 1836, when their
patents were taken out, there was no vessel propelled by a screw
in existence. Experiments, indeed, had been made in England,
in America, and in France, showing that by means of a screw,
a vessel might be driven through the water. But the recollection of these experiments had in a great measure died out,
and what remained of it operated rather as a discouragement
than a provocative to enterprise, since it carried the presump-
tion that if the mode of propelling by the screw had been found
satisfactory it would not have been relinquished.*

Shortly after Ericsson's patent was granted, the *Francis B.
Ogden*, a vessel 45 feet long, 8 feet beam, and 3 feet draught,
was built for the purpose of effectually testing the power of the
screw, and launched upon the Thames in the spring of 1837.
Two propellers, 5 feet 3 inches in diameter, were so fitted to
the stern of this vessel that either could be used. "So successful was the experiment that when steam was turned on for
the first time, the boat at once moved at a speed of upward of
ten miles an hour, without a single alteration being required
in her machinery. This miniature steamer had such power,

* Treatise on the Screw Propeller. By John Bourne, C.E. London, 1852.

too, that she towed a schooner of one hundred and forty tons burden at the rate of seven miles an hour, and the American packet ship *Toronto* at the rate of more than four and a half knots an hour against the tide." "This fact," Mr. Sargent tells us, "excited no little interest among the boatmen of the Thames, who were astonished at the sight of this novel craft moving against wind and tide without any visible agency of propulsion, and, ascribing to it some supernatural origin, they united in giving it the name of the *Flying Devil*. But the engineers of London regarded the experiment with silent neglect." *

In the summer of 1837, Ericsson invited the Lords of the British Admiralty to take an excursion in tow of his experimental steamboat. The *Ogden* was taken to Somerset House, the headquarters of the British Navy, and lashed alongside the Admiralty barge containing the First Lord, Sir Charles Adams; the Surveyor of the Navy, Sir William Symonds; the Hydrographer, Captain Beaufort, and Sir William Edward Parry, the hero of five expeditions to the Arctic seas, who had recently assumed the duties of the newly created office of "Comptroller of Steam Machinery for the Royal Navy." Other gentlemen of scientific or naval distinction accompanied this party. The results of the expedition are best told in the language of Mr. John O. Sargent, the friend of Ericsson for half a century. He described it while the circumstances were still fresh in recollection, in his lecture delivered before the Boston Lyceum in December, 1843,* as follows:

In the anticipation of a severe scrutiny from so distinguished a personage as the Chief Constructor of the British Navy, the inventor had carefully prepared plans of his new mode of propulsion, which were spread on the damask cloth of the magnificent barge. To his utter astonishment, as we may well imagine, this scientific gentleman did not appear to take the slightest interest in his explanations. On the contrary, with those expressive shrugs of the shoulder and shakes of the head which convey so much to the bystander without absolutely committing the actor, with an occasional sly, mysterious, undertone remark to his colleagues, he indicated very plainly that though his humanity would not permit him to give a worthy man cause for so much unhappi-

* Sargent's Lecture on the Late Improvements in Steam Navigation, etc.

ness, yet that "he could an' if he would" demonstrate by a single word the utter futility of the whole invention.

Meanwhile the little steamer, with her precious charge, proceeded at a steady progress of ten miles an hour, through the arches of the lofty Southwark and London Bridges, toward Limehouse, and the steam-engine manufactory of the Messrs. Seaward. Their lordships having landed and inspected the huge piles of ill-shaped cast-iron, misdenominated marine engines, intended for some of his Majesty's steamers, with a look at their favorite propelling apparatus, the Morgan paddle-wheel, they re-embarked and were safely returned to Somerset House, by the disregarded, noiseless, and unseen propeller of the new steamer.

On parting, Sir Charles Adams, with a sympathizing air, shook the inventor cordially by the hand, and thanked him for the trouble he had been at in showing him and his friends this *interesting* experiment; adding, that he feared he had put himself to too great an expense and trouble on the occasion. Notwithstanding this somewhat ominous finale of the day's excursion, Ericsson felt confident that their lordships could not fail to perceive the great importance of the invention. To his surprise, however, a few days afterward, a friend put into his hands a letter written by Captain Beaufort, at the suggestion, probably, of the Lords of the Admiralty, in which that gentleman, who had himself witnessed the experiment, expressed regret to state that their lordships had certainly been very much disappointed at its result. The reason for the disappointment was altogether inexplicable to the inventor, for the speed attained at this trial far exceeded anything that had ever been accomplished by any paddle-wheel steamer on so small a scale.

An accident soon relieved his astonishment, and explained the mysterious givings-out of Sir William Symonds, alluded to in our notice of the excursion. The subject having been started at a dinner-table when a friend of Ericsson was present, Sir William ingeniously and ingenuously remarked, that "even if the propeller had the power of propelling a vessel, it would be found altogether useless in practice, *because* the power being applied in the *stern* it would be *absolutely impossible* to make the vessel steer." It may not be obvious to everyone how our naval philosopher derived his conclusion from his premises; but his hearers doubtless readily acquiesced in the oracular proposition, and were much amused at the idea of undertaking to steer a vessel when the power was applied in her stern.

But we may well excuse the lords of the British Admiralty for exhibiting no interest in the invention when we reflect that the engineering corps of the empire were arrayed in opposition to it; alleging that it was constructed upon erroneous principles, and full of practical defects, and regarding its failure as too certain to authorize any speculations even of its success. The plan was specially submitted to many distinguished engineers, and was publicly discussed in the scientific journals; and there was no one but the inventor who refused to acquiesce in the truth of the numerous demonstrations proving the vast loss of mechanical power which must attend this proposed substitute for the old-fashioned paddle-wheel.

Mr. Francis B. Ogden was a gentleman well known at that time to travelling Americans, as Consul of the United States at Liverpool. He was a liberal-minded man and one whose practical experience in steam navigation made him an invaluable ally to Ericsson. Though not an engineer by profession, Mr. Ogden had been distinguished, Mr. Sargent tells us, " for his eminent attainments in mechanical science, and is entitled to the honor of having first applied the important principle of the expansive power of steam, and of having originated the idea of employing right-angular cranks on marine engines. His practical experience and long study of the subject—for he was the first to stem the waters of the Ohio and Mississippi, and the first to navigate the ocean by the power of steam alone—enabled him at once to perceive the truth of the inventor's demonstrations; but not only did he admit their truth, he also joined Captain Ericsson in constructing the first experimental boat," and to this boat his name was given.

In Mr. Ogden Ericsson found an attentive listener to his engineering ideas, and a warm sympathizer with projects so novel that they confused the mind of the average Englishman, who hates a thing merely because it is new. To a man pursued almost to his death by the tribe of the 'twill-never-doists, acquaintance with such a man as Ogden was like the shadow of a great rock in a weary land. " How I hate that expression ' it will never do,' " says Hayden—the unfortunate artist to whom England owes its possession of the Elgin marbles—in his " Lectures on Painting and Design; " " it has always been the favorite watch-cry of those in all ages and all countries who look on all schemes for the advancement of mankind as indirect reflections on the narrowness of their own comprehensions."

This was not Ogden's first venture with Ericsson, for I find the record of an obligation he entered into in 1831, binding himself in the penal sum of £20,000 as assignee for Ericsson of the rights in the United States "to a certain invention, being an improvement in the application of steam for mechanical purposes." This is evidently the steam-drum, in which William Laird also invested. Ogden, being a citizen, took out the patent in the United States, and assigned to Ericsson one-half interest. It was through Mr. Ogden, too, that Ericsson applied at Washington, in 1837, for a patent for his propeller.

"One thing is forever good: that one thing is success." "Will it pay?" is the supreme test of success in contemporary appreciation of mechanical improvements, and Ericsson's inventions, as we have seen, did not always pay. Sometimes because the result he sought could be more economically accomplished in other ways, if less efficiently, and as often because a long educational process was required to convince those he wished to benefit of their need of what his genius had provided for them. The reception, no less than the conception, of new ideas necessitates evolution, and this is a weary world for those who see much beyond their fellows. Ericsson's investments in "futures," as they would be called on the exchanges, were too heavy, and the financial difficulties resulting from this imprudence were increased by the enforcement of an obligation assumed on behalf of a friend. The firm of Braithwaite & Ericsson had failed, and the bailiffs were on the track of the junior member. So, for a time, he enjoyed the hospitalities of "The Fleet" as a foreign debtor. In the year 1837, so disastrous to many others, he took the benefit of the "act for the relief of insolvent debtors," and secured his discharge in bankruptcy.

We had in our navy at this time, a sailor, Robert F. Stockton, who united qualities rarely found in combination. An accomplished and experienced officer, showing an intelligent interest in all that concerned his profession, he was at the same time a man of fortune and family influence, as well as an important factor in the politics of his native State of New Jersey, afterward representing it in the Senate of the United States. Lieutenant Stockton was building the Delaware & Raritan Canal, and had invested in it his fortune, and that of his family. The financial difficulties of 1837 compelled him to visit England to procure the means for completing the canal. There he made the acquaintance of Ericsson, no doubt through Mr. Ogden, who was a fellow-Jerseyman, and a representative, as Stockton

himself was, of a family honorably identified for several generations with the history of the State.   Robert Ogden, the
grandfather of one, was a member of the Continental Congress,
and the ancestor of the other was one of the signers of the
Declaration of Independence. ,

Thus it happened that Ericsson and Stockton were brought
together just at the time when the inventor of the propeller was
most in need of influential assistance to enable him to develop,
in some more congenial clime, schemes in danger of perishing
under the chilling influence of British hostility and indifference.   To Stockton the State of New Jersey is indebted for
the early development of her railroad and canal system, and
his experience in this work, supplementing his naval training,
led him to give much attention to the construction of steam
engines, and the subject of applying steam to war vessels at a
time when most naval officers were still insisting upon the advantages of sails.

Stockton was induced to accompany Ericsson in one of his
excursions on the Thames on the *Francis B. Ogden,* and at
once appreciated the value of the invention received with such
cool indifference by the officials of the British Navy.   He comprehended immediately the revolution it was destined to work
in naval warfare, and this was sufficient to fix his attention
without reference to its commercial value.

His perceptions were quick, his self-reliance was unlimited,
and he was nearly as energetic as Ericsson himself in carrying
out a plan once conceived.   A single trip from London Bridge
to Greenwich was sufficient to induce him to at once order from
the inventor two iron boats for the United States, to be fitted
with his steam machinery and propeller.

"I do not want," said Captain Stockton, "the opinions of
your scientific men; what I have seen this day satisfies me."

A dinner at Greenwich ended this excursion and Stockton, who added oratory to his other accomplishments, made a
speech declaring to Ericsson, "We'll make your name ring on
the Delaware, as soon as we get your propeller there."

Returning to the United States, Stockton was, in December,
1838, promoted to captain and ordered to the Mediterranean as
fleet-captain on board the flag-ship of Commodore Hull.   He

was also made bearer of despatches to the American Minister to the court of St. James, and improved the opportunity of his visit to England to thoroughly inform himself as to the condition of the marine armaments of Great Britain. He also found time to witness the trial of the screw steamer built for him, the *Robert F. Stockton*, and for further consultation with his friends Ogden and Ericsson. It would have been impossible to find two men better fitted to assist Ericsson in the realization of his ambitious schemes with reference to marine propulsion, for the studies and experience enabling them to comprehend his plans had not closed their minds to new suggestions. "Stockton was, moreover," as Philip Hone says in his "Diary," "not one of the timid sort, and did not often find his modesty crossing the path of his undertakings." *

The *Stockton* was launched in the river Mersey on July 7, 1838, and immediately fitted with her double cylinder, direct-acting engine and the patent spiral propeller. After several highly satisfactory trials with her at Liverpool, she was, on January 12, 1839, tried on the river Thames, in the presence of Captain Stockton, Mr. Ogden, and about thirty other gentlemen invited to witness her performance. The London *Times* of that date mentions as present several distinguished British and Swedish naval officers, Mr. Vignoles, and other engineers, and Major-General Sir John Fox Burgoyne—a natural son of the Burgoyne of Saratoga surrender, the engineer-in-chief in the attack on New Orleans, repulsed by Jackson, and the father of a son destined, thirty years later, to fall a victim, as a captain in the British navy, to Cowper Coles's attempt to rival Ericsson in marine construction. Sir John was at this time Chairman of the Board of Public Works and Commissioner of Steam Navigation, etc., in Ireland.

The results obtained with this vessel were considered at the time most extraordinary. The *Times* described them at length, announced that they appeared "quite conclusive as to the success of this important improvement in steam navigation," and forecasted "important changes in steam navigation" from its introduction. The *Robert F. Stockton* was an iron steamboat, seventy feet in length on deck and ten feet beam, drawing

* Diary of Philip Hone, vol. i., p. 273.

three feet of water and propelled by a fifty-horse power engine. Of such engines the *Times* said :

> They may be made much stronger and more compact than ordinary marine-engines, in consequence of the power being applied directly to the shaft which works very near the bottom. This for sea-going vessels will be very important, and their original cost may be considerably reduced, as all the paraphernalia of shafts, wheels, wheel-guards, etc., will be dispensed with. We were struck with the great regularity of the motion, not the slightest jar being perceptible. The engines consist of two cylinders sixteen inches in diameter with eighteen-inch stroke, and are worked by steam, of a pressure varying from thirty-five pounds to fifty-five pounds to the square inch, their construction is extremely simple and evinces a knowledge of steam machinery by the inventor which is calculated to give additional confidence in the success of his propeller in all the varieties of its application for the canal, river, or ocean navigation.

The *Stockton* was built at Birkenhead, on the Mersey, by Messrs. John & Macgregor Laird, who were the pioneers in building iron vessels, one of their boats, the *Alburka*, having been sent with the Landers to Africa to explore the Niger.* From them, no doubt, Ericsson obtained thus early, ideas on the subject of iron ship construction of which he was able, later in life, to make most effective use.

Some gentleman, whose knowledge of the text of Shakespeare was obtained at second-hand, objected to one of his plays on hearing it for the first time, because it was too full of familiar quotations to do credit to the author's originality. Ericsson was the subject of similar criticism in his old age. His knowledge of and experience with many mechanical contrivances in common use to-day dated so far back of any existing recollection that he was supposed to have copied from others what he, in fact, originated himself, or certainly first brought into use. The spectacle of saucy little steam-tugs drawing huge vessels after them at will, so familiar now in American waters, was wholly unknown to British seamen in 1838. So strange, indeed, that the stolid watermen watched the feats of towing on the Thames with the sort of curiosity attending a balloon ascension, as an entertaining exhibition in dynamics, wholly disconnected from any relation to the daily business of

* Fairbairn's History and Progress of Iron Ship Building, p. 4.

life. Even the commendation of the *Times* could not arouse in conservative British ship-owners, or naval officers, the ambition to avail themselves of this new power.

Just previous to this, in the winter of 1837, Ericsson's propeller had been fitted with great success to a canal boat of ten horse-power called the *Novelty*, plying upon the canal between Manchester and London, and realizing a speed of eight or nine miles an hour. "This," says Bourne, "is the first example of a screw boat being employed for commercial purposes; but this boat was in a short time laid up, owing to the failure of her owners. In the early part of 1839 another iron steamer, 70 × 7 feet, with 14-horse-power engines, was built by Mr. J. T. Woodhouse, and fitted with Ericsson's propeller to run on the Ashby-de-la-Zouche Canal, near Leicester, England. She attained a speed of nine to ten miles in deep water. These experiments were not repeated, and it required a struggle of years to persuade the British public and British officials of the value of the screw." *

In his petition of 1850 to the Privy Council Ericsson tells us that the success attending these several vessels was, at the time, faithfully and favorably recorded in the *Times* newspaper, *Mechanics Magazine*, the *Civil Engineers and Architects Journal*, and the *London Journal of Arts and Sciences*.

Although the importance, usefulness, and practicability of the invention were thus established, and public attention attracted to it, "yet so little was it then understood and such was the opposition and indifference of engineers and others interested in the invention that no benefit resulted to the inventor."

Ericsson further called the attention of the Privy Council to the fact that his patent " was the earliest in date, and that in a book recently published by Bennet Woodcroft, Professor of Machinery in the University College of London, on 'The Origin and Progress of Steam Navigation,' it is admitted that your petitioner, John Ericsson, accomplished for the screw propeller in America and in England what Fulton did for the paddle-wheel in the former country,† which testimony your pe-

---

* A Treatise on the Screw Propeller, by John Bourne, p. 88. London, 1852.
† See Woodcroft's Sketch of the Origin and Progress of Steam Navigation, p. 102. London, 1848.

titioners submit is the more valuable as proceeding from one who is himself the inventor of an improved propeller, and to whom your petitioners were wholly unknown. The efforts of your petitioners, and particularly your petitioner, the said John Ericsson, have mainly contributed to the introduction and practical application of the screw as a marine propeller to the almost incalculable benefit of this great commercial country."

This petition presents very fully, in formal language, a history of its author's claims to the screw propeller. Various nations have claimed it for their citizens, just as they have claimed the steam-engine and other useful inventions. In front of the Polytechnic School at Vienna stands a bronze monument, erected in 1863, by a national subscription, to the memory of Joseph Ressel, the Austrian to whom his countrymen ascribe the first use of the screw. Ressel's first drawing was made in 1812, while he was a student in the University of Vienna ; his first experiments were made in 1826, with a barge driven by hand, and February 11, 1827, an Austrian patent was issued to him. In 1829 he applied his screw to a boat with an engine of six horse-power and made for a time six miles an hour. Then a steam-pipe burst and the police, whose heads were more occupied in those days with the plots of Carbonari than with scientific investigation, put an end to further experiments.

It is a curious fact that John Bourne, who devotes a treatise to the screw propeller and describes one hundred and twenty-six different inventions, does not so much as mention the original of the Austrian monument. In 1823, Captain Delisle, of the French Engineers, presented a memorial to the Minister of Marine describing a proposed method of propelling vessels by means of a submerged screw. No attention was paid to it and it was forgotten until revived in after years to furnish a pretext for the invasion of Ericsson's patent in France where his propeller was the first introduced and obtained a wide acceptance. Weighing Ericsson in the balance with his chief rival, Smith, Bourne says : " Ericsson, previous to his connection with the screw, was an accomplished engineer ; Smith was only an amateur, with almost everything except the leading idea to learn. Ericsson's mechanical resources gave him means of overcoming difficulties such as Smith did not possess ; and

7

Smith had therefore to accept expedients then usual among engineers as his starting-point, whereas Ericsson could reject those expedients in favor of others which his own ingenuity suggested. Thus, in bringing up the speed of the screw, Smith had to submit to the use of gearing, because that was the expedient which was approved by orthodox engineers; but Ericsson threw the dogmas of engineers to the winds, and coupled the engine immediately to the propeller." *

In March, 1845, Ericsson made affidavit that before the year 1833 he had devoted much time and attention to the invention of stern propellers, having been appointed by a carrying company in London to conduct numerous experiments in propelling canal-boats with submerged propellers in the London & Birmingham Canal. In 1833 his attention was particularly directed to the subject of oblique propulsion, on the principle for which he afterward obtained letters patent in England. He employed Elias Harrison, afterward Chief Engineer on the U. S. S. *Princeton*, to fit stern propellers of various patterns to a canal boat called the *Francis* and belonging to Messrs. Robins & Mills, forwarders, 128 London Wall. All of these propellers were connected with the engine with a cylindrical iron shaft projecting through the centre of the stern-post and worked below the water-line. They were placed between the rudder and the stern-post, and were protected by an overhang which also gave support to the rudder from above; wheel and rudder being supported from below by a flat iron bar bolted to the after end of the keel, extending beyond it and turning in the space between this and the overhang. The same device was, toward the end of 1834, applied by Ericsson to a new canal boat called the *Annatarius* built by Robins & Mills, the overhang in this case forming part of the boat itself. These facts are stated in an affidavit made by Harrison, who further states that the screw was thus put into practical operation on the *Annatarius* "before May, 1835, this deponent having been employed by the aforesaid Robins & Mills as chief engineer running the said boat for many months from that time."

Farmer Smith's attention was not directed to the subject of screw propulsion until 1835, but he preceded Ericsson with his

* Bourne's Treatise on the Screw Propeller, p. 90.

English patent. It was dated May 31, 1836, Ericsson's July 13, 1836, or six weeks later. That the latter carried his invention into practice at once is shown by his statement and that of Count Von Rosen to the Privy Council, as well as by contemporary newspaper accounts.

The *Mechanics Magazine* of June 3, 1837, described the towing of the American packet ship *Toronto*, of six hundred and thirty tons burden, on June 28, 1837, and published the certificates of the pilot and mate that the vessel was towed "at the rate of four and a half knots an hour against the tide." Two years later the same vessel was again towed by another propeller, and this led to some confusion of dates, upon which has been founded a denial of the original performance. The *Enterprise*, built for the Ashby-de-la-Zouche Canal, ran there for one season, but without profit to her owner. She was accordingly transferred to the Trent and Mersey where she met with great success as a steam-tug hauling coal barges.

Among Captain Ericsson's papers appears a letter from Count Von Rosen enclosing this financial statement. It presents a very interesting condensed history of his early relations to the propeller.

ERICSSON'S PATENT PROPELLER.

DR.

				£	s	d
1836.	To cost	of first experimental model................		27	14	10
	"	" patent........		150	0	0
1837.	"	" Robins & Mills' canal boats machinery...		1,264	17	2
Jan.	"	" model No. 2........		26	12	6
April	"	" experimental boat *Ogden*		394	16	11
Nov.	"	" canal boat *Robin No. 1*.................		282	13	8
1838.						
Jan. 1,	"	" engine and propeller of the *Robert Stock-ton*		1,529	2	6
May 7,	"	" Robins' canal boat.....................		208	10	7
" 19,	"	" Robins' experiment....................		115	8	1
Aug.	"	" model No. 3		44	0	9
" 24,	"	" Rossière rotary engine and propeller.....		516	11	2
" "	"	" " " " " "		80	5	2
" "	"	" engine and propeller *Stockton*..........		37	12	3
Dec. 7,	"	" " " " "		66	13	8
" 31,	"	" Captain Ericsson's maintenance		94	3	0
1839.	"					
Jan. 1,	"	" *Stockton* machinery....................		196	11	3
" 19,	"	" No. 3 rotary engine and propeller........		404	17	8
" 25,	"	" Rossière's rotary engine and propeller....		304	16	10

			£	s	d
1839.					
Feb. 15,	To cost of *Stockton* machinery.....................		180	7	0
May 25,	" " " "	....	248	19	7
" " "	" 3 models.............................		149	11	5
June 5,	" engine and propeller for canal boat *Ashby-de-la-Zouche*		562	17	9
" 25,	" semi-rotary engine and propeller		802	18	2
Sept. 2,	" Captain Ericsson's maintenance..........		600	0	9
Nov. 5,	" Robins' canal boat.......		27	17	6
Dec. 31,	" Captain Ericsson's maintenance..........		50	0	0
1840.	*Stockton* machinery.....................		47	0	0
Jan. "	" Robins' canal boat.......		15	13	6
July, "	" Captain Ericsson's maintenance..........		249	12	0
Dec. 31. "	" " " "		50	0	0
1841. "	"				
			8,730	6	1

CR.

			£	s	d
1837.					
April 5,	By cash *Ogden* and *Stockton* boats.................		95	0	0
May 16,	" " " "		170	0	0
Sept. 13,	" old material canal boats		250	0	0
Oct. 2,	" cash Robins & Mills...........................		455	6	11
1838.					
Jan. 25,	" " *Ogden* and *Stockton*		350	0	0
March 1,	" " Robins		130	0	0
" 5,	" " "		415	15	8
April 22,	" " *Ogden* and *Stockton*		400	0	0
May 19,	" " " "		156	9	4
June 8,	" " Robins.......................		99	3	7
28,	" " Rossière.......................		100	0	0
Aug. 24,	" " "		160	0	0
Oct. 2,	" " *Ogden* and *Stockton*.......................		550	0	0
1839.					
Jan. 5,	" " Rossière		180	0	0
Feb. 20,	" " *Ogden* and *Stockton*.......................		442	11	0
July 6,	" " " "		572	12	0
Aug. 3,	" " *Ashby-de-la-Zouche*		290	0	0
Dec. 31,	" old material, Robins...........................		50	0	0
1840.					
Jan. 4,	" cash *Ogden* and *Stockton*.......................		770	18	9
Feb.	" " Robins		49	12	5
Aug.	" old material, Robins...........................		25	10	5
			5,712	19	8
	Balance.............................		3,017	6	5
			8,730	6	1

		£	s	d
	Balance........................	3,017	6	5
1846.	Cash *Amphion*.................	1,500	0	0
		1,517	6	5
	Law expenses.................	156	0	0
		1,673	6	5

CHAPTER VII.

REMOVAL TO THE UNITED STATES.

Adventurous Voyage of the Stockton Across the Atlantic.—Subsequent
History of the First Screw Steamer.—Recognition of Ericsson's
Claims to the Screw.—Robert Fulton's War-steamer.—Naval Oppo-
sition to the Use of Steam.—Award of a Gold Medal for the Steam
Fire-engine.—Early Use of Propeller in American Waters.—Erics-
son's Personal Appearance and Habits.—Mrs. Ericsson Joins her
Husband.

UNDER date of May 30, 1839, this entry appears in the
published "Diary of Philip Hone."

Among the maritime exploits with which these adventurous times
abound, the arrival, on Wednesday last, of a little steam schooner, called
the *Robert F. Stockton*, from England, was one of the most remarkable.
She sailed from Gravesend on April 13. She is only ten feet wide and
seventy feet long, and her burden is thirty tons. She is built entirely
of wrought sheet-iron, and is intended as a towing vessel on the New
Jersey Canal. The commander is Captain Crane. She performed her
voyage in forty-six days, with no serious disaster except the loss of one
seaman, who was washed off this little cockle-shell by one of the seas
which were constantly sweeping her decks. Never, I presume, was the
western ocean crossed in so small a craft. There was not room enough
to lie straight nor to stand erect. This little vessel lies near the Battery,
and is visited by hundreds of curious persons, anxious to realize the
possible truth of the nursery story about the "three men of Gotham"
who "went to sea in a bowl." *

Crane was a captain in the American merchant marine and
a most intrepid sailor, as this experience shows. His crew consisted of four men and a boy, and he made the passage under
sail alone. In admiration of his daring the New York authorities presented him with the freedom of the city. The little tug

* Diary of Philip Hone, 1828–1851. Edited by Bayard Tuckerman. Vol.
i., p. 362.

was set to work on the Delaware & Raritan Canal, and nearly thirty years after was still doing duty as the *New Jersey.* On November 17, 1866, Bennet Woodcroft, then Librarian of the British Patent Office, wrote to Ericsson expressing a desire to purchase the original engines of this vessel, to place them in the Patent Office Museum—"not only for their historical value, but also to put an end to F. P. Smith's false claim to any invention in regard to screw boats or their first introduction." Ericsson replied: "The *Robert F. Stockton* (*New Jersey*) is still in operation as a tow-boat after twenty-five years' constant service.

The Stockton crossing the Atlantic.

The original engine was some time ago taken out. It will give me great pleasure to send it to you free of cost, if not broken up."

The *Stockton,* or *New Jersey,* was at this time in the possession of the Messrs. Stevens, of Hoboken. Ericsson offered to replace the old engine with a new one, but without avail, and on August 15, 1873, he wrote: "Nothing could induce the Messrs. Stevens, who claim to be the originators of screw propulsion, to permit the machinery of the *real* pioneer screw vessel to be placed in your museum. Accordingly, some time ago, the *Robert F. Stockton* was hauled out of the water and cut up, each plate being separated from the others, while the machinery was broken up and put into the melting-pot. So careful were the parties mentioned to prevent the smallest part to remain as a proof that the remarkable vessel once existed, that 'not a vestige now remains,' says my informant, who has access to the premises where the vile act of destruction took place. A meaner proceeding cannot well be imagined, but I expected nothing else, since it leaked out during the negotiation what the old machinery was wanted for."

This letter was in response to one from Mr. Woodcroft of a month earlier, saying: "The benefit you have conferred on the world by the screw propeller is beyond computation. If I could obtain the original engines, in whatever state they now are, I should be proud of them as a trophy, to be placed in the Patent Office Museum in London, where they would be side by side with Miller's experimental engine that drove a paddle-wheel boat in 1788; Watt's steam-engine, by which circular motion was first given to a shaft; Bell's engine that drove the first practical paddle-wheel steam-boat in Europe in 1812, on the Clyde; Stephenson's locomotive, the *Rocket*, and your locomotive, the *Novelty*. If you could possibly point out the way in which I could obtain them, I would spare neither expense nor trouble." This is what was thought at the British Patent Office of Ericsson's claim to the screw propeller, after a generation of trial, investigation, and controversy.

"Not only did Captain Stockton order on his own account the two iron boats," says Mr. Sargent, "he at once brought the subject before the Government of the United States and caused numerous plans and models to be made at his own expense, explaining the peculiar fitness of the new invention for ships of war. So completely persuaded was he of its great importance in this aspect, and so determined that his views should be carried out, that he boldly assured the inventor that the Government of the United States would test the propeller on a large scale; and so confident was Ericsson that the perseverance and energy of Captain Stockton would sooner or later accomplish what he promised, that he at once abandoned his professional engagements in England and set out for the United States."

Speaking of the screw propeller, Mr. Sargent says further : "The circumstances under which this invention was devised and prosecuted, the perseverance with which it was followed up by Ericsson, through all discouragement and neglect, and its ultimate success in its *precise original shape* prove it to have been the result, not of a happy accident, but of patient reflection and scientific calculation. It was not hit upon, but was wrought out; it was not suggested, but elaborated; demonstrated in theory to the inventor's own satisfaction before it was submitted to the test of successful experiment." *

Ericsson was at this time superintending engineer of the Eastern Counties Railway, one of the principal lines centring in the British metropolis, designed by Mr. Braithwaite and opened in 1839. For this road Ericsson built a machine of his own contrivance for constructing embankments. He resigned his position and started for New York November 1, 1839, in the steamer *Great Western*, the pioneer of the first line of Atlantic steamers.

The *Great Western* had a stormy passage and did not arrive in New York until November 23d, so Ericsson had an opportunity of realizing the difference between planning ships on shore and sailing in them on the sea, for he was dreadfully sea-sick. "Before May 26, 1826," he says, in a letter written in 1875, "I hailed from Sweden, after that date up to November 1, 1839, I hailed from England, and since November 23d, same year, I have been a steady New Yorker."

It does not appear to have been Ericsson's original intention to become a resident of the United States, for I find among his letters the following from his friend Ogden, to whose friendly suggestions his journey to the New World was in no small measure due :

OAK DALE, Thursday Night.

MY DEAR ERICSSON : I have just got through with a lot of letters for you to take with you to the United States, but I have determined to put them into your hands myself, and to bid you good-by in person. I am going up to town on Saturday night, and on Sunday morning shall go directly to Swartwout, wherever he may be—if you have not yet learned, inquire either of Miller, in Henrietta Street, or of Blood, 12

---

* Sargent's Lecture on Improvements in Steam Navigation.

North Audley Street, but at all events hold yourself ready to dine with us on Sunday, somewhere, where you will get much information on the subject of your transatlantic tour.

Remember me kindly to Madam and believe me,

Yours truly,

FRANCIS B. OGDEN.

At the time of Ericsson's transfer to the United States there were no steam vessels in our navy. In 1813–14 Robert Fulton had built his *Demologos* or *Fulton*. This was the first war-steamer ever built, and into her Fulton introduced a variety of devilish contrivances for confounding an enemy ; furnaces for red-hot shot, submarine guns sending one hundred pound balls twelve feet below the water-line, and an engine for discharging an immense column of water upon decks and through portholes. The *Fulton* was never entirely completed, the war with England which had called for her construction having ended. She was converted into a receiving ship and stationed at the Brooklyn Navy Yard. There she was blown up in 1829, whether by accident or design has never been settled, and a large number of persons on board of her were killed.

In 1837–38 a second *Fulton* was built. Though this vessel attained a high speed, she was entirely unsuited to naval purposes, and in 1839 was lying a useless hulk at the Brooklyn Navy Yard. Stockton was an ardent advocate for the introduction of steam into the naval vessels already in service, and his conferences with Ericsson had satisfied him that it was possible with a vessel on an entirely new plan to convince the most conservative of the value of steam. By act of March 3, 1839, Congress had authorized the construction of three ships of war, and it was Stockton's confident assurance that he would be allowed to build one of these that prompted Ericsson to prepare the plans of a steam frigate in England and bring them with him to this country. Every detail for such a vessel had been most thoroughly considered, and the plans included not only the model of the vessel but her engines and motive power, her guns, and the method of mounting, aiming, and firing them.

Unexpected difficulties attended the carrying out of the project Stockton and Ericsson had conceived between them. A powerful service sentiment resisted innovation of every sort, as it always has done and always will do. "Do you not know," Ericsson once wrote, "that you can never convince a sailor?" "The head of the Navy Department," so says Stockton's biographer, "is generally a politician more solicitous to obtain popularity among the officers than competent to discharge judiciously the functions of his office. He listens, therefore, to the voice of the superannuated officers, who, with professional dogmatism, denounce all novelties, and pronounce all innovations dangerous. The application of steam to national ships-of-war from the first was resisted by many naval officers, and had to encounter the most stubborn prejudices and most determined opposition. It was confidently asserted by the old captains that steam vessels would be worthless except for purposes of transportation." *

An officer of the navy, Captain William M. Hunter, submitted a plan for a vessel with submerged wheels on the sides and Stockton urged the building of a steam frigate after the designs of Ericsson. It was finally decided to build one vessel on each plan. There was delay in carrying out the purpose of the Navy Department, and work was not begun until 1842, upon the vessel proposed by Stockton and called the *Princeton*, after the city of his residence.

Meanwhile Ericsson found abundant occupation. Just after his arrival here the Mechanics' Institute of New York, taking alarm at the destructive fires devastating the city, in January, 1840, offered its great gold medal as a prize for the best plan of a steam fire-engine. With his previous experience, Ericsson had no difficulty in securing this prize. In this engine he adhered to his early system of using a blowing apparatus to generate steam, in deference to the prevailing opinion that the sparks from an engine using the "steam-blast" would endanger the wooden houses so common at that day. The engine used in 1829, at the Argyle fire, had six horse-power and threw one hundred and fifty gallons of water in a minute to the height of one hundred feet. It took twenty minutes to get up steam. The new engine got up steam in ten minutes, had the power of one hundred and eight men, and threw three

* Life of Commodore Robert F. Stockton.   New York, 1856.

thousand gallons of water in a minute through a 1½-inch pipe to a height of one hundred and five feet. It weighed two and one-half tons.

The main purpose of Ericsson's visit to the United States was to introduce his propeller to American waters. In a letter to his friend Sargent, dated January 24, 1845, he says: "I visited this country at Mr. Ogden's most earnest solicitation, to introduce my propeller on the canals and inland waters of the Union. I had at the same time strong reasons for supposing that Stockton would be able to start the 'big frigate' for which

Steam Fire Engine awarded a Prize by the American Institute, 1840.

I had prepared such laborious plans in England. On arriving here I soon found that Captain S. had not that power with the administration he had told me in England—where he once assured me he could get my propeller introduced in the American navy at once. He, on one occasion, expressed himself thus: 'I will let you have,' or 'you shall have' the 'finest frigate in the American navy'—meaning to try the propeller on.

"Stockton's inability to do anything with the navy induced me at once to turn round and see what could be effected with private individuals. The result was the fitting out of the *Clar-*

ion, the *Vandalia*, on the lakes, the steamboats *Propeller, Erics-son*, and a barge for the Canadian Government, all running on the St. Lawrence. Various other vessels were in contemplation, when at last Captain Stockton ordered his four iron boats, for which he never paid me one cent. The steamboat *Ericsson*, on the Delaware, and numerous other propeller vessels were successively commenced, all without the least assistance from Captain Stockton, who all the while threw cold water on my endeavors."

In a letter to Captain Stockton, dated "Astor House, New York, August 31, 1840," Ericsson called attention to the fact that his "journey to this country" was undertaken "for the sole purpose of carrying out patents in which yourself and Mr. Ogden are equally interested with myself." He stated that Mr. Ogden had agreed to loan him £150, and asked for a similar loan from Stockton, adding, "Your refusal would be unwelcome news, I can assure you." His gun-lock was at that time being tried at Sandy Hook, and he had great hopes of profit from that. He says, in concluding his letter, "Mr. Ogden tells me you are about starting an ocean steamer at Philadelphia—I will not express my apprehensions that the news are too good to be true."

The canal barges for Stockton were vessels of six feet draught and two hundred tons burden, $100 \times 22\frac{1}{2}$ feet. They were built early in 1842 and ran from Philadelphia, two of them to Albany and two to Hartford. They were ordered through Ericsson from a New York builder named Cunningham, and were the occasion of some unpleasantness growing out of circumstances the significance of which is not now apparent. In a letter dated November 1, 1842, Stockton says: "There seems to be no end to the misunderstanding between us." In this letter he also says: "What I have done for you, the trouble, pain, anxiety, suspense, and inconvenience which I have undergone in my desire to serve you—not myself, seem to be altogether overlooked by you, and you seem to accuse me of having made use of your services for my own ends and afterward to refuse you what you thought was your just due. I was not disposed to submit to this in silence and was desirous to know whether you intended to make any charge for any other services you have rendered, because I did not wish unexpectedly to be reminded of them."

This seems to have been simply a phase of the old quarrel between client and patron. "I hope," said Dr. Johnson, in his famous letter to Lord Chesterfield, "it is no very cynical asperity, not to confess obligation where no benefit has been received, or to be unwilling that the public should consider me as owing that to a patron which Providence has enabled me to do for myself." Stockton's confident assurances had thus far resulted in nothing tangible, and whatever assistance he might receive, the proud-spirited engineer believed to be due from a public servant to one who was himself seeking public ends. He felt that he was superior to Stockton in every respect, except the possession of wealth and influence, and he was by no means disposed to accept the position, in which it was sought to place him, of an "ingenious mechanic" developing the ideas of a progressive naval officer.

The increase of intelligence has in some measure relieved the men of brains from their position of slavish dependence upon men of position, but their emancipation is not yet complete, as Ericsson discovered. He struggled through life to assert the dignity of his profession, and we shall see how constantly his uncompromising spirit kept him at war with circumstances. From his cradle almost he had had the command of men; the sense of strength which superiority in any department gives was active within him, and in his field he was inclined to be as autocratic as one who controls the resources of an empire.

Among those who witnessed the early trials of Ericsson's propeller in England were two American ship captains and ship owners, Messrs. Russell E. & Stephen E. Glover, of New York. The Glovers were enterprising men and they determined, without waiting for others, to apply the screw to the *Clarion*, a vessel they were building to run between New York and Havana. This was the fourth vessel to receive the Ericsson propeller; the *Ogden* being the first, the *Stockton* the second, and the *Vandalia*, plying between Oswego and Chicago, the third. Four vessels were put on the Rideau Canal and St. Lawrence, viz., the *Baron Toronto*, *Royal Barge*, *Propeller*, and *Ericsson;* seven sailed from Philadelphia to various ports; one was on the Erie Canal; four on Lake Erie; two, besides the *Vandalia*, ran from Oswego to Chicago; two from New York to Canada;

one was put on the James River Canal and one on the Delaware. This makes in all twenty-four merchant vessels receiving the Ericsson propeller before the *Princeton* went into commission, February, 1849. There was besides the Revenue Cutter *Jefferson* on Lake Erie.

Great interest in this new motor was awakened by the discussions in the New York papers at the time the *Clarion* was built in 1840, and its obvious adaptability to the necessities of American shipping was soon made apparent. From a list prepared in 1843 by Lieutenant Johnson, a Swedish naval officer, acting under the instructions of his Government, it appears that the propellers at that time numbered in all forty-two ; one built in 1839, six in 1841, nine in 1842, and twenty-six in 1843. The history of the introduction of steam navigation on United States waters shows that several years before screw propulsion had assumed importance in England the carrying trade of our great lakes was to a large extent conducted by screw vessels. On April 6, 1841, Captain James Van Cleave and Mr. Benjamin Isaacs purchased the right to use the Ericsson propeller on the lakes. The *Vandalia* was their first vessel, and on December 1, 1841, her owners reported that she had proved a great success. "She has astonished us all," they said.

At a still earlier date the canal barge *Ericsson*, built from the plans of her namesake, made her first voyage from Rockville to Montreal, forty miles in sixteen hours—no great speed, the significance of the voyage being in the ability shown to master the rapids. Another propeller *Ericsson*, built in 1842, to run on the Delaware & Chesapeake Canal, between Philadelphia and Baltimore, carrying passengers and freight, proved so great a success commercially that two other vessels, the *Cumberland* and the *Baltimore*, were ordered and the "Ericsson Line" established, greatly to the discomfort of the Philadelphia, Wilmington & Baltimore Railroad, with whose business it most seriously interfered. The railroad was compelled to reduce its fares one-half. It finally persuaded the State of Delaware to impose a prohibitory toll on passengers going on the propeller line, but this did not restore its freight business. The Ericsson line of steamers was incorporated by the State of Maryland in 1844, and it is still in operation with five propellers.

Out of it has grown the New York & Baltimore Transportation Company, equipped with eight steamers and plying daily between Baltimore & New York.

When he first came to New York Captain Ericsson took up his residence at the Astor house, in those days a famous hos-

The Vandalia—Pioneer Propeller on the Lakes.

telry, especially affected by New Englanders, Daniel Webster making his home there when in the city and the New England Society there doing yearly homage to Plymouth Rock. Among the New England habitués of the place was Mr. John O. Sargent, a lawyer of Massachusetts birth, who to his legal learning united fine abilities as a writer and much experience as an editor. He had founded the *Collegian* when a student at Harvard in 1830, had for four years, 1834–37, contributed the political articles to the Boston *Atlas*, and was at this time associated with James Watson Webb in the conduct of the New York *Courier and Enquirer*. The New Englander and the Swede had a common fondness for a good glass of sherry, and were accustomed to linger over their wine after the "fifteen minutes for refreshments" Americans had left the dining-room. Thus they fell into conversation, conversation led to acquaintance, and acquaintance ripened into a friendship lasting to the end of Ericsson's life, Mr. Sargent, who was eight years his junior, surviving him.

Immediately after his arrival in New York, Ericsson established business relations with the "Phœnix Foundry," which about this time passed under the control of two young men, Messrs. Hogg and De Lamater. With the junior partner, Mr. Cornelius H. De Lamater, his relations became very intimate, and their associations of business and friendship continued through life.

Another of Ericsson's early acquaintances in New York was Mr. Samuel Risley, to whom I am indebted for a description of his appearance, his characteristics, and his personal habits at this time. Mr. Risley says:

My first acquaintance with Captain Ericsson, or rather my first sight of him, I think, occurred in the summer of 1839.* He had brought with him from England a working model of the propeller engine he had designed for the war steamer *Princeton*, and a twelve-inch wrought-iron gun. The model engine referred to was erected in the Phœnix Foundry engine works, West Street, New York, and put in operation there. Captain Ericsson would frequently visit the works, bringing with him friends and Government naval officers to witness its working. Of these I think Mr. Ogden was one, Captain Stockton, of the United States Navy, the promoter of the building of the *Princeton*, another.

Captain Ericsson all his life was careful of his personal appearance; at the time I refer to he was exceptional in dress, not dandified, but more in keeping with the present morning call attire than an ordinary day habit. A close-fitting black frock surtout coat, well open at the front, with rolling collar, showing velvet vest and a good display of

* This must have been in 1840, as Ericsson did not arrive until the last of November, 1839.

shirt front, a fine gold chain hung round the neck, looped at the first button-hole of the vest and attached to a watch carried in the fob of the vest. Usually light-colored, well-fitting trousers, light-colored kid gloves, and a beaver hat completed the dress. To this add a well-built military figure, about five feet ten and one-half inches in height and well set up, with broad shoulders and rather large hands and feet; the head well placed and supported by a military stock round the neck. Expressive features, blue eyes, and brown, curly hair, fair complexion. His head was about medium size,* his mouth well cut, upper lip a little drawn; the jaw large and firm-set, conveying an expression of firmness and individual character.

Up to the summer of 1842 I was in constant attendance upon the Captain, being a sort of factotum to him in preparing his models. At that time he boarded at the Astor House where I first met his wife. He was very reserved about his models and inventions and seemed to have a mortal dread of their being discovered. I remember once, at a later period than I am now referring to, we shook hands and I pledged myself most solemnly not to reveal a discovery of his that at the time he considered of vital importance to the caloric engine, but which on trial was disappointing to him. It, however, led up to uses by which he profited eventually.

Ericsson's manner with strangers was courteous and extremely taking. He invariably made friends of high and low alike. With those in immediate contact in carrying out his work he was very popular. He had few intimates of his own social level. Mr. John Osborne Sargent, brother of Epes Sargent, was one of them. With such I think he would be very hearty, open, and frank, and he was a good talker.

In the fall of 1842 the Captain employed me to superintend the building of an iron screw steamer at Richmond, Va., for the navigation of the James River and Kanawha Canal, in that State. Owing to the shallow water in the canal, the *Governor McDowell*, as the vessel was christened, was put to other use, although the result of the experiment was in the main satisfactory. She was followed by another steamer propelled by paddles, but again the difficulty of running the boat through about three feet of water was insurmountable. The Captain was at the trial of the *McDowell* and was introduced to the Governor, after whom the boat was named. Being present at the interview, I had an opportunity of seeing both men at their best, the Governor gracious and affable and withal dignified, Ericsson lifting his hat and holding it above his head while bowing respectfully, then replacing it and shaking the hand held out to him by the Governor.

The following year I went with the Captain to 95 Franklin Street as his assistant, and remained with him until the fall of 1846, when I left him to go to China. During the period I was with him he accomplished

* Twenty-three inches in circumference. He was about five feet seven and one-half inches tall.

an immense amount of work. He would work out designs in pencil and I would make fresh drawings from them in detail. He gave up this practice, he informed me, after I left him and gave particular attention to all details, working out every screw in finished drawings. He said he profited by it in the end.

Ericsson's habit of life at that time was to breakfast at 8.30 A.M. dine at 4 P.M., with a cup of tea and toast at 7 P.M. He usually went to the engine works to see how his work was progressing in the forenoon, but as a rule he spent about fourteen hours a day at his drawing-board.

In designing he was marvellously quick, and with his scale and a pencil he would sketch almost equal to a finished drawing. He had been thoroughly grounded in Euclid and his conceptions of mechanical movements were clear and distinct. He had great method and order in laying out his work and its continuance after was easy to him—more, in fact, a pleasure than a labor. His mechanical resources in designing were practically unlimited. The engines in the caloric ship *Ericsson* were a remarkable evidence of his superiority in this respect. In some respects his wonderful inventive faculty may have acted as a drawback to the successful working out of his plans. Had he, for instance, given more time to the improvement of the steam-engine in his earlier days it is not improbable that he would have outstripped all competitors in its development.

During this time he designed the iron steamer *Iron Witch* as a passenger day boat between New York and Albany. In this he introduced the compound principle in the engine, using the steam expansively in a second cylinder. The boat attained a speed of about seventeen miles an hour, as well as I remember, but was not fast enough to outrun the old line boats, and she was withdrawn from the route.

About 1845 I made drawings from a sketch by Captain Ericsson for a further improvement in the compound principle in the steam-engine. I think a model was also made and a patent applied for.

I have remarked that Captain Ericsson was, at this period of his life, exceptionally handsome in personal appearance, and that he was equally attractive in dress and bearing. To me, from my first intercourse with him to the last, he was always gentle, kind, and considerate. In habit of life he was frugal, but in carrying out his mechanical conceptions, or in the elaboration of them, money was not considered.

I last saw Captain Ericsson on July 1, 1887, at his home, Beach Street, New York. Being on my way to England, I called to say good-by; we had not met for several years. He was very cordial, going over his daily habits of life, his work, the improvement of the steam-engine, the sun motor, and the lunar investigations. He was in good health and spirits, and laughingly told me that he was going down by gravitation only at the rate of about three-fourths inch in seven years. Twice, on taking my leave, he shook hands, and bid God bless me, repeatedly saying good-by. My last letter from him is dated November

[Mrs. John Ericsson.]

9, 1888. In it, in reference to his health, he writes : "I very seldom quit my drawing-table before 11.00 P.M, and not once in the course of the year go to bed before half an hour past midnight. Brain, muscle, and eyes, thank God, all hold good."

Mrs. Ericsson did not accompany her husband to the United States, but soon followed him. Crossing the ocean in the middle of winter, in one of the uncomfortable boats of that time, she had a trying passage, arriving in a state of complete exhaustion. She remained with Captain Ericsson for a time at the Astor House, and until they transferred their residence to No. 95 Franklin Street, where he had his office as well as his home. This was a fine house in that day, and stories of John's extravagant living went back to Sweden, as would appear from a letter received from his mother at this time. Do not, he said, in reply, "put any faith in the gossip about our 'lavishing.' There are people who cannot understand that one can live in a grand house, wear fine clothes, and yet starve. As to my wife, her elegant garment is a black dress which I gave her five years ago, and yet she gains everybody's attention."

Mrs. Ericsson was a woman who would attract attention in any dress. She was above the medium height; in fact, quite as tall as her husband, who was five feet seven and one-half inches. A trifling masculine in her type, but bearing herself with grace, her beauty and dignity of manner made her a noticeable figure wherever she went. Her husband was proud of her beauty, and she was equally proud of his talents, but his mind was too much occupied with his work to leave him opportunity for those domestic interchanges which are the recreation of leisure hours. His wife was not a woman to be neglected, and, as her husband expressed it, was "jealous of a steam-engine." It is not the habit of imperious beauties to admit even a Frankenstein to rivalry, and Mrs. Ericsson soon tired of the isolation in which she was left. She did not like America, and as her husband was engaged in a desperate struggle with fortune, it was finally decided that it was best for her to return to her relations in England until Ericsson found the opportunity, that never came, to join her there. He made such allowance for her support as his means admitted of from time to time, and they continued in correspondence up to the day of her death, without again meeting.

Ericsson appears to have stripped himself for the battle he was constantly waging against conservatism, and it left him little leisure for anything else. A tender-hearted and affectionate man in his way, his intellect dominated his affections, and he was to an unusual extent independent of them. They were with him rather sentiments than motive forces, and he gave himself small opportunity for their cultivation. His love for his mother was always controlling with him, and while she lived he continued in constant correspondence with her, though there were times of intense absorption in his work when even she for the moment seems to have been forgotten. His check-book gives proof, however, of his constant recognition of the claims of filial duty, as well as of his obligation as a husband. It seems to have been his wish that his wife should share his fortunes in the United States, for a letter to him from her sister shows that on one occasion she refused to leave England after he had paid her passage across the ocean. This letter was written just after Mrs. Ericsson's death, and in it her sister says, that "Amelia's" last words were, "I have always been a trouble to you all. Forgive me."

CHAPTER VIII.

THE SCREW IN WAR VESSELS.

Screw Vessel Ordered for the Navy.—Captain Stockton calls Ericsson to His Aid.—His Testimony to Ericsson's Ability.—The Direct-acting Screw System.—Stockton's Injustice to Ericsson.—The Guns, "Oregon" and "Peacemaker."—Disastrous Explosion of the Stockton Gun.—President Tyler Loses Two of His Cabinet.—Universal Excitement.—Success of the "Princeton."—Other Naval Vessels Rendered Obsolete.—Ericsson's Physical Strength.

"WHILE busily engaged," said Ericsson, in a letter already quoted from, " and perfectly independent of Captain Stockton, so far as the introduction of the propeller went, I unexpectedly received a letter from him in the fall of 1841, asking me to meet him at Princeton, N. J. There he informed me that he had received orders to build a steamer of six hundred tons for the navy. He at this interview consulted me as to the best dimensions for such a vessel. I made a sketch on the spot, and after some discussion he agreed to my proportions. He then desired me to make out a general plan for the whole ship, arrangement of steam machinery, etc. I went to New York, and in about a week returned to Princeton, with such general plans, and with these Captain Stockton was delighted. I also brought an estimate of the cost of the steam machinery, made at his particular request. The maximum of the estimate was seventy-five thousand dollars. Captain Stockton told me he would put it down at one hundred thousand dollars, on which I remarked that it was too much ; to this he replied, ' I want to make ample allowance for paying you for the use of patents,' or words to that effect. Captain Stockton, having made his formal arrangements with the Government and fixed on Messrs. Merrick & Town* as the builders of the engines, desired Mr. Merrick

* Concerning the machinery of the *Princeton*, Mr. J. Vaughan Merrick, the son of one of the builders, says in a letter to the author of this biography :

to go to New York to receive my instructions with regard to the engines. Captain Stockton not only desired me to make the plans and superintend the manufacture of the engines, but he frequently complimented me as the only man in America capable of doing it.

"At a dinner given by Captain Stockton to the Corporation of Princeton on the day the *Princeton* was launched at Philadelphia, he told his guests he had been all over the world in search of a man that could invent or carry out what he thought was necessary to make a complete ship of war; he had at last found that man. 'He is,' he said, 'my friend here by my side, Captain Ericsson,' and he desired the company to drink my health with 'three times three.' Such were his sentiments then concerning the man who, in May, 1844, had dwindled into an 'ingenious mechanic,' 'a mechanic of some skill.' Again, on board the *Princeton*, at a public trial in New York Bay, Captain Stockton proposed my health to hundreds of respectable gentlemen in these words: 'Captain Ericsson, the most extraordinary mechanical genius of the present day.'"

This was said by Ericsson in a letter written in 1845 to Mr. John O. Sargent in the confidence between client and attorney, and the writer further says: "I am ready to swear to the contents if needful." Letters not necessary to produce here, as they form part of the official record at Washington, show these facts: On May 27, 1841, Captain Stockton wrote to the Secretary of the Navy transmitting a model for a steam ship-of-war

---

" The machinery of the *Princeton* was of a novel type, and I believe has never been copied (certainly not in the United States), although its performance was good, and its location in the hull was low—an excellent point for war vessels of light draught. The writer, at a later period, when a draughtsman in the Southwark Foundry, made several sets of drawings of the details of these engines for foreign governments (the art of blue printing not having been invented). The originals were the handiwork of the inventor, and were beautiful specimens of work. It was one of Ericsson's great peculiarities that his design sprang from his brain in so perfect a shape that there was little to do except to embody them in the drawings. I think that Ericsson's career proved that the *pencil*, as well as the pen, is mightier than the sword. Napoleon did not effect greater changes in the face of Europe than has Ericsson produced in naval warfare, and these latter are lasting, while the former have long since passed into other forms."

and asking that Lieutenants E. R. Thomson and William Hunt be detailed to assist him in preparing the drawings to show the character of the vessel proposed. This request was granted on June 1, 1841. September 21st, Commodore Charles Stewart, known as "Old Ironsides," from the frigate *Constitution* which he immortalized, was informed that the Secretary of the Navy had authorized the construction at the Philadelphia Navy Yard, commanded by him, of "a steamer of six hundred tons on the plan proposed by Captain Stockton; steam to be the main propelling power upon Ericsson's plan." He was further informed that Captain Stockton had been requested "to prepare a draft of the plan of the steamer."

The origin of the plan proposed by Captain Stockton is indicated in a letter addressed by him to Ericsson more than two months previous to this, in July, 1841. In this letter he said:

In making up the estimate of the cost of the ship, it will be necessary to consider what must be put down for the use of your patent-right. It will be necessary, therefore, for you to write me a letter, stating your views on that subject. As a great effort has been made to get a ship built for the experiment, I think you had better say to me in your letter that your charge will hereafter be (if the experiment shall prove successful) ——, but, as this is the first trial on so large a scale, I am at liberty to use the patents, and after the ship is tried Government may pay for their use in that ship whatever sum they may deem proper.

To this Ericsson replied as follows:

NEW YORK, ASTOR HOUSE, July 28, 1841.

To CAPTAIN R. F. STOCKTON:

SIR: I have duly received your communication on the subject of my patent-right for the ship propeller and semi-cylindrical steam-engine; in reply to which I beg to propose that in case these inventions should be applied to your intended steam-frigate, all considerations relating to my charge for patent-right be *deferred* until after the completion and trial of the said patent propeller and steam machinery. Should their success be such as to induce Government to continue the use of the patents for the navy, I submit that I am entitled to some remuneration; but, considering the liberality that thus enables me to have the utility of the patents tested on a very large scale, and the advantages which cannot fail to be derived in consequence, I beg to state that whenever the efficiency of the intended machinery of the steam-frigate shall have been duly tested, I shall be satisfied with whatever sum you may please to recommend, or the Government see fit to pay for the patent-right.

I am, sir, your obedient servant,

JOHN ERICSSON.

In a letter to Sargent, written a few years later, "February 15, 1845," Ericsson said: "I do not understand why Captain Stockton wanted the services of Lieutenants Hunt and Thomson *in connection with the plans* of the *Princeton*, excepting as a vehicle of communication between him and myself. As such, these gentlemen certainly were useful, but in no other manner, as neither of them pretends to the slightest knowledge of mechanics. The making of a plan for a common wheelbarrow requires far more knowledge in mechanics than possessed by these officers. Captain Stockton himself, on the other hand, never made a plan in his life."

Stockton's whole stock in trade as a naval designer appears to have been the model of a vessel prepared by Ericsson when they were together in England. "In the summer of 1839," Ericsson tells us in one of his letters, "I prepared a model of a war screw-steamer of two thousand tons, with a set of detailed drawing plans, for Captain Stockton. These plans and this model Captain Stockton presented to the United States Navy Department in the fall of 1839." This was before Ericsson arrived in this country.

Again Ericsson says:

I am the father of the *direct-acting* screw system. On leaving England for this country the whole engineering world opposed me, and ridiculed the idea of driving engines fast enough to turn the screw *directly*. I, however, adhered to my plan, and built over *twenty* direct-acting engines, not one of which ever failed, before a single individual followed my system. Smith and the whole Archimedean screw fraternity advocated the cog-wheel system, and the Maudsleys, Watts, Rennies, Seawards, and Napiers all built cog-wheel engines for the British Government with such bad success that the screw system was on the eve of being discarded from the navy. In the meantime some forty propeller vessels had been fitted out in this country under my patent, all with direct-acting engines; and presently the *Princeton* appeared in the Mediterranean, and the eyes of the naval authorities of England were opened and the direct-acting system insisted on. The host of great engineering

houses now all entered the field, and all sorts of direct-acting engines
were planned by men who had no experience in the working of engines
of quick action. I say, without hesitation, that most of their engines
are disgraceful to the profession. These boasted engines do not even
hold out during the trial trips over the measured mile, in the placid
waters of Stokes Bay. Did you ever hear of the direct-acting engines of
the *Princeton* being out of order during her remarkable cruise? It is,
I believe, on record that this ship was under steam for forty consecutive
days and nights, at Vera Cruz.*

Captain Stockton's orders "to superintend the building of
said steamer [viz., the *Princeton*], under the Commandant of
the Navy Yard in Philadelphia," were dated at Washington,
September 22, 1841, and addressed to him at Princeton, N. J.
Immediately upon their receipt, Captain Stockton appears to
have visited Philadelphia for he wrote from that city, October 2, to Ericsson in New York:

I will meet you at the depot at Princeton on Tuesday morning, if
you can make it convenient to dine with me on that day; you may return to New York in the night train. I have received orders to build a
ship of six hundred tons; I have remonstrated against it. [He wanted
a larger vessel.] In the meantime I wish to converse with you on the
subject. R. F. S.

"Tuesday" was the 5th. As the result of the conference
on that day, apparently, Stockton wrote from Philadelphia,
October 8, saying to "Captain Ericsson, Astor House, New
York:"

I wish you would make the drawings of a ship with the dimensions
we spoke of. I will go to Washington as soon as you can send them to
me. Put both bow and stern to her, and make her midship section according to the plan we spoke of at my house.

Next followed a series of calls for one thing and another.
October 13th Stockton wished "a drawing of the amidship
section with engine, as well as the others." October 17th he
called for various details which he was required to send to
Washington, "cost of hull, equipments, etc., etc., as well as for
the engines, displacement, metacentre, centre of gravity, centre

* Letter to John O. Sargent, dated May 5, 1854.

of flotation, five midship sections, etc." "You are so much better skilled in these matters," he says, very truthfully, "that you will have these all ready by the time I get through my work, when I propose to take them all to Washington."

November 21, 1841, the working drawings for the engines were called for; April 13, 1843, the "drawings for the wheel and gun-carriage." Altogether one hundred and twenty-four working drawings were furnished by Ericsson, occupying, with the sketches, skeleton plans, and diagrams necessary in their construction, two hundred and seven days of the time of a man who could do in one day double the work of an ordinary draughtsman; one hundred and thirteen days were devoted to actual superintendence at New York and Philadelphia, and in travelling to and fro. This was but part of the labor to which Ericsson gave two of the best years of his life. It was the strictly professional service of an engineer, and could not by any honest possibility be included in Ericsson's expression of his willingness to leave the question of the *payment for his patents* to the generosity of the Government.

He was, besides, put to no inconsiderable expense during the two years for office expenses, travelling expense, postages (which were a serious matter in those days), and the like. The manufacturers of the machinery, guns, gun-carriages, etc., testified that they did their work from Ericsson's drawings and under his directions. Stockton gave his assurance over and over again that if the vessel succeeded there would be no difficulty about pay, and a letter from him to Ericsson, dated Philadelphia, February 2, 1844, shows that he acknowledged the obligation by a partial payment of $1,150.

It is necessary to be thus specific in order to lay the basis for a proper understanding of the action taken by Captain Stockton upon the account rendered for these services when this account was referred to him by the Department. By this time the man whose genius he had extolled in England, and to whom he had held out such brilliant anticipations; the one man he had hunted the world over to find, who could build a complete ship; the only man in America capable of making the engines she required, etc., had become "a very ingenious mechanic by the name of Ericsson."

In the letter dated February 2, 1844, here referred to, Stockton said: " Will you send me a bill and receipt for the $1,150 which I paid you for services rendered in constructing and superintending machinery, etc., for the U. S. ship *Princeton*. I will include it in the *Princeton's* expenses, and repay myself for the advance in that way if I can." In a note accompanying this letter Ericsson says: "The preceding letter for the first time suggested to Captain Ericsson that any difficulty was anticipated in securing him an adequate compensation for his services in the construction of the *Princeton*." When Ericsson's account was referred by the Department to Stockton he sent in reply a letter which extinguished Ericsson's hope of obtaining pay for his services out of the appropriation for the *Princeton*, to which it was properly chargeable. The events immediately succeeding the completion of the vessel explain this change of attitude toward the man Stockton had before extolled.

I have mentioned the fact that Ericsson brought with him from England a wrought-iron gun of his own designing. This gun was built at the Mersey Iron Works, near Liverpool, and was forged of the very best material, as the manufacturers asserted. Still, it had the defect of a forged gun ; strong longitudinally, it was weak transversely and opened cracks under the proof firing in rear of the trunnions, and thus near the butt of the gun. To remedy this, Ericsson adopted an expedient now in universal use. Hoops three and one-half inches thick, made of the best American wrought iron, were shrunk onto the breech of the piece up to the trunnion bands. These hoops were arranged in two tiers, one above the other, in such a manner as to break joint, and they were so perfectly matched as to appear like a single band.

That this expedient proved entirely successful is shown by the fact that the gun is still intact, and is now (1890), on exhibition at one of our Navy Yards, after having been fired some three hundred times with charges varying from twenty-five to thirty-five pounds of powder (enormous in that day) and a two hundred and twelve-pound shot. In 1842, before going aboard the *Princeton*, this gun was fired from one hundred and twenty to one hundred and fifty times, after being banded ; and aimed by its designer, the ex-Swedish artillerist, Ericsson, it pierced a target of four and one-half inches of wrought iron. This target is also still to be seen.

Thus the discovery that this thickness of armor was no protection against artillery fire was made by Ericsson many years in advance of others.

Fired by Ericsson's example, Stockton aspired to build a gun of his own. He had one forged at Hamersley Forge and sent it to the Phœnix Foundry, New York, to be bored and finished under Ericsson's directions. It was of the same calibre as the imported gun, viz., twelve inches, but a foot more in diameter at the breech, and much heavier. This Stockton gun was considered at the time to be a remarkable specimen of workmanship, and great confidence was placed in its strength, because of the supposed superior quality of American iron; it was believed to be capable of sustaining the explosion of any amount of powder that could be put into it, having been thoroughly tested by charges varying from twenty-five to fifty pounds. It was the largest mass of iron that had at that time been brought under the forging hammer, and had a massive appearance by the side of its slender companion on the *Princeton*.

But this appearance of strength was deceptive. The fibrous quality, giving strength to the iron, was in some way destroyed in the process of manufacture, and the specific gravity of the metal reduced nine per cent. below that of ordinary iron. This fact was not discovered until it was too late. Ericsson had a natural partiality for his own gun and advised Stockton to use it for the purpose of exhibition instead of the *Peacemaker*, as the second gun was called, but he does not appear to have doubted the sufficient strength of the Stockton gun.

Describing the trial of this gun a newspaper letter, dated New York, January 17, 1844, says:

Instead of being placed on the ground in some remote corner, as is usual in proving guns of not one-third of her calibre, such was Stockton's confidence in this wrought-iron piece that the proving was actually performed on board a small vessel of some twenty feet beam and seventy feet in length. This appears the more astonishing when we consider that the charge was fifty pounds of powder; and a charge that might well be required for the capacious maw of a gun fifteen feet long, with a bore of twelve inches, carrying a ball of two hundred and thirteen pounds weight, and itself weighing ten tons.

So much for Captain Stockton's big gun—the largest piece of wrought-iron in the world, and forged in this city, of American iron !

Here, where four short years ago they could not forge an ordinary steam-engine shaft ! There was a christening scene on board the *Princeton* yesterday, and from a font of champagne this magnificent piece of ordnance was appropriately baptized the *Peacemaker*. *

In his diary under the date of February 20, 1844,† John Quincy Adams says :

The House of Representatives yesterday adjourned over till to-morrow, for the avowed purpose of enabling the members to visit the *Princeton*, a war-steamer and sailing vessel combined, with the steam machinery of Ericsson's propeller, all within the hull of the vessel and below the water-line. This vessel, the "gimcrack of sundry other inventions" of Captain Stockton himself, was built under his directions, and was commanded by him. She was ordered round here to be exhibited to the President and the heads of the Executive Departments, and to the members of both Houses of Congress to fire their souls with a patriotic ardor for a naval war. On Saturday last, by invitation from Captain Stockton, the vessel was visited by the President, the Heads of Departments and Senators, and for this day, at eleven o'clock, Captain Stockton has issued a card of invitation to every member of the House of Representatives, besides a general one in the *National Intelligencer* this morning. I went with Isaac Hull Adams to Greenleaf's Point, and thence embarked in the *Princeton's* barge on board that vessel.

I was punctual to the hour of eleven and the first of the company that came. Captain Stockton received me with great politeness, and showed me all the machinery of the ship. Afterward upward of a hundred members of the house came on board. The two great guns are called the *Peacemaker* and the *Orator* [*Oregon*]. A salute was fired from the carronades, and the *Peacemaker* was three times discharged.

Eight days later, February 28th, we find this entry : †

Dies iræ. I had received an invitation from Captain Robert F. Stockton to another party of pleasure, with the ladies of my family, on board the war-steamer *Princeton*. We declined the invitation. I had engaged to dine at six o'clock this evening with Mr. Grinnell and Mr. Winthrop, in company with Mr. Pakenham, the new British Minister.

* Boston Post of January 20, 1844.
† Memoirs of John Quincy Adams, Comprising Portions of His Diary, from 1795 to 1848. Edited by Charles Francis Adams. Vol. xi.

. . . While we were at dinner, John Barney burst into the chamber, rushed up to General Scott, and told him with groans that the President wished to see him ; that the great gun on board the *Princeton*, the *Peacemaker*, had burst and killed the Secretary of State, Upshur ; the Secretary of the Navy, T. W. Gilmer ; Captain Beverly Kennon ; Virgil Maxey ; a Colonel Gardiner, of New York, and a colored servant of the President, and desperately wounded several of the crew. General Scott soon left the table, Mr. Webster shortly after, also Senator Bayard. I came home before ten in the evening.

29th. At the House, immediately after the reading of the Journal, a message was received from the President, announcing the lamentable catastrophe of yesterday, bewailing the loss of his two Secretaries, with others, and hoping that Congress will not be discouraged by this accident from going on to build more and larger war-steamers than the *Princeton*.

The biographer of Commodore Stockton * says :

During the progress down the Potomac the great guns of the *Princeton* had been again and again discharged, until public curiosity appeared to be satiated. The company had returned below, and at the festive board the voice of hilarity resounded through the proud ship. Some of the guests had commenced retiring and were renewing their scrutiny of the different parts of the ship. Captain Stockton had risen to offer a toast complimentary to the Chief Magistrate of the Republic. As he rose, with his wine-glass filled in his hand, an officer entered and informed him that some of the company desired one of the great guns to be again discharged. Captain Stockton shook his head and saying, " No more guns to-night," dismissed the officer. He soon again returned, while Captain Stockton was speaking on the subject of his toast, with a message from the Secretary of the Navy, expressive of his desire to see one of the big guns fired once more.

This message Captain Stockton considered equivalent to an order, and immediately went on deck to obey it. He placed himself upon the breech of the gun, aimed and fired. Feeling a sensible shock, stunned and enveloped in a cloud of smoke, for an instant he could not account for his sensations. But in a few seconds, as the smoke cleared, and the groans of the wounded and the shrieks of the bystanders who were unhurt resounded over the decks, the terrible catastrophe which had happened was revealed. He was severely hurt, but the strength of his intellectual powers, now intensely concentrated, sustained him. Calmly and clearly his voice pealed over the elements of confusion and disturbance ; a few brief orders, recalling his men to a sense of duty, were given, the dead and wounded ascertained, and all proper dispositions respecting both

* Life and Speeches of Robert F. Stockton. New York, 1856.

being made, when, as he turned to leave the sad scene, he fell into the arms of his men, exhausted physically and was borne insensible to his bed.

"There were two hundred ladies on board," Philip Hone tells us:

But, fortunately, they were all below, dining and drinking toasts. The noise of mirth and joviality below mingled with the groans of the dying on deck. By this circumstance they were saved. Not one of the ladies was injured. But oh, the anguish of wives and daughters at the sight of the mangled remains of their husbands and fathers. Nothing so dreadful has ever happened in this country, except the shipwreck of the *Rose in Bloom* and the conflagration of the Richmond theatre. The wife of Governor Gilmer was on board. The story of her woe is melancholy and touching in the extreme. Her lamented husband entered upon the office of the Secretary of the Navy a few days since, and the estimation in which he was held is proved by his nomination having been unanimously confirmed without debate by the Senate. Mr. Gardner's two daughters were also witnesses of their father's death. President Tyler gave a new instance of folly and bad taste in a toast that he gave at the entertainment which terminated so tragically on board the *Princeton*. It was: " Oregon, the *Peacemaker*, and Captain Stockton." Oregon is the bone of contention at this time between Great Britain and ourselves, to settle which difficulty a new minister has just landed on our shores. It is a subject which requires to be handled with the greatest delicacy. The *Peacemaker* is the great gun which was to hurl defiance at Great Britain or any other nation which might stand between the wind and Colonel Benton's popularity. Captain Stockton is the fire-brand which was to ignite the whole ; and in the excited state of the public mind on this subject, the President gives this mischievous sentiment. The *Peacemaker* at the same moment broke the peace in the manner which has been described, and amidst the melancholy reflections arising from this fatal day's excursion will be mingled a feeling of contempt for this act of folly.*

David Gardiner, one of the victims of the disaster, was a descendant of the lords of the manor of Gardiner's Island, off the east coast of Long Island. His remains were carried to the White House, and the event resulted in the marriage of his beautiful daughter, Julia, to President Tyler.

The injuries of Captain Stockton were, fortunately, only

* Diary of Philip Hone, 1828-1851, edited by Bayard Tuckerman, vol. ii., p 207.

slight. He soon recovered and demanded a Court of Inquiry to investigate the question of his responsibility for this sad accident, turning his rejoicing into mourning. This court exonerated Stockton from all blame. In their report they referred to the consultations held by him "with three gentlemen possessing from their scientific acquirements and practical experience on such subjects, very superior qualifications in questions of this character; and whose opinions were entitled to high respect, Mr. William Young, of the West Point and other foundries, Captain Ericsson, and Francis B. Ogden, Esq."

During his triumphant exhibition of his pet vessel, Stockton had apparently forgotten Ericsson, and an examination of the contemporary accounts of her performances shows how little was said of him in connection with this triumph of naval construction. This neglect was so marked that a writer in the *Brother Jonathan*, a New York newspaper of March 2, 1844, was tempted to say:

We apprehend that it will be necessary for his sober friends to provide the gallant admiral of the great Tyler squadron with a strait jacket. What with revolutionizing New Jersey by his eloquence, and the art of naval warfare by his inventions, he is in a fair way of having his head turned. If we can believe all we see in the newspapers, he will hardly be satisfied till the nation shall give him an opportunity with his steamer *Princeton*, to annihilate a few British squadrons, and burn down the city of London. We do not desire in the least to detract from the credit to which Captain Stockton is entitled for the construction of the *Princeton*. He deserves praise for having put himself in the hands of a thoroughbred engineer, and for having acquiesced in his suggestions and followed his advice.

A remarkable result has been accomplished, manifesting a fertility of invention and a skill in construction which indicate the mind and the hand of a master in theoretical and practical mechanics. The nation is well aware to whom our navy has been indebted for this new wonder, and we should not be surprised even if Congress should some day attain the information which Captain Stockton has withheld in his recent report to the Secretary of the Navy. It is not a little surprising that in commending to Congress the numerous striking inventions and constructions which give his single ship her boasted advantage over entire navies, he should have omitted to mention even the name of the individual who had invented, planned, and superintended the whole of them.

The report here referred to was forwarded by Stockton February 5, 1844, after the *Princeton* had received her armament on board and was fitting for sea. He dwelt with enthusiasm upon the "great and obvious advantages" she possessed "over both sailing ships and steamers propelled in the usual way." With engines lying "snug in the bottom of the vessel out of the reach of an enemy's shot," showing no chimney and "making no noise, smoke, or agitation of the water (and, if she chooses, no sail) she can surprise an enemy," and "at pleasure take her own position and her own distance."

The *Princeton* was the only war vessel that then possessed these advantages ; she had by far the most formidable guns afloat and could "throw a greater weight of metal than most frigates, with a certainty heretofore unknown." "By the application of the various arts to the purposes of war on board the *Princeton*," said Stockton, "it is believed that the art of gunnery for sea service has, for the first time, been reduced to something like mathematical certainty. The distance to which these guns can throw their shot at every necessary angle of elevation, has been ascertained by a series of careful experiments. The distance from the ship to any object is readily ascertained with an instrument on board, contrived for that purpose, by an observation which it requires but an instant to make, and by inspection without calculation. By self-acting locks the gun can be fired accurately at the necessary elevation—no matter what the motion of the ship may be. It is confidently believed that this small ship will be able to battle with any vessel, however large, if she is not invincible against any foe. The improvements in the art of war, adopted on board the *Princeton*, may be productive of more important results than anything that has occurred since the invention of gunpowder. The numerical force of the navies, so long boasted, may be set at nought. The ocean may again become neutral ground ; and the rights of the smallest, as well as the greatest nation, may once more be respected."

All of this was true, and it was further true that to the genius of John Ericsson were due these changes which inevitably revolutionized naval methods and speedily compelled the reconstruction of every great navy. This important fact Cap-

9

tain Stockton omitted to mention in his report. The name of
Ericsson did not appear there, and he left it to be inferred, if
he did not directly state, that it was to Stockton himself that
the country was indebted for this marvel of a naval vessel. In
a measure this was true. While it is not certain that Ericsson
might not have otherwise obtained an opportunity to develop
in practice the ideas he had elaborated a dozen years before, it
is evident that this opportunity did come to him in 1842–44,
through Stockton. The two men were necessary to each other,
and if there had been a sufficiently generous recognition of this
fact on both sides, even the disaster attending the *Peacemaker*
might not have prevented them from together accomplishing
great results for our navy.

The history of gun construction shows how much tentative
effort is required to develop even a sound theory in ordnance,
and in the half century and more that has passed since Ericsson drew the plan of his twelve-inch gun nothing has occurred
to show that he was mistaken in contending, as he did to the
last, that he was on the right track with his forged and hooped
gun. On the contrary, the development of heavy ordnance
thus far has been precisely in his direction. The two men
upon whom we principally depended throughout our Civil War
for heavy guns, Major T. J. Rodman and Captain Robert C.
Parrott, both testified that their inventions dated from studies
prompted by the bursting of the *Peacemaker.*[*]

"I do not pretend," said Parrott, "to be the inventor of
the idea of putting a band on the gun, because that thing has
been tried before, but I believe my gun is the first banded gun
that was ever actually introduced into the service of any country as part of its armament." This is perhaps true in the sense
in which the word "introduced" is here used, for the ill fate
of the *Peacemaker* prompted the transfer of the *Oregon* to a
Navy Yard, where it has since remained. But the idea was
there, and had our ordnance officers kept their heads, and
availed themselves of the talent and experience Ericsson was
ready to place at their disposal, they might have led the world
in ordnance from that time on. As to his own forged and

---

[*] Report of the Joint Committee on the Conduct of the War. Second Ses
sion, 38th Congress, vol. ii., pp. 99, 136.

hooped gun he always contended that none of his works furnished better evidence of his thorough knowledge of dynamics
and his practical experience of the strength of materials.
Twenty one years ago he declared that nothing more reliable
had, up to that time, been produced, and this declaration
may be repeated now. Stockton's imitation was not Ericsson's
gun.

" 'The United States Government having been the first to
introduce heavy wrought-iron ordnance, why does it not continue to build guns of that material?' European artillerists
repeatedly put this question. Probably the answer will be
found in the fact that, although having in the meantime successfully constructed wrought-iron ordnance of considerable
size, the first essay at building heavy guns for naval purposes
proved most disastrous." *

As to the gun-carriage and the "friction gear," by which the
recoil of the gun was controlled, nothing more reliable was
contrived until Ericsson undertook the handling of the enormous monitor ordnance. Of the *Oregon* its author says: " Experienced commodores at the time protested loudly against the
proposition to ' mount the monster gun' on board a vessel so
lightly built as the *Princeton*, insisting that, among other difficulties, the breeching would tear her upper works to pieces.
It was urged by the opponents of my new system that the
handling of such guns at sea would prove impossible, the constructing carriages of sufficient strength being pointed out as
impracticable; while the imprudence on the part of the Navy
Department of intrusting such matters to mere engineering
skill was severely criticised. In spite of the remonstrances,
however, Captain Stockton's influence with the Government
prevailed. In the meantime the problem of handling the
twelve-inch gun received due attention. Calculations of the
dynamic equivalent of the recoil convinced me that a moderate
resistance, if continuous and uniform, would suffice to bring the
piece to rest in less space than that required by breeching.
Friction, being the simplest means of obtaining a continuous resistance, was accordingly resorted to." *

* Contributions to the Centennial Exhibition. By J. Ericsson. 1876.

The instrument for measuring distances, spoken of in Stockton's report, Ericsson had just invented, and in 1851 it was awarded a prize at the London Exhibition. It worked automatically, dispensing with calculations and indicating the range by the movement of a hand upon a dial. The self-acting gun-lock was invented by him as early as 1828, and shown to the head of the British Ordnance Department, Sir Henry Vane. It was proposed to appoint a board of officers to test Ericsson's gun-lock in actual practice. As this would disclose the secret of the invention, and the British Government refused to enter into an agreement to pay for it if the trial was successful, the instrument was locked up in a safe until 1839. Then it was shown to Captain Stockton, who was quick to perceive its value, though most unwilling to accord to the inventor proper credit for it.

In the semi-cylinder engine of the *Princeton* Ericsson took especial pride. Of it, Chas. B. Stuart, Engineer-in-Chief of the United States Navy, said, in his work on "The Naval and Mail Steamers of the United States," published in 1853.

The semi-cylinder engine of the *Princeton* is unquestionably the most remarkable modification of the steam-engine that has ever been carried into successful practice. A vibrating piston of a rectangular form moving in a semi-cylinder is an old mechanical device. Mr. Watt, in his celebrated patent, embraced this plan of transmitting the motive force of steam to machinery. Since his time, several engineers have attempted to build engines on this plan, but without success. In common with Mr. Watt, they have adopted the single semi-cylinder with packing against the piston-shaft. Ericsson's plan differs materially from these various attempts, he having introduced double or compound semi-cylinders of different diameters with double pistons placed in opposite directions on the piston-shaft, both being acted upon by the steam at the same time, their differential force being the effective motive power of the engine. The combination of two such double semi-cylinders, arranged so as to transmit their power in directions nearly rectangular to a crank-pin common to both, also contributes to the complete success of this singular engine.

The device of the blower, worked by a separate small steam-engine, first introduced, as we have seen, in 1831, in the steam-packet *Corsair*, enabled Ericsson to substitute for the ordinary fixed smoke-stack, offering in action a target for shot, a telescopic chimney. This could be used when natural draught was desired, and lowered when the blowers were at work. His engine as a whole was regarded by experts as one of the most remarkable features in the vessel, weighing, as it did, less than one-half as much as British marine engines of equal power, and occupying but one-eighth the space. The moving parts were so light that the quantity of matter to be kept in motion was hardly one-sixth as great. The compactness of Ericsson's engine as compared with the engines of British naval vessels at that time, is shown by the two illustrations given on the next page.

A semi-cylinder engine had been applied to the *Stockton* in 1838, and the model of the engine for the *Princeton* was brought by Ericsson with him from England. The link motion applied to it was that introduced by him in 1830 into his locomotives *King William* and *Queen Adelaide*, subsequently into the *Stockton*, and later on into hundreds of screw-propeller engines. The engine was first introduced on the *Stockton* and patented in 1839.

A committee of the American Institute was appointed to visit the *Princeton* and report upon this "important experiment in steam navigation." They announced that this vessel was "in every way worthy of the highest honors of the Institute —a sublime conception most successfully realized, an effort of genius skilfully executed, a grand, unique combination, honorable to the country as creditable to all engaged upon her." The chairman of this committee was Commodore George C. De Kay, a gentleman of high reputation and large experience in ship construction. The Secretary was Professor James J. Mapes, Vice-President of the Institute, and among its members was Professor James Renwick, the physicist.*

The sensation produced by the *Princeton* wherever she appeared is shown by the description given by two eye-witnesses, John O. Sargent and Francis B. Ogden, of a trial of speed between the naval vessel and the pioneer steam-packet between New York and Liverpool. The occasion was the departure of

* The other members were J. S. Drake, H. Meigs. Adoniram Chandler, Philip Schuyler, Geo. F. Barnard, Gordon J. Leeds, and Thomas S. Cummings.

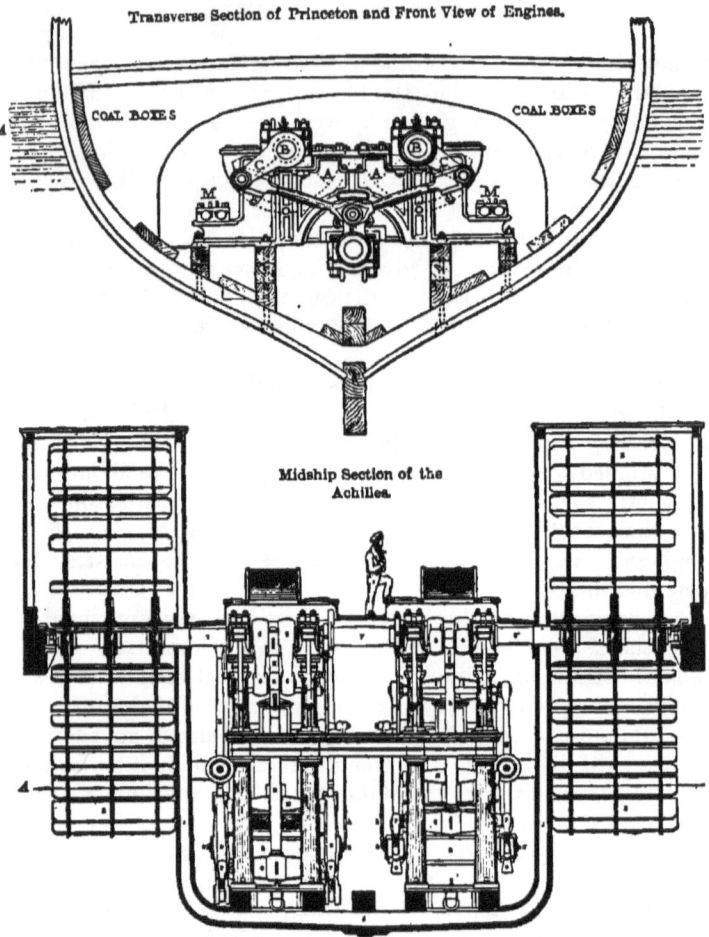

Transverse Section of Princeton and Front View of Engines.

COAL BOXES   COAL BOXES

Midship Section of the
Achilles.

Engines and Paddles of H. M. S. Achilles.*

* The location of the engines and the propeller of the *Princeton*, and the engines and paddles of the *Achilles*, with reference to the water-line at *A*, shows what a complete revolution Ericsson effected in the matter of protection against shot and shell. His early use of coal protection is also shown, but not the relative size of the engines, as the diagrams are not drawn to the same scale.

the *Great Western* upon one of her transatlantic voyages, October 19, 1843. Describing the scene, Mr. Sargent says:

The Battery and the piers were thronged with an expecting multitude. At her appointed hour the *Great Western* came plowing her way down the East River, under circumstances which manifested more than ordinary effort. She was enveloped in clouds of steam, and of dense black smoke ; her paddle-wheels were revolving with unusual velocity, leaving a white wake behind her, that seemed to cover half the river with foam ; and with her sails all set she was evidently prepared to do her best in the anticipated race. As she passed the Battery she was greeted with three hearty cheers, and a fair field with no favor was all that she seemed to challenge, and the least that all were willing to allow her.

She had left Castle Garden about a quarter of a mile behind her, when a fine model of a sailing ship, frigate-like, appeared gliding gracefully down the North River, against the tide, without a breath of smoke or steam to obscure her path—with no paddle-wheels or smoke-pipe visible—propelled by a noiseless and unseen agency, without a rag of canvas on her lithe and beautiful spars—but at a speed which soon convinced the assembled thousands that she would successfully dispute the palm with the gallant vessel, celebrated throughout the world, and everywhere admitted to be the queen of the seas. Such is the march of improvement in the arts. The newcomer was the United States War Steamer *Princeton*. The agent by which she was moved was Ericsson's propeller. She soon reached and passed the *Great Western*, went round her, and passed her a second time before they had reached their point of separation. In a moment, practical men began to speak lightly of their hitherto favorite paddle-wheel, and the propeller that they had shrugged their shoulders at, and amused themselves with for some years of doubtful experiment, rose into altogether unexpected favor." *

Of the numerous screw steamers planned by Ericsson, the *Princeton* was the only one built under his superintendence. The others were constructed from drawings made in his office. He was extremely particular about the quality of both materials and workmanship, and his thoroughness in inspection is shown by a story told of him which also illustrates his enormous physical strength.

On one occasion, during the construction of an engine at Delamater's, a certain casting appearing to him doubtful as to soundness, Ericsson ordered it broken up. And, possibly sus-

* Sargent's Lecture on Steam Navigation. New York, 1844.

pecting that blowholes might be plugged, or the suspected piece made to do duty in some way, he insisted on having it broken on the spot. Some stalwart workmen accordingly attacked it with heavy two-handled sledges, but, failing to make an impression, they desisted at length, saying: "We will put it under the drop by and by." His quick temper rose at this, but he spoke not a word; with his right hand he snatched the sledge from the nearest man, and in an instant it whirled like a meteor before the eyes of the astonished spectators, the ponderous tool driving its head at the first stroke through the shell of the dubious casting, making it a hopeless wreck. He tossed away the sledge as if it had been a jackstraw, and turning on his heel, strode away with the remark : "Now you *may* put it under the drop." *

So thorough was the work upon the *Princeton* that after serving through the Mexican War, and doing more duty than any other naval vessel, she was sent to Europe without being repaired. Her success was the final triumph of the principle of screw propulsion. It was most fortunate for Ericsson, in his contest with the adverse opinion of authority, that he was able to present his new motor in a remarkably perfect condition at the start. Yet his proposition to substitute the propeller for the paddle-wheel was received with ridicule by all officialdom.

Government officers at Washington, enjoying a high reputation for scientific attainment, proved, to the satisfaction of themselves and their fellows, that the *Princeton* never could attain a speed of five miles an hour; she was able to make over twelve, and this was relatively equal to eighteen or twenty miles now. The most prominent of the Government naval constructors assured his Department that a mere glance at the propeller intended for the *Princeton* was sufficient to convince the practical eye of the absurdity of the scheme, " the surface of the blades was too small for the body to be propelled." The President of the United States was warned by Government engineers that utter failure would attend the attempt to use engines constructed on such erroneous mechanical principles as those of this vessel. The learned Franklin Institute condemned the vessel, and the builders of her engines received in-

* Scientific American, December 14, 1889.

timations from the members of the Institute that they ought not to be parties to this waste of the public money.

Indeed, public opinion has been so misled by statements finding their way into standard publications, encyclopedias and the like, that one who undertakes to set forth the plain facts concerning Ericsson's inventions must expect even now to be condemned as a partisan. His engines, using a half cylinder instead of a whole cylinder, have been confounded with the one patented by Watt, to which they bear only the most superficial resemblance. Ericsson understood that it was possible to make circular pistons tighter than those of his semi-cylinder engines, and he introduced this modification into engines, made otherwise on the plan of his *Princeton* engines, and put into the *Daylight* and the *Penguin*.

Returning to the biography of Captain Stockton, we learn that the construction of the *Princeton* " confuted the ignorance and antiquated dogmas of the Washington Naval Bureau. Her speed and sailing qualities, her admirable model, the impregnable security of her motive power (being placed below water-line), and her powerful armament made her an object of universal admiration. Wherever she appeared immense crowds gathered to witness her evolutions and inspect her machinery. She was kept in continual service from the time she was launched until the antipathy of the blundering incapables who controlled the Bureau of Construction at Washington directed her to be broken up. On her visit to the Mediterranean she attracted the attention of the curious and of the skilful engineers of every naval power; and, while the United States neglected to multiply such cheap and efficient auxiliaries of naval defence after her model, England and France profited by the experiment, and their navies are now [1856], crowded with powerful steamers, many of them built on the model and possessing all the peculiar characteristics of the *Princeton*." *

As soon as he gave his attention to marine engineering, which was shortly after his arrival in England in 1826, Ericsson saw clearly that three conditions were essential to the introduction of steam into war vessels: first, the instrument of propulsion must be beneath the water; second, the machinery

* Life of Stockton, p. 81.

must also be placed below the water-line to be protected from shot, and finally, the draught of the furnaces must be made independent of a smoke-stack liable to be shot away at any moment. All of these indispensable conditions were fulfilled in the *Princeton* and he enjoyed the gratification of finding his old antagonists of the British Admiralty compelled to follow his lead.

When he left England Ericsson entrusted his interests to the guardianship of Count Adolph E. Von Rosen. In 1843 Count Rosen received an order from the French Government to fit a forty-four gun frigate, the *Pomone*, with a propeller on Ericsson's plan, and with engines of two hundred and twenty horse-power to be kept below the water-line, as in the *Princeton*. In 1844 the English Government gave Count Rosen instructions to fit the *Amphion* frigate with a propeller and with engines of three hundred horse-power. These were also to go below the water-line.

Aside from the *Victory*, fitted out by Ericsson in 1828, " these were the first engines in Europe which were kept below the water-line. They were also the first direct acting horizontal engines employed to give motion to the screw. The air-pumps, which were also horizontal, were double-acting, and were furnished with canvas valves to diminish the shock incident to the shutting of large apparatus where so high a speed had to be maintained. Both vessels were completely successful. The speed engaged to be given was five knots an hour. The speed of almost seven knots an hour was actually attained." *

The designs for the machinery of this first British naval steamer carrying a propeller were made in New York by Ericsson. He had made scores of plans before he finally decided that the application to vessels of war of side propellers was inadmissible, because of their exposed position, the difficulty of actuating them with the propeller shaft under water, and the additional power required because of the breadth of the beam.

"When the *U. S. S. Princeton, propelled by Ericsson's screw* and armed by *Ericsson's wrought-iron gun*, was launched the war between armor and projectiles began. Heretofore the

* Vide Bourne's Treatise on the Screw Propeller, p. 89.

means of propulsion by steam had been by machinery entirely above the water, and exposed to an enemy's fire: the screw did away with this great drawback, removing the working-beam and paddle; compact engines in the hull, giving motion to a propeller protected in part by the element in which it acted. The centre of gravity was also lowered, and, the paddle-boxes being removed, there was less surface to armor, and less target to hit.

"The *Princeton* was in reality Ericsson's first monitor, giving a warning on both sides of the Atlantic of the changes that were to ensue. Congress resounded with eulogies of the genius which would enable us in the near future to defy the navies of Europe. Parliament, perceiving the error the admiralty had made in driving the Swedish inventor from England, voted large sums of money to build trial propellers and built-up guns. The British foundries were ready for the emergency; stimulated by the success of their first iron steamers, they hastened to increase their plant so as to include the fabrication of armor plates for iron men-of-war. The age of iron had begun." *

* Development of Armor as Applied to Ships. By Lieutenant Jacob W. Miller, U.S.N. Proceedings U. S. Naval Institute, No. 10, 1879.

CHAPTER IX.

STOCKTON'S TREATMENT OF ERICSSON.

Ericsson Declines to be Held Responsible for the *Princeton* Disaster.—
Anger of Stockton.—Payment for the *Princeton* Refused.—Correspondence with the Navy Department.—Application to Congress.—
Testimony of Dionysius Lardner and Professor Mapes.—Legislative Injustice.—The Court of Claims Allows the *Princeton* Claim.
—Congress still Refuses to Pay it.—Stockton as a Duellist.—Stevens's Bomb-proof.

WHEN the *Peacemaker* exploded with such fatal results
Captain Stockton bethought himself of Ericsson. If he
was not disposed to share the credit of success with him he
was quite ready to give him his full measure of responsibility
for disaster. It was on the programme that Ericsson should
accompany the *Princeton* when she was ordered from New
York for exhibition to convince the public officials at Washington of her value. He proceeded accordingly to the foot
of Wall Street at the appointed time, expecting to be taken
aboard there, but the vessel carrying his fortunes, not less than
those of Stockton, steamed by without stopping for him.*

From Washington came the echoes of the cannon celebrat-
ing the triumphs of the ambitious naval captain, of the speeches
sounding his praises, and of the clinking of the glasses in
which delighted visitors drank his health. There was no music
in all this for the man who had spent so many years in developing the ideas thus coolly appropriated. He was in no state of
mind, therefore, to obey with alacrity the summons that came
for him to appear and assume the responsibility for the one de-
fective feature in the vessel and its equipment ; so he left his

* I make this statement upon the authority of Mr. Samuel W. Taylor,
for many years the confidential secretary of Captain Ericsson, from whom he
obtained this information.

associate to his own explanations. His agency in the success of the *Princeton* had been, as he believed, most ungenerously ignored, and he did not propose that criticism for disaster should be diverted from Stockton to himself. Ericsson's reasons for declining to respond to the summons calling him to Washington are given in this letter:

NEW YORK, March 1, 1844.

DEAR SIR: Your letter of the 28th did not reach me until 5 o'clock this afternoon. The awful calamity which you relate was therefore known to me twenty-seven hours before the receipt of your communication, but for the joyful intelligence of *Captain Stockton's safety* I am still indebted to you. Your request for me to come on immediately, whilst yet the funeral knell is piercing the air of Washington, you can readily imagine is not very agreeable.

How differently should I have regarded an *invitation* from Captain Stockton a week ago! I might then have had it in my power to render good service and valuable counsel. *Now* I can be of no use. I must be permitted to exercise my own judgment in this matter, and I have to state most emphatically that since Captain Stockton is in possession of an accurate working plan of his exploded gun my presence at Washington can be of no use, should an investigation of the causes of the sad accident be deemed necessary.

The circumstances attending the loading, quantity and strength of powder, weight, nature, and fit of ball, etc., of course *I* cannot inquire into. On the other hand, any detailed information from the forge as to the quantity of metal and the mode of proceeding with the forging from day to day, and also a similar statement from the Phœnix Foundry, showing the quality of the chips or borings in every part of the gun I can readily procure whilst remaining here.

With the sincerest wish that Captain Stockton may now have sufficiently recovered to bear with the fatigue of hearing you read this, I am

Yours truly,

J. ERICSSON.

WM. H. THOMPSON.

The haughty naval officer never forgave this defection, as he considered it, and in his mind it was ascribed to other motives than those of wounded professional pride. "If Ericsson had not been a —— coward," he once said to Sargent, "there would have been no trouble about his getting his money for the vessel."

As it was, Stockton prevented the payment of Ericsson's bill from the appropriation for the *Princeton*, and there was no possibility of his obtaining remuneration for the two years he had devoted to the Government work, and for the charges to which he had been subjected, except by the tedious and uncertain process of an appeal to Congress.

With a bill made out in due form, and amounting altogether to $15,080, Ericsson sent this letter:

CITY OF NEW YORK, March 14, 1844.

SIR: I have the honor to transmit to you, annexed, the bill for my services as engineer in planning and superintending the steam machinery, armament, etc., of the U. S. steamer *Princeton*, and for certain inventions therein specified.

I beg leave to state that the *per diem* charge of five pounds sterling includes all my office, travelling, and other professional disbursements, and barely covers my expenses for the time during which I have been occupied on this important national work.

Of the value of the inventions which I have introduced in the *Princeton*, the results of much previous labor and outlay, it does not become me to speak. On this subject I can only refer to the recent official report of Captain Stockton, and to the report made by the American Institute of New York at Captain Stockton's request, a copy of which is herewith enclosed. In any point of view, I trust that my professional charges will be deemed reasonable by the Department, for it has been my intention to make them so. When the sum total of charges is compared with the magnitude of the work that has been performed, it will exhibit a moderate compensation for services of such variety and extent.

I have the honor to be your most obedient servant,

JOHN ERICSSON.

To the HON. THE SECRETARY OF THE NAVY.

The charge was for two hundred and thirty days at five pounds a day, and $5,000 for services, specified as follows:

For services rendered in inventing, designing, and perfecting the following improvements connected with the arts of naval warfare and with steamships of war, and applied to the U. S. steamer *Princeton*, viz. :

The heating apparatus, by which a great saving of fuel is effected, which has never before been attained ;

The new gun-carriage, by which not only the heaviest piece of ordnance can be handled by a few men, but which so gradually checks the recoil that the ship receives no injurious shock ;

The sliding chimney and mechanism by which that great desideratum, the absence of a projecting chimney in a ship of war, has been attained; and

The spirit-level, by which the elevation of a piece of ordnance may be readily ascertained with the utmost precision. . . .

A reply came at once from the Department stating that the account had been received and "referred to Captain Stockton for report." Twenty-five days passed and Ericsson again wrote saying: "The great length of time which I devoted to this work compelled me to incur pecuniary liabilities which render it necessary for me to solicit as early an attention to my account as may be consistent with the multiplicity of business."

No reply. Again he wrote, a month later (May 8, 1844), suggesting that it might be necessary for him to apply to Congress, and asking such information as would enable him "to judge of the propriety or necessity of making such an application." This time an answer came at once, saying that the Department was waiting for Stockton, and the next day this letter was received:

NAVY DEPARTMENT, May 11, 1844.

SIR: A letter has this day been received from Captain Stockton which contains the following paragraph in relation to your claims:

"In regard to Captain Ericsson's bill, which was sent to me at the same time, I must say that, with all my desire to serve him, I cannot approve of his bill; it is direct violation of our agreement as far as it is to be considered a legal claim upon the Department."

With such an unfavorable expression of opinion, the Department cannot allow your claim.

I am respectfully yours,

J. Y. MASON.

Captain J. ERICSSON, New York.

Nine days after the date of this letter Stockton sent this communication to the Department:

PRINCETON, May 20, 1844.

SIR: In answer to your last communication of the tenth instant, on the subject of Captain Ericsson's account, a copy of which had been previously sent to me by the Department, and which I could not approve, I have the honor further to state:

That it has given me great pleasure to acknowledge on all proper occasions the services of Captain Ericsson's mechanical skill in carrying out my well-intended efforts for the benefit of the country and, although I am still free to do so, yet my duty to the Government, and not more than a proper regard for myself, require me to say, that I was quite surprised to learn that he had presented *any claim or demand whatever*, against the Department, for services rendered to me in fitting the *Princeton;* nor was my surprise at all diminished on the perusal of his accounts to find that he had been so extravagant in all his demands.

That the Government may have a proper understanding of the true position of Captain Ericsson toward the Government and myself in regard to any demand he has made or may see fit to make for services before alluded to, however *eminent and laborious* they may turn out to be, it seems to be proper here to state some of the circumstances connected with my first acquaintance with him and his subsequent visit to the United States.

Previous to my acquaintance with Captain Ericsson I had proposed to the President of the United States and the Navy Department to construct a steamship-of-war, whose machinery should be entirely out of the reach of shot. Pursuing my inquiries on this subject a few years afterward in England, I was informed by Mr. Francis B. Ogden, our Consul at Liverpool, that a very ingenious mechanic by the name of Ericsson had been devoting much time and attention to the matter of submerged wheels. He afterward introduced him to me ; subsequently I had constructed in England, under his immediate superintendence, an iron boat with submerged wheels, and which boat was afterward sent to the United States. I also had constructed under his direction an engine similar to the one now on board the *Princeton*, which was also sent to the United States.

Having obtained these two models, I took my leave of Captain Ericsson, not knowing that I should ever again see him, and not supposing that his personal services would be ever required or desired by me. I had the fullest confidence that all that I wished could be done quite as well by the mechanics in the United States as by Captain Ericsson. I had no idea that Captain Ericsson intended to come to the United States until I received a letter from him announcing his arrival in New York. I have invariably given him to understand in the most distinct manner, whenever the subject was alluded to, that I have no authority from the Government to employ him, and that if he received anything, that it must be altogether gratuitous on the part of the Government, that considering the great opportunity he, as an inventor, would have to introduce his patents to the world by the aid of the Government, I did not think it proper for him to make a charge for their application to the *Princeton*, in all of which he has concurred as far as I know, up to the time of his presentment of his extraordinary bill.

It appears, then, in the first place, that Captain Ericsson came to the United States without my invitation or approbation, and allow me further to add, much to my surprise and annoyance. Having thus thrust himself upon me, and believing him at that time to be a mechanic of some skill, *I did not employ him, but I permitted him, as a particular act of favor and kindness,* to superintend the construction of the machinery of the *Princeton,* on the success of which he had placed so much of his future hopes and expectations. Captain Ericsson himself considered, at the time he thus volunteered his services, that the opportunity afforded him to exhibit to the world the importance of his various patents, would be a satisfactory remuneration for all his services in getting them up on so magnificent a scale.

In giving you this brief and general statement of my views on the subject of your letter of the 10th inst., I have endeavored to avoid everything not directly connected with the subject of your inquiry.

Your obedient and faithful servant,

R. F. STOCKTON.

To Hon. JOHN Y. MASON, Secretary of the Navy.

It thus appears that Captain Stockton, after delaying a report upon Ericsson's claim for services as long as he could, finally took a position concerning it which was in flat contradiction of his own previous action and of oral and written promises to Ericsson. The distinction between a claim for patent fees and one for professional services is too obvious to suffer them to be for a moment confounded. Besides, Stockton was held by the strongest obligations that can bind an honorable man to urge upon the Government Ericsson's title to the recognition of his patent claims, for these had been made contingent only upon the success of the *Princeton* and its complete success was not questioned. Even were the facts as stated they would not justify Stockton's position, and if the letter does not actually misstate facts it does furnish an example of the *suppressio veri, suggestio falsi.*

"To the Honorable the Congress of the United States," "John Ericsson, of the City of New York, Civil Engineer," accordingly addressed a memorial setting forth the facts, as shown by a series of twenty-six letters and documents accompanying the petition, and saying in this temperate language: "It is suggested by Captain Stockton that your memorialist has no 'legal claim' upon the Department. By this expression Captain Stockton does not intend to deny that the services alleged have been rendered—that the work for which your memorialist claims compensation has been done by him and well

10

done—nor that the United States are in the present enjoyment of the unpaid results of your memorialist's labor and
invention. . . . A claim founded on such considerations
and so verified, your memorialist cannot well distinguish from
a 'legal claim.'"

Ericsson then quotes the letters which passed between him
and Stockton in July, 1841, with reference to his leaving the
matter of payment for his patent rights to the Government, and
continues: "This your memorialist presumes to be the agreement which Captain Stockton alleges to be directly 'violated'
by the account which your memorialist has submitted to the
Department. It is true that your memorialist consented thus
to leave the amount of his patent fees to what Captain Stockton should 'recommend,' or the Government should see fit to
pay. Six months have elapsed since the ship was tried. Four
months have elapsed since Captain Stockton reported to your
honorable body that the *Princeton* can make greater speed
than any sea-going steamer or other vessel heretofore built, and
expressed his belief that she would prove 'invincible' against
any foe. Meanwhile the Government has not seen fit to pay
your memorialist anything for his patent rights. Meanwhile
Captain Stockton has not been pleased to recommend that anything should be paid to your memorialist for his patent rights.
And when your memorialist calls upon the Department—*not*
for the patent fees in question—but for the bare repayment of
his expenditures and compensation for his time and labor in
the service of the United States—still leaving his patent
charges to their own voluntary action—he is told that the
'Government cannot allow his claim,' and the presentation of
his bill, 'if it is to be considered a legal claim upon the Department,' 'violates an agreement.'

"This agreement, it is obvious, had reference *only* to the
patent rights in question and not to the services of your memorialist as engineer, his expenses in that capacity, nor to his
compensation for the numerous inventions and improvements
unconnected with the engine and propeller which were subsequently introduced in the *Princeton*. Your memorialist never
contemplated that these services should be gratuitously rendered,
and it would require certainly a very clear and unequivocal ex-

pression of such an intent on his part to lead any one to a conclusion so extraordinary.

"Under these circumstances your memorialist is compelled to apply to your honorable body for relief, and would respectfully solicit the attention of your honorable body to the verified accounts he has the honor to transmit to them. The advances which your memorialist has made on account of the United States and the great length of time during which he was devoted to this work without compensation have exhausted his resources, and the refusal of the Department to entertain his claim leaves him no recourse but that of making a direct appeal to the representatives of the American people.

"All of which is most respectfully submitted by
"Your obedient servant,
"JOHN ERICSSON."

The documents accompanying this memorial were the official orders directing Stockton to build the *Princeton*, a series of letters from Stockton calling upon Ericsson for the plans, designs, superintendence, travelling, etc., charged for in his bill, and affidavits from Professor Dionysius Lardner, Professor James J. Mapes, and Robert Schuyler, setting forth that the charge of £5 per day was not only moderate but far less than such exceptional professional services might properly command. There were also letters and contracts showing that the specifications called for "a semi-rotary engine on Ericsson's patent principle" and for his propeller, and that the work upon the equipment of the vessel was done from his designs and under his superintendence. The sequence and order of these letters, together with their text, shows that while Stockton stood before the Department as sponsor for the *Princeton* he was dependent for every detail of its equipment upon Ericsson's skill and experience. Yet in his official report upon the completion of the vessel Ericsson's name does not appear, nor is there any allusion to him in the message of President Tyler to Congress transmitting this report, February 12, 1844.

"Of this," wrote Mr. Sargent at the time to Senator Morehead, "Captain Ericsson does not complain. But not satisfied with deriving all the *credit*, Captain Stockton is altogether inactive in procuring Captain Ericsson compensation for his services. Whether or no this arises from a desire to keep Ericsson altogether out of view, and then monopolize all the credit you can judge as well as I. Stockton has taken all the *glory*. In his report he even speaks of ' submerged wheels,' to avoid an allusion to ' Ericsson's propeller,' and besides all this suffers Ericsson to go without remuneration for his laborious, valuable, and unremitted services for two years. Ericsson was the author and maker of the whole thing, that is to say everything about her in which she differs from others. Bills for constructing for the United States the most formidable ship of war that floats the seas, and that has excited the wonder and admiration of so many thousands of our citizens, sleep on the table of the Secretary *unpaid*. His letters on the subject remain unanswered. Is not this disgraceful to the navy ?" The Naval Committee of the House of Representatives unanimously reported a bill to pay Ericsson $15,080, but it was defeated by a narrow majority. In 1848, a similar bill was defeated by an unfavorable report from the Senate Naval Committee.

For eight years nothing further was done in Congress. Meantime, the Act of February 24, 1855, established a Court of Claims to adjudicate upon questions in dispute between the Government and individuals, reserving to Congress the right to approve or disapprove the decisions of the Court. On March 26, 1856, the Senate of the United States ordered Ericsson's papers to be referred to the Court of Claims. The Court united in a decision granting him $13,930, and referring this award to Congress in the usual form for approval. This was the amount of his bill for $15,080—less $1,150 he had received, including the thousand dollars referred to in his correspondence with Stockton. Ten days after this judgment the Senate committee reported a bill providing for the payment of this net sum. In the United States Senate on May 14, 1858, an earnest speech in support of the claim was made by the Hon. Stephen R. Mallory, representative from Florida, whose experience as Chairman of the Naval Committee had made him familiar with the value of Ericsson's services. " There was no experiment in the *Princeton*," Mr. Mallory said. " The exper-

iment had been made at great cost by Captain Ericsson. He
had exhausted every dollar he had on earth in making the experiment. . . . The *Princeton* is the foundation of our
present steam marine. It is the foundation of the steam marine of the whole world. . . . The qualities which the
Princeton had we have translated into other vessels, but we
have never excelled her. . . . If he had volunteered his
services, I ask, when the country has reaped these great advantages by them, is it just, is it generous, is it magnanimous in the
American people to refuse him this paltry compensation? A
letter from Stockton, written in 1853, was interpreted by the
Court of Claims as showing that he merely held that there was
no legal contract and not that no service was rendered. The
Court of Claims did not accept Stockton's view of the case and
finding in his letters, as well as elsewhere, proof that payment
of some sort for service was expected, granted Ericsson the
amount asked for."

There the matter has rested from that time to this. Congress neglected to appropriate the money, and the bill for
Ericsson's relief, like so many other meritorious measures,
after running the usual course, disappeared in the sandy wastes
of legislative talk. The decisions of the Court of Claims adverse to the claimants against the Government were concurred
in at that time without examination. The decisions in their
favor were sent to a committee, where, in the language of one
of its members, you needed "law, equity, evidence, and inspiration to get anything."

The justice of his demand being recognized, and the Court
of Claims having reported in its favor, Ericsson had every
reason to believe that his money would soon be received.
Thus he was tempted to give to the collection of his "claim"
time which he might have devoted to more profitable pursuits,
and was kept for years in a constant state of irritation and
anxiety. The chief theme of his discourse with his friend Sargent, in a long series of letters, extending over a number of
years, was the injustice of Congress, and his favorable opinion
of American methods did not grow apace. At the conclusion
of a long letter on this subject, he writes: "I will say no more;
the gross injustice in the whole matter makes me nervous, far

more than if doomed to decapitation in twenty-four hours." He was constantly harassed for money at this time, and subjected to endless embarrassment and humiliation. For this the law afforded no possible redress against the Sovereign Congress. The Navy Department did finally, in 1848, allow him two thousand dollars for the use of his patented engine but his bill for two years' services devoted to the construction of the *Princeton* still stands as an unpaid judgment against the Government.

If an "ingenious mechanic" had rendered service under like circumstances to an architect employed to build a house, can there be any doubt that he would not only have had a legal claim against the owner of the house but a lien upon the property as well? A claim that is legal as against an individual is not under our system enforceable against the Government; that is all. Judge Story, in his "Commentaries on the Constitution," points out the serious defect of both Federal and State constitutions in failing to provide any means of enforcing a just claim against the State, such as exists in England under what is called a petition of right to the Court of Chancery. "Cases of the most cruel hardship and intolerable delay, have," said Judge Story, "already occurred, in which meritorious creditors have been reduced to grievous suffering, and sometimes to absolute ruin, by tardiness of a justice which has been yielded only after the humble supplication of many years before the legislature."

Such is Ericsson's case, and in this instance the United States has availed itself without compensation of the experience acquired at great cost by a private individual, and has continued to make use, from that day to this, of ideas undoubtedly originated and first applied by him, without payment for the service rendered. If this does not violate the letter it certainly does offend the spirit of the constitutional requirement that private property shall not be taken for public use without just compensation; for property, as the United States Supreme Court has said, " is a word of large import."

In 1866 a competent engineering authority declared that no screw propeller engine " has since been constructed to go below the water-line which surpasses that of the *Princeton* in trust-

worthiness, durability, strength, lightness, and mechanical ex-
cellence of performance.   It was simpler and had fewer parts
than any propeller engine ever put into a war steamer."   Ericsson was the pioneer in applying power directly to the shaft
turning the screw, so as to get rid of the complication of belts
or gearing, and the engine of the *Princeton* was the first example of this type.   It marked a new departure, and was at
the time openly and unsparingly ridiculed by all the experts
who examined it.   In spite of them and their wisdom it did
its work so perfectly and accurately that it wore out one hull,
and another was built expressly for it.

Whatever feeling Ericsson may have had toward Captain
Stockton, it did not survive the occasion.   In his Contributions to the Centennial Exhibition, 1876, he gives some account
of his transactions with him (Chapter XXVI.) making no allusion to the differences between them, and speaking of him as
" that enterprising and spirited officer."   Ericsson's published
references to Stockton were all dignified and free from passion,
though in one of his private letters, written in 1844 when he was
smarting under the sense of recent injustice, he does speak of
" the deep rascality of that letter of Stockton's."   In another
private letter, also written at that time, he said : " Give Stockton time and he will produce *certificates* that gun, carriages,
heaters, engines, and propeller of the *Princeton* are all failures.
Ten to one he will make me out to be the Government's debtor
—only give him time."   Francis B. Ogden, who had a pro-
prietary interest in the propeller, shared its inventor's opinion
as to the hostility of Captain Stockton.   Writing concerning
some of Ericsson's difficulties, he said (in a letter dated June
25, 1849) :

I enter feelingly into your disgust at the unfair decision of juries and
judges ; but, my dear friend, you have a recuperative hundred horse-
power in your favor in your own inexhaustible resources.   Write me
immediately and more frequently—tell me what you are doing—where
is Stockton and what is he about—has he influence with the present administration ?   If he has I need not ask how he employs it.   I have it
from the best authority that he has sworn to ruin me—as well as yourself.   I should like to have him within *ten paces,* with all his boasted
chivalry and *devil-may-care deeds.*   What is Robert Stevens doing ?   Will

his *shot-proof* frigate ever be afloat, or his *thirty mile* steamers ever astonish the world ?

The " ten paces " has reference to Stockton's early reputation as a duellist. At one time, when feeling between British and American officers ran high, just after the War of 1812, Stockton accepted challenges to fight all the captains of the British regiment then garrisoning Gibraltar. Several meetings took place and Stockton had a most adventurous escape from arrest after wounding his adversary in one of them.

How deeply Ogden was interested in his partner's success is shown by these extracts from letters written by him to Ericsson from Liverpool.

February 3, 1842. As soon as any money comes in that you can spare do let me for God's sake have a little for old scores, for I do assure you I am still devilish poor, although Stockton's acceptance has kept me afloat for the present, and I hope for better times some day hereafter.

February 18, 1842. I am delighted with your satisfaction at the coming in of the works of the frigate, and with the rapid progress you are making; and I do not allow myself to put in a hypothetical *if* as to the success of the iron boats. [These were the four canal barges ordered by Stockton.] I look upon that as settled. Had Stockton come forward three years ago, as he ought to have done, his property would have been at this day worth twice what it is; never too late, however.

Liverpool, April 3, 1842. Count Von Rosen has had two interviews with the Lords of the Admiralty, and seems to think that they favored the idea of giving your propeller a trial. I have written to President Houston, of Texas, urging him to let me build him an iron ship, fitted with Ericsson's propellers and armed with Paixhan guns."

May 20, 1842. My chief, nay for a time to come my only dependence is in your success, and as I embarked with you heart and soul, and have never for one instant faltered, but have stuck by you in good report and evil, and as far as it was in my power have assisted you and promoted your views, I feel quite certain of all your exertions in my favor. My head is yet above water, but I tell you in sincerity that I have not money to go to market with. I have property here worth four times as much as it would now sell for. I have debts (good in time) due from the United States to the amount of $15,000, from which I cannot now realize a shilling.

Your arrangement with the Lake people I approve highly of, for in the first instance, a peppercorn is of more importance than any sum that might be recovered or rather jeopardized by the uncertainty of the law.

I am rejoiced at the prospect your iron boats will open, and indeed I look upon the thing as fairly before the public, sink or swim, according to its own merits. Of the result I have not the least doubt. Such is Robert Stevens's standing that it will not be advisable to come out against his plan until you are in successful operation—then plunge a 240-pound shot into his citadel, and don't take it for granted because he says so that his " Pa " was the inventor of the propeller. Bring him down to particulars and you will find it to have been quite a different thing. Should he attempt to introduce it into his iron bomb-proof, make no stir about it until the thing is complete, and Congress has acted upon your claim. Then you will have ground to go upon.

June 3, 1842. Since the fate of the *Clarion*, no sea-steamer, I suppose, will be started until the *Princeton* sets the question at rest, which I trust it will do to the satisfaction of all the world except Robert Stevens, who of course will be an unbeliever until he can establish his claim to it in the name of his ' Pa,' who tried everything and succeeded in nothing. The Marquis of Worcester was a fool to him with his " Cento " ; Stevens was a Millio.

These familiar letters show the relations existing between the two men to whom we are chiefly indebted for the steam propeller—to Ericsson because of the engineering ability and persevering energy devoted to the solution of a problem so long baffling mechanics—to Ogden because of the sound nautical judgment and personal influence which contributed to its early introduction. The *Clarion* of the Havana line, alluded to here, was the first ocean steamer fitted with the propeller. Stevens's " bomb-proof " was the iron-clad vessel begun by Robert L. Stevens at Hoboken, in 1843, carried on during his lifetime at heavy expense, and continued after his death by General George B. McClellan, Stevens having left a million dollars for this purpose in his will. It was never completed, and was finally sold for old iron and broken up. Stevens's battery as well as the *Princeton* originated in the Oregon boundary troubles of President Tyler's administration and the " fifty-four forty or fight " sentiment of that day, which demanded that the boundary line between the United States and the British possessions should extend to latitude 54° 40′ N.

In 1842, April 14, an act of Congress was passed authorizing a contract with Mr. Stevens for an iron-clad steam vessel, a joint commission of army and navy officers having decided, after experiments at Sandy Hook, that four and a half inches of armor were proof against existing ordnance. Similar experiments in England led to similar conclusions. Before Stevens's vessel was begun Ericsson and Stockton had shown that this thickness of armor could be easily pierced, and the contract with Stevens was changed accordingly.*

In this and in other ways Ericsson and the Stevens antagonized, for among the numerous claimants for the screw was John Stevens, who experimented with it in 1804. Ogden's letters quoted here appear to be the echo of Ericsson's own sentiments concerning Stevens. Ericsson's antagonisms were, however, directed against acts rather than individuals, as even his friends sometimes discovered to their cost. He was too large-minded to indulge in antipathies merely personal. Confident in his own abilities he asked only for a fair field and no favor, and his feelings of hostility never survived their occasion, as was shown in still another instance when he rebuked with dignity a correspondent who assumed upon his supposed hostility to his Rainhill antagonist, George Stephenson, to speak slightingly of him. It was not his habit to speak ill of others and he was always ready to rebuke those who imagined that they could turn what they assumed to be his hostilities to their personal account. Favors done him were written on adamant; injuries were inscribed upon the waters. When he had acquired wealth some one sought to annoy him by writing from abroad, that a movement was on foot to erect a monument to one of the numerous claimants to the invention of the screw. Ericsson's response was a check for five hundred dollars as a contribution to the monument.

* See American Cyclopedia of Biography, article R. L. Stevens.

CHAPTER X.

SUCCESSES AND FAILURES.

General Introduction of the Screw.—Adopted for the British Navy.—
First Use of Twin Screws.—Ericsson's Business Methods and Fi-
nances.—Auxiliary Steam Vessels.—Their Use During the War with
Mexico.—The *Massachusetts* General Scott's Flag-ship.—The *Princeton* Claim Again.—Failure of the *Iron Witch.*—Business Associations with R. B. Forbes.—Ericsson's Work for the Government.—
Competitive Trial of Screw-vessels.—Rival Claims to the Invention
of the Screw.—Contests in the Courts.

ERICSSON'S occupation with the *Princeton* continued for
two years, from September, 1841, to September, 1843.
During this period, as already stated, twenty-five vessels trading
in American waters received the screw, besides the original imported tug *Robert F. Stockton*. By the end of 1843 the list of
screw vessels afloat on this side of the Atlantic had extended
to forty-two. They are enumerated and described in the report
of the Swedish Lieutenant Johnson referred to on page 110.
Speaking of this report, an English authority says:

> The fate of mechanical inventions is much like that of the seed in
> the parable. The invention must fall on a proper soil and be nurtured
> by favorable circumstances of time and place, in order to bloom into
> success. The application of the steam-engine to navigation was of
> greater necessity to the large extent of the rivers and lakes of the Unit-
> ed States than with ourselves ; and Fulton did right to take his marine
> engine back to his own country. For similar reasons the screw pro-
> peller worked its way into use there much quicker than with ourselves.
> It is worthy of notice that Ericsson applied his propeller to upward of
> sixty vessels in America before any other form of propeller was adopted,
> nor is it less worthy of remark that the adoption of his propeller proved
> a great commercial success from the start, many of the original vessels
> being now, after fifteen years of service, in good working condition.*

* The London Engineer, May 11, 1866.

The machinery of these early vessels was built in New York, Philadelphia, and Oswego.

During the two years principally devoted to the *Princeton* time was found for other work. June 24, 1843, engines upon a new principle were experimentally tested in a canal barge called the *Black Diamond*, and the next year a model was deposited in the Patent Office, June 8, 1844, and a patent applied for June 24th. October 6, 1843, Rufus K. Page, of Hallowell, Me., was given the right for eighteen months to negotiate "on joint account" with "any prince, power or sovereignty," except France, for applying Ericsson's propeller and engines to vessels on the Mediterranean and the Black Sea. In 1842 back action engines were planned, and in 1843 they were applied to the Revenue cutter *Legaré*, and afterward to H. M. S. *Amphion*, the first British war vessel fitted with the Ericsson propeller. They are described as "a species of steeple-engine laid upon its side." The steeple-engine is one familiar to travellers on American rivers. The guides to the connecting-rod rise vertically along the crank-shaft, and require for their accommodation the high frame rising above the deck like the steeple of a country church.

In 1843, too, twin screw engines were applied to the steamship *Marmora*, these consisting of two independent beam engines placed transversely in the ship, the beams operating close under the deck. This was the first practical application of the twin screw system. Single cylinder screw engines were also applied in a peculiar manner to numerous freight vessels on the canals and rivers of the United States, to adapt them to the necessities of navigation in shallow waters. The piston-rod and driving-crank were so connected by cog-wheels as to move in opposite directions through equal arcs in equal times.

Soon after his arrival in New York Ericsson opened an account in the bank of "Manhattan Company," a corporation chartered in 1799 under the pretence of introducing water into New York, and owing its existence to a scheme of Aaron Burr's for neutralizing the influence in New York City of Hamilton and the Federalists. With this ancient and substantial institution Ericsson continued to bank until his death. In his series of check-books are found the only accounts he ever kept, for, whatever his accomplishments, book-keeping is not to be included among them. Departing from the strictly legitimate uses of the check-book, he filled his up with memoranda of various sorts—most useful for biography, if somewhat disturbing to the cashier's idea of the fitness of things. Here is to be found the only consecutive account that has been preserved of Ericsson's transactions from day to day, and from year to year. His check-books tell in their way the story of their owner's personal peculiarities, and with mute eloquence testify to his generosity, his kindness of heart, his strict integrity, and, most of all, to his overmastering disposition to spend his money upon his ideas rather than upon himself. There was for him no resting-place of ease, of Sybaritic enjoyment, or even of personal comfort, as most men regard comfort. Always just beyond lay the goal of higher attainment.

The account in these check-books begins with July, 1844, and one or two of the books before 1844 have disappeared. The sum to Ericsson's credit at this time was $5,361.16, and the deposits during the previous six months had amounted to $21,-423.33. For six weeks from July 1 there were no deposits: then on August 15, 1844, $3,700 went into the bank, and the next day $3,500 more. Meantime checks had been drawn for these items :

Payments on account of machinery contracted.	$2,897	14
For patent expenses on the propeller.........	316	93
Salaries of office assistants...................	80	00
Rent for one month.........................	128	00
Marble bust from H. Kneeland (on account)..	70	00
For "Duck" (Mrs. Ericsson)................	150	00
For personal expenses.....................	150	00
Total........................	$3,792	07

Substantially thus runs the account from month to month. It shows that as soon as he was released from his obligations to Stockton, Ericsson found abundant and profitable occupation. Had his honest bill against the Government received recognition, he would have had to his credit nearly twenty thousand dollars on July 1, 1844, less than five years after he landed, a stranger, in the country; by no means an inconsiderable

sum for any professional man in those days, and especially
for one starting life anew in a strange country. During the
entire year 1844 Ericsson's receipts were nearly forty thousand dollars, $39,121.16, and the year following they were
more than double this, or $84,536.84. In these two years, as
his records show, he was carrying out contracts for steam-ma-
chinery for seven or eight steam vessels. One of these was
the Revenue cutter *Legaré*, another the Revenue cutter *Jefferson*, and a third the 188-ton twin screw propeller *Midas*.
The *Midas* belonged to Messrs. J. M. & R. B. Forbes and W.
C. Hunter, and was the first American steamer to pass the Cape
of Good Hope, and the first to ply in Chinese waters. She
sailed from New York November 4, 1844, and fell a victim to
neglect and bad engineering. Her boilers were ruined and
she was transformed into a sailing vessel.

The *Midas* was followed by the auxiliary steam bark
Edith, 450 tons, belonging to Robert B. Forbes and Thomas
H. Perkins, Jr., two of the most enterprising of Boston
merchants and ship owners in the China trade. Mr. Perkins who, during the War of 1812, served on a private armed
ship, and took part in several naval engagements, was familiar
with navigation, as was also Mr. Forbes. Both of them were
men of rare force of character, of far-sighted views, and independent judgment. It was with such men that Ericsson
always succeeded best. It was only the timid worshippers of
precedent who feared him. The "opium war" of 1842 had
opened five treaty ports in China to foreigners, and as there
was an active contest for their trade the *Edith* was built with
a fine model and a full rig, to enable her to run between India
and China in competition with the fast English opium clippers.

Speaking of this vessel's trial trip, Ericsson wrote: "The
Edith went four and a half miles in twenty-seven and a half
minutes, being at the rate of nine and eight-tenths miles per
hour (statute). My guarantee was, as you will recollect, seven
statute miles. This result far exceeds anything that has attended the application of my propeller, and that it should be
so in this particular case, being the first in which my patent invention for unshipping the propeller has been applied, is most
gratifying." The *Edith* sailed from New York January 18,

1845, and was the first American steamer to visit British India and the first square-rigged propeller that went to China under the American flag.

On March 11, 1845, Ericsson acknowledged the receipt of $1,000, patent fees, from Messrs. Forbes & Perkins for the propeller and shipping apparatus of the *Edith*, and agreed to protect them against adverse claims for patent fees.

In February, 1845, Ericsson wrote to Sargent, saying: "*In confidence*, our Boston friends have about made up their minds to build at once a large packet with my auxiliary propeller for the Atlantic. I am almost crazy with joy in consequence. It is by far the most important move yet."

The owners of the *Edith* were so well satisfied with her performance that they resolved to follow her with another auxiliary screw-steamer, that is, a vessel rigged as a sailer but fitted with engines and a propeller to be used as occasion required. This was the *Massachusetts*, 770 tons, old measurement, belonging to Mr. Forbes and some friends. She had the same general arrangement as the *Edith* for turning up her propeller out of the water and was, like her, full-rigged with double topsails and masts and spars aloft, so that she could either steam or sail. She was intended for the transatlantic trade, and left New York on her first voyage, September 16, 1845, as the pioneer steam packet between the United States and England under the American flag. Neither of these two vessels was successful commercially, for reasons explained by Mr. Forbes in his volume of " Personal Reminiscences." They met the fate that usually overtakes the pioneers in any enterprise, and their ill success was in no way connected with Ericsson's work, which was done to the entire satisfaction of the owners of the vessels. Fortunately, the Mexican War created a demand for transports and these vessels were chartered and afterward bought by the United States. The *Massachusetts* carried Winfield Scott to the siege of Vera Cruz and was after the war employed on Lighthouse service. She was rechristened *Farallones* and was finally sold and transformed into a sailing ship called the *Alaska*. The *Edith* was lost in a fog off Santa Barbara Cove while in charge of an officer of the Navy.*

* Personal Reminiscences. By Robert B. Forbes, pp. 210-216.

Mr. Forbes sent to the Navy Department a most flattering account of the *Massachusetts* and proposed that Ericsson's propeller and unshipping gear should be applied to a frigate, declaring that it was his "greatest ambition" to build a ship of war for the navy to be used as a merchant vessel until occasion required its service, for war. At this time Ericsson's attorney Mr. Sargent wrote from Washington that the Committee of Congress was proposing to cut down the *Princeton* claim to $6,000 and pay him that. To this he replied, saying: "So far from refusing the $6,000 recommended, I gladly accept it as a godsend, since I have for several weeks past made up my mind to receive nothing whatever. I am now on the point of concluding very favorable contracts with gentlemen in the East, which in another year will make me independent of Government. Hence, $6,000 will be of far greater importance to me *now* than *three* times that amount this time twelve months, and I have good reason to believe that Stockton has sworn vengeance against me and that it would be a very heavy sacrifice indeed that he would not make to purchase my downfall." This letter throughout shows how sound a judgment Ericsson had even in matters where his interest might seem to blind him to the facts.

Early in 1845 (says Mr. Forbes in his Reminiscences), I signed a contract to build an iron steamer to be called the *Iron Witch*. My associates were J. M. Forbes, J. K. Mills, W. S. Wetmore, John E. Thayer, Edward King, M. O. Roberts, and John Ericsson, the eminent engineer, who designed her, and expected her to beat all competitors on the North River. Hogg & Delamater were the builders. She had sea-going inclined engines of great power, intended to operate small paddle-wheels. She was very nicely built, and had superb engines, plenty of boiler, fire, and grate surface. All American engineers, who had long pinned their faith on the beam-engine and long stroke, with wheels of large diameter, predicted the failure of the *Iron Witch*. On trial, it was found that she could just beat the old *Troy*, but stood no chance with the more modern boats on the route to Albany. She ran for a time in charge of Captain Roe, continually losing money; when it was determined to try an experiment suggested by Ericsson; namely, to remove her side-wheels, and put on geared side-propellers; with these she made no increase of speed, and added much to the vibration. Some five or ten thousand dollars were thus wasted, and the material went into the scrap-heap.

The *Iron Witch*—known in my books originally as the *Allegania*—

proved to be a grand failure. Her machinery being very massive, it was concluded to put it into a sea-going steamer. A contract was made with Mr. Brown, who built the *Falcon*, taking the *Iron Witch's* hull in part payment. He fitted her with an ordinary beam-engine; and, for a long time, she ran in connection with some railroad on the North River. The *Falcon* was sold to George Law, and, I believe, was the first to run in connection with the Chagres and Panama route to California. It will readily be conceived that the *Iron Witch* spec resulted in a heavy loss to all concerned. The wise men of Gotham, who predicted her failure, had no doubt that her powerful engines would revolve her small wheels up to any desired speed; but they said she would not go fast. Ericsson had no doubt of his power to work up to more than thirty turns, and had full faith that she would go over twenty miles per hour. The result proved that no amount of steam could get the wheels beyond about thirty turns; and with this she went about seventeen statute miles, or just enough to beat the old *Troy*. With an active competition under the control of such men as Daniel Drew, this slow rate was a failure.

A speed was guaranteed " six miles per hour faster than the average run of the boat *Empire* upon the Hudson River," and the gentlemen advancing the money to build the vessel were to have one-half the patent right for the Hudson River and one half of all profits the *Iron Witch* and all other boats similarly equipped might earn upon that stream. Success would have made Ericsson a rich man, but success did not come. Altogether, this was one of the most trying experiences of his life, and failure left him in a position from which nothing but great abilities could have extricated him.

Ericsson's accounts show that a little over ninety thousand dollars was expended on the *Iron Witch*, and nearly one-half of this amount was furnished by Mr. Forbes and his brother. The vessel had double engines and in these the steam was worked highly expansively and on a new plan. As both paddle-wheels and propeller were applied to her, an excellent opportunity offered for a comparison of the two, greatly to the advantage of the propeller. In a letter dated April 3, 1846, Ericsson wrote:

The *Witch* ran yesterday up and down the Hudson eighteen miles each way in one hour and fifty-five minutes on 16½ pounds of steam in the boilers, all we could carry without foaming. Her speed at that low pressure (only one-third of what we intended to carry) is conclusive as to our ultimate success. . . . In a few weeks we will show the fast-

11

est vessel now in the world, and perhaps, the fastest ever to be seen propelled by *steam* force.

Ericsson's idea was, that great speed could be obtained by
the use of small wheels, and over eighteen miles an hour was
certainly by no means a contemptible result, but it was not sufficient to give him and his associates the monopoly of steam navigation on the Hudson, which he had confidently hoped to secure.
For the invention he filed a caveat August 23, 1845. In it he
describes himself as an alien, who has declared his intention of
becoming a citizen of the United States. The amount lost by
Mr. Marshall O. Roberts, of New York, in this enterprise was
sufficient to threaten him with pecuniary embarrassment, but
his fortunes took a happy turn just then and within the next
ninety days he was able to console himself with the addition of
half a million dollars to his possessions.

The business associations formed at this time between Ericsson and Forbes resulted in personal friendship, and this continued for nearly half a century, or until the death of Ericsson,
followed within a few months by that of Mr. Forbes. The
shipmaster's ill ventures in the steamship line in no way affected his confidence in the engineer, and he was in the habit
of consulting him upon all occasions. He asked his opinion as
to the rig of ships, as to the introduction of salt water into
cities, and concerning a great variety of subjects which occupied the busy brain of this energetic and public-spirited Yankee
skipper and merchant. In a letter written just after Ericsson's
death, giving some account of his early acquaintance with him,
Mr. Forbes said: " This brief sketch of my intimate association
with Ericsson, covering a long period of time and much correspondence, never interrupted by an hour of unfriendliness,
proves that, while a man of positive convictions, he never gave
me any offence, and proved a firm friend and able correspondent nearly up to his death." *

* Letter from R. B. Forbes to the Army and Navy Journal, March, 1889.
In a letter addressed to Mr. Forbes in 1883, Ericsson said with reference to
the introduction of salt water into seaboard cities : " The subject was brought
to my notice thirty years ago (*i.e.*, 1853). I have ever since taken much interest in the matter, and strongly advocated the salt-water system. It is only
a question of time when it will be introduced, as the steam engine demand
has already increased to such an extent that fresh water cannot be supplied.

Ericsson in 1844 planned an iron tow-boat, built by Otis Tufts for the Boston underwriters, and named the *R. B. Forbes*. She had great power, applied to twin screws, was the first twin screw propeller built in New England and was generally recognized as the most powerful tug-boat in the United States. After a service of fifteen years in Massachusetts waters, during which she towed ·the huge ship *Great Republic* around to New York, the *Forbes* was sold to the United States and, in 1862, towed a frigate into action during Du Pont's attack on Port Royal. On her way along the coast, soon after, she ran ashore and was burnt to prevent her falling into the hands of the enemy. The specification for this vessel, dated July 13, 1844, provides for water-tight bulkheads.

Objections to the screw arose at the beginning because of the practice of cutting out the stern of vessels to make room for it. Ericsson accordingly carried the propeller shaft on the side of the stern-post, working it abaft the rudder and securing the further advantage of deeper immersion. This device was first applied to the *Edith* and *Massachusetts* with great economy of fuel, and in 1849 was adopted for the U. S. war steamer *San Jacinto*, 1,460 tons, whose beautiful lines gave opportunity for a striking exhibition of this new method of applying the screw. A precisely similar vessel, the U. S. S. *Saranac*, was fitted with the ordinary side-wheels and the two vessels were tried together under similar conditions, the result clearly demonstrating the superiority of the screw vessel. Now, a naval power would as soon think of building a vessel without engines as without the screw. To meet the early objection to the screw, Ericsson built his ships precisely on the model of sailing vessels of the first class, with similar lines in the run and similar form of stern, the perforation in the hull for the propeller shaft being the only indication of a steamer.

In 1840 Mr. Isambard Kingdom Brunel, the younger of the two eminent engineers of that name, recommended as the result of his investigations into the merits of the screw, that it be adopted on board the steamer *Great Eastern*. Previous to this, Captain Richard Clayton, R.N., made six voyages across

For the steam-boiler salt water is nearly as good as fresh. Other purposes are too numerous to mention."

the Atlantic in the pioneer vessel of the first transatlantic line, the *Great Western*, to note the exact performance of her paddles and engines on behalf of Mr. Brunel. The attention of the Admiralty was called to Mr. Brunel's conclusions concerning the screw, and Sir E. Parry, Controller of Steam Machinery, proposed that he should apply the propeller to a naval vessel to be built for the purpose of experimenting with it.

When his engines were approaching completion, Mr. Brunel inquired as to the progress of the ship and ascertained that the vessel ordered had never been laid down. As the result of his inquiries he was sent for by Sir George Cockburn, the First Naval Lord. In his room was a model of the stern of an old-fashioned three-decker with the whole lower deck exposed through openings designed to make room for the screw. On this model was written "Mr. Brunel's mode of applying the screw to Her Majesty's ships." Pointing to this Sir George said:

"Do you mean to suppose that we shall cut up Her Majesty's ships after this fashion, sir?"

Mr. Brunel smiled and disclaimed all responsibility for this ridiculous application of the screw. "Why, sir," said the First Lord, "you sent it to the Admiralty." This was denied, and investigation showed that it came from the office of the Surveyor of the Navy, the gentleman who had three years before reported that a vessel could not be steered with the power applied at the stern.[*] Mr. Brunel's experience shows how useless was Ericsson's attempt to overcome the interested or prejudiced judgment of Mr. Symonds. It was not until two years later that Mr. Brunel got his vessel, the *Rattler*, and so thoroughly demonstrated the advantages of the screw that in 1845, eight years after Ericsson's excursion with the Admiralty lords, twenty of Her Majesty's vessels were ordered to be fitted with the screw.

The unique engines of the *Massachusetts* furnished the model for the screw vessels of Sweden, and her horizontal double-acting air-pumps were extensively copied in the British and American navies. The back-acting engines applied to the United States Revenue cutter *Legaré*, so named after an Attorney-General of the United States, were copied with slight modifications into the British screw-steamer *Amphion*. In

[*] Life of I. K. Brunel, Civil Engineer, p. 285.

1844 and 1845 Ericsson applied to several vessels vertical engines for working twin screws independently of each other.
These were so unpopular at the time with engine-drivers that
he discontinued their use but they have since come into favor.
Numerous freight steamers on the canals and lakes were fitted
with machinery especially adapted to their use.

Ericsson's plan of coupling the engine directly to the propeller shaft met with great opposition, but in the end his judgment prevailed, and the rapid introduction of the propeller is

Auxiliary Steam-packet-ship Massachusetts.

no doubt due to his early appreciation of the necessity of getting rid of the clumsy gearing through which motion had been
transmitted to paddle-wheels. The change involved a difficulty
with the valves of the air-pump. After many experiments he
finally overcame it by using valves of canvas resting on per-
forated plates. These were first applied to the *Massachusetts*
and attracted great attention from engineers. On this vessel,
also, he first discarded the hoop used to strengthen his original
propeller, securing the same result by bracing the blades diagonally.

By 1849 the screw propeller had been applied to twenty-four steamers belonging to the United States Government. Four were naval vessels—the *Princeton ;* the *Water Witch*, a harbor tug; the *Scourge*, a purchased steamer, and the *San Jacinto*, 1,461 tons. Three of these vessels were built by the Treasury Department, the *Jefferson, Legaré,* and *Spencer,* and seventeen were merchant vessels—purchased for transport service by the Quartermaster-General of the army, General Jesup, during the war with Mexico. Various forms of propellers were tried on these vessels, six having Ericsson's propeller and some a flat-bladed propeller invented by Loper, who claimed to have improved upon Ericsson.

During the winter of 1846–47 Ericsson spent much time in Washington seeking for Government work to retrieve his fortunes, after the miscarriage of his plans in connection with the *Iron Witch.* He made a most favorable impression upon the Secretary of the Treasury, Robert J. Walker, and was consulted by him with reference to changes required to improve the Revenue cutters, being also requested to go to Pittsburg to take charge of alterations in the Revenue cutter *Robert J. Walker.* The Secretary gave him orders for the introduction of his system for supplying fresh water from the boilers of steamers, and altogether Ericsson received so much encouragement that he wrote, April 27, 1847: "Appearances now indicate that I reached the climax of misfortune in putting propellers into the *Iron Witch,* and that I am henceforth to taste some of the sweets of my long and laborious career."

He was then in the forty-fourth year of his age, and had been for over thirty years continuously at work, but the end of his probation of disappointment and comparative poverty was not yet. He was even then engaged in a struggle that proved to be one of the most bitter he was destined to know during a long life full of conflict and opposition.

"The triumphs of genius," says Dr. Dionysius Lardner, "are not unattended with alloy. The moment that any invention proves to be successful in practice a swarm of vermin are fostered into being to devour the legitimate profits of the inventor, and to rob genius of its fair reward. Captain Ericsson, so long as his submerged propeller retained the character of a mere experiment, was left in undisturbed possession of it; but when it forced its way into extensive practical use—when it was adopted in the United States navy and in the Revenue service—when the coast of this country witnessed its application in numerous merchant vessels—when it was known that in France and England its adoption was decided upon—then the discovery was made for the first time that this invention of Captain Ericsson's was no invention at all—that it had been applied since the earliest dates in steam navigation. Old patents—some of which had been still-born, and others which had been for years dead and buried—were dug from their graves, and their dust brought into courts of law to overturn this invention and wrest from Captain Ericsson his justly-earned reward." *

When in 1838 Ericsson applied for a patent at Washington he appears to have had some difficulty at first in obtaining it, owing to a supposed interference with a patent granted to one Jesse Ong, of North Huntington, Pa., May 23, 1837, or nearly a year after Ericsson had procured his patent in England, but before his application for it in the United States had been filed. He was informed, however, by the examiner of the Patent Office that the similarity was confined to the principle, the application being new, and he heard nothing more from Ong. The principle of the propeller was then so little understood that any revolving wheel seems to have been mistaken for it, whether this was intended to turn under or above water, at the stem or stern, or even at the side. As late as May 17, 1873, Sir E. J. Reed wrote to Ericsson: "The action of the screw propeller is a subject which has not been exhaustively, or in my opinion, satisfactorily dealt with by any English writer."

From Abo, in Finland, Samuel Owen wrote to the London *Engineer*, December 22, 1871, saying: "John Ericsson took the idea from my father's propeller, which was shown to him at the time." To this Ericsson, in a letter to John Bourne, replies with characteristic directness:

This assertion I have to state is an unqualified untruth, the communication addressed to the *Engineer* being the first intimation I have that the steam-engine builder Samuel Owen, in Stockholm, at any time

* Popular Lectures on Science and Art, New York, 1846.

conducted experiments relating to stern propulsion. With reference to the drawing of Mr. Owen's propeller wheel, published in the *Engineer*, it is scarcely necessary to call your attention to the fact that it could not have been intended to operate under water, since the blades are attached to a centre-piece and arms, which, if immersed, would to a great extent neutralize the propulsive energy of the wheel. Mr. Owen possessed too much practical knowledge to support the blades in such a manner had he intended his wheel to operate under water. Evidently, then, the wheel which Mr. Owen's son mistakes for a *screw propeller*, was simply a transverse stern wheel provided with flat blades placed obliquely. It will be observed that the drawing published in the *Engineer* furnishes no evidence that Mr. Owen had any conception whatever of a screw propeller, his flat blades and solid centre-piece and arms being incompatible with the principles of a screw.

The claim to priority giving Ericsson the most trouble in the United States was that of J. B. Emerson. This was founded upon a patent originally taken out May 23, 1837, for improvements in the steam-engine and improvements in propelling. Ericsson showed that no draughtsman could by any possibility construct from the specifications filed by Emerson a propeller containing the distinctive and patentable features of his own device. The Patent Office at Washington, with its records, was burnt in 1836 and inventors were granted the privilege of refiling their papers. Taking advantage of this privilege, Emerson filed in 1841 drawings, and again in 1846 amended drawings, embodying in them features obtained from the plans of Ericsson's screw previously recorded. At the time Ericsson obtained his patent a thorough examination was made by the Patent Office of all previous devices, and the originality of his device established so far as the Patent Office could do so. This examination was repeated in 1846 at the request of the Navy Department, and with the same result. No attempt was made by Emerson to introduce his propeller into actual use; it never went beyond a record in the Patent Office. But when he found that Ericsson had achieved success, he brought suit for infringement, sought to restrain him by injunction, and busied himself with travelling along the lakes, where the Ericsson propeller was coming rapidly into service, demanding royalties for its use. He also gave public notice through the newspapers that no patent fees could be safely paid to Ericsson, and by a long and vexatious litigation kept him worried for many years. After the issue of this notice nothing further could be collected for the patent, and Ericsson's income from this source was at once cut off and the expenses of litigation took its place.

Emerson finally memorialized Congress asking $15,000 as compensation for the use of his patented "spiral propellers" on Government vessels. His memorial was referred to Engineer-in-chief of the United States Navy, Charles H. Haswell. He reported against Emerson's claims as covering a form of propeller-blade employed neither by Captain Ericsson nor Captain Loper and "positively impracticable for any useful purpose." This was the opinion of an expert whose professional training enabled him to estimate at their true value vague resemblances that confused courts and bewildered juries.

As Messrs. Hogg & Delamater were the parties defendant, they had been subjected to the expenses of litigation, and on February 24, 1847, Ericsson executed on their behalf an assignment of all his patent rights in the propeller. This assignment specifies the original patent of 1838, a patent for improvements dated November 5, 1840, the patent of December 31, 1844, for an "unshipping apparatus," and the patent of September 9, 1845, for an elliptical propeller. A circular issued by Ericsson contains this announcement:

The patentee offers to dispose of his right at the rate of $3.50 per ton register measurement for vessels of 1,600 tons and upward, with an increase of ten cents per ton for vessels below that tonnage, thus:

		Per ton.			Per ton.
For vessels of 1,600 tons....	$3 50	For vessels of 800 tons	$4 30
" " 1,500 "	.... 3 60	" " 700 "	..... 4 40
" " 1,400 "	.... 3 70	" " 600 "	..... 4 50
" " 1,300 "	.... 3 80	" " 500 "	.... 4 60
" " 1,200 "	.... 3 90	" " 400 "	..... 4 70
" " 1,100 "	.... 4 00	" " 300 "	..... 4 80
" " 1,000 "	.... 4 10	" " 200 "	..... 4 90
" " 900 "	.... 4 20	" " 100 "	..... 5 00

J. ERICSSON, Patentee,
95 Franklin Street.

NEW YORK, *March* 15, 1849.

Many persons occupied their day dreams with speculations upon the possibility of screw propulsion; some experimented with screws more or less impracticable in form or in the method of applying them; Ericsson alone invented a submerged screw, so complete at the outset in its mechanical details that it was capable of immediate use. Further, his large experience in mechanical construction enabled him to determine the best methods of applying his propeller to vessels of various kinds. What is absolutely the best form of screw is not even now determined, nor is the theory of its operation placed beyond discussion. As for the screws invented since Ericsson demonstrated the advantages of this method of propulsion, their name is legion. For a time he received a royalty on his patent, but he was forced to maintain his rights against constant aggression. And, at the end of a long and expensive contest in the courts, it was finally decided that the invention of the screw could not be protected in the United States by a patent.

Nevertheless, the demonstration of the efficiency of the screw which converted the world dates back to the building of the United States steamer *Princeton* and its engines, in 1842-44, by John Ericsson, or from his plans and under his supervision. All who have investigated the subject, as such authorities as Scott Russell, Bourne, and Woodcraft have done, will accept the dictum of the "Encyclopædia Britannica," that "a small vessel fitted with a propeller patented by Ericsson was the *first* brought into practical use." Long after steam had been applied to navigation, battle-scarred and experienced old admirals in the British service were declaring that a sailing ship would always beat a steamship, and that steam could never be depended upon. The control such unconvincible gentlemen exercise over naval affairs in England has resulted in the British Admiralty's always following, instead of leading, in the march of improvement. Long after the screw had demonstrated its efficiency, the English dockyards continued to turn out the good old-fashioned paddle-wheel steamers, and in the end they were obliged to adapt these as best they could to the new motor. Ericsson's early antagonist, Sir William Symonds, who prevented the Admiralty from considering his invention when it was offered to them in the beginning, continued to resist for twenty-two years longer the idea of adopting the screw in war-vessels.

When in 1850 Ericsson appeared by counsel before the Queen's Privy Council and asked for the extension of his English patent, it was necessary to prove that his propeller was an invention and a meritorious one, and that the time covered by the original patent had not been long enough to sufficiently remunerate the inventor. The proof on all these points appears to have been found sufficient, as the application for renewal was granted. Ericsson's counsel was Sir F. Thesiger, late Attorney-General, afterward Lord Chancellor, and finally, as Baron Chelmsford, one of the leaders of the Conservative party in the House of Lords. Mr. Thesiger served in his youth as a midshipman in the navy, and was better fitted than most attorneys and judges in those days to understand the distinctive features of Ericsson's invention. He showed that the only propeller in use before 1836 was the Archimedean screw, and one with arms like the vanes of a smoke-jack; he pointed out the advantages and indicated the essential differences between these and his client's invention, which offered the first "efficient means of screw propulsion known to the scientific world." He described the difficulties encountered in endeavoring to secure the recognition of the screw in England from the Admiralty and others, and demonstrated that there had been thus far an actual loss on the patent of £3,271 16s. 2d. This did not include these further items taken into account between these parties in interest in their private settlement, viz., "Captain Ericsson's time, three years, £1,500; M. Hobin's time, eight years, £2,400; Count von Rosen's time, ten years, £5,000."

Mr. Thesiger gave some account of the litigation resulting from the rival claims in England to the invention of the screw, ending finally in the union of the several interests, and called as a witness Mr. Bennet Woodcroft, whose patent for screw propulsion, taken out in 1832, had been extended. Mr. Woodcroft said in his testimony: "The parties having patents for the screw propeller have united; they are Messrs. Smith, Lowe, Ericsson, Blaxland, and myself. After fighting each other for many years, we have got tired of it and want to be amicable."

By the Attorney-General. You were to be a partner in the profits!

Answer. Profits! We have had none.

Question. Did not Captain Ericsson first introduce a fixed shaft, or a shaft running horizontally below the water-line?

Answer. Yes, Captain Ericsson did.

Question. He was the first that introduced the shaft running below the line of the water through the stuffing-box outside the stern?

Answer. Yes.

Various witnesses were called to establish Ericsson's title to the screw, and after listening to this testimony and to the arguments, the Council reached their conclusions as thus recorded:

The Attorney-General. I understand your lordships to grant this extension upon the same terms and the same conditions as Mr. Smith's?

Mr. Baron Parke. Yes.

The Attorney-General. And further, the Crown using it may employ engineers to make it?

Mr. Baron Parke. Yes.

Of this judgment the London *Mechanics' Magazine* said at this time:

The Attorney-General demanded that a condition should be attached to the prolongation, to the effect that the Government should have the use of the patent and with it of all the other patents for the screw propeller gratuitously. The argument relied on to extort this concession appears to be worthy of the narrow-minded policy, which has almost invariably characterized the treatment of inventors by the authorities of this country. As our readers well know, the proprietors of the various screw patents have been at law with each other for some years—they receiving the shells while the lawyers swallowed the oysters; and when they finally make peace and have a prospect of getting a few of the oysters for themselves, they are coolly told by the Attorney-General— " You are going to make some money now, so you can bear to be fleeced a little." This is really the truth of the matter. If people want to use the screw propeller in their national capacity, why should they not pay for it the same as they would have to do in their individual capacity?

The Admiralty subsequently made an award of £20,000 for the use of the screw. This sum was divided among the five inventors whose names are given above by Mr. Woodcroft. The proportion coming to Ericsson was by him made over to Mrs. Ericsson who was living in England at the time of the award. To his associate, Count Von Rosen, he had previously (July 15, 1845) assigned his patent rights " within England, Wales, and the town of Berwick on Tweed and all his Majesty's colonies and plantations abroad." This was necessary to enable him to carry on litigation in England. " Berwick on Tweed," then a free town, independent of both England and Scotland, now constitutes a county by itself.

Count Von Rosen took charge of the introduction of Ericsson's propeller in France. At the end of ten years of constant effort, he reported that it had established its superiority with the public and the government, "but," he adds, " I have experienced nothing but disappointment and discouragement at seeing the invention, when its merits were acknowledged, boldly infringed upon and pirated by the very people who showed themselves at first most averse to it. Now (February 8, 1848) there are upward of 5,000 horse-power of engines, made or in course of construction, applied or to be applied to screw-ships on our system. On these, a large amount of patent fees are due, for which I shall be obliged to sue."

The claim made on behalf of John Ericsson to the honor of substituting the screw for the paddle-wheel has been hotly disputed. In the end, when all the evidence is sifted, his name will be associated with that great advance in steam navigation, as the name of Watt is associated with the steam-engine, Fulton's with the steamboat, and that of Morse with the telegraph. Let them build monuments as high as they may to others, they can never overshadow the memorial which the impartial judgment of the future will accord to Ericsson.

As a screw is reported to have been introduced into England from China early in the seventeenth century, its origin may be referred to a period as remote as the invention of the windmill, or the smoke-jack it so much resembles. Still, it is to Ericsson, unquestionably, that we owe the revolution in steam navigation resulting from the demonstration of the possibilities of the screw propeller.

How important his labors in this regard were, in establishing the supremacy of steam upon the ocean, is shown by the calculation made in 1852 that the cost of £198 14s. 3d. for transporting four hundred tons of merchandise over a distance of five hundred miles with a full-powered paddle vessel, was actually reduced by using a screw vessel of auxiliary power to £60 12s. 6½d. or seventy per. cent.* In this difference lies the solution of the problem of competition with sails.

Any device, from a smoke-jack to a windmill, with arms turning upon a centre, or having the spiral motion of the screw, was considered sufficient to antagonize Ericsson's claims to priority. "The principle of the propeller," Mr. Sargent tells us, "was first suggested to the inventor by the analogies of nature, and a study of the means employed to propel the inhabitants of the air and deep. He satisfied himself that all such propulsion in nature is produced by oblique action; though, in common with all practical men, he at first supposed that it was inseparably attended by loss of power. But when he reflected that this was the universal principle adapted by the great Mechanician of the universe, in enabling the birds, insects, and fishes to move through their respective elements, he knew that he must be in error. This he was soon able to demonstrate, and he became convinced, by the strict application of the laws which govern matter and motion, that no loss of power whatever attends the oblique action of the propelling surfaces applied to Nature's locomotives."

In connection with his studies of the propeller at this time Ericsson applied to the equipoise rudder his plan of investigating the operation in nature of the mechanical laws, as would appear from a letter written twenty years later to Mr. Robert B. Forbes. In this he said:

NEW YORK, September 29, 1857.

MY DEAR SIR: I note with profound satisfaction that you have been in the habit of swearing by me. Swear on; my opposition to the equipoise rudder furnishes no *just* ground for your withdrawing your confidence. You say that the several engineers that you consulted all pronounced in favor of the equipoise; you mean that all of them agreed that the rudder could be worked with very little power and that it would steer. Any person of ordinary intelligence could see all that. The *drag* inseparable from this steering apparatus, this "vile contrivance" as you

* John Bourne's Treatise on the Screw Propeller, p. 183. London, 1852.

remember I called it at our interview, requires, however, some knowledge of hydro-dynamics to determine. Your suggestion is far from being correct that my knowledge on the subject is mere theory. All my early propeller experiments in England were made in boats steered by equipoise rudders. I know the *critter* to pieces, and so do the canal men of Europe, who no longer favor this machine, invented for the lazy at the expense of force and time. You will admit on reflection that a rudder to be theoretically perfect should form an elongation of the vessel and be if possible, devoid of thickness. The Great Constructor of the craft of the deep, not only carries out this theory but adds *flexibility* to the rudder, which renders its action absolutely perfect by presenting the greatest angle at the aft end.

The current of water, instead of being forced violently from its course along the body is *gradually* deviated on meeting the rudder, thereby causing a minimum retardation to the moving body, removing at the same time the greatest action to the extreme end, where the leverage is greatest. Although we cannot, with all our boasted ingenuity, imitate this beautiful property of flexibility which Omnipotence employs, we can at least construct our rudder so as to form an *elongation of the vessel.* As the thin stern-posts of iron vessels admit of a rudder almost devoid of thickness, we are enabled in that class of vessels to do all that theory demands. Let us, then, not introduce a detached body to be towed abaft the vessel.

I note particularly what you say of the small angle required by your rudder. There is a fixed law in dynamics that "every deviation from a straight line of a moving body is attended with a given diminution of speed or momentum." Do not suppose that there is any way to cheat this law.

Very truly yours,
J. Ericsson.

CHAPTER XI.

THE ERICSSON HOT-AIR SHIP.

The Perfection Engine.—Plans for a War Vessel.—Ericsson Employed by the United States Government During the War with Mexico.—Elected Honorary Church Member and Becomes a Citizen.—Honors from England.—His Temperance Principles.—Prosperity and Adversity.

DURING the years in which Ericsson was so constantly occupied with the application of his ideas to the practical purposes of navigation, and in defending himself against the efforts to rob him of the fruit of his industry, he still found time to develop various new inventions. He designed in 1846 an apparatus for heating the feed-water of boilers, and a high-pressure condensing steam-engine with two single-acting cylinders, the diameter of one being five times that of the other. This engine was patented in America and in other countries. It received the special attention of Professor Dionysius Lardner, the British writer and lecturer on Physical Science, who had been Professor of Natural Philosophy and Astronomy in the London University until domestic difficulties led to his transfer to the United States. During his residence in New York, Dr. Lardner devoted several months to the theoretical study of Ericsson's engine, and he continued these investigations after his removal to Paris. He estimated that Ericsson's engine showed an economy of fuel equalled only by the engines used in the mines of Cornwall.

Lardner endeavored to introduce this engine into France, and there was an amiable dispute between him and its inventor as to whether he should receive any remuneration for this service. On August 23, 1849, he wrote to Ericsson from Paris, saying : " After the services you formerly rendered me, I think you need not have felt much hesitation in accepting my aid without thinking of compensation in any shape. I can assure you that I would act for you as zealously and carefully as for myself. However, seeing what your sentiments are on this point, I believe that it will be best for you that I should at once acquiesce in your proposition of accepting a fifth of the net profits for France, if through my exertions the patent should be rendered productive." As Professor Lardner had gathered $200,000 from a lecturing tour in the United States, he was much more independent in his circumstances than Ericsson was at this time.

In the spring of 1846, the House Committee on Naval Affairs of the 29th Congress considered the subject of employing steam for naval armaments and sent a circular to various persons, asking an opinion as to the practicability of rendering, an iron vessel shot-proof. Among the replies accompanying the report of the Committee (Report No. 681, H. R., 29th Congress, 1st Session) is one from John Ericsson. He argued that "the weight of a floating body is prescribed within such narrow limits as to preclude the possibility of making the side of a vessel of sufficient thickness to prevent penetration by heavy projectiles. He recommended, therefore, a system of watertight bulkheads, so distributed that less than one-fortieth of the ship's displacement would be occupied by water entering through a shot-hole. He proposed also to strengthen the bows so that they would deflect a shot when the vessel was fighting bows on, the method he always favored. He forwarded a plan for a 1,200-ton iron vessel. This he proposed to build, and arm with two 12-inch and four 8-inch guns, for $415,000. She was to be 200 feet long by 36 feet beam, and to make "fifteen miles an hour at sea in pretty rough weather." Three of his guns were to be placed within the line of the protected bow, one was to train over the stern, and the other two were to be placed amidships. These guns were to be mounted on circular railways and the engines of the vessel were to be partially protected by stowing the coal in water-tight bulkheads over the engine-room.

This Congressional inquiry antedates by nine years the appearance, during the Crimean War, of the first French armorclads. Ericsson's rejection in 1846 of the idea of undertaking

12

to protect the ordinary war-ship against shot, cleared the way
for his final conclusions as to the only possible type for a completely protected armored vessel.   He advanced step by step in
his study of battle-ships, until his mastery of the subject enabled him to act at a critical moment with the utmost promptness and decision, while others were yet lingering in the preliminary stages of discussion.   This diagram of the deck plan
of the vessel he recommended to Congress also suggests the
monitor idea of all-round fire.

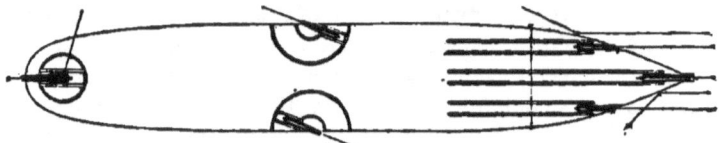

Deck Plan of Ericsson's War Vessel of 1846.

The committee in their report called attention to the fact
that the *Princeton* was the first ship ever constructed with her
machinery and propeller so arranged as to be secured from an
enemy's shot, and urged that " this fact should hereafter be the
governing principle in the construction of a steam navy." They
also said : " The machinery and propeller of this ship were invented and arranged under the superintendence of that eminent
civil engineer, Captain John Ericsson."   The committee recommended the building of twelve iron war steamers and one iron
frigate, but beyond the competitive trial of the paddle-wheel
Saranac and the screw vessel *San Jacinto*, already recorded,
and the building of the 23-gun paddle-wheel steamer *Sus-
quehanna*, nothing was done.   This was in the line of Congressional precedent.   In 1816 the national legislature had decided that the navy must be gradually increased and improved.
So, for the next twenty-three years they spent an average of
$600,000 a year in partially building frigates and seventy-fours,
erecting houses over them at a large expense, and then leaving
them to rot on the stocks, while the men who were to man
them were deprived of the opportunity to practise their profession, which the commissioning of these vessels would have
given them.

This was one of the most trying periods of Ericsson's history, and at times he was driven nearly distracted by pecuniary difficulties. In full reliance upon the justice of Government he had expended $6,000 in money, besides his time, in the work upon the *Princeton*. This involved him in debt, and he was constantly harassed by the attempt to meet over-due obligations out of an empty purse. His check-book shows balances to his credit during the two years ending with May, 1846, varying from $1,000 to nearly $14,000, but much of this was expended in completing contract work. On May 5, 1846, he was reduced to $38.54, and against the entry of this ominous balance he has made a memorandum in Swedish to the effect that it was a most discouraging exhibit for so many years of hard work. He had not even then touched bottom, and $23 was at one time the limit of his credit with the bank. September 16, 1846, he wrote to Mr. Sargent, saying:

"I received your letter of the 14th yesterday afternoon, and opened it with trembling hand. My worst fears were realized, and I turned nearly crazy for a few minutes. In my despair I resorted to the expedient of asking Delamater to help me, and he has done so for to-day, appropriating the funds he has for meeting a bill at the end of next week. Now, if in addition to my anxiety already experienced, I should ruin the young man's credit by not being able to refund the money by next Wednesday I shall have to cut my throat."

"It is unfortunate," said Ericsson, in a previous letter, "that I have allowed the supposed payment of my *Princeton* claim to enter into my *financial* calculations, as, in all probability, it will be the means of throwing me on my beam ends; still more unfortunate is it that immediately on the success of the *Princeton* I did not pack up my traps, make a present of my inventions to the United States, and recross the Atlantic with a grateful heart to find my retreat left open, an advantage which I do not now enjoy." *

From this condition of pecuniary distress Ericsson was for a time relieved by the fortunate sale to the Government of the steamer *Massachusetts*, in which he had a part interest, and by the receipt, December 27, 1847, of a payment of

* Letter to John O. Sargent, New York, July 20, 1846.

$4,300 for the application of his fresh water apparatus to that vessel.

A portion of this year was occupied with a careful study of oscillating engines, and on June 17, 1847, he wrote to the Committee on Engines of the United States War Steamers that he had "succeeded in removing the principal imperfections of this simple instrument for transmitting the force of steam for purposes of locomotion." He was also called upon by the United States Treasury Department for a report upon the alterations required in the Revenue cutter *Polk*, and he presented to the War Department a plan for an iron steamer to navigate the Gulf of Mexico and the Rio Grande. This was a time of war, and the Government were looking in all directions for an improvement in the means of transporting troops and supplies to Mexico.

The apparatus for condensing into fresh water the steam generated by the boilers of ocean-going vessels was applied in 1848 to the *Alabama*, a steamer belonging to the Quartermaster's Department of the United States Army to the U. S. S. *Edith*, then fitting out for the Pacific, and to the Revenue cutter *Legaré*. The profit on the $10,725 received for this service constituted nearly all of Ericsson's income for this year. But his frugality in personal expenditure enabled him even then to respond to the calls of duty and affection, as is shown by his remittances to his wife in England and his mother in Sweden. A report to the Quartermaster-General stated that there was a saving of twenty-five per cent. in fuel from the use of the fresh water apparatus, and that it condensed all the steam generated during an entire day, with full fires and engines stationary. The captain of the *Alabama*, after a voyage from New Orleans to Chagres and back, said :

The condensing apparatus for making fresh water for use of passengers and crew works admirably, furnishing one thousand two hundred gallons, if necessary, for twenty-four hours, enabling us to dispense with at least three thousand gallons of water, which weight can be carried in fuel or cargo. We drank this water from choice during the whole voyage ; it is clear as the purest spring water.

Unfortunately, iron had been used for the tubes instead of copper, and these were rapidly destroyed by the galvanic action resulting from the use of copper in the vessel itself. So the inventor's confident expectation that his apparatus would be introduced into other Government vessels, and ultimately into the Atlantic steamers, was not realized.

In January, 1847, Ericsson was in Philadelphia experimenting in the use for locomotives of anthracite coal, which had been first employed on steamboats in place of wood ten years earlier. January 5th he wrote: "Christmas and New Year's have played the devil with my work on the Reading road. We are now at work again, and probably this week we shall know something more of burning anthracite than we now do." He was not an observer of holidays, and all days were much the same with him.

Ericsson became a naturalized citizen October 28, 1848, and his correspondence for 1848 contains the only political allusion I have been able to find. The Democrats had nominated as their candidate for President, General Lewis Cass, of Michigan, and for Vice-President, General W. C. Butler, of Kentucky. Writing to his enthusiastic Whig friend, Sargent, May 31st, on the eve of the Whig National Convention, Ericsson said: "Opposed by two generals your party cannot surely think of any other man than the victorious soldier whose military lustre is untarnished by a single spot or speck. I therefore take it for granted that Taylor will be nominated." He sympathized with his friend's enthusiasm, but personally he took very little interest in the contentions dividing parties at that time. It was not until slavery became the main issue in the contest that his earnestness was aroused. He was hostile to slavery from the beginning, and was accustomed to say that he could conceive of nothing meaner than the desire of one man to live on the toil of another.

1849 was another trying year for Ericsson. His receipts from all sources were only two thousand dollars and at the end of this year he records against his balance of $132.32 on his check-book this legend, written in Swedish: "A beautiful balance indeed to start the new year with. One gives much for little as he grows older and more used up." He was occupied in 1849 in an unsuccessful attempt to secure a contract for an immense pumping-engine for a new dry dock at the Brooklyn Navy Yard. "You must know," he wrote to his agent at

Washington, "that I built in Europe a machine raising 3,000 gallons of water per minute to precisely the same height as will be requisite at the Brooklyn dock by means remarkably simple, durable, and efficient and cheap. But as we have no dry docks in England or on the continent, I could not profit by my beautiful machine. Now, however, is a chance of making a little fortune."

Ericsson was a pioneer in the attempt to solve the difficult problem of introducing steam power upon the canals of the United States. In 1844 he entered into a contract with Charles Dimmock,* of Richmond, Va., to build small steamboats for canal navigation. It was agreed that they were to exceed the horse-boats in speed, and as they failed in this he became involved in an unfortunate litigation with the purchaser. With his usual hopefulness he had guaranteed results which the conditions of canal navigation made it impossible for him to realize. In October, 1849, he entered into a contract with James S. French, of Old Point Comfort, Va., to build for him for $3,000 a model locomotive, to test French's invention for obtaining greater adhesion to the rails and security against derailment with lighter locomotives. This engine, called the *Climber*, was to be used on an experimental road authorized by the Virginia Legislature.

In 1849 Ericsson secured a patent for his " independent action condenser." It provides for condensing the exhaust steam from a marine engine by passing it through tubes, around which circulates cold water from the sea, the water flowing in a direction opposite to that of the escaping steam. The water is supplied by a pump, worked by an auxiliary engine so as to be independent of the action of the engine running the vessel, and can either be returned to the boiler to be again converted into steam or used for other purposes. This invention is described at length in Ericsson's volume, "Contributions to the Centennial Exhibition," and appears to be an improvement upon his previous condensers. In 1847 a board composed of three naval engineers, and four other experts, reported to the Secretary of the Treasury on this appar-

* An ex-army officer, West Point graduate, and native of Massachusetts, who died in the Confederate service in 1863 as General Dimmock.

atus as applied to the revenue cutter *Legaré*, saying, at the conclusion of a very flattering report:

We cannot but congratulate ourselves and the profession with which we are connected that you have seen fit to test this experiment by the construction of the apparatus upon which we have been called to report. Such encouragement identifies in the merits of success the patron with the improvement, and is honorable to yourself no less than to the nation in whose service you have bestowed it.

They reported a saving of 7.56 per cent. in fuel, " and altogether, independent of the loss of heat by the presence of scale in the boiler when salt water is used, and from leaks incurred by the oxidizing effects of salt water."

A number of minor inventions were sent to the Crystal Palace Exhibition of 1851. For an alarm barometer a prize medal was awarded. The tube of the common barometer was so enlarged at the upper end that the mercury in falling ran out of the lower end and into a cup, so adjusted that its weight set loose a catch and released the hammer of a gong moved by a spring. An index regulated the altitude of the mercurial column at which the gong would sound, thus giving notice of sudden changes.

The Croton Aqueduct Department of New York adopted, after a series of careful experiments, a fluid meter of Ericsson's invention, measuring the flow of water by plungers of definite size working between stops. He also patented a meter for measuring fluids by a calculation of the velocity with which they passed through apparatus of different dimensions.

In 1851 a pamphlet was published in London entitled " Brief Explanation of some Philosophical and other Instruments placed in the United States Division of the Industrial Exhibition of All Nations, Hyde Park, London, by John Ericsson, Knight of the Order of Vasa, Member of the Royal Academy of Sciences, Stockholm; Corresponding Member of the Franklin Institute, Philadelphia; Member of the Royal Academy of Military Sciences of Sweden; Hon. Member of the American Institute, New York, &c., &c., &c." It was accompanied by this dedication:

To His ROYAL HIGHNESS PRINCE ALBERT :

ILLUSTRIOUS PRINCE—In laying before your Royal Highness the accompanying Brief Statement of some Philosophical and other Instruments placed in the Industrial Exhibition of All Nations, it is my duty
to state that these mechanical productions, the result of much labor,
would never have been put before the public in the complete form they
now appear, but for the encouragement extended by your Royal Highness to all nations alike—an encouragement entitling your Royal Highness to the gratitude of the whole civilized world, and the results of
which mark an epoch in the annals of mankind.

Your Royal Highness's most humble Servant,

J. ERICSSON.

NEW YORK, June 16, 1851.

Included in the brief explanation are seven of Ericsson's
inventions—the instrument for measuring distance at sea ; the
hydrostatic gauge for measuring the volume of fluids under
pressure ; the reciprocating fluid meter ; the alarm barometer ;
the pyrometer for measuring high temperatures; the rotary
fluid meter, and the sea-lead. Lithographic illustrations of
these several instruments accompanied the text. The various
distinctions referred to in the title-page of this pamphlet were
conferred upon him after he left England in 1839. In 1843,
the Franklin Institute elected him a corresponding member,
in recognition of the service rendered in designing the steam
fire-engine, for which the New York Mechanics' Institute
awarded the only gold medal it has ever bestowed upon an inventor. In 1847 the Royal Academy of Sciences of Stockholm
elected Ericsson an honorary member ; in 1850 the Swedish
Government bestowed upon him the distinction of Knight of
the Order of Vasa, and in 1852 the Royal Military Academy of
Sciences of Sweden elected him an honorary member.

The studies into the nature and application of heat as a mechanical force, begun by Ericsson at the time of his youthful
invention of the flame-engine, were continued at intervals for
three score years and ten, or until the end of his active and useful life. At a very early date he discovered the fallacy of the
conclusions concerning high temperatures resulting from the
use of Wedgewood's method of measuring these by gauging
the dimensions of a cylinder of clay before and after heating it
in a furnace. This measurement gave 21,637 degrees as the

temperature of iron melted in cupola furnaces. Ericsson satisfied himself that this was at least six times too great, and the actual temperature proved to be 2,786 degrees. The invention of the pyrometer was one result of these studies. Ericsson's method of measuring high artificial temperatures by the expansion of confined gases has since been shown to be one of the most reliable of the dozen different methods tested, and he was a pioneer in this field of investigation, as in so many others. Of the others none have been superior, except perhaps Siemens's method, recently adopted, of measuring temperatures by changes in resistance to electricity.

After his removal to the United States in 1839, Ericsson continued his experiments with hot air as a motor, building eight caloric engines for experiment between 1840 and 1850. Seven of these cost together $9,400 and the eighth $7,000. He gradually enlarged the dimensions of these experimental engines from the fourteen inches of his original model to sixteen inches and then to thirty. Into these engines he introduced the principle of "regeneration," as he called it, or transfer of the heat from the outgoing to the incoming air by passing the currents alternately through a metal box or chest filled with wire meshes.

Theory, he said, "clearly indicates that, owing to the small capacity for heat of atmospheric air—that beneficial property which the Great Mechanician gives to it as a fit medium for animated warm beings to live in—and, in consequence, also, of the almost infinite subdivision among the wires, the temperature of the circulating air in passing through the regenerator of the caloric engine must be greatly changed. Practice has fully realized all that theory predicted, for the temperatures at x and z [that is, at the points of entrance to and exit from the regenerator] have never varied during the trials less than 350 degrees, when the engine has been in full operation; indeed it has been found *impossible* to obtain a differential temperature of less magnitude with sufficient fires in the furnaces. The great number of disks, their isolated character, and the distribution of the air in such a vast number of minute cells, readily explain the surprising fall and increase of temperature of the opposite currents passing the regenerator, and which constitutes the grand feature of the caloric engine, effecting, as it does, such an extraordinary saving of fuel by rendering the caloric not converted into work active over and over again." *

Letters from Ericsson show that he was at work upon his caloric engine in 1847. Early in December of that year a model engine was sent from the factory and set up in his room at No. 95 Franklin Street for experiment. On December 23d, he wrote to Sargent : " The caloric is very nearly finished. It will beyond all question succeed. Never felt so sure in my life." Six weeks later, January 14, 1848, he wrote: "I am at this moment under lock and key with Harrison, who is engaged in the secret operation of stuffing the guts of the regenerator of the caloric, which is in all other respects ready for trial. I have had pressure, and all is tight. The thing must go."

But not yet, for January 20th he wrote again, saying: "The caloric is not yet completed; a deposit of water, occasioned by the pressure of atmospheric air within the machine, has given me trouble, great trouble. The steam formed from this water has produced inflammation in the stomach of the regenerator. Cold applications have been resorted to without reducing the undue temperature. All that medical skill can effect will be done, and no fears need be apprehended as to the safety of the patient."

On the principle that troubles never come singly, Ericsson at this time, as he wrote another correspondent, " suffered the pains of the damned," having been obliged to lose three of his strongest back teeth, to cure the toothache. A few days later, January 27th, he reported concerning the ailing one, for whom he himself served as physician, that " the patient is yet laboring under his intestine complaints, caused by water in the stomach, but his physician entertains strong hopes of a complete cure." On February 2, 1848, he wrote :

" I fear the unexpected difficulty cannot be got over without a material change in the apparatus. ' Take nothing for granted' is an excellent precept in all mechanical combinations where the physical agents are called upon to coöperate. Understand me, I have not discovered anything wrong in the

* Contributions to the Centennial Exhibition, p. 429.

principle of the motive engine, practical difficulties alone have presented themselves in a new quarter. Bent as I am on doing something great in my line, I thank God that I have the vast steam engine improvement to fall back upon, scarcely inferior in importance, whilst more readily convertible into dollars. So don't be alarmed, we shall still go to London together."

This indicates a purpose of visiting England, which was never realized.

Five days elapsed and again, on February 7, 1848, Ericsson wrote : "I have, after serious reflection, decided on making the requisite alteration in the caloric, the new parts are all on hand and probably in two weeks I start again. The new difficulty I met with took me aback for a day or two, but I feel now as warm and confident as ever—now, don't laugh at me when I tell you 'next time' the thing will go off without a screw to alter. I can hardly be mistaken in supposing that I now see all the difficulties that can have any *material* bearing on the operation of the great principle in practice. I am shocked to think that for a single moment I should have contemplated relinquishing my gigantic scheme."

February 15th "the alteration of the caloric was more than half completed " and the inventor was " in fine spirits and full of confidence." In another fortnight he was able to announce that all difficulties had been overcome and the caloric engine was ready for trial. March 3d he reported, saying : " I wrote last Saturday that the caloric was ready for trial. So it was, excepting some hard ingredients for its stomach which it does not take five minutes to cram in. Now these ingredients, however simple, the manufacturer did not let me have until last night—confound him! On starting the affair this morning everything went straight off, as I had calculated, and, as you suppose, the thing does everything but talk. I am writing under the click-clack of the machine, and have not time to go into particulars now."

We may be sure that this "click-clack" was music in the ears of Ericsson, and these letters indicate the intense delight he took in his chosen work of mechanical creation. "Caloric does work," he wrote, on March 8th, "and not a single practical detail remains to be removed."

The engine here alluded to was followed by others, as we have seen, and finally, in 1851, the work of developing this new motor had advanced to the production of a ninth experimental engine, this costing $17,000, having two feet stroke and two compressing cylinders of forty-eight inches diameter. The regenerator of this engine contained an aggregate of 13,520,000 meshes for each working cylinder, the two thus distributing the air through more than twenty-seven million minute cells, there being, necessarily, as many small spaces between the disks as there are meshes. As there were 228,000 feet, or forty-one and one-half miles of wire in each regenerator, the metallic surface presented was equivalent to that of four boilers, each forty feet long and four feet in diameter. The regenerator occupied but two cubic feet and the boilers would fill 1,920 times that amount of space. After putting a moderate quantity of fuel into the furnace, the engine worked for three hours without fresh fuel, and it frequently worked for one hour after the fires had been drawn. But eleven ounces of fuel were consumed per horse-power per hour. It was estimated that nine ounces were required to make good the loss of radiation into the air in contact with the exterior of the machine, only two ounces being lost in the process of transferring the heat to and from the regenerator.

1851 was one of Ericsson's prosperous years. He had entered upon 1850 with some sarcastic reflections concerning the very unsatisfactory showing of $132.32 to his credit at the Manhattan Bank, but by January, 1851, his balance had increased to $8,690.10. More than that, his improved caloric engine was regarded as a success, and there is an entry in his accounts recording the receipt of ten thousand dollars from William Bloodgood and Dr. C. Dellinger for ten per cent. interest in the foreign patents. Previous to this he had disposed of interests in his American patents to Edwin W. Stoughton, subsequently United States Minister to Russia, and to Messrs. Tyler and J. Bloodgood, the entries indicating the sale of two tenths interests to the two gentlemen last named for $11,000.

In January, 1852, the King of Sweden sent to Ericsson his sincere congratulations on the success of his test caloric engine.

"The regularity of action and perfect working of every part of the experimental thirty-inch engine, completed in 1851," says Ericsson, "and above all its apparent great economy of fuel, inclined some enterprising merchants of New York in the latter part of 1851 to accept my proposition to construct a ship for navigating the ocean, propelled by paddle-wheels actuated by the caloric engine. This work was commenced forthwith, and pushed with such vigor that within nine months from commencing the construction of the machinery, and within seven months of the laying of the keel, the paddle-wheels of the caloric ship *Ericsson* turned around at the dock. In view of the fact that the engines consisted of four working cylinders of one hundred and sixty-eight inches diameter, six feet stroke, and four air-compressing cylinders of 137 inches diameter, and six feet stroke, it may be claimed that, in point of magnitude and rapidity of construction, the motive machinery of the caloric ship stands unrivalled in the annals of marine engineering. The principal engineers of New York all expressed the opinion that a better specimen of workmanship than that presented by the huge engines of the caloric ship had not been produced by our artisans at that time." *

The *Ericsson* was certainly a singularly bold undertaking, and it shows the confidence her designer inspired in business men that he should have been able to obtain the money to build her. Her principal owner was Mr. John B. Kitching, a young man of wealth and enterprise. Another gentleman interested was Mr. Edward Dunham, president of the Corn Exchange Bank of New York.

The cost of the vessel was about half a million dollars, her engines costing $130,000. Her length was 260 feet, breadth 40 feet, and draught 17 feet, tonnage nearly 2,200. The keel was laid in April, 1852, she was launched five months later, September 15, 1852, and went on her trial trip January 4, 1853. Thus in nine months, or half the time ordinarily required at that date for completing a vessel of her class, Ericsson had pushed to completion this vessel of novel design and including so many new and untried problems of construction. It is a remarkable illustration, not alone of his industry, energy, and

* Contributions to the Centennial Exhibition, p. 432.

skill in management, but of the completeness of his preliminary
preparation in the way of designing and planning. He could
carry in his head every detail of the most complicated construction, and when his drawings were completed every bolt was
in place, every screw where it should be, and he was able to
keep several establishments busied on different parts of his
mechanism with the certainty that when the several parts were
brought together, they would fall into adjustment without
change—provided his working drawings had been strictly followed. He was most exacting in his requirements and he
thoroughly understood what good work was. So if the work
upon the *Ericsson* was hurried, it was in no respect slighted.

Up to that time no finer or stronger ship had been built in
the United States. Indeed, the agreement with the builders
required that the vessel should be "the strongest ever built in
New York," and Ericsson was not the man to let such a stipu-
lation become a dead letter enactment. The *Scientific American* totally condemned the principle of the caloric ship, and
persistently predicted its failure, but in fairness it said : " We
heartily wish success to Captain Ericsson and his compatriots,
for patriots they certainly are. The caloric ship *Ericsson* is a
marvel of faith and enterprise, their energy and spirit deserve
success and the praise of the whole world. The caloric ship
has new and very excellent features about it. The designer
and constructor of its machinery have shown themselves to have
long heads and skilful hands. We have seen nothing to compare with the castings. It is safe and comfortable for passengers, and it saves the firemen from the pandemonium of our
steamship." * If these had been the days of forced draught
with fire-rooms at 180°, this comparison would have been still
stronger. Comfort, as well as safety, was involved in Ericsson's grand scheme for substituting hot air for steam at sea.

A week after her trial trip, on February 11, 1853, "the
representatives of the Press " and others were invited to take a
trip on the *Ericsson*, and the papers of the day following contained glowing accounts of her success and most confident predictions of a coming revolution in locomotion. During the trip
the gentlemen present appointed a committee to draft appro-

* Scientific American, New York, January 22, 1853, p. 149.

priate resolutions, and these were adopted with enthusiasm. The members of the Committee were Richard Grant White, Professor James J. Mapes, and Freeman Hunt, all gentlemen then and since well-known in New York. One of these resolutions declared, "that the peculiar adaptability to sea vessels of the new motor presented to the world by Captain Ericsson, is now fully established and it is likely to prove superior to steam for such purposes."

In a speech on this occasion Professor Mapes said: "I consider there were but two epochs of science—the one marked by Newton, the other by Ericsson." "The inventor to whom this unwholesome flattery was paid," says his critic of the *Scientific American*, "rebuked the speaker with manly modesty." Some years later (July 20, 1875) Ericsson wrote to this paper saying:

After having completed the general design of the motive engines of the caloric ship, and finding that in proportion to the power exerted by the 72-inch trial engine, a speed of five miles an hour called for cylinders of 168 inches diameter, 6 feet stroke, I hesitated in undertaking the construction. But for the encouragement received from some of our leading commercial men who were consulted on the subject, the caloric ship would not have been built. Let me add, that all united in the opinion that if a speed of seven miles could be produced, the work ought to proceed. Francis B. Cutting, the eminent patent lawyer, who took a greater interest in the scheme than probably anyone else, stated emphatically during a conversation at the Union Club, that if I felt sure of being able to produce a rate of *five* miles an hour, I ought not to hesitate, reminding me of Fulton and *his first* attempt.

I have never before communicated the above facts to anyone, excepting a few intimate friends; nothing short of my integrity having been assailed in your columns would have induced me to make a statement which I had reserved as an accompaniment to my account of the world's first and last big air-engine.

I abstained, in my letter of Saturday, from adverting to your editorial reference to "the Ericsson hot-air stock-jobbers," confident that you had inadvertently made the damaging remark.

Replying in the same month (July 7, 1875), to a complimentary letter from his associate in the caloric ship enterprise, Mr. J. B. Kitching, Ericsson said: "Your remark about the caloric ship gratifies me more than I can express. There was more engineering in that ship than in ten *Monitors*. I regard the hot-air ship as by far my best work, it was simply a mechanical marvel. The four 168-inch working cylinders and four air-compressing cylinders of 137-inch diameter, sink the *Great Eastern* machinery into insignificance."

The *Scientific American* seems to have struck the only jarring note in the general chorus of approval and prophecy, and to this Ericsson made no objection, but the suggestion that he was a party to a stock-jobbing operation, or that the gentlemen associated with him could have any other motive for investing so much money in a new venture than the obvious one, could not pass without notice. It is, of course, impossible to prove a negative, but such a charge was not only opposed to the facts and probabilities of the case, but it is contradicted by the whole course and tenor of a life as absolutely free in its way from any suggestion of the kind as that of Simon Stylites; for Ericsson, if he did not dwell on a pillar apart, was equally removed from the ordinary currents of sordid calculation by his devotion to ideas.

"The age of steam is closed," declared one of the admirers of the caloric ship the next day, "the age of caloric opens. Fulton and Watt belong to the past. Ericsson is the great mechanical genius of the present and the future." Somewhat too enthusiastic as to the ship, but not so far wrong as to her designer.

The *Baltic* and the *Pacific*, two vessels of the Collins line at that time offering themselves for comparison, each used fifty-eight tons of coal in twenty-four hours; the four furnaces of the *Ericsson* consumed six tons in the same time. With this amount eight pounds pressure per square inch was obtained, and a regular speed of seven miles per hour, with a possible eight. Critics declared that the difference in the coal consumption was due to the difference of speed. Ericsson replied that the consumption of coal was nearly all due to radiation, that increased power and speed would not result in corresponding increase in coal consumption, and that on a large scale, much of this radiation would be prevented. The question was never tested. Difficulties innumerable assailed an engine working at a temperature of 444° and constantly subject in all of its parts to the destructive influence of dry heat, burning out its lubricants, loosening its joints, and rapidly destroying its working members by oxidation.

After being thrown open to curious visitors for a day or two the *Ericsson* started on a trip to Washington, February 16, 1853, arriving there in safety after a stormy passage, and without injury to her machinery, which was so utterly unlike anything before seen on board ship as to invite the distrust of all properly constituted sailors. Her four huge working cylinders were arranged in pairs along the centre of the vessel, two forward and two aft of the midship section, and each 14 feet, or 168 inches in diameter. Instead of resting in the usual manner on the keelsons these cylinders, each of 924 feet, or 691 gallons cubical contents, were suspended, like enormous camp-kettles, over the furnace fires. Above the working cylinders were an equal number of supply cylinders or single acting pumps, $11\frac{5}{12}$ feet, 137 inches, in diameter. Eight piston-rods, each 14 feet long, connected the mammoth pistons of each set of cylinders, and these pistons had a total area of 43 cubic feet.

Though the pistons, with their connecting-rods, weighed upward of fifty tons, so perfect was the frame-work supporting this weight and that of the cylinders that Captain Sands of the navy, who, with Ericsson, accompanied the ship to Washington, was able to report to the Secretary of the Navy that not the slightest movement was observed in any part, even when the vessel was passing through a gale and rolling very heavily. Ericsson expected to attain a pressure of twelve pounds with his engine, and calculated that this would give a speed of ten or even twelve miles an hour, but it was found impossible to exceed eight miles. Still, this was all that had been promised, and the failure in speed alone would not have secured the condemnation of the vessel if there had been sufficient prospect of increasing it.

Considering the time, no bolder feat of marine engineering has ever been accomplished; so that it was truly said that the caloric ship was at the same time a commercial failure and one of the greatest mechanical triumphs of the day. An effort was made to secure an appropriation from Congress for building such a vessel, but it met with no success.

13   —

Soon after his arrival in Washington with the vessel, Ericsson issued this invitation:

CALORIC SHIP ERICSSON,
OFF ALEXANDRIA, March 4, 1853.

Captain Ericsson requests the pleasure of the Company of the members of the Virginia Legislature on board the new caloric ship *Ericsson* for the purpose of inspecting the improvements made by this new mode of propelling vessels, which will afford facilities to commerce by reducing the rates of running ships with motive-power even to that of sailing vessels.

For the purpose of enabling the members of the Legislature to visit the vessel with least possible loss of time, Captain Ericsson will cause her to be at Acquia Creek either on Monday or Tuesday morning as may be most convenient to them, and he will therefore be obliged by answer in time to enable him to move the ship from Alexandria to Acquia Creek.

J. COOK, Clerk.

The Virginia legislators were entertained by a speech from the inventor, for he could be eloquent on occasion with the eloquence of earnest conviction and assured mastery of the particular subject he discussed. He was not a man of varied knowledge, or of culture in that sense, but what he did know he knew thoroughly, and as the stream of a given volume gains additional power by running in a narrow channel, so did the concentration of his thought give added force to Ericsson's vigorous personality. He was accustomed to great intensity of expression, he had exceedingly clear and positive conceptions concerning matters he understood, and was indifferent to everything else.

In return for the courtesy shown them, the Virginia Legislators invited Ericsson to dine with them, but he had left Washington before the invitation reached him. He did dine, however, at the capital with Washington Irving, who was then engaged in researches connected with his work upon the life of Washington.

CHAPTER XII.

APPLICATIONS OF THE HOT-AIR PRINCIPLE.

Sinking of the Ericsson in New York Harbor.—It is Raised and Takes
the Seventh New York Regiment to Richmond.—Its Use during
the Civil War.—Attempts to Apply Hot Air on a Large Scale Abandoned.—Its Application to Small Motors.—Speculations as to the
Moral Results to Follow their Adoption.—Prince Krapotkin's Opinion.—Large Demand for the Caloric Engine.—Its Advantages and
Profits.

AFTER the caloric ship returned to New York from Washington, it was decided to make changes in her engines to
increase their efficiency and correct defects revealing themselves
in actual practice. Ericsson seems to have counted too confidently on his regenerator, and the heating power was insufficient. Blowers were therefore added to force the draft and
make good the deficiency in the area of grate surface. The
Ericsson was finally made ready for another trial, and took a
trip down New York Bay on March 15, 1854. A second trip
followed on April 27th, and the next day Ericsson wrote to
Mr. Sargent, concerning the results as follows :

At the very moment of success—of brilliant success—fate has dealt
me the severest blow I ever received. We yesterday went out on a private
preparatory trial of the caloric ship, during which all our anticipations
were realized. We attained a speed of from twelve to thirteen turns of
our paddle-wheels, equal to full eleven miles an hour, without putting
forth anything like our maximum power. All went on magnificently
until within a mile or two of the city (on our return from Sandy Hook),
when our beautiful ship was struck by a terrific tornado on our larboard
quarter, careening the hull so far as to put completely under water the
lower starboard ports, which unfortunately the men on the freight deck
had opened to clear out some rubbish, the day being very fine. The
men, so far as we can learn, became terrified and ran on deck without
closing the ports, and the hold filled so rapidly as to sink the ship in a

few minutes. I need not tell you what my feelings were as I watched
the destructive element entering the fireplaces of the engines, and as
the noble fabric, yielding under my feet, disappeared inch by inch. A
more sudden transition from gladness and exultation to disappointment
and regret is scarcely on record. Two years of anxious labor had been
brought to a successful close, the finest and strongest ship perhaps ever
built was gliding on the placid surface of the finest harbor in the world
and within a few cable lengths of her anchorage ; yet, with such solid
grounds for exultation, and with such perfect security from danger, a
freak of the elements effected utter annihilation in the space of a few
minutes.

As it was impossible under these circumstances to demonstrate the capacity of the vessel, a certificate of her performance
on the trip that ended thus disastrously was prepared and
signed.by five persons who witnessed it. They united in saying
that the engines of the vessel were worked up to " twelve turns
per minute against quite a smart breeze." An average pressure
of seventeen and one-half pounds was carried in both furnaces,
and a mean pressure at the time of closing the cut-off valve of
twelve and one-half pounds per square inch. This gave eleven
miles an hour through the water, the wheels being thirty-two
feet in diameter. The excursion being merely preparatory to
a regular trial trip, the consumption of fuel was not ascertained.
These witnesses estimated it at a little less than nine tons for
twenty-four hours.

In response to Sargent's letter of condolence, Ericsson said :
" You are quite right in thinking that it takes something more
to kill me than the sinking of a ship, though it carried down
the results of twenty years of labor. I am in abundant pin-
money, having brought out some small inventions kept back
by the absorbing caloric."

The same day, May 1st, he wrote : " The ship is up, much
to the sorrow of numerous wise men who predicted that the
thing could not be done. Pray present my warm thanks to
Commodore Smith for the prompt manner in which he ordered
his officers to put the ship on the Government Dock. Gentlemen are so confoundedly scarce in these diggings that it is quite
refreshing to me to come in contact with the officers of the
Navy now and then." This was Commodore Joseph E. Smith,
Chief of the Naval Bureau of Yards and Docks from 1846 to

1869. Of him we shall hear more in connection with Ericsson's work.

After examining the caloric ship, Ericsson reported on the 19th of May that twelve thousand dollars would be required to put her machinery in order. It was finally decided to take out her caloric engines and convert her into a steamer. Though the economy of fuel in hot-air engines was very considerable, it was accompanied by too great a sacrifice of space, and too great an outlay of machinery, to permit competition with the steam-engine at its best estate. Each of the four "regenerators" of the engines on the caloric ship contained fifty disks of one-

The Caloric Ship Ericsson.

sixteenth inch wire netting, each disk measuring six by four or twenty-four square feet. As the open spaces in each disk measured one-half this, or twelve square feet, there was no appreciable resistance to the passage of the air to and from the cylinders, Ericsson tells us. But the expansion of the air in the supply-cylinders, resulting from the great volume of the vessels containing the wires through which the air passed, seriously diminished the effect from the working cylinders.

After her transformation into a steamer, the *Ericsson* was chartered, in 1858, to carry the Seventh New York Regiment to Richmond, Va., on the occasion of transferring to Hollywood

Cemetery the remains of James Monroe, Ex-President of the United States. She was subsequently used during the Civil War as a Government transport, and with her four small smoke-stacks was conspicuous in the picturesque group of vessels assembled at the capture of Port Royal, S. C., by Commodore S. F. Du Pont. After serving as a transport for a time she was fitted up with a battery of small guns and sent cruising after a Confederate vessel. She was finally converted into a sailer and employed by the British Government in carrying coal to one of their stations in the Pacific.

In his Centennial volume (p. 438) Ericsson says of this vessel: "The average speed at sea proving insufficient for commercial purposes, the owners, with regret, acceded to my proposition to remove the costly machinery, although it had proved perfect as a mechanical combination. The resources of modern engineering having been exhausted in producing the motors of the caloric ship, the important question has forever been set at rest: Can heated air as a motor compete on a large scale with steam? The commercial world is indebted to American enterprise—to New York enterprise, for having settled a question of such vital importance. The marine engineer has thus been encouraged to renew his efforts to perfect the steam-engine, without fear of rivalry from a motor depending on the dilatation of atmospheric air by heat."

Though Ericsson was able in after years to speak so philosophically concerning his defeat in the matter of the caloric ship, we may be sure that the experience at the time was most bitter and humiliating. Nothing better illustrates his energy and force of character, and his unfailing confidence in his own mechanical conceptions, than the fact that he still continued his labors upon his caloric engine. The triumphant assertion of his friends that "the age of steam had closed; that of caloric had opened," was falsified. He was compelled to submit to the gibes of his enemies and the laughter of a world that takes no account of efforts whose results are for the future: but he was not discouraged. When told that the name of his friend and associate in the caloric enterprise, Mr. John B. Kitching, stood very low in Lombard Street in consequence of his connection with this invention, Ericsson indignantly replied that the caloric was " a boon to humanity, and was another step in the progress of man ordained by God."

On April 23, 1853, in a letter to the London *Builder*, he had said :

> The caloric engine is destined ere long, its opponents notwithstanding, to be the great motor for manufacturing and domestic purposes, because of its entire freedom from danger alone. It is destined assuredly to effect much in dispensing with physical toil with the laborer. The artisan of moderate means may place it in his room, where it will serve as a stove while turning his lathe, at the same time purifying the atmosphere by pumping out the impure air and passing it off into the chimney. In fine, it will heat, toil, ventilate, and always remain harmless. All this will soon be exhibited in practice and save critics from racking their brains to discover theoretical mistakes and practical imperfections.

The caloric engine was finally made available for many commercial purposes, but its inventor was obliged to postpone further attempts to supersede steam.   The radical vice of all air-engines employing a cylinder and piston, is the necessity for using very large engines and very high heat in order to secure the necessary difference of temperature between the two sides of the piston.   This speedily burns out the machine, as iron becomes red hot at 650° C.   Lubricants are decomposed, packing destroyed, and, by the expansion of the metal, joints are loosened and the whole structure weakened.   But partial success came only at the end of efforts and struggles on the part of Ericsson such as would have discouraged anyone but an inventor.   What he endured is told in this letter addressed by him to his associates in the caloric enterprise, Messrs. Stoughton, Tyler, and Bloodgood, January 16, 1855.

> You will not be surprised to learn that for want of means I have, after prolonged struggles, at last been compelled to abandon the prosecution of the invention which formed the subject of our several agreements four years ago. Whilst I refrain from dwelling on the painful disappointment I experience in being thus forced to abandon the grand idea of the wire system which, together with that peculiarly simple arrangement of inverted cylinders, formed the principle of the improved caloric engine which you joined me in prosecuting, I feel bound emphatically to state my conviction that this extraordinary system of obtaining motive power will some day be perfected.

I repeat now what I stated to you at our first interview, that on the principle of the improved caloric engine under consideration more motive power may be obtained from a mess of metallic wires of two feet cube than from a whole mountain of coal, as applied in the present steam-engine. Every experimental trial made has more than realized my anticipations as regards the rapidity and certainty of depositing and returning the caloric on this remarkable system. The practical adaptation *alone* has presented difficulties. In justice to myself, allow me here to remind you that I have had no funds at my disposal for making experiments. The large test engine intended for the London Exhibition was built in all essential features like my original thirty-inch cylinder engine, that being deemed complete, the difference being mainly the application of two pairs of cylinders. The engine of the caloric ship, again, was a perfect copy of the large test-engine, differing only in size and in having four instead of two pairs of cylinders. The magnitude of the ship and the consequent heavy responsibility forbade the slightest deviation from the engine which had been found to work satisfactorily. Accordingly, and most unfortunately, not a single point was gained by these undertakings, not a step was made in advance. The small engine built at Springfield indeed established an important fact. It corroborated my opinion that the inverted single-acting cylinders were indispensable to practical success. It has naturally been supposed by the public that I have had ample—enormous—funds at my disposal for making *experiments*, and hence that the resources of the very principle of the new motor have been exhausted. How utterly at variance with fact are these suppositions! Except as stated in the small Springfield engine, no funds have been expended *experimentally*, and therefore the improved caloric engine, with its inverted cylinders and wire regenerator, this day stands where it did when you first witnessed the operation four years ago. But though unavailable for practical purposes it yet rests on immutable physical laws which by money, labor, and patience will assuredly secure a great boon to mankind. There can be little doubt that $50,000, about ten per cent. of the cost of the caloric ship, expended in experiments would teach the proper practical application of the wire system to obtain that available force which so far has not been properly realized.

Truth and candor compel me now to notice that during the four years in which I have labored unceasingly in a common cause, for a joint benefit, I have been left wholly unsupported by those holding the largest interest in the patent. I have during that period defrayed expenses and incurred liabilities exceeding $30,000 in the prosecution of the patents in which I hold very little more than one-fourth interest. I desire to be distinctly understood not to abandon the invention in which we are mutually interested. I only stop for want of funds—without money I can do nothing, and my only capital is my intellect and my time. Try what you can do. I am ready to work with all my energies.

Only furnish funds, and we will show practically that bundles of wires are capable of exerting more force than ship-loads of coal.

In the mean time I find myself on the verge of ruin. I must do *something* to obtain bread and vindicate to some extent my assumed position as the opponent of steam. Accordingly I have determined to return to my original caloric engine. The plan is less brilliant—less startling —but as it proved to yield power practically twenty years ago, so it will again. At any rate, it cannot fail to be sufficiently useful to save its author from starving. I am sanguine, you know, and I therefore expect confidently to succeed on my old field. If so, I may yet take up the invention in which you have an interest, on the principle which compels metallic threads to yield more force than mountains of coal. Thus I may once more devote individual means and *exertions* to a common interest.

Thus, with many heartburnings, Ericsson, through force of sheer necessity, abandoned his efforts to further develop his caloric system as a universal motor to supersede steam. The spirit of prophecy was upon him, but he prophesied to deaf ears. He believed then, as he had believed for a quarter of a century at least, what is now generally accepted, that the displacement of the steam-engine is essential to future industrial progress. To the British Association for the Advancement of Science, Sir Frederick Bramwell declared, in 1888, that those who should attend the centenary of the Association in 1931 " would see the present steam-engines in museums, treated as things to be respected and of antiquarian interest, by the engineers of those days, such as were the open-topped steam cylinders of Newcomen and of Smeaton to ourselves, and that the heat engine of the future will probably be one independent of the vapor of water."

Ericsson had not lost the confidence of his friends, not even of those whose money had been spent in his caloric ventures thus far, and in the end those who continued to assist him had no reason to regret their confidence. With their help he built four little engines with 15-inch cylinders, costing $500 or $600 apiece, and intended for lecture-room models; an engine of 16-inch cylinder, sent to France, and one of thirty inches intended for the Crystal Palace Exhibition in New York. Eight other models and test engines were built at a cost altogether of $18,-400, and patents for improvements were issued dated July 31,

1855, and December 14, 1858. The engines of the steamer were covered by a patent issued in 1851.

Within three years of his announcement to his associates, in January, 1855, of his determination to make the caloric engine a source of profit, Ericsson's manufacturers were able to report that the "caloric engine is no longer a subject of experiment, but exists as a perfect, practical machine, daily at work in manufactures and diversified uses." By the end of 1857 the work of introducing the perfected engine had begun with domestic motors of 6 and 8-inch cylinders, and seven large establishments were at work upon their construction.

Next came the 12-inch engine. This was an excellent pumper and could do light rotary work. It was succeeded by the 18-inch cylinder engine with power sufficient to drive two or three printing presses. This was followed by the 24-inch cylinder, capable of doing most hoisting work and exhibiting an increase of power in excess of the increased consumption of fuel. Finally, before the end of 1858, an engine with a cylinder of thirty-two inches in diameter was built and set up in one of the Government warehouses in New York for hoisting work.

Five years before (1853) Ericsson had agreed to build a caloric engine of sixty horse-power for the Washington Navy Yard, but he does not appear to have been called upon to do so. Still earlier than this, in 1848, Mr. Sargent had suggested that he should build a fifty horse-power engine for exhibition in Washington. To this suggestion he replied: "I must observe in regard to the caloric that if I had any confidence in justice at Washington I would not hesitate to build the fifty horse-power engine, but I well know that I am as likely to be cheated as patronized there—you know that too."

A thousand caloric engines were sold within two years, and soon more than three thousand were engaged in working printing presses, and hoisting-gear for warehouses, docks, and ships; in mines and mills; for pumping, irrigating land, and supplying villages with water; in various operations on farms and plantations, and in numerous other mechanical employments. If it was found inadequate to move a great ocean steamer with sufficient speed, it was satisfactorily tested in the propulsion of boats and pleasure yachts; in short, wherever a limited, economical, safe, independent, and self-managed motive-power was required, Ericsson's caloric engine was in demand.

The Fitchburg Railroad of Massachusetts reported that a caloric engine belonging to them had pumped in one year 1,600,000 gallons of water at an expense of $25 for fuel and oil, and $25 for the time of an engineer. The New York Central Railroad, which had forty-eight of the engines in use, reported that they performed an "incredible amount" of labor for the "small quantity of fuel consumed." One engine, at an expense of eleven cents a day, was doing the work of five men who received $125 a month, or $5 a day. An attempt was made to substitute the caloric engine for the horses then used in drawing their cars through the city of New York. The New York *Evening Post*, the *Hartford Times*, the *Dutch Reform Messenger*, and forty newspapers altogether, employed this motor and sounded its praises the country over. Stimulated by the interest in caloric, a little paper called *The Ericsson*, and having for its motto "Improve on Improvements," was started in 1853, in Fond du Lac, Wis., then a place of two or three thousand inhabitants.

Caloric engines were also in extensive use on the sugar plantations in Cuba and in the Southern United States; they were at work abroad in England and Ireland, and especially in Sweden, several establishments in this last country having engaged engines under license, the inventor with characteristic generosity making over the proceeds of his royalties in Sweden to his sister living there.

At the agricultural fair of Ostergothland, the most important province of Sweden, the first prize was awarded, in January, 1859, to an Ericsson caloric engine. The Swedish journals particularly noticed that this engine, in its present efficient form, differed altogether from that of the "caloric ship," and that it resembled in essential features the engines elaborated and built by Captain Ericsson in London, between the years 1827 and 1833. A working model of one of these engines was carried from London to Stockholm in the spring of 1833, by Colonel Nils Ericsson, brother of the inventor. It was pointed out as a remarkable instance of the correctness of first conceptions that

Captain Ericsson, after spending thirty years of intense labor, should find himself just where he started. The striking feature of the new engine, aside from the novel principle involved, was the mode by which the supply-air was introduced into the machine, and in this it was identical with the model engine alluded to. The singular achievement, recognized by engineers, of effecting the very dissimilar requisite movements of supply and working pistons by one crank-pin dates back to 1833, and the idea of placing the fire within the cylinder was practically exemplified by Captain Ericsson in London, as long ago as 1827.

The distinguishing merits of the engine were its economy, portability, simplicity, and non-liability to explosion. Added to this, is the superior advantage, in certain localities, of requiring no water. In Texas and California it was used for purposes of irrigation; in Louisiana for the operation of cotton-gins, on account of the diminished risk of fire and freedom from explosion. One caloric engine is reported to have exploded in Cuba, but the exact cause of the explosion was never ascertained.

The hot air engine was found of special value in lighthouses. It required no water, and water is liable to freeze in exposed situations and to fail altogether in others. Its freedom from the danger of explosion, the ease with which it could be managed by the ordinary light-keeper, and the service it rendered in heating his quarters also commended it to favor, though it was more bulky than the steam-engine, and cost fifty per cent. more. Ericsson examined carefully into the question of applying it to canal boats, but decided that it had too little power in proportion to its bulk and weight.

For similar reasons his plans for using it as a motor for horse-cars were not carried out. Its most ingenious application was to the work of compressing air so that it could be conveyed from a reservoir wherever it was needed. It was applied in this way by an establishment in New York employing five or six hundred hands with sewing-machines. Ericsson was very much amused by his experience with a handsome factory girl who invited him to a competition. She ran her sewing machine with her foot, against the caloric engine, and "—— me,"

said he, in telling the story, "if she didn't beat me to fits."
But as his engine could run all day and all night her defeat was
certain in the end.

I find no evidence that Ericsson ever gave attention to the
study of electricity, though he did invent, in 1859, an "improvement in actuating and regulating the speed of telegraphic instruments" by compressed air, conveyed to the telegraphic instruments in different rooms of a building, from a central
motor.   "Allow me to remind you," said Ericsson, in a letter
to one of his Swedish friends, "that I am an engineer and
designer rather than an inventor.   Is the capacity for construction gained during the experience of a lifetime, an invention?   Edison, in his ignorance, discovers or invents; Ericsson, acquainted with physical laws, constructs."   This was
not said in any spirit of disparagement toward Edison, for
whose talents and accomplishments Ericsson had the highest
respect.

CHAPTER XIII.

THE REGENERATIVE PRINCIPLE.

Receipts for Patent Fees.—Report on the Hot-air Engine by Dr. F. A. P. Barnard.—Application of the Regenerative Principle by Sir William Siemens.—Faraday's Continued Faith in It.—Its Application to the Steam-engine.—Professor E. N. Horsford's Investigation of the Caloric Engine.—Its Progress During Thirty Years.—Ericsson Receives the Rumford Prize.

ASIDE from marine motors, Ericsson expended altogether about $60,000 upon twenty-five test machines while perfecting the caloric engine. His accounts show that more than one-half of this sum was returned in patent fees in a single year, after the invention was on the full tide of success. He had parted with interests in it from time to time until at length he retained only one-half, but his books record the receipt of $16,555.21 from this half in 1860, after deducting payments for the cost of collecting. This shows a total receipt of $35,-000 for patent fees during the year, and the price received previous to this for partial interests indicates that the patent-right as a whole was valued at $100,000. In a letter to Mrs. Stoughton, dated October 31, 1870, Ericsson said: "Edwin [Mr. Stoughton], during conversation when he last called at 36, did me the great injustice of hinting that I 'never complete anything.' The *fact* is that I never leave an invention while anything can be done to it within my power (or within the power of man ?). Since he *advised* me to abandon the caloric engine I have perfected fifty-six inventions, all carried into practice. Upward of three thousand caloric engines have been built in the meantime, the patent having yielded more than $100,000. Do me the favor to impress all this on the mind of my unjust friend."

The attempt to apply the hot-air engine to the purpose of

navigation was economically a failure, but as a means of education to Ericsson it was worth far more than it cost, as the sequel will show.   Even after this failure was recorded, Robert Hunt, F.R.S., in his "Supplement to Ure's Dictionary of Arts, Manufactures, and Mines," declared that "we may, notwithstanding this result, safely predict, from the investigations of Messrs. Thomson & Joule, that the expansion of air by heat will eventually, in some conditions, take the place of steam as a motive power."

Sir William Siemens told the British Association in August, 1882, that "the gas or caloric engine combines the conditions most favorable to the attainment of maximum results, and it may reasonably be supposed that the difficulties still in the way of their application on a large scale will gradually be removed."   "Before many years have elapsed," he said further, "we may find in our factories and on board our ships engines with a fuel consumption not exceeding one pound of coal per effective horse-power per hour, in which the gas-producer takes the place of the somewhat complex and dangerous steam-boiler. The advent of such an engine, and of the dynamo machine, must mark a new era of material progress at least equal to that produced by the introduction of steam-power in the early part of our century."

Sir William spoke from experience, for he had spent many years of his life in seeking to apply the regenerative principle which so fascinated Ericsson, and was a firm believer in its effectiveness.   Commencing his studies into the application of heat fifteen years after Ericsson, he had the advantage of the sounder theories concerning its nature established by the investigations of Joule in England and Mayer in Germany, during the years from 1842 to 1849.   Siemens contended that Ericsson's partial failure with his respirator or "regenerator" was due to a mistake in its application, resulting from an acceptance of the mistaken theory of the nature of heat, current at that time, and a consequent neglect to provide sufficient heating apparatus.   This is also the explanation of Dr. Frederick A. P. Barnard, LL.D., late president of Columbia College, New York.   Speaking of Ericsson's early engine, with the "regenerator," Dr. Barnard says:

"The engine, it will be seen, was remarkably simple in construction. It also performed very well in practice, so far as its performance was merely a question of mechanics. But it failed because the heating arrangements were inadequate to the demand made upon them. Mr. Ericsson did not expect to be dependent on his furnaces for the supply of more than a moderate fraction of the heat which each successive charge of air was to receive. It was his anticipation that the regenerators would serve to transfer so large a quantity from each charge to the next that it would be necessary to provide for a little more than the always inevitable loss by mere radiation. This anticipation was not realized and in fact could not be, since no account was taken of the large amount of heat necessarily transferred into work." *

At the time of his invention of the hot-air engine Ericsson held the opinion that equal increments of heat produced equal increments of power, whatever the medium used, and that the resulting force suffers no diminution; so that the effects may be reproduced indefinitely by transfer from one medium to another, or from one portion of the same medium to another portion. Whatever the loss of heat in an engine from radiation and conduction there was, according to this theory, no loss from the exertion of power. Rumford's experiment in boiling water with heat generated by friction dates back to 1798, but the doctrine of the mutual convertibility of heat and mechanical action, or of heat as a mode of motion, was only gradually establishing itself while Ericsson's thoughts were occupied with his inventions, and it was not until 1862 that Professor Tyndall commenced the series of lectures that did so much to make the theory generally known.

In a paper read before the London Institution of Civil Engineers, session of 1883–84, on "Heat and its Mechanical Application," Professor Fleeming Jenkin, F.R.S., said of Sir William Siemens: "The fact that such a man spent so many years of his life in endeavoring to adapt the regenerator to the internal combustion engine served to show, what I believe to be certain-

* Paris Universal Exposition, 1867, Machinery and Processes of the Industrial Arts and Apparatus of the Exact Sciences. By Frederick A. P. Barnard, LL.D., U. S. Commissioner.

ly the truth, that in that idea lies the future of internal combustion in general; that by the application of the regenerator
we shall be able to so much lower the temperature of rejection as in a marked manner to increase the efficiency of the
engines."

The fact that such a man as Ericsson gave so many years
of his life to the study of this expedient, and that he believed
in it to the end, has equal significance.

Sir William Siemens applied the regenerative principle to
the steam engine, taking out his first patent for his improvements in this line December 22, 1847. His biographer tells us
that he did not claim the regenerative principle as an original
discovery, but "it was looked upon by engineers as unsound in
principle, and its application had very little beneficial result.
Mr. Siemens saw not only its theoretical correctness, but its
great practical value, and the wide success it afterward attained fully justified his views. The regenerative principle
was undoubtedly sound, and he had devoted ten or twelve of
the best years of his life to its application. During this time
he had the support of many eminent engineers, the practical
aid of two of the best manufacturing firms in the country, and
the funds of a powerful commercial association. Neither theoretical knowledge, nor practical experience, nor ingenuity, nor
skill, nor money, nor perseverance, nor influence was wanting.
But in spite of their promised advantages, the regenerative
steam-engine would not supplant the simple machine of Watt." *

The final result was the application of the Siemens regenerative furnace to mechanical operations, for which a high temperature is required, such as smelting and glass and pottery
manufacture.

During the years of experimental research devoted to this
improved engine, Siemens met with the difficulties that had
assailed Ericsson in the way of "leaks, destruction of working
parts, undue consumption of fuel, imperfect action and so on."
In the Siemens' regenerator the exhaust steam deposits its heat,
to be taken up by the cold water on its way from the condenser
to the "hot well." It was found that the gases escaping from
the furnace at a temperature of 4,000° F. could be cooled

* Life of Sir William Siemens. By William Pole. Vol. i., p. 79.
14

down in a regenerator to between 200° and 400°. Siemens provides for the passage of heated vapor, or vapor and steam, and atmospheric air through regenerators of fire brick laid with open spaces. Of his furnace Dr. Siemens said : " The greatest heat that can be produced by direct combustion of coke and air is about 4,000° F. But with my regenerative furnace I should have no difficulty in going up to 10,000°, in fact, to any degree the material composing the furnace can be made to stand."

The most intense terrestrial combustion that we can command, Professor Tyndall tells us, is that of oxygen and hydrogen, and the temperature of the pure oxy-hydrogen flame is 8,061° C.=14,542° F. The sun Siemens considered to be a gigantic specimen of one of his own regenerative gas furnaces. He likened its action to that of a centrifugal blowing fan, revolving with enormous velocity and drawing in upon its polar surfaces the gaseous matters circulating in a highly attenuated state in space ; subjecting them to enormous friction and expelling them at the solar equator at a temperature estimated by Ericsson at 4.035.584° F., to commence anew the cycle of change.

The entrance of Siemens upon a line of investigation followed by Ericsson fifteen years before him is interesting testimony to the fascinations of the regenerative theory. Michael Faraday seems never to have lost faith in it, for the last lecture he ever delivered was on the Siemens regenerative furnace. This was June 20, 1862, or nearly thirty years after his attention had first been directed to the principle involved in it by Ericsson's invention of 1833. As early as 1838 Ericsson had conducted a series of experiments with a view to adapting the regenerative principle to the steam-engine, as Siemens did later on. Though the result hoped for was not accomplished, it was found that most valuable use could be made of the heat then wasted in condensing the steam, and the surface condenser was the result. The latest patent for this was taken out in the United States in 1849, and it is described in Ericsson's " Contributions to the Centennial Exhibition," chapter xxix.

The extent to which the efficiency of the marine engine has been increased by this device is illustrated by an example quoted by Mr. W. T. Harvey, before the Engineering Section of the Bristol, England, Naturalists' Society, showing that a vessel, the *Juno*, saved nine and a half tons of coal per voyage, or nine per cent., by a change from a jet condenser to the surface condenser, the engines working at the same pressure, thirty pounds, indicating the same horse-power, 1605, and making the same speed, 14.1 knots.

In 1887 the German Bureau of Statistics estimated the power of steam-engines then at work as the equivalent of forty-six million horses or a thousand million men, double the working population of the earth. Four-fifths of this power has been brought into action during the last quarter of a century, or since Ericsson terminated his labors upon the caloric engine. In his "Contributions" (p. 443) Ericsson tells us that "steam engineers, finding by the extraordinary demand for caloric engines that very moderate power was a great desideratum, have perfected the steam-motor until it almost rivals the caloric engine in safety and adaptability; consequently, the demand for caloric engines has been greatly diminished of late. Yet this motor can never be superseded by the steam-engine, since it requires no water, besides being absolutely safe from explosion. There are innumerable localities in which an adequate quantity of water cannot be obtained, but where the necessities of civilized life call for mechanical motors; hence the caloric engine may be regarded as an institution inseparable from civilization."

In a letter written to Professor E. N. Horsford, then Rumford Professor in Harvard University, Ericsson said :

NEW YORK, January 19, 1861.

SIR : Your letter to Mr. Sargent, which indicates that you are investigating the origin and development of the caloric engine, induces me to present to you the enclosed table relating to the compression of atmospheric air. The relations of volume, temperature, and pressure expressed in this table you will find somewhat different from the result of Regnault's and Joule's investigations on the subject—I will not question the theoretical accuracy of their deductions but I claim that my table, as it records what actually takes place during compression on a large scale, is of more value to practical engineering. It is proper to add that the leading facts exhibited in this table were established by the writer long before the commencement of the investigation of the distinguished savants alluded to. The trial of the caloric engine of 1833 clearly proved that a compression of ten pounds to the square inch above the atmospheric pressure caused an elevation of temperature of more than 80°. At that time, you will remember, Dalton's theory prevailed, which admitted only 50° increase of temperature for reducing atmospheric air to half volume. It is proper further to observe that the inclosed table, which I request that you will do me the honor to accept, is founded on actual results produced by long-continued compression with cylinders varying from thirty to one hundred and thirty-eight inches diameter.

I annex a very brief explanation, as you will comprehend the nature of the table at a glance.

I am, sir, with great respect, your obedient servant,

J. ERICSSON.

PROFESSOR HORSFORD.

Tracing the progress of the caloric engine during a period of thirty years, from its first suggestion to the final completion of the work upon it in 1858, we find that it originated in the flame engine, described in the paper sent to the Institution of Civil Engineers, London, in the year 1827. This had two cylinders with a piston in each cylinder. In 1837 a fly-wheel and regenerators were added, and in 1839 two pistons were put into one cylinder, one a supply piston and the other a working piston, and a device was added for compressing the air at the instant of its passage from the supply cylinder to be heated. Next, through a series of experimental engines, the grand thirty-inch engines of the caloric ship were evolved. In 1855 the supply piston was changed so as to work *in equilibrio* at the time when the working piston was nearly stationary, and in 1856 was added the quickened motion at the conclusion of the inward stroke of the supply piston. Finally, in 1858, came a device to keep the lubricated surface of the cylinder at a temperature below that at which the oil suffers injury, by turning upon it an alternating blast of cold air. Thus was answered the objection that the hot-air engine could never be made successful because of the impossibility of securing the lubricants from destruction. The ingenious combination of movements in this engine so excited the admiration of Professor Horsford as to lead him to say: "It is difficult to conceive of a higher theoretical and mechanical triumph."

The engine consisted of a single horizontal cylinder. To one end of this fire was applied, and at the other end were two pistons alternately approaching and receding from each other, in such a manner as to produce internal pressure during the outward stroke of the outer piston. Both pistons were connected to the same crank-pin, and the peculiar and contrary motions of the two pistons were produced by lever movements. The solution of the problem of imparting motion to the two pistons required compliance with nine distinct conditions, and the result was one of the most remarkable mechanical conceptions of our time. "It is as impossible," said Professor Horsford, "to go into detail with each of Captain Ericsson's air engines as it would be to review the discussions of the caloric engine in which Ericsson, Rankine, Joule, Napier, Regnault, Barnard, Norton and a crowd of other writers, French, German, English, and American, have taken part. No one who comprehends the action of Stirling's earlier engine, or of Ericsson's of 1833 or 1837—which, with the regenerator attached, would do an amount of duty to which it was utterly inadequate with the regenerator detached ; or of the action of the caloric engine of 1858, or of Wilcox's, which with the escape and supply ports closed, and the air of the working cylinder returned alternately to and received from the supply cylinder, will run for a long time after the fire has been withdrawn—can now doubt, that upon the main point, the function of the regenerator, the claim of Ericsson had been sustained."

Wilcox's engine was a reproduction, in 1859–60, with some modification in details, of Ericsson's engine of 1837 with flywheel and regenerator. The earlier caloric engine of 1833 was the first of a series on the different plan of alternately heating and cooling a body of compressed air without the use of a regenerator. "In comparing the earlier with the later engines," said Professor Horsford, "there is a marked development of the capabilities of the principle, and corresponding progress in invention." *

---

* These quotations are from the address accompanying the presentation by the American Academy of Arts and Sciences of the Rumford premium of a gold and silver medal "awarded to John Ericsson for his improvement in the management of heat, particularly as shown in his caloric engine of 1858."

If Ericsson's caloric engine did not realize all his sanguine expectations, it certainly accomplished a great work, and its inventor had the satisfaction of knowing that he alone had met with any considerable success in the attempt, so frequently made during the previous half century, to substitute another motor for the steam-engine. Canada, by a special act of Parliament, granted Ericsson the privilege of a patent for his caloric engine, "as if the said John Ericsson had been a subject of Her Majesty, and resident of this province." In announcing the result in a letter from Toronto, May 21, 1861, a friend said: "In the passing of this bill nothing gave me more pleasure than the just tribute paid to your talents and energy. The Legislature generally is opposed to special legislation, and have made an exception in your case. I do not hesitate to say that no other man would have obtained it but yourself, and the ground of it was your untiring zeal in the cause of science, and the great benefit the whole world derive from the exercise of your talent and energy. For once, at any rate, merit has carried the day."

In his address in 1888, before the British Association, already referred to, Sir Frederick Bramwell said:

The working of heat engines without the intervention of water, by the combustion of gases arising from coal and water, is now not merely an established fact, but a recognized and undoubted commercially economical means of obtaining motive power. Such engines, developing from one to forty horse-power, and worked by ordinary gas supplied by gas-mains, are in most extensive use in printing-works, hotels, clubs, theatres, and even in large private houses, for the working of dynamos to supply electric light. But, looking at the wonderful petroleum industry, and at the multifarious products which are obtained from the crude materials, is it too much to say that there is a future for motor-engines worked by the vapor of some of the more highly volatile of these products—true vapor—not a gas, but a condensable body capable of being worked over and over again? Numbers of such engines, some of as much as four horse-power, are now running, and are apparently giving good results—certainly excellent results as regards the compactness and lightness of the machinery.

Ericsson was a pioneer in this field, and his caloric engine opened the way for the coming revolution, not only by its direct agency, but still more effectively in the way that most useful in-

ventions accomplish their object, by stimulating further invention and suggesting improvement in the line of the original
investigation. In spite of the wonders accomplished by modern
machinery, serious and well-founded objections are urged against
it on ethical grounds, for its tendency is to destroy the individual initiative and to lessen independence of character. For
thousands of little work-shops, each the centre of moral influences out of which have developed our best types of citizenship, we have substituted a single great manufactory where the
principle of the interchangeability of parts is applied to the
artisan as well as to his products. Each workman is one of a
thousand, so shaped to pattern that any one may be substituted
for any other. The factor of individuality, so essential to manly development, is thus, so far as possible, eliminated.

No man understood this tendency of modern mechanical
development better than Ericsson. "The close observer of
labor-saving machines," he said,* "is well aware that of late
years the legitimate bounds have been passed, and that we are
rapidly encountering the dangers of intellect-saving machines,
by introducing mechanical devices for effecting everything
which hitherto has been the result of the healthful combination
of intellect and muscular effort. At this moment hundreds of
thousands of human beings are employed in working a treadle
or turning a crank, vacant spectators of what their muscles effect; not the least tax on their intellect. Unfortunately, the
number of persons thus occupied is being augmented with a
rapidity only known to those who study the records of mechanical invention. It is needless to speculate on the effect upon
our race which this dispensing with intellect, and the substitution of monotonous muscular labor, will produce in course of
time. The evil is manifest.

"It will be asked, 'is there no remedy?' A motor of such
properties that it can follow the thousand mechanic denizens
into their corners would obviously meet the difficulty. It is
claimed that the caloric engine possesses these properties. It
works as well when made to exert the power of one man as
that of twenty. It is actuated by the air of the surrounding
atmosphere and requires no engineer; it can be managed by

*Letter to the editor of the London Times, May 23, 1860.

any person of common intelligence; is wholly free from danger; the cost of fuel which it consumes amounts to less than five per cent. of the manual. labor employed to exert equal force." Again he says: "The steam-engine requires water, which prevents its use in millions of instances in which we want motors to relieve human drudgery. We cannot trust that dangerous agent to the care of our wives and children, but the caloric engine we safely may. We can turn the key to the room which contains it, and the humble artisan may, without apprehension, ply his tool while this harmless servant turns the crank and cooks his food."

Five years later, when his triumphs in other fields had made his name universally known, Ericsson said (November, 1865): "The satisfaction with which I place my head on the pillow at night, conscious of having through my little caloric engine conferred a great boon on mankind—though the full importance of that boon will not be understood until the lapse of perhaps another century—is far greater than any satisfaction the production of an engine of war can give."

"The division and subdivision of functions," says Prince Krapotkin, one of the most conspicuous representatives of the modern socialistic element, "have been pushed so far as to divide humanity into castes almost as firmly established as those of old India. First the broad division into producers and consumers; little-consuming producers on the one hand, little-producing consumers on the other hand. Then amid the former, a series of subdivisions, the manual worker and the intellectual worker, sharply separated; and agricultural laborers and workers in manufactures. Amid little-producing consumers are numberless minute subdivisions, the modern ideal of a workman being a man or a woman, a boy or a girl, without the knowledge of any handicraft, having no conception whatever of the industry in which he or she is employed, and only capable of making all day long and for a whole life, the same infinitesimal part of something; from the age of thirteen to that of sixty pushing the coal cart at a given spot of the mine, or making the spring of a penknife, or the eighteenth part of a pin. The working classes have become mere servants to some machine of a given description; mere flesh-and-bone parts to some immense machinery ; having no idea about how or why the machinery is performing its rhythmical movements. Skilled artisanship is swept away as a survival of the past which is condemned to disappear. For the artist who formerly found æsthetic enjoyment in the work of his hands, is substituted the human slave of an iron slave."

It was against this tendency, constituting so great a danger to modern society, that Ericsson struggled, and with intelligent purpose, as the letter I have quoted shows. He had a profound sense of the dignity of labor ; his early years had been spent among working people, and those of the very best class ; and though he found but little leisure for the polite interchanges of " society " and had as little taste for them, his heart and his hand were always open to " plain people."

One hundred years ago when Benjamin Thompson was made a Count of the " Holy Roman Empire" he chose for his title the name of the place, Rumford (now Concord), N. H., from which he fled sixteen years before to escape the coat of tar and feathers in preparation for him, because of his supposed hostility to the local sentiment of opposition to the rule of England. Among the numerous proofs he gave of magnanimous forgetfulness of this episode in his history is to be numbered the gift of $5,000 to the American Academy of Arts and Sciences to found a prize, bearing his name, for the most important discoveries in light and heat.

Though the prize was founded in 1796, it was not until forty-three years after that the Academy, in 1839, found anyone who was in its judgment worthy of the award. Then the gold and silver Rumford medals were bestowed upon Robert Hare, of Philadelphia, whose subsequent wanderings in the unscientific ways of spiritualism have not diminished his earlier credit as a chemist and philosopher. To Hare, the prize was granted in recognition of his invention of the oxy-hydrogen blow-pipe, and his improvement in galvanic apparatus. Another interval of twenty-three years elapsed before it was proposed to bestow the prize a second time, though the fund had meantime increased to nearly thirty thousand dollars, and a still larger sum, the proceeds of its investment, had been expended, under authority of the State Court, in ways not contemplated in the original gift.

In 1860 the subject of bestowing the Rumford prize upon John Ericsson was brought to the attention of the Academy. The question as to his title to it was referred to the standing committee of the Academy having this matter in charge. At the five hundred and sixth meeting of the Academy, held two years later, April 6, 1862, Joseph Lovering, Hollis Professor of Mathematics and Natural Philosophy at Harvard College, from a majority of the Rumford Committee presented the following report :

> The Rumford Committee, having examined the subject of hot-air engines, and the recent improvement in their construction made in America, ask leave to report as follows :
> The Rumford Committee does not recommend that the Academy should award the Rumford premium for the alleged recent improvements of Mr. Ericsson in the hot-air engine, nor for his engine as at present constructed.
> MORRILL WYMAN, JOSEPH LOVERING, JOSEPH WINLOCK.
> CAMBRIDGE, April 8, 1862.

On behalf of himself and Daniel Treadwell, a former Rumford Professor, E. N. Horsford, presented the following :

> The minority of the Rumford report :
> That they dissent from the opinion of the majority, in that they believe the improvements in the caloric engine of Mr. Ericsson which he brought out in 1858 are such as to entitle him to the Rumford Medal.
> They see the evidence of high inventive talent, of patient thought and prolonged and persevering experimental research, in the practical solution on a large scale of the various problems underlying the hot-air engine, especially in the compact arrangement of the supply and working pistons; the telescopic tube, the fire-pot and the regenerator in a single cylinder, thereby economizing heat and space ; in the device for protecting the lubricating material of the packing of the working piston, by exposing it at each stroke to the current of entering cold air ; and in the system of cranks, rock-shafts, bars and their connecting rods by which the varied, complicated, but necessary motions of the supply and working pistons are regulated and connected with each other and the fly-wheel.
> The minority recommend that the Rumford Medal be awarded to Mr. Ericsson for his improvements in the management of heat, particularly as shown in his air engine of 1858.
> E. N. HORSFORD, DANIEL TREADWELL.
> CAMBRIDGE, April 8, 1862.

Thus were two professors of mathematics, one of Harvard and the other of the Naval Academy, and one physician, arrayed in judgment against two Rumford Professors, both celebrated for inventive capacity and experience. Who should decide? The two reports were received and the question of choosing between them was discussed by their authors, the merits of the hot-air engine being the subject of controversy. The discussion was continued at an adjourned meeting on April 22, 1862, and again at a meeting held May 13th, when Professor Louis Agassiz, Drs. Jacob Bigelow and Charles Pickering of Boston, Benjamin Peirce, Professor of Astronomy and Mathematics at Harvard, and Messrs. Washburn and Guy joined in the discussion. This controversy between practical invention and theoretical criticism was so earnest and determined that it was decided to refer the question to the annual meeting for settlement. Finally, at an adjourned annual meeting, held on June 1, 1862, on motion of Professor Horsford, seconded by Professor Treadwell, this resolution was finally adopted :

Resolved that the Rumford premium be awarded to John B.* Ericsson for his improvements in the management of heat, particularly as shown in his caloric engine of 1858.

The account here given of the award of the Rumford Medal to John Ericsson in 1862 somewhat anticipates this event in the order of chronology, yet it belongs naturally to a period occupied with studies destined to be laid aside for a time, and only for a time, in deference to the demands of the most imperative public obligations.

* The resolution is thus recorded in the published minutes of the Academy.

CHAPTER XIV.

PERSONAL HISTORY.

Ericsson's Associates and Friends.—His Interest in European Politics.—
He Meets with an Accident.—Submits to a Surgical Operation.—
His Physical Condition.—His Acquaintance with Professor J. J.
Mapes.—His Favorite Authors.—His Mathematical and Linguis-
tic Acquirements.—His Relations with Mr. Delamater.—Personal
Anecdotes.—His Physical Vigor.—Hopes to Live a Century.

WHEN we pass beyond the limits of Ericsson's workshop,
we find very little to record concerning his movements
during the twenty years succeeding his removal to New York,
in November, 1839. For a portion of this time his associate,
Mr. John O. Sargent, was residing in Washington, and intercourse with him was maintained by a correspondence devoted
chiefly to the dry details of business. Succeeding Mr. Sargent
as Ericsson's legal adviser came Mr. Edwin Wallace Stoughton,
whose connection with the important patent cases of Goodyear
and others, soon after his admission to the bar in 1840, had
brought him into prominence in this line of practice. The acquaintance with Mr. Stoughton, begun in 1850, continued until
his death in 1882. Ericsson's accounts show that Mr. Stoughton not only invested to a moderate extent in his caloric ventures but helped him to tide over some of his pecuniary difficulties while at work on his hot-air engine in 1855–56. Their
relations, originally those of attorney and client, extended
to personal friendship and social intercourse. Mr. Stoughton
was fond of his joke, and though Ericsson was less given to
jesting himself, he enjoyed humor in others, and when they
were together a jolly laugh would upon occasion well up from
the depths of the capacious lungs that filled his expansive
chest. He would occasionally drop in upon Mr. and Mrs.
Stoughton for an evening's chat. European politics were
among the topics of discussion during the Crimean war, and he
gave vigorous expression to the sympathy he felt, in common

with his countrymen, in the efforts of the allies to weaken the
power of Russia.   As Ericsson was a Knight of the Order of
Vasa he was familiarly spoken of by the Stoughtons as "Sir
John," and among his letters are found numerous notes from
Mr. Stoughton thus addressed.   That he occasionally respond-
ed in the same vein is shown by this letter:

"Sir John Ericsson" presents his compliments to Lord Counsellor
Stoughton, and regrets inexpressibly that previous engagement will
prevent his having the honor of meeting the Judges of the Court of Appeal, Tuesday next.

If anything could add poignancy to the regret which Sir John feels
at being prevented from putting *his* feet under the mahogany—more
properly the *oak*—of the Lord Counsellor, it is the fact that such a rare
selection of the Learned's feet will be under the same on this momentous occasion.

HASH SQUARE, April 6, 1867.

LORD COUNSELLOR STOUGHTON.

Sometimes Ericsson would take a Thanksgiving dinner
with his friends, the Stoughtons, and this New England festi-
val appears to have been the only one that received his homage.   It was on Thanksgiving day in 1854 that he lost the
second finger of his right hand while superintending some work
at the Delamaters', and he had, ever after, a superstition concerning the observance of the day.   If, as sometimes happened,
he lost sight of the calendar it was only necessary for his secretary to hold up an admonitory finger with "Remember,
Captain!" and the answer came promptly, "True, I forgot; no
work on Thanksgiving."   On the day he found such occasion to
remember, Ericsson was overseeing some work at Delamater's.
Noticing one of the men reaching forth to steady a vibrating connecting-rod, he shouted, "Be careful! you will lose your hand!"

Involuntarily his own hand went out, and his finger dropped
upon the floor.   Picking it up, the owner turned to his friend,
Delamater, who stood by, exclaiming, "See, Harry, what I have
done!"   Dropping the severed finger into his pocket, and ty-
ing a piece of tape around the stump to stop the hemorrhage,
he got into a carriage, drove home, and sent for a surgeon.
When the doctor came a further amputation was found necessary.
Refusing to take ether, the wounded man held out his maimed
hand, and calmly looked on while the surgeon operated.

That evening, a friend, Professor Mapes, called, alarmed by the reports he had received of the accident. He found Ericsson busied at his drawing-board with the pencil in his left hand. Answering the anxious inquiries concerning his condition, he said, quietly, "I expect to be obliged to use my left hand hereafter, and thought it best to commence practising with it."

This anticipation was, fortunately, not realized, for the hand did its owner good service for thirty-five years longer.

About this time Ericsson was greatly disturbed by the appearance of an angry swelling on the right-hand side of his jaw. This proved to be a malignant pustule. The physicians consulted agreed in the opinion that an operation was necessary, but to this Ericsson objected because of the disfigurement that would result, declaring that he would much rather die than be so scarred. Finally, a young doctor was found who was confident of his ability to cure without the knife. This was Dr. Thomas M. Markoe, then an assistant of Dr. Delafield, of New York, and since one of the best-known practitioners in New York. Dr. Markoe's treatment resulted so satisfactorily that his patient soon recovered, and he naturally conceived a warm regard for the young physician.

The partner of Mr. Stoughton was Mr. William Dodge, the son-in-law of Ericsson's old friend, Professor James J. Mapes, and the husband of Mrs. Mary Mapes Dodge, the editor of the *St. Nicholas Magazine*, New York. Professor Mapes was an inventor, as well as chemist of reputation, and a civil engineer holding high rank as an expert in patent cases. The acquaintance with him began soon after Ericsson's removal from England, and their relations were cordial and intimate.

The professor's house was one of the very few where the busy engineer was accustomed to visit, and he was a favorite in the household, the children running to meet him when his well-known ring was heard at the door. By the family of Professor Mapes Ericsson is remembered as a most genial and kindly man, who had an exceptional faculty for interesting himself in what interested others. Professor Mapes was accustomed to propound to him his chemical theories, especially one he held concerning the "progression of the primaries," and for this at least he always found a sympathetic listener in Ericsson, and one whose quick apprehension and intelligent comment were of service in clarifying his own ideas. Ericsson being a foreigner by birth, his thorough command of English, and his exact use of words and terms was a subject of remark. It could hardly be otherwise, however, with a man so precise in all things, after a daily experience for over twenty-five years with a language he had learned in his youth.

When Professor Mapes changed his residence to Newark, N. J., Ericsson extended his visits to that place, a rare instance upon his part of enterprise in the line of social accomplishment. His calls were usually made on Sunday afternoon, and he was fond of discussing philosophy with Professor Mapes, who was accustomed to say that Ericsson was the only man of whose intellectual ability he stood in awe. The professor considered himself an adept in mathematics, but acknowledged his master in Ericsson, who was one of the few in New York at that day familiar with the "Mécanique Celeste" of La Place. Two copies of La Place's great work were to be found in Ericsson's library; one a five-volume edition in the original French, published "An VII" (1797), when the author was a plain citizen of the Republic, the other Bowditch's translation, published in 1829, and bearing the name of "Marquis de La Place" on the title-page. The last was Ericsson's working copy, and it shows the marks of study, it being his custom to underscore what he wished to recall, with a red or black lead-pencil and mark a reference to it on the fly-leaf.

Ericsson also kept among his favorite authors Bishop Horsley's edition of Sir Isaac Newton's complete works, the first two volumes printed in 1779. The treatise "Philosophiæ Naturalis Principia Mathematica" in the third volume was one of his favorite studies, and he always found delight in reading it. In the fourth volume he has marked some of Newton's observations on the nature of light, and his declaration of the absurdity of the theory of innate gravity, and more especially the discourse on light and color. In this Newton declares that though he has argued the corporeity of light, it was "without any absolute positiveness." Under this statement Ericsson has drawn a line in red pencil and appended to his reference to several pages he has marked along the margin the words "very interesting." Newton's remarks concerning the propagation of light by vibrations in the ether attracted his particular attention, for the reason that he had some theories of his own concerning the ethers, holding that there were several. On this subject he used to engage in lively discussions with Professor Mapes. Ericsson was a most entertaining talker upon any subject that occupied his attention, and he was unusually fluent in speech, few men exceeding him in rapidity of utterance. He read French but could not speak it. He knew something of Spanish and Greek and could get along in these languages with the help of a dictionary. That he had some knowledge of German is indicated by this extract from a letter to Mr. Epes Sargent concerning a translation by his brother, Ericsson's special friend :

MY DEAR SARGENT: The great poet having kindly forwarded his "Last Knight" I am going to discharge the pleasing duty of thanking and complimenting him. The knowledge of the German displayed in his translation amazes me. I have "Der letzte Ritter" before me and find with admiration that in description your brother actually excels the original; but as German sentiment cannot be rendered into English, the spiritual part falls a little short, though not much. John has immortalized himself.

Ericsson's library was limited to a few hundred volumes, nearly all on scientific and professional subjects; the three or four novels appearing among them had evidently strayed out of place or belonged to some assistant, hungering for a bit of fiction to relieve so much grim reality. His reading was almost entirely confined to works connected with his special studies, the leading engineering and scientific periodicals, and two or three Swedish papers. Speaking once of the journals he received from Sweden, he said: "It is a perfect enjoyment to read, in my leisure moments, these papers. I always feel then as if I were in my dear Sweden. You don't know, perhaps, that I never read Swedish books."

Captain Ericsson disliked to be called a mathematician, though he was proud of the title of geometrician. He was accustomed to say that the ordinary mathematician had no reasoning power, or he would not disguise his processes in symbols that nobody but one of his own class could understand. It was his theory that articles upon mechanical subjects should be so written that a school-boy could understand them. The symbols are only required in the process of the higher mathematics, such as those of astronomy. A letter addressed to one of his clients by Ericsson shows at once his methods of calculation and his opinion upon the subject of confusing ideas with symbols. He said:

NEW YORK, September 12, 1864.

MY DEAR SIR: The proper thickness of a *square* cast iron plate will be obtained by the following:

Multiply the side in feet (or decimals of a foot) by $\frac{1}{4}$ of the pressure in pounds, and divide by 850 times the side in *inches*. The quotient is the square of the thickness in inches.

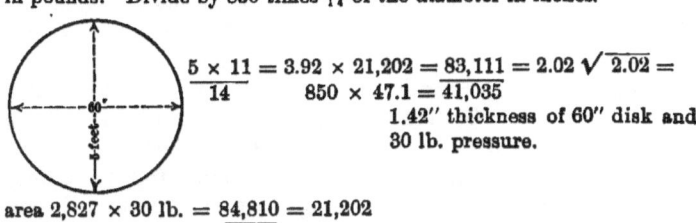

$$3{,}600 \;\square\; \times 30\,\text{lb.} = \frac{108{,}000}{4} = 27{,}000$$

$$5 \times 27{,}000 = \frac{135{,}000}{51{,}000} = 2.64 \;\sqrt{2.64} = \underline{1.62''}$$

thickness of a square plate 60 × 60" with 30 lb. pressure.

5 feet.

$850 \times 60 = 51{,}000$

For *circular* plate.

Multiply $\frac{11}{14}$ of the diameter in feet by $\frac{1}{4}$ of the pressure on the plate in pounds. Divide by 850 times $\frac{11}{14}$ of the diameter in inches.

$$\frac{5 \times 11}{14} = 3.92 \times 21{,}202 = 83{,}111 = 2.02 \;\sqrt{2.02} =$$

$$850 \times 47.1 = \overline{41{,}035}$$

1.42" thickness of 60" disk and 30 lb. pressure.

area $2{,}827 \times 30\,\text{lb.} = \dfrac{84{,}810}{4} = 21{,}202$

diameter $\dfrac{60 \times 11}{14} = 47.1''$

Yours very truly,

J. ERICSSON.

A great mathematician would cover half a dozen sheets with figures to solve the above problem.

15

With Mr. Cornelius H. Delamater, the engine manufac-turer and proprietor of the Phœnix Foundry, New York, Ericsson continued in intimate relation for a longer time than with any other man. Mr. Delamater was a clerk in this foun-dry when it began work on the engines of the *Princeton*, in January, 1842, and his acquaintance with Ericsson grew out of the latter's relations to this establishment. He had the great-est confidence in Ericsson's ability, and the highest admiration for his character, and when fortune favored him was always ready to assist in carrying on his enterprises. Their friendship was founded upon mutual respect and mutual advantage, and though their relations became at times somewhat strained, owing to Ericsson's hasty temper, there was a solid foundation of good will to settle down upon after the tempest had blown over.

Mr. Delamater's interest in the success of their joint under-takings, as well as good will toward his associate, would at times tempt him upon the dangerous ground of criticism. Ericsson was a severe censor of his own work, and as he had exhausted criticism before his work reached the machine shop, he was not accustomed to invite any favors in that line. It was not absolutely impossible to convince him that he was wrong, but the successful attempt came as near as possible to a solution of the lyceum problem as to the result of an encoun-ter between an immovable obstacle and an irresistible force. Doubts and suggestions already disposed of in his own mind so often returned to him through the fears of others, that he be-came accustomed to treat criticism with indifference.

On one occasion when Ericsson was finally convinced that a piece of mechanism he had spent much time upon was defect-ive, he sent it flying across the room and against the mantel-piece, to the serious disturbance of its offending internal econo-my. This was the only announcement he made as to his con-clusion concerning it. He demanded the most rigid observance of every detail in the drawings provided for the guidance of his workmen, and they were hugely delighted when they found in one case where they had been furnished with designs for a piece of mechanism requiring the introduction of gas, that "the old man" had omitted to include the vent-hole in his otherwise complete drawing. Such instances of oversight were so rare as to be a subject of comment forever after. Generally Ericsson was quite safe in saying, as he was accustomed to do when suggestions were offered to him, " Have you my drawing ? " " Then follow that." Mr. Watson, the editor of the *Engineer*, New York, tells this story of him :

Charles Nelson, at one time draughtsman in the Old Novelty Works in this city, had charge of the engines of the *Columbia*, designed by Captain Ericsson, and when the engines were done it was customary in those days to get the length of the piston-rod from the engine itself, so that there would be no mistake in cutting the keyway on the piston-rod. Nelson was down in the *Columbia's* cylinder with a baton about fourteen feet long, getting clearances, etc., when Captain Ericsson came on board by chance and stood right over him. He roared out : " What are you doing there, sir ? "

" Getting the length of the piston-rod, Captain Ericsson."

" Is it not on the drawing, sir ? "

" Yes, sir."

" Then why do you come here with sticks, sir ? Go and get the length from the drawing, sir. I do not want you to bring sticks when the drawing gives the size."

Charles Bernard, an old New York engineer, recently told us of another similar instance of Ericsson's accuracy. John Mars was putting in the engines of the old *Quinnebaug*, and one of the details was a small connection as crooked as a dog's hind leg. Mars tried to get it in its place for a long time, but failed, and finally went to Ericsson and told him the rod could not be got in. Ericsson said :

" Is it right by the drawing ? "

" Yes, sir," said Mars.

" Then it will go in," said Ericsson ; and when Mars tried it again it did go in.

Mr. Watson further says of Captain Ericsson :

An incident as to his leniency and consideration for others may be related here. The foundry foreman of a certain marine engine works in this city said he once made a large casting for a surface condenser for Captain Ericsson, and it was so peculiar in some respects that the proprietors of the work and the foreman of the foundry would not guarantee it. They feared it would crack by shrinkage strains across the corners. Ericsson said he would guarantee it, but when it was cast and had thoroughly cooled, it was found to be cracked just where it was expected to. Ericsson was notified, and came down to look at it.

" Can you make another one with what you know now ? " said Ericsson. The foreman said he thought he could.

"Make me another one," said Ericsson, and that was all there was about it.

Incidents like these, varying only in kind, could be related endlessly, for in his long life of constant professional activity he was always coming in contact with workmen and others, and was always the principal actor.

Ericsson was unquestionably the foremost man of his time in his profession, and while he was careful of his reputation and jealous of his standing as an engineer, he was not jealous of individuals or others in the profession, unless, indeed, they went out of their way to stir him up; then he was relentless. We have heard Captain Ericsson mention many well-known American engineers and their work; he always gave credit where it was due.

Ericsson was thoroughly familiar with the practical details of machine work, but it was his custom to give the most exact directions for carrying out his plans and leave their execution to others. When on rare occasions he did interfere, it so disturbed the routine of the work-shop that he lost more than he gained. He was not a "mechanic," as Stockton called him, but an engineer; that is "one devoted to the science and the art of utilizing the forces and materials of nature," and directing those who handle machinery or the tools of some craft. The only machines he employed himself were those of the scientific investigator; the only tools, those of the designer and draughtsman.

Like most men of aggressive convictions, Ericsson was more fond, when talking upon subjects he understood, of presenting his own ideas than of listening to what was said in reply, for every man, as Euripides says, "occupies himself with that in which he finds himself superior." He was never given to gossip of any sort, although sufficiently vigorous at times in his denunciation of those who angered him. To the ordinary topics of conversation he was indifferent. The policies of Government, especially as related to questions of armament, occupied his thoughts, but with politics in the lesser sense he never concerned himself, and it is doubtful if he ever voted during the forty years of his American citizenship. He prided himself upon his physical vigor, as he had good reason to do. It displeased him to note the signs of advancing age, and when gray hairs announced the unwelcome advent of his declining half century, he invoked the aid of art to deceive time. He made no concealment of the fact, however, explaining to his friends that he did not dye for their benefit but to gratify his own æsthetic taste. He disliked, he said, to see his gray locks reflected from his mirror.

The barber, who came once a week, on one occasion so over-emphasized his art that Ericsson, while entertaining a visitor soon after, found himself the object of unusually critical observation. When the visitor had bidden him good-by he questioned his assistant as to the cause and was told that the barber had transformed what nature intended to be a Scandinavian brown into an oriental black, making a most comical alteration in the appearance of the great engineer, and doing violence to the scriptural declaration that we cannot make one hair black or white. So the barber was sent for and kept at work until Ericsson was restored to himself.

He would occasionally visit the theatre and that he was not indifferent to the charms of histrionic art is shown by a little circumstance. When Fanny Kemble was giving her readings in this country in 1858, she applied through a friend to Ericsson asking him to design for her a reading-desk to meet certain requirements. When it came to the question of paying for it, the gallant Captain wrote a polite letter to the intermediary, asking Mrs. Kemble to accept the service, as an expression of his high appreciation of her contributions to the art of dramatic interpretation.

To this Mrs. Kemble replied saying: "I wish you would present my compliments to Captain Ericsson and tell him I am very grateful to him for his great courtesy and kindness. His letter will be treasured among my collection of valued autographs and my table preserved and honored among my goods and chattels as the most magnificent piece of furniture could never deserve to be."

Delving in a dusty heap of engineering designs and calculations, I came upon a paper which seems to shine out from the mass like a diamond from its kindred carbon of the coal-heap. It was a list of forty Swedish songs in Ericsson's delicate handwriting, which was as dainty as a woman's when he wrote carefully. There were two copies of the list. One contained the titles in Swedish ; the other the Swedish names with a transla-

tion in English. Among the titles were such as these: "And
Woman's Destiny is Certain," "Resolve and Act are One with
Woman," "Who are You, My Girl?" "It is so Sweet in
Spring," "Young Lady, in Your Springtime," "I Possess Such
a Handsome Wife," "Give Me while yet My Wife," "And
Sunset Parts," "O Robert, Cruel is Our Parting," "Bacchus
Calls His Lamb."

"E'en in our ashes burn the wonted fires." Here was the
busy engineer who had governed his life, as nearly as possible
to all appearances, by the exact calculations of machine work,
turning aside, as he neared the end of his third score, to revive
his recollections of the songs he had no doubt sung in the days
when he indited sonnets to the Northern Lights from under the
shadows of the Jemtland forests. It would be a great mistake
to infer from this sober narration of engineering achievement
and scientific study that John Ericsson had any sympathy with
the chemist, who refused to marry because his analysis of woman detected in her composition nothing beyond a combination
of sundry salts with water. His reasons for living solitary, instead of following the admonition to "dwell together in families," were sufficient, but they by no means implied indifference
to woman. That he had a high appreciation of the obligations
of marriage is shown by this letter addressed to a young bridegroom:

NEW YORK, July 20, 1860.

MY DEAR SIR: Your notice was too short to admit of my being
present at the very interesting ceremony at Christ Church last Wednesday. A reluctant absentee on the solemn occasion, allow me now to
offer my cordial congratulations. Not simply do I hope that you may
enjoy all happiness, which married life under favorable circumstances is
so well calculated to bestow. I am delighted to find that all commend.
your choice, yet I cannot refrain from giving you as a friend advice not
to expect too much of your wife. Remember well that you will yourself
fail to meet the *just* expectations of her whose destiny is now entwined
with your own, and whose happiness in life is now so completely at your
mercy. Pardon this phrase, which I select with a friend's anxious desire
that you should duly contemplate your high responsibility at the very
outset of your, so to speak, new experience,
Yours truly,
JOHN ERICSSON.

Ericsson had a hope that he might prolong his days well on to the completion of a century, but as to that he had no anxiety. His only wish was to retain to the end his capacity for work, since with him idleness was misery. He had no resources outside of his absorbing devotion to work, and as is the case with all men whose lives are prolonged, those in whom his deepest affections centred nearly all passed away before him. Domestic relations he could hardly have been said to have had at all. In his way an admirer of women, he was never willing to meet them on their own terms, for he regarded them rather in the light of a diversion for his leisure than as companions in the serious matters of life. The experiences of his early manhood are hidden in obscurity, for he remorselessly destroyed nearly all the letters and documents relating to his career previous to the year 1861, when his success was established. Here and there comes a flash of light to reveal his characteristics, but nowhere do I find any indication of a purely sentimental or intellectual relation to the opposite sex. He was kindly, he was generous, he was considerate, and in his relations to his kin most affectionate, as his letters show, but the attempt to accommodate himself to feminine sensibilities assumed with him a place among the less important duties of life.

As some of Ericsson's most intimate friends were lawyers, it is evident that he had no prejudice against the members of the legal profession. Yet his experience with courts had not predisposed him in favor of professional methods and the endless worry and expense attending the defence of his rights against infringement had given him a dread of litigation. On one occasion when a steamship company refused to pay his modest bill of five hundred dollars, for showing them how to remedy a defect in one of their engines which was beyond the skill of their own engineers, he was persuaded to bring suit. All went well until he received the necessary summons to appear as a witness. To this he refused to respond, and let his case go by default rather than submit himself to the badgering of the lawyers. Had the rule of ancient Greece prevailed, and suitors been required to plead their own causes, he would have won almost any case, for he was a master of persuasive discourse upon any subject that he understood. He was more than

once the victim of the ignorance concerning mechanical questions prevailing, especially in former years when courts and
juries were more easily misled in technical matters by resem-
blances that did not indicate perfect similarity. When Ericsson
came to New York Professor Mapes was almost, if not quite,
the only consulting engineer in the city, and professional
knowledge had hardly passed beyond the period when a physician was considered competent, after a week's study in a library, to design the capitol at Washington, and when it was
easy for a man who knew a little more than his neighbors to
persuade them that he knew everything.

CHAPTER XV.

INCEPTION OF THE MONITOR.

Ericsson's Preparation for His Great Work.—His Struggles with Professional Jealousy.—Dealings with the Navy Department Previous to 1861.—Presents Two Sub-aquatic Systems of Attack to the Emperor of the French.—History of Armored Vessels.—Outbreak of the Civil War.—Prompt Action of the Confederate Authorities.—Ericsson Offers His Services to President Lincoln.—Is Called to Washington.—Dramatic Interview with the Board on Armor-Clads.—The Monitor Ordered.

" EACH thing, both in small and in great, fulfilleth the task which destiny has set down," and it is only when we discard the theory of chance or accident, that the history of such a man as Ericsson becomes clear to us. Then, through all the seemingly tangled web of circumstance, we are able to trace the evidences of over-ruling purpose, and to see how incidents, apparently without connection, stand in orderly relations one to another as essential parts of an intelligent design. Ericsson's early training on the Göta Canal; his studies of artillery and of military engineering in the camps of Jemtland; his observation of the behavior of raft-like structures in the storms sweeping over the Swedish lakes; his experience in the difficult and but little understood work of marine construction, in the handling of men and choice of material; his unceasing studies into the possibilities of applying old principles in new ways, and his constant effort to emancipate himself from the slavery of routine—all these were to have a part in the great work involving the interests of a nation, the hopes of humanity. All the strength and experience gathered by the exercise of his great powers for nearly half a century were needed now, to meet the strain of a demand to which no other living man was adequate, for whatever part others may have borne in the events succeeding the election of Abraham Lincoln, in 1860, the contribution of John Ericsson to the cause of National Unity was as unique as it was important.

When the storm which had been gathering through so many years of political commotion burst over Fort Sumter, in the spring of 1861, Ericsson was in the fifty-eighth year of his age. He had the constitution and the vital force of a man of forty; an experience in actual accomplishment such as few acquire even in the longest lifetime, and this experience was of a nature to make his services of the greatest value to his adopted country. Yet no place could be found for him at a time when the public security demanded the services of every man capable of assisting it. High commissions in the military service were obtained by men whose lives had been spent in making speeches or manipulating politics, and they were bestowed on foreigners of every degree of military experience or inexperience. Search lights were turned in all directions to discover men who might aid the Government; but not a ray of light fell upon John Ericsson.

The difficulty was not that he was unknown, but that he was too well known—at least at Washington, and in those bureaus of the Navy Department with which his abilities and his experience would naturally associate him. Since his work in 1842–43 upon the *Princeton*, he had been engaged more or less with Government matters; but with the bureaus he was no favorite. From their point of view he was a failure. They preferred the safe waters of precedent, while it was his mission to sail the high seas of discovery. Without judging between them, it is sufficient to say that Ericsson and the Government officers, to whom he looked for approval, were seldom in accord.

Writing to Sir John Burgoyne during the Crimean War, Brunel, the great engineer, said: "You are the first professional man of high official rank I have met with ready to assume the possibility of a man who is neither R.E. nor R.N. [Royal Engineer or Royal Navy] having an idea worth attending to." Brunel had taken to the Lords of the Admiralty a suggestion, prompted by his anxiety to assist his adopted country in the contest wherein it was allied with his native France. This suggestion was rejected without a hearing, as the suggestions of Ericsson and so many others have been rejected from time to time by these Lords Paramount of official stolidity. From boards Brunel turned to brains and made his appeal to Palmerston, who referred his proposition for report to Sir John Burgoyne, inspector of fortifications, lieutenant-general and second in command of the British forces in the Crimea. In a letter to the Prime Minister, enclosing a favorable report, Burgoyne suggested that in dealing with the eminent engineer "there was need of the exercise of tact, arising from his thorough independence, which rather requires that he should be courted than merely given permission to work out his plans, and his great dislike to negotiate with the authorities of the Admiralty."

No man knew better than Sir John how the interests of the Government are sacrificed to the conceit of office; to the disposition of small men in large places to make arrogance supply the place of ability. In a letter to Brunel, General Burgoyne, speaking from large experience, thus explained the secret of the antagonism so often arising between public officers and men of ability in private station who seek to serve the Government:

First, there is our own jealousy, pride, and conceit, of which you all complain, and with much reason, originating in a false idea that we should be admitting a culpable want of knowledge in our own business by obtaining assistance from others; then another false conception, that because in all these things there are certain military considerations involved, of which civilians must be comparatively ignorant, therefore it is that only a military man can devise them; whereas it is generally much more easy for us to make you masters of the military conditions, than to obtain from you what is necessary for the rest.

At the same time there is usually great fault on the side of the civilian projectors; they put us down for a set of ignoramuses and do not admit that there can be any military considerations that can be of the least consequence, or that they do not know by intuition. Hence the most outrageous propositions, which the projectors, however, cling to with pertinacity, and call us bigots, narrow-minded, and fools because we will not adopt them.*

Here is an explanation of some of Ericsson's difficulties. As a civilian, seeking to influence naval administration, he

* Life and Correspondence of Sir John Burgoyne, pp. 365-66.

realized the disadvantages of what is known to military men as fighting on exterior lines. He was often thwarted by interference with his plans, as in one instance whereof he bitterly exclaims, in a private letter: "In the name of God is not my position cruel? The scoundrels have prevented my furnishing plans or giving directions; and now that they have failed, they attribute this failure to having worked to my plans!" This was no uncommon experience with him.

"In the name of common sense," he says in another letter, "should an engineer's *experiments* militate against his works intended for practical purposes? If so, experiment should be conducted by those only who are incapable of constructing anything. Am I not the originator and founder and perfector of war steamers, under-water machinery and entire system? Did any of my screw-engines ever fail? EXPERIMENTS with condensers, fresh-water apparatus, boilers, etc., etc., are matters apart that must not be confounded with *engines built* for *practical* purposes. I say damned is the injustice of calling him 'wild' who has originated with his wildness and perfected war propulsion!" This is vigorous language, but no more vigorous than Ericsson's experience justified.

"You have heard me say," he writes again, "that no man can tell by any process of reasoning how a new form of boiler may answer. I have always contended that the subject is *not susceptible of previous determination*. Not so with the *new form* of engine to be worked by *steam already generated!* I profess to be able to determine that point on mechanical data. In that respect I never was mistaken, for out of some fifty distinctly different forms of steam-engines I never yet failed in a single instance; with *steam* at *command* I have always produced a perfect working engine. All the world predicted failure in the case of that most novel form of engine of the *Princeton*. But all the world proved wrong, but mark, I had the steam furnished by boilers of *known* and approved form."

These letters were written seven years before the outbreak of the American Civil War had directed universal attention to Ericsson's signal ability. From them, and from other letters, it appears that he was striving to impress his views upon the Navy Department at Washington and was met by a spirit of hostility and distrust which paralyzed his efforts to serve the country. Even his sober statement as to what experience had made possible to him was gauged by the capabilities of feebler men; the giant was accused of extravagance because he would not limit his powers of performance to those of the dwarfs. It was supposed that two years would be required to build a war steamer, and Ericsson's offer to do the same work in eight months subjected him to suspicion. Concerning this he wrote to Mr. Sargent, saying:

New York, April 20, 1854.

My dear Sargent: I have your letter of the 17th, relative to your interesting interview with the Secretary of the Navy. I feel a little nettled at the Hon. Secretary's doubting my statement as to the time of building the *Ericsson*. Please present to him the enclosed document on the subject.

I note that the Secretary thinks my assertion that a screw steamer may be built in *eight* months a "wild" one. After he has perused the document alluded to, he will think otherwise. Did I promise to build such a vessel in five months he would be justified in thinking me wild, though he could by no means prove his position. Should I, however, promise to do the work in *six* months it would be quite possible for me to redeem such promise. The steamship *Massachusetts*, without extraordinary exertion, was built, hull, engines, and all, and under steam in six months.

The machinery of a screw steamer contrasted to the gigantic eight-cylinder engine of the caloric ship, is absolutely insignificant. Indeed, had I the entire control of building, I should feel impatient at spending more than five months in *building* a screw engine.

One word as to my promise to build a vessel that would blow half a dozen English or French screw ships out of the water. Dobbin will scarcely find it so difficult to repress his merriment at the suggestion as did Mr. Lord, of the British Admiralty, on my proposing to them the application of the propeller to their men of war *exactly as the thing is now done*. Pray put me in the right with the Hon. Secretary. I do not propose to build the destructive vessel, I only say that in eight months such a vessel *could* easily be constructed.

Yours very truly,

J. Ericsson.

John O. Sargent, Washington.

He was at this time perfecting his system of "sub-aquatic attack," and his ill-success at Washington no doubt had its in-

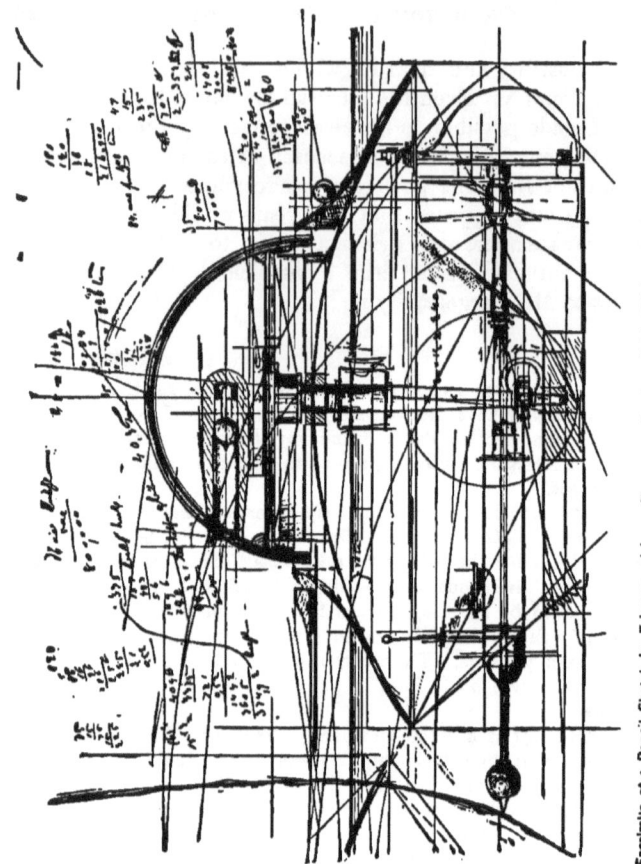

Facsimile of a Pencil Sketch by Ericsson, giving a Transverse Section of his Original Monitor Plan with a Longitudinal Section drawn over it.

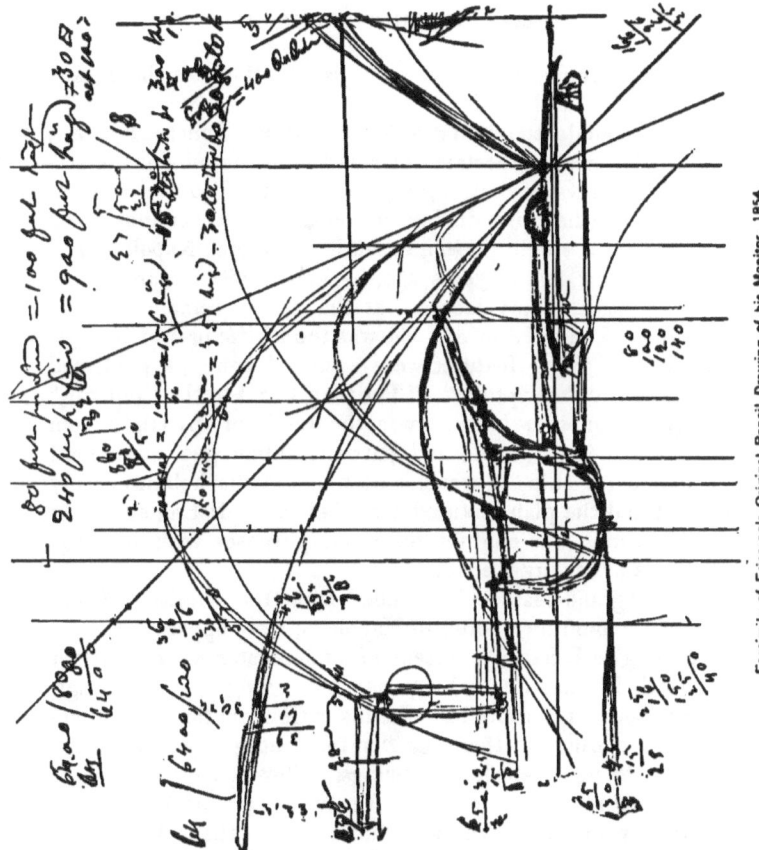

Facsimile of Ericsson's Original Pencil Drawing of his Monitor, 1854.

fluence in prompting him to turn his attention elsewhere, as it will be seen that he did.

In a confidential letter written to John Bourne, Ericsson said : "The great importance of what I call the sub-aquatic system of naval warfare strongly presented itself to my mind in 1826. Yet I have not during this long interval communicated my ideas to a single person, excepting Emperor Napoleon III. What I knew twelve years ago, he knows with regard to the general result of my labors, but the details remain a secret with me. The monitor of 1854 was the *visible* part of my system, and its grand features were excluded from its published drawings and description." "The plan I sent to the Emperor," he says, in another letter, "was the result of my study from youth. An impregnable and partially submerged instrument for destroying ships of war has been one of the hobbies of my life. I had the plan matured long before I left England. As for protecting war engines for naval purposes with iron, the idea is as old as my recollection."

The "grand features," excluded from the published drawings of the monitor offered to Napoleon, were apparently those pertaining to Ericsson's system of under-water attack. After his death I found among his papers two autographic drawings, shown here in fac-simile. In his "Contributions," Captain Ericsson speaks of them as "unfortunately lost," alluding, perhaps, to more finished drawings. Those given here show clearly the ideas developed on the *Destroyer* of 1878. The emergency of our Civil War did not call them forth, and they were no doubt reserved for an occasion that did not arise until declining years warned their author that there was danger that they might die with him. They would have been developed promptly enough in the event of an attack by a naval power upon either Sweden or the United States.

The original inspiration to Ericsson's studies in naval defence was the protection of his native Sweden against foreign aggression, and especially against the encroachments of Russia, whose hostility to Sweden was among the vivid recollections of his early youth. His letter was sent to Napoleon, September 26, 1854, through the Swedish Consul at New York, and the

Swedish Minister in Paris. Concerning his purpose in laying the matter before the Emperor, he says: "My object was to cause the destruction of the fleets of the hereditary enemy of my native land. Strange to say, no sooner did my communication reach its destination, than news came that the fleet at Sebastopol had been voluntarily consigned to those subaqueous regions which I had had in view. Deeply regretting what had occurred, I ceased to labor in the matter until our civil war broke out, when I took it up with great enthusiasm and finally elaborated some points of detail; cautiously waiting, however, to move until England and France should, by overt act, espouse the cause of our enemies—a cause which involved the perpetuation of the bondage and a firmer riveting of the shackles, for another century, of four million of persons whose only crime was their color, the inevitable consequence being that at the end of that century this fair portion of our planet would have contained some forty millions of bondsmen. But the echo of the guns at Hampton Roads had its effect. It was deemed imprudent to send fleets of wooden vessels among enemies so fertile in mechanical expedients and so enterprising as the Americans."

"I imagined," he said further, in a letter to Assistant-Secretary Fox, of the Navy Department, "that I had a very valuable idea and kept it secure accordingly."

The Emperor of the French does not appear to have been sufficiently impressed with this idea to make use of it, and the receipt of the plans was simply acknowledged with the usual formal reply of courteous thanks as follows:

MONSIEUR: The Emperor has himself examined with the greatest care the new system of naval attack which you have submitted to him. His Majesty directs me to have the honor of informing you that he has found your ideas very ingenious and worthy of the celebrated name of their author; but the Emperor thinks that the result to be obtained would not be proportionate to the expenses or to the small number of guns which could be brought into use. Although not disposed to make use of your inventions the Emperor appreciates all their merit, and directs me to thank you for this interesting communication.

The plans and description sent to the Emperor were accordingly put aside, and the dust of nearly seven years had accumulated upon them before another motive appealed to Ericsson with sufficient strength to induce him to make them available for the purposes of warfare. "This motive," as he explains, "was that of serving the Union cause by constructing vessels capable of defeating the *Merrimac* and other Confederate iron-clad vessels."

In July, 1861, Mr. Delamater, who had been Ericsson's associate in so many of his engineering enterprises, wrote to him from Washington, saying: "I am treated well: have had two evening interviews with Mr. Secretary Welles, one of them alone in my own room, yet I have no expectation of any contract or immediate good to result to me or to us from my present stay. I am remaining to finish off Mr. Isherwood if possible, which I think I owe it to my country to do. Mr. Welles seems to have taken a fancy to me and I have avoided pressing any special purpose, and altogether my position appears to be strangely disinterested. Am to see Mr. Welles this evening at his request. I have given Isherwood an Irish hoist, and if I only knew who in the navy to aid, might almost finish the job."

As Ericsson and Delamater had various interests together it does not follow that this visit had any relation to the proposed iron-clads. Indeed, the allusion to Ericsson's old antagonist, Mr. Isherwood, chief of the Naval Bureau of Steam Engineering, would indicate that it was to the work of his department that Mr. Delamater's efforts were directed.

The subject of iron-clad vessels had at that time just begun to attract the attention of Congress, and no appropriation for building such vessels was yet available. In his report dated July 4, 1861, the Secretary of the Navy, Mr. Gideon Welles, called attention to the efforts of foreign governments, and particularly France and England, to provide themselves with "floating batteries or iron-clad steamers" adding: "I would recommend the appointment of a proper and competent board to inquire into and report in regard to a measure so important, and it is for Congress to decide whether, on favorable report, they will order one or more iron-clad steamers, or floating batteries."

The submission of Ericsson's plans to the Emperor Napoleon had been followed the next year, 1855, by the appearance in the attack upon Kinburn, during the Crimean War, of three French floating batteries clad with 4½-inch plates, the *Lave*, the *Devastation*, and the *Tonnante*. Three years later, in 1858, Napoleon ordered the construction of four armor-plated steam frigates, *La Gloire*, *L'Invincible*, *La Normandie*, and *La Couronne*. These were all the armored vessels France had in commission at the beginning of 1861. Two others, the *Solferino* and *Magenta*, had been launched, and twelve more were on the stocks. England had at sea her *Warrior, Black Prince, Defence, Resistance*, and *Royal Oak*, with five other armor-clads launched and eleven more under way. This refers to sea-going vessels only. None of these ships had any resemblance to the vessel suggested by Ericsson to Napoleon in 1854, except in their significant departure from the precedent of wooden walls, upon which so much reliance had hitherto been placed.

The conditions calling for armor plating had actually existed for forty years, or ever since the introduction, in 1819, by one of the soldiers of the First Napoleon, General Henri Joseph Paixhans of the system of firing explosive shell directly at an object, instead of from mortars on an ascending and descending curve through the air, as before.*

The attention of the British Admiralty was called in 1834–35 to the advisability of adopting iron for ships of war. Iron

---

* In response to a letter from Rear-Admiral S. B. Luce, U.S.N., claiming this invention for General George Bomford, U.S.A., whose "columbiad" was known at an earlier date, Ericsson wrote this letter:

NEW YORK, December 10, 1885.

DEAR ADMIRAL: Shortly after my arrival in this country, 1839, I became intimately acquainted with Colonel Bomford and Commodore Perry. The latter had just returned from England and France, where he had studied naval ordnance under instructions from the Navy Department. The result of his journey was considered very important at the time, as he brought a full report of the success of the then recent labors of General Paixhan; he also brought complete drawings of Paixhan's perfected shell gun, which was at once adopted by the Navy Department at Washington for the two large paddle wheel steam frigates, *Mississippi* and *Missouri*, then being constructed.

I had frequent interviews with the two United States officers mentioned, as I brought plans of a screw steamship-of-war, for which Congress at once granted an appropriation. Of course General Paixhan's brilliant invention and its important bearing on naval warfare was frequently adverted to dur-

targets were ordered to be prepared at Woolwich for experiment with a 32-pounder smooth-bore gun at a range of only thirty yards. Iron was condemned as a result of these experiments, and the Admiralty fell back upon the old wooden walls, as the only vessels calculated for the purposes of war. This decision against a change retarded everything in the shape of progress until the adoption of iron-clads in the French Navy compelled England to follow the lead of Napoleon in 1855.*

As early as 1845 an American engineer, Mr. R. L. Stevens, had undertaken to experiment with armor, and in the year that Ericsson sent the model of his monitor to France had begun, as has been already stated, the construction of an iron-plated ship.

The results of shell-firing upon naval warfare were not made apparent until the Crimean War. Then Napoleon III., who prided himself upon his knowledge of artillery, was greatly chagrined to find how much the French navy was at a disadvantage in the contest with the Russian forts in the Black Sea. If he did not take Ericsson's plans, he certainly adopted the suggestion of armor defence and built five armor-clads, England following in humble imitation with an equal number on the same general plan. The guns at this time had so much the advantage that the Russians were able to steam into Sinope and in a single morning destroy the Turkish fleet, to shut out Sir Charles Napier from Cronstadt, and to defy the allied fleets at Sebastopol. Of the British experience in the Black Sea Lord Dundonald, one of the bravest sailors that ever trod a quarter-

---

ing the said interviews, yet Colonel Bomford in my presence never claimed the new gun as his invention.

In connection with *coast defence* the "columbiad" was often spoken of, a gun particularly described in the enclosed extract from Colonel Benton's Ordnance and Gunnery, published at New York, 1867. I also enclose a brief extract from Appleton's Cyclopedia of 1864, vol. xii., page 145.

With reference to the "bomb cannon" for firing hollow shot charged with powder, I beg to observe that during my early studies of artillery, previous to 1820, such a gun was not even then regarded as a novelty.

I have deemed the foregoing explanation necessary in answer to your assumption that I have. in my *Century* article, inadvertently deprived General Bomford of the credit of being the originator of a system known in Europe before his time.   I am, Admiral, yours truly,

J. ERICSSON.

* Fairbairn on Iron Ship Building.

deck, asserted that the Russian shells made it impossible to continue the vessels under fire, and it was considered no disgrace to declare, after three shells had exploded in one ship, it was not possible to find men "fools enough to stand to the guns." " The man who goes into action in a wooden vessel is a fool," said Sir John Hay, "and the man who sends him there is a villain."

The Confederate Secretary of the Navy in 1860 was Mr. Stephen R. Mallory, of Florida, who had served for several years in Congress as Chairman of the Naval Committee. He had been, as we have seen, a champion of Ericsson, and in a speech in Congress, made in May, 1858, had shown intelligent appreciation of the revolution in naval warfare accomplished by the *Princeton*. Mr. Mallory was much better informed in nautical matters than Mr. Welles, Secretary of the Navy in the Cabinet of Mr. Lincoln, and more prompt to recognize the changes in naval warfare. Two months before the Federal Secretary of the Navy had made his halting suggestion to Congress on the subject of armored vessels the head of the Confederate naval service had spoken on the same subject in these distinct terms, in a letter to the Chairman of the Confederate Naval Committee dated May 8, 1861 :

I regard the possession of an iron-armored ship as a matter of the first necessity. Such a vessel at this time could traverse the entire coast of the United States, prevent all blockade, and encounter, with a fair prospect of success, their entire navy. If, to cope with them upon the sea, we follow their example, and build wooden ships, we shall have to construct several at one time, for one or two ships would fall an easy prey to their comparatively numerous steam frigates. But inequality of numbers may be compensated by invulnerability, and thus not only does economy, but naval success, dictate the wisdom and expediency of fighting with iron against wood without regard to first cost.

Naval engagements between wooden frigates, as they are now built and armed, will prove to be the forlorn hopes of the sea, simply contests in which the question, not of victory, but of who shall go to the bottom first, is to be solved. Should the committee deem it expedient to begin at once the construction of such a ship, not a moment should be lost.

Mr. Mallory's action was as decided as his words. Without waiting for an appropriation, on July 11, 1861, he approved plans submitted to him by Chief Engineer William P. Williamson, Lieutenant John M. Brooke, an ex-officer of the United States Navy, and Naval Constructor John L. Porter. These plans provided for raising and altering into an iron-clad, the U. S. frigate *Merrimac*, of 3,500 tons and 40 guns. This had been burnt and sunk at the Norfolk Navy Yard when it was abandoned in April, 1861. With but one establishment in the South capable of furnishing her armor, the Tredegar foundry, the work upon the *Virginia*, as she was rechristened, was slow, and in this delay Ericsson found his opportunity.

On August 3, 1861, President Lincoln approved an act of Congress, authorizing the appointment of a Board asked for by Mr. Welles. An advertisement inviting proposals for iron-clad steam vessels was issued from the Navy Department, and August 8th Commodores Joseph Smith and Hiram Paulding and Commander Charles H. Davis were appointed a board to examine plans. Twenty-six days later Ericsson prepared the letter to President Lincoln which follows, as appears from a copy of it in his handwriting found among his papers:

NEW YORK, August 29, 1861.

SIR: The writer, having introduced the present system of naval propulsion and constructed the first screw ship of war, now offers to construct a vessel for the destruction of the rebel fleet at Norfolk and for scouring the Southern rivers and inlets of all craft protected by rebel batteries. Having thus briefly noticed the object of my addressing you, it will be proper for me most respectfully to state that in making this offer I seek no private advantage or emolument of any kind. Fortunately I have already upward of one thousand of my caloric engines in successful operation, with affluence in prospect. Attachment to the Union alone impels me to offer my services at this fearful crisis—my life if need be—in the great cause which Providence has called you to defend. Please look carefully at the enclosed plans and you will find that the means I propose to employ are very simple—so simple, indeed, that within ten weeks after commencing the structure I would engage to be ready to take up position under the rebel guns at Norfolk, and so efficient too, I trust, that within a few hours the stolen ships would be sunk and the harbor purged of traitors. Apart from the fact that the proposed vessel is very simple in construction, due weight, I respectfully submit, should be given to the circumstance that its projector possesses practical and constructive skill shared by no engineer now living. I have planned upward of one hundred marine engines and I furnish daily, working-plans made with my own hands of mechanical and naval structures of various kinds, and I have done so for thirty years. Besides this I have received a military education and feel at home in the science of artillery. You will not, sir, attribute these statements to any other cause than my anxiety to prove that you may safely entrust me with the work I propose. If you cannot do so then the country must lose the benefit of my proffered services. If, on the other hand, you decide to act, please telegraph and I will at once wait upon you in Washington. I respectfully submit that in the former case you return the plans, honored with your signature, to testify that I have discharged the duty of laying this important matter before you.

I cannot conclude without respectfully calling your attention to the now well-established fact that steel-clad vessels cannot be arrested in their course by land batteries, and that hence our great city is quite at the mercy of such intruders, and may at any moment be laid in ruins, unless we possess means which, in defiance of Armstrong guns, can crush the sides of such dangerous visitors.

I am, sir, with profound respect, your obedient servant,

J. ERICSSON.

To His Excellency ABRAHAM LINCOLN, President of the United States.

It is not for me, sir, to remind you of the immense moral effect that will result from your discomfiting the rebels at Norfolk and showing that batteries can no longer protect vessels robbed from the nation, nor need I allude to the effect in Europe if you demonstrate that you can effectively keep hostile fleets away from our shores. At the moment of putting this communication under envelope it occurs to me finally that it is unsafe to trust the plans to the mails. I therefore respectfully suggest that you reflect on my proposition. Should you decide to put the work in hand, if my plan meets your own approbation, please telegraph and within forty-eight hours the writer will report himself at the White House.

It was fortunate for Ericsson that the naval board on iron-clads were so ignorant as they were of the subject committed to their decision. Beyond a general distrust of and prejudice against armored vessels they had no opinion concerning them, and no predilections in favor of any special system. Embarked upon unfamiliar waters, they were ready to listen to anyone who offered to pilot them safely into harbor. In their report to the Secretary of the Navy, dated September 16, 1861, they frankly said: "Distrustful of our ability to discharge this duty, we approach the subject with diffidence, having no experience and but scant knowledge in this branch of naval archi-

tecture." Their disposition was to favor vessels for coast and
harbor defence, as undoubtedly formidable adjuncts to fortifications on land. " For river and harbor service," they declared,
" we consider iron-clad vessels of light draught or floating batteries, thus shielded, as very important." Their final conclusion
was to meet the immediate demand by calling for " vessels invulnerable to shot, of light draught of water, before going into
a more perfect system of large iron-clad sea-going vessels of
war." So far, then, their disposition was in favor of such a
vessel as Ericsson proposed.

The three vessels the Board recommended for adoption
were the Ericsson floating battery ; a broadside vessel of 3,296
tons, afterward known as the *Ironsides,* and the *Galena.* The
plans for this last vessel were presented by Mr. C. S. Bushnell,
of New Haven, Conn., who was subsequently associated with
Ericsson in building the *Monitor.* Telling the story of his experience with the Board Mr. Bushnell said, in a letter written
some years ago to Secretary Welles:

The Board examined hundreds of plans, good and bad, and among
others that of a plated gunboat called the *Galena,* contrived by S. H.
Pook, now a constructor in the navy. The partial protection of iron bars
proposed for her, seemed so burdensome that many naval officers warned
me against the possibility that she might not be able to carry the weight
of her armament.

I met Mr. C. H. Delamater on the steps of Willard's Hotel in Washington just after I had secured the contract for the *Galena.* When I
told him that several naval men doubted whether the vessel would be
able to carry the stipulated amount of iron, he advised me to consult
the engineer Captain John Ericsson, of New York, as one whose opinion
would settle the matter definitely and with accuracy. Acting upon the
advice of Mr. Delamater, I went to New York on the following day and
laid the plans of the *Galena* before Captain Ericsson, asking whether
the vessel would be able to carry the specified armor. I gave him the
data necessary for his calculations and he told me to call the next day
for his reply. This I did and received the answer. " She will easily
carry the load you propose and stand a six-inch shot at a respectable
distance."

At the close of this interview Captain Ericsson asked me if I had
time just then to examine the plan of a floating battery, absolutely impregnable to the heaviest shot or shell. I replied that this problem had
been occupying me for the last three months, and that considering the

time required for construction, the *Galena* was the best result I had been able to obtain.

He then produced a small, dust-covered box, and placed before me the model and plan of the *Monitor*, explaining how quickly and powerfully she could be built, and exhibiting with characteristic pride a medal and letter of thanks received seven years previously from Napoleon III. For it appears that Ericsson had invented this battery during the Franco-Russian War, and out of hostility to Russia had presented it to France, hoping thus to aid in the defeat of Sweden's hereditary foe. The invention, however, came too late to be of service and was preserved for another issue.

I was perfectly overjoyed when, at the close of the interview, Captain Ericsson entrusted the box with its precious contents to my care. You doubtless will remember my delight with the plan of the *Monitor*, as I followed you to Hartford, where you were spending a few days, and astounded you by saying that the country was safe because I had found a battery which would make us masters of the situation, so far as the ocean was concerned. I left New York that night and went to Hartford direct, without stopping at my home in New Haven, so eager was I to save time in bringing this great discovery to the knowledge of the Navy Department.

You were much pleased and urged me to lose no time in presenting the plan to the Naval Board at Washington. I at once secured the co-operation of wise and able associates, in the persons of the late Hon. John A. Griswold, and John F. Winslow, of Troy, both friends of Governor Seward (Secretary of State) and large manufacturers of iron plates, etc. Governor Seward furnished us with a strong letter of introduction to President Lincoln, who was at once greatly pleased with the simplicity of the plan, and agreed to accompany us to the Navy Department at 11 A.M. the following day, and aid us as best he could. He was on hand promptly at 11 o'clock—the day before your return from Hartford. Captain Fox (Assistant Secretary of the Navy) together with a part of the Naval Board were present.* All were surprised with the novelty of the plan. Some advised trying it ; others ridiculed it. The conference was finally closed for that day by Mr. Lincoln's remarking :

"All I have to say is what the girl said when she stuck her foot into the stocking, It strikes me there's something in it ! " †

The following day Admiral Smith convened the full board, and I presented as best I could the plan and its merits, carefully noting the remark of each member of the board. I then went to my hotel quite sanguine of success, but only to be disappointed the following day.

* Several naval officers were also present unofficially.

† Mr. Bushnell was given a pasteboard model of the *Monitor*, admirably illustrating the easy method of training the guns by rotating the turret. It was this that struck Lincoln, and which he held in his hand when he remarked about the girl and her stocking.

For during the hours following the last session I found that the air had been thick with croakings that the department was about to father another Ericsson failure.

Never was I more active than in proving that Ericsson had never made a failure; that on the contrary he had built for our Government the first steam war propeller ever made; that the bursting of the gun was no fault of his, but of the shell, which was not made strong enough to prevent its flattening up with the pressure of the explosion behind it, making the bursting of the gun unavoidable; * that his caloric principle was a triumphant success, but that no metal had yet been found to utilize it on a large scale. I succeeded at length in getting Admirals Smith and Paulding to promise to sign a report advising the building of one trial battery *provided* Captain Davis would join with them. On going to him I was informed that I might "take the little thing home and worship it, as it would not be idolatry, because it was in the image of nothing in the heaven above or on the earth beneath or in the waters under the earth."

One thing only yet remained to be done. This was to get Ericsson to come to Washington and plead the case himself. This I was sure would win the case, and so informed you, for Ericsson is a full electric battery in himself. You at once promised to have a meeting at your own room if I could succeed in inducing him to come. This was exceedingly doubtful; for so badly had he been treated, and so unmercifully maligned in regard to the *Princeton*, that he had repeatedly declared that he would never set foot in Washington again.

Nevertheless, I appeared at his house next morning precisely at nine o'clock, and heard his sharp greeting:

"Well, how is it?"

"Glorious," said I.

"Go on! go on," said he with impatience. "What did they say?"

"Admiral Smith says it is worthy of the genius of an Ericsson."

The pride fairly gleamed in his eye.

"But Paulding—what did he say of it?"

"He said it was *just* the thing to clear the rebels out of Charleston with."

"How about Davis?" he inquired, as I appeared to delay a moment.

"Captain Davis," said I, "wants two or three explanations in detail that I couldn't give him, and Secretary Welles wishes you to come right on and make them before the entire board in his room at the Department."

"Well, I'll go, I'll go to-night."

* Mr. Bushnell might have said further that it was not Ericsson's gun that burst, but the one Stockton had copied from it, and which had, in some way, been so injured in the forging that the crystals were of abnormal size. Nor was it reinforced as Ericsson's gun was.

From that moment I knew that the success of the affair was assured. You remember how he thrilled every person present in your room with his vivid description of what the little boat would be, and what she could do, and that in ninety days time she could be built, although the rebels had already been four months at work on the *Merrimac* with all the appliances of the Norfolk Navy Yard to help them. You asked him how much it would cost to complete her. Two hundred and seventy-five thousand dollars he said.

Then you promptly turned to the members of the Board, and one by one asked them if they would recommend that a contract be entered into for her construction with Captain Ericsson and his associates. Each one said, " Yes, by all means." And then you told Captain Ericsson to start her immediately ; and the next day in New York a large portion of every article used in her construction was ordered, and a contract immediately entered into between Captain Ericsson and his associates and T. F. Rowland at Greenpoint, for the most expeditious construction of the most formidable vessel ever made.

It was arranged that after a few days I should procure a formal documentary contract from the Naval Board, to be signed and executed by the Secretary of the Navy, Captain Ericsson, and associates.

I regret that this part of the matter has been misunderstood and misjudged, as though you had made terms heavier or the risk greater than you ought. The simple fact was that after we had entered upon the work of construction, and before the formal contract had been awarded, a great clamor arose, much of it due to interested parties, to the effect that the battery would prove a failure and disgrace the members of the Board for their action in recommending it.

For their own protection, therefore, and out of their superabundant caution, they insisted on inserting in the contract a clause requiring us to guarantee the complete success of the battery, so that in case she proved a failure Government might be refunded the amounts advanced to us from time to time during her construction. To Captain Ericsson and myself this was never an embarrassment. But to Mr. Winslow, as indeed to Mr. Griswold also, it seemed that the Board had asked too much. But I know that the noble old Admiral Smith never intended that we should suffer. And among the many fortunate things that the nation had occasion to be grateful for—like the providential selection as President in those dark days of the immortal Lincoln, who knew how to select a man for the head of the navy who united diplomatic skill and judgment with absolute promptness, with a private Secretary [Mr. W. Faxon], who never left his desk at night with a thing undone that could be done to assure success that day—was the appointment of Admiral Smith to the charge of the Navy Yards, who always seemed to sleep with one eye open, so constant was his watchfulness and so eager his desire that the entire navy should be always in readiness to do its part in the overthrow of the Rebellion.

I am confident that no native-born child of this country will ever forget the proud son of Sweden, who could sit in his own house and contrive the three thousand different parts that go to make up the complete hull of the steam battery *Dictator*, so that when the mechanics came to put the parts together not a single alteration in any particular was required to be made. What the little first monitor and the subsequent larger ones achieved is a part of history.

One of my associates—as noble and generous a man as it is the lot of one ever to meet on earth—John A. Griswold, has gone to his rest, and fast shall we each and all follow, but it may be a pleasure to those who should love our memory to find with your preserved records of those trying times this memorandum of the unrecorded private negotiations that resulted in the opportune meeting of the "cheese-box" on a raft with the ponderous *Merrimac* at Hampton Roads March 9, 1862.*

Ericsson proceeded to Washington on the night of September 13, 1861, arriving there the next morning after the tedious journey in ill-ventilated and over-crowded cars, which was the penalty of a summons to the capital in those days. With him journeyed the usual crowd of soldiers hastening to join their regiments; office-seekers, loaded down with testimonials as to their "claims;" civilians of every grade—eager to enlighten the Government with their wisdom, to assist it with offers of service, or to worry it with crude suggestions as to the conduct of the war. To the authorities of Washington the great engineer was only one of the motley gathering of patriots, to whose suggestions, to whose entreaties, and to whose reproaches even they had grown accustomed and indifferent. He proceeded at an early hour upon his arrival in the capital to the Navy Department. Describing his reception there, in a private letter he says:

NEW YORK, November 16, 1877.

MY DEAR SIR: I enclose extract of Mr. Bushnell's letter to Ex-Secretary Welles concerning the *Monitor*. As Mr. B. only relates his own personal experience, I have to add that on going to Washington and entering the room occupied by the Board over which Commodore Smith presided I was very coldly received, and learned to my surprise that said Board had actually rejected my *Monitor* plan, presented by Mr. Bushnell. Indignant, my first resolve was to withdraw, but a second thought prompted me to ask why the plan was rejected. Commodore

---

* This is printed from a MS. copy found among Ericsson's papers.

Smith at once made an explanation showing that the vessel lacked stability. This warmed me up, inducing me to enter on an elaborate demonstration proving that the vessel had great stability. My blood being well up, I finished my demonstrations by thus addressing the Board :

"Gentlemen, after what I have said, I deem it your duty to the country to give me an order to build the vessel before I leave the room."

The three commodores then entered into some conversation among themselves which I did not take note of, at the conclusion of which I was asked to call again at 1 P.M. On making my appearance Commodore Paulding called me into his room and in a very cordial manner asked me to repeat my explanation about the stability of the vessel. I complied, having in the meantime drawn a diagram presenting the question in a very simple form. My explanation lasted about twenty minutes, at the end of which the frank and generous sailor said :

"Sir, I have learned more about the stability of a vessel from what you have said than I ever knew before."

Commodore Smith then desired me to call again later in the day. On making my second appearance I was asked to step into Secretary Welles's room, who briefly told me that the commodores had reported favorably and that accordingly he would have the contract drawn up and sent after me to New York, desiring me in the meantime to proceed with the work. I returned at once, and before the contract was completed the keel-plate of the intended vessel had already passed through the rollers of the mill. Little did I dream that the contract would contain a clause compelling my associates to guarantee the success of the vessel, and in case of the stipulations about invulnerability, etc., etc., not being fulfilled, to refund the money advanced by the Department during the progress of the work. Had Secretary Welles on calling me into his room told me that such a guarantee would be demanded, the *Monitor* would not have been built.

One word more. The *Monitor* was brought under the enemy's guns at Hampton Roads before the last instalment of the contract had been paid !

The foregoing will enable you to form your own judgment as to the merit due to the Navy Department in the *Monitor* matter. Let me observe, however, that in building other vessels I was warmly and cordially supported by the Assistant Secretary, Mr. G. V. Fox.

Yours very truly,

J. ERICSSON.

P.S.—I have had neither time nor inclination to make a fair copy of the foregoing communication in my own hand.

Captain E. P. DORR, Buffalo.

CHAPTER XVI.

BUILDING THE FIRST MONITOR.

Partnership with Messrs. Bushnell, Winslow, and Griswold.—Interview with Thomas F. Rowland.—Laying the Keel of the *Monitor.*—Building and Launching of the Vessel.—Mishaps by the Way.—Herculean Labors.—Doubts and Criticisms of Commodore Smith.—Payments for the Vessel Delayed.—Cost and Profit.

IN a letter written April 25, 1862, Ericsson said: "A more prompt and spirited action is probably not on record in a similar case than that of the Navy Department, as regards the Monitor. The committee of naval commanders appointed by the Secretary to decide on the plans of gunboats laid before the Department occupied me less than two hours in explaining my new system. In about two hours more the committee had come to a decision. After their favorable report had been made to the Secretary I was called into his office, where I was detained less than five minutes. In order not to lose any time the Secretary ordered me to 'go ahead at once!' Consequently, while the clerks of the Department were engaged in drawing up the formal contract the iron which now forms the keel-plate of the *Monitor* was drawn through the rolling mill." This was said at a time when the country was all aglow with the success of Ericsson's opportune little vessel, and it does not conflict with the fuller statement of a later date in the last chapter.

The keel was laid October 25, 1861, steam was applied to the engines December 30th, the *Monitor* * was launched Jan-

---

* The origin of the name is explained by this letter to Gustavus V. Fox, Assistant Secretary of the Navy :

NEW YORK, January 20, 1862.

SIR : In accordance with your request, I now submit for your approbation a name for the floating battery at Greenpoint. The impregnable and aggressive character of this structure will admonish the leaders of the Southern Rebellion that the batteries on the banks of their rivers will no longer present

nary 30, 1862, and practically completed February 15, 1862. She went on her first trial trip and was turned over to the Government February 19, 1862. She was put into commission under the command of Lieutenant John L. Worden, U.S.N., February 25, 1862. Her steering gear was adjusted on a second trial; on her third, March 4th, she tried her guns, and a board of naval officers who conducted the trial reported favorably upon her performance. Professor MacCord, who was Ericsson's assistant at the time he built the *Monitor*, has given some interesting particulars of the circumstances attending its construction.

Ericsson followed it with keen and critical eye until the launch, and then his visits to the ship-yard became infrequent. As the "*Monitor* type" of engine had already been fully tested in the *Judith*, the *Daylight*, and in other vessels, he contented himself with the report of the Government engineers on the one in the new battery. When the trial trip came, neither engine nor steering gear worked properly, and one of the daily papers made it the text of a "crushing" article under the heading of "Ericsson's Folly." Her designer was called an incapable schemer, and sternly rebuked for the sin of wasting the resources of the country.

The motive engines were not in proper adjustment, the steering gear would not work freely, and between the two the vessel proved unmanageable.

The events of that dismal day must have vexed Ericsson's very soul, but the manner in which he bore them was strikingly characteristic. Had they been trifling things he would have been exasperated, as his custom was, and exasperating, too, when small affairs went wrong; but under heavy burdens his broad shoulders never bent, and he looked always squarely in the face of grave misfortunes with calm and resolute eyes. It is true that on his return to Franklin Street, where he then resided, there was a somewhat portentous cloud upon his face, and no wonder; but it was not the forerunner of a storm.

barriers to the entrance of the Union forces. The iron-clad intruder will thus prove a severe monitor to those leaders. But there are other leaders who will also be startled and admonished by the booming of the guns from the impregnable iron turret. "Downing Street" will hardly view with indifference this last "Yankee notion," this monitor. To the Lords of the Admiralty the new craft will be a monitor, suggesting doubts as to the propriety of completing those four steel clad ships at three and a half million apiece. On these and many similar grounds, I propose to name the new battery *Monitor*.

Your obedient servant,

J. ERICSSON.

The drawings, for whose accuracy the draughtsman was responsible, were found to be correct and the error was traced to a superintendent of the engine works, whom Captain Ericsson had once described as "too stupid to make a blunder." His error was so quickly rectified that it alone would not have delayed the vessel. The rudder was found to be somewhat over-balanced, the weight forward of the rudder-post being too great. It was not the time nor was Ericsson the man to indulge in idle speculations as to the cause of this error, but, says Professor MacCord, "had he adopted the remedy suggested to him it is morally certain that the battle between the giant and the pygmy would not have occurred when and where it did. This remedy was neither more nor less than the replacing of the balanced rudder by one of different form. I do not know where the idea originated, nor do I say that any formal proposal was made, but in some way the Captain became aware of an intention of the naval authorities to have the vessel put in the dry-dock and fitted with a new rudder. The hot Scandinavian blood flushed his cheek, his eyes gleamed, his brow darkened; and this time the storm broke in all its fury. With the full volume of his tremendous voice, and with a mighty oath, he thundered: 'The *Monitor* is MINE, and I say it shall not be done.' Presently he added, in a tone of supreme contempt: 'Put in a new rudder! They would waste a month in doing that; I will make her steer just as easily in three days.' My recollection is that it was done in less time. No change in the rudder was even thought of, and the change in the steering-gear was the simplest possible. . . . Considering how precious were the moments then, the suggestion of a new rudder might well excite his indignation and disgust. But the Captain's wrath was chiefly roused by the idea of any official interference with the vessel, as yet unpaid for and wholly in his own hands; which was perfectly natural in view of his treatment by the Government in this and other matters."

To add to the chapter of blunders, Engineer Stimers on the trial trip temporarily disabled both gun-carriages by turning the compressor wheels the wrong way. Far the most important of these mishaps, that fixed the hour of the *Monitor's* appearance at the very crisis of fate, "was the trouble with the steering-gear, though from the simplicity of the remedy it might appear the most insignificant; and it was this that brought into the boldest relief the prominent traits of the Captain's character. His keen mechanical instinct, quick decision, firmness of resolve, his fiery spirit, his energy in action, were all conspicuous; but all these were dominated by self-reliance and his pride in originality.

"He loved to do his own work in his own way, and his fertility of expedient was something marvellous; to quote his own words on another occasion, 'If I ever do get into a scrape, I know exactly how to get out of it;' and men unlike him, as most men are, were more likely than he to follow the lines laid down by others. He had said, 'The *Monitor* is mine,' and his she was, in another and to him a far dearer sense; from turret to keel-plate, from rudder-shoe to anchorwell, every distinctive feature was the creation of his brain, every detail was stamped with the evidence of his handiwork." *

Under the hand of the master the work upon the battery was pushed to a speedy completion, in spite of miscarriages that would have been fatal to less able management. "They are amazed at Washington," wrote Mr. Griswold on January 8th, "that within the hundred days the battery will be completed."

Ericsson was officially notified, by letter dated September 21, 1861, that his proposition for an iron-clad gunboat had been favorably reported upon, and the actual contract for the construction of the battery was agreed upon October 4, 1861. On September 27, 1861, by formal contract with Messrs. Bushnell, Griswold & Winslow, he stipulated that all net profits or losses were to be divided equally among the four, the three associates agreeing to advance all money needed for the construction of the vessel. It was also agreed that in the event of the further construction of similar batteries the same division of loss or profits was to be made.

There was at this time at Greenpoint on the East River,

* Ericsson and His Monitors, by Professor Charles W. MacCord (formerly Chief Draughtsman for Captain John Ericsson), North American Review, October, 1889.

opposite New York, a young man named Thomas F. Rowland,
who had just commenced business as a ship-builder. He was
full of energy and enterprise, anxious to identify himself with
Government work, and had visited Washington with the model
of a vessel he proposed to build, having a turret mounted on a
railroad turntable. Though he carried with him an influential letter of introduction, he was not able to get near enough
to the Secretary of the Navy to present his plan until he met
Mr. Welles one evening at Willard's Hotel; then he had the
satisfaction of securing a prompt hearing, and an equally
prompt rejection of his proposals. On his return to New York,
Mr. Rowland was invited by Captain Ericsson to call upon him
at his office in Franklin Street. There he was shown the model
sent to Napoleon in 1854, and satisfied that he could claim no
priority for his idea of a turret. He was next informed of the
order received from the Government for an iron-clad battery.
Then turning to him, Ericsson said, "You want money; I want
fame. You can do the mechanical work on this vessel in your
ship-yard, but it is my conception, and it must be understood
that it was built here in my parlor." After some discussion it
was agreed that 7½ cents a pound should be paid for the work
upon the hull, and on October 25th an agreement to that effect
was entered into between John Ericsson and his associates, and
Thomas F. Rowland, Continental Iron Works, Greenpoint,
New York.

Another account states that on the day preceding this interview three strangers had appeared at Mr. Rowland's works
and sounded him upon the subject of the price he would
charge for building the hull of an iron vessel, suggesting 4½
cents per pound. When he called upon Ericsson the next
day he found the great engineer with head and body bent
over his drawing-table absorbed in his work upon the *Monitor*
plans. Glancing from his work for an instant, Ericsson said
abruptly:

"Tom, my boy, what are you going to charge me to build
my iron vessel?" Thinking of his previous interview with his
interrogators, who proved to be Messrs. Winslow, Griswold &
Bushnell, Rowland answered at a venture: "Nine cents a
pound." "Tut, tut, Tom!" cried Ericsson, without lifting his

eyes from his work, " it must be done for $7\frac{1}{2}$ cents ; " and this was the price agreed upon.

The contract with Mr. Rowland stipulated that the work was to be done to the satisfaction of Captain Ericsson, who reserved the right to determine what number of men should be employed, and the number of hours they must work to complete the contract in the shortest possible time, this being "in consideration of the liberal price paid."

Work was commenced on the day the contract was signed, October 25, 1861. The vessel was launched at Mr. Rowland's risk, and to prevent it from plunging under water when it slid from the ways, he constructed large wooden tanks to buoy up the stern as it entered the water. The turret was entrusted to the Novelty Iron Works, and all the machinery to Delamater & Co. By this division of labor work was hastened, still further time being gained by pushing the men night and day. The vessel in all of its parts was designed by Ericsson. Hull, turret, steam machinery, anchor-hoister, gun-carriages, etc., all were built from working drawings made by his own hands, furnishing the rare example of such a structure in all its details emanating from a single man. " The allegation that I received aid in designing the *Monitor*, and other work during the war," said Ericsson, in a letter of May 28, 1877, to General George B. McClellan, " is absolutely false. The entire labor of preparing the original working plans was performed by myself, every line being drawn by my own hand."

The details were sufficiently numerous. Besides keeping the several establishments at work, the terms of the agreements with Mr. Rowland and the Novelty Works required that they should be provided with the material which they were to put into shape for the hull and the turret-plates, bars, rivets, etc. Everything had been so carefully arranged by the able engineer that no trouble or delay was experienced in carrying out his part of the undertaking. Within one hundred working days from laying the keel-plates of the hull, the vessel was completed and the engines put in motion under steam. No greater despatch is recorded in the annals of mechanical engineering. The battery would have been finished even sooner than it was had the Government been more prompt in its payments under the contract, and enabled the contractors to keep a larger part of their force busied nights as well as days.*

Though the work was done in haste it was not done carelessly or incompletely. Time was saved, not by neglect of necessary finish but by simplifying the design of the vessel in every way to meet the required conditions. Thus the hull was merely an iron tank, with the sides sloping, instead of being rounded, so as to admit of employing ordinary mechanics under proper supervision. Good workmen were scarce, for the dominant military spirit had called to the field of battle the best men in every calling. While the work progressed at Greenpoint, L. I., Ericsson was there every day superintending it, and nearly all day. In the early morning, before going to the ship-yard, and far into the night after his return, he was occupied at his desk, drawing plans, preparing specifications, and conducting a constant correspondence with the Navy Department and others. A story is told in this connection illustrating his extraordinary physical strength. During one of his visits of inspection he tripped over a heavy bar of iron. Turning to two workmen, he asked them to remove it; but they said it was too heavy. Nettled at this refusal, and as if in contempt for the excuse, he made no reply, but stooping he picked up the bar with his own hands, carried it without assistance across the shop, and threw it on a scrap-heap. Amazed at this display of energy on the part of a sexagenarian the men procured assistance at noon time and weighed the bar, finding that it showed upon the scale nearly six hundred pounds.

From Ericsson's desk the drawings, numbering at least one hundred, went directly to the workshop, without waiting to be traced. Yet the plans were none of them mere copies from

---

* A similar feat had previously been performed in England, according to Sir Thomas Brassey, when in 1855-56, during the Crimean war, three ironclad floating batteries of 2,000 tons burden and 300 horse-power, the *Thunderbolt*, *Erebus*, and *Terror*, were built by private ship-yards in three months. What he includes in the term *built* he does not explain however. The *Monitor* was a vessel of 776 tons. Her extreme length was 172 feet; breadth, 41½ feet; depth of hold, 11½ feet; draught of water, 10½ feet; inside diameter of turret, 20 feet; height of turret, 9 feet; thickness of turret, 8 inches; side armor, 5 inches; deck plating, 1 inch; diameter of propellers (2), 9 feet; diameter of steam cylinders, 36 inches; length of stroke, 26 inches.

existing models. Everything had to be contrived anew, to meet the wholly novel conditions of life in a submerged structure. Even the waste of the ship's crew was gotten rid of by an ingenious contrivance, with an air-pump attached. By this means the natural law of hydrostatics was so far overcome as to admit of openings in the hull below the water-line. Waste matter was dropped into a pipe closed at the lower end. The upper end of the pipe was then shut, the lower end opened in its turn and the force-pump turned on, driving out the water in the pipe with its contents. A ship's surgeon who omitted an essential part of this ceremonial found himself suddenly projected into the air at the end of a column of water rushing up from the depths of the ocean and pouring into the ship.

The Original Monitor.

It was estimated by Isaac Newton, the first engineer of the *Monitor*, that she contained at least forty patentable contrivances. Ericsson was urged by Mr. Newton to secure patents for these, but he declined to do so. He was strangely neglectful all through life of this means of protecting his property rights. Numerous as were his patents, they by no means represented the full measure of his ingenuity, and many of them were taken out to secure for himself, as well as for others, the right to use his own inventions.

Ericsson's inventions were not the result of waking dreams, but of the studious application of the resources of a mind well stored with engineering and mechanical lore to the solution of new problems. He did not disregard precedent or experience, but he compelled them to his service instead of following them with blind obedience. It was his habit to wait until he was ready to present his engineering conceptions in practical form before announcing them.   Thus they had opportunity to ripen in his mind and to gain in clearness and completeness with growing experience.   The conception of a *Monitor*, as part of his mental history, was nearly half a century old when it was put into execution to meet the exigencies of war.

"You assume correctly," he wrote to Mr. G. V. Fox, on October 5, 1875, "that the plan of the *Monitor* was based on the observations of the behavior of timber in our great Swedish lakes.   I found that while the raftsman in his elevated cabin experienced very little motion, the seas breaking over his nearly submerged craft, these seas at the same time worked the sailing vessels nearly on their beam ends."

Working as he did, from first to last, upon plans already matured in his own mind, if they were not committed to paper, Ericsson always resented the imputation that his *Monitor* must be an imperfect vessel because it was built in haste.   "No improvement," he said in 1867, "has been made in the original *Monitor*.   On the contrary, that vessel was both theoretically and practically a more perfect vessel for defence than any of the numerous monitors afterward built by me, excepting only the pilot-house."   This was said in a letter written by his secretary at his dictation, and concluding as follows :

"Respecting this structure, Captain Ericsson particularly directs me to say, in reply to your impertinent insinuation that the present pilot-house of the monitor vessels is not his invention, that it originated with him and was perfected by him, and that whoever insinuates that this structure in its conception, theory, and every part of its detail, is not the invention of Captain Ericsson, utters a gross falsehood."

An entry in Ericsson's diary showed that in August, 1861, previous to the acceptance of his plans by the Navy Department, he spent a day in planning a stationary pilot-house to be placed on the top of the revolving turret.*   Time did not admit of the introduction of this feature into the original *Monitor*, and it was reserved for use in those of later construction.   The complications involved in adapting it to its intended position,

* A copy of this entry was published by Captain Ericsson in the Army and Navy Journal.

as well as the lightness of the original turret, made it necessary to adopt the necessary expedient which was justly subjected to the criticism of those who had to fight the *Monitor*. It is not true, however, that the plan of putting the pilot-house on top of the turret was first suggested by the engineer of the *Monitor*, after the vessel had gone into action.

Necessary changes were made in the plans of the vessel as the work progressed, to meet the emergencies of the time, and when she was completed slight defects were discovered, but these were easily remedied. The constructor was favored with numerous suggestions for change and supposed improvement, none of which were heeded.

Ericsson's work during that three months was herculean. Nerves and sinews needed to be of steel. The least halting, even trifling delay, confusion of mind, or weakness of body, and the story of Hampton Roads might not have been written. It was well for the United States that the question how to build an impregnable fighting vessel was entrusted to an engineer of such versatility, thorough experience, and freedom from prejudice in favor of existing forms. The entire resources of modern engineering knowledge were thus brought to bear upon the solution of the problem of an impregnable battery, armed with guns of the heaviest calibre then known, hull shot-proof from stem to stern, rudder and propeller protected against the enemy's fire, and above all having the advantage of light draught.

It was proposed to build a vessel that could navigate the shallow Southern rivers, and the draught was limited to eleven feet. This absolutely compelled the adoption of the plan of a sunken hull. It was manifestly impossible to carry the weight required to protect a high-sided vessel. The adoption of a covered cylindrical turret followed logically, from the necessity for protecting guns and gunners. The plan of revolving this turret on a vertical axis, was adopted to secure an all-around fire while the vessel remained stationary, as it was clearly impracticable to manœuvre the battery in narrow rivers. The slight draught of the vessel brought the propeller and rudder near the surface; to protect these the deck was extended over the hull at the stern and also at the bow, where the anchor, hanging in a cylindrical well, could be lowered and lifted by machinery within the hull without exposing the crew.

The steam machinery, as well as the quarters of the crew, were located below the water-line to protect them against shot, and they were further protected by extending the armored part of the vessel some distance over the sides. With this overhang, shot could not reach the vulnerable hull. Thus, as J. Scott Russell in his work on "Naval Architecture" declares, the *Monitor* is "a creation altogether original, peculiarly American; admirably adapted to the special purpose which gave it birth. Like most American inventions, use had been allowed to dictate terms of construction, and purpose, not prejudice, has been allowed to rule invention." The monitors are, Mr. Russell further says, "successful by the rigidity and precision with which they fit the end and fulfil the purpose which was their aim. By thus frankly accepting the conditions he could not control, the American did his work and built his fleet."

The Chief of the Bureau of Yards and Docks, who represented the Navy Department in the construction of the *Monitor*, was Commodore Joseph Smith, a noble sailor who had grown old in the service which he entered as a midshipman in the year 1809. He had been an officer for more than half a century, was thoroughly in sympathy with the traditions and prejudices of his profession, and though the earnest eloquence and able demonstration of Ericsson had for the moment convinced his judgment, there was an under-current of doubt, and this kept him constantly uneasy and distrustful. "The old Commodore is fidgety at times," wrote one of Ericsson's friends from Washington, "and may provoke you by his own anxieties, but he has confidence in you, and he has no confidence in anybody else. So give the old man his tether, and let him fret a little when he feels like it."

This encouragement to forbearance seems to have been needed, for the suggestions, doubts, and forebodings showered upon Ericsson from Washington, must have been trying to a man so overwhelmed with the responsibilities of a venturesome undertaking, in the success of which was involved not only his own reputation but the interests of a nation. September 25, 1861, Commodore Smith wrote:

> I am in great trouble from what I have recently learned, that the concussion in the turret will be so great that men cannot remain in it and work the guns after a few fires with shot. I presume you understand the subject better than I do.

It would have been well if he could have rested content with this conclusion, but his own conversion was recent, if hopeful, and his convictions were too feeble to enable him to resist the doubting suggestions of others. Ericsson's judgment upon this point was not founded on theory; it was the result of personal experience in firing heavy guns from little huts while he was an officer in the Swedish army. Yet he had the greatest difficulty in dispelling this obvious fallacy, as to the effect of firing guns in a turret with muzzle protruding, and it is not strange that Commodore Smith should have been affected by it. A few days later, October 11th, he wrote:

> I understand that computations have been made by expert naval architects of the displacement of your vessel, and the result arrived at is that she will not float with the load you propose to put upon her, and if she would she could not stand upright for want of stability, nor attain a speed of four knots. Relying upon your calculations, I had no computation of displacement made. I have had some misgiving as to her stability as well as sea-worthiness on account of the abrupt termination of iron to the wooden vessel; I have thought the angle should have been filled up with wood thus, to ease the motion of the vessel in rolling. I believe when you look into cause and effect you will come to the same conclusion. But if the whole thing is to be a failure this will be of little consequence. I am extremely anxious about the success of this battery. The Government wants some dozen of them if they prove successful. I want to go to New York, but I am now so afflicted with rheumatism I can but barely walk.

This was a personal letter, and in an official communication dated the same day Ericsson was reminded that, "You are responsible for the successful working of your vessel in all its parts." Three days later it was suggested that the vessel would "prove a failure," as the anxious Commodore had calculated her

displacement and found that she would not float. His estimate
of her displacement was thirteen hundred tons; the actual displacement of the vessel, when launched and in fighting trim,
with her stores, guns, and ammunition on board, was one thousand tons with 321 square feet of immersed midship section.
The Commodore suggested such a change in the vessel as
might in his opinion " save her from the possibility of failure ; " but which would, in the judgment of her better informed
designer, have sacrificed one of the essential features of his
system.

"I shall be subjected to extreme mortification," wrote Commodore Smith in this letter, " if the vessel does not come up
to the contract in all respects; having taken for granted as
correct your statement of the power and capacity of the battery,
without going into the calculations of weight and displacement,
and relying on the validity of the contract, I assumed a great
responsibility in recommending in haste (to meet the demands
of the service) your plan.   Your specifications state the engine
to have a power of four hundred horse. I am advised that
that power will not give the speed you guarantee.   I am aware
of your known reputation for scientific and practical skill as an
engineer, hence the reliance I placed upon you."

It does not appear to have occurred to the worthy Commodore that " extreme mortification," trying as that must be,
would be one of the least of Ericsson's sufferings if he should
fail in his great undertaking. And more than this, that he
had a claim to honor, and confidence, and consideration beyond
any that mere official position could give him. With an enormous burden upon him, and every minute intensely occupied,
Ericsson was obliged to deprive himself of necessary rest and
sleep that he might act as schoolmaster for the naval veteran,
and guide his timid steps along the path he was himself tread-
ing with the assurance of ripened experience. On October
11th, he sent to Commodore Smith this essay on stability, which
he found frequent occasion to repeat in his after-experience
with naval experts.

I have the honor of laying before you the enclosed transverse section
of my battery for the purpose of proving its stability. In order to do this

in the simplest manner, the vessel is represented as being heeled over one foot at the extreme beam. By reference to the plan you will find that at this extent of heeling over, the centre of gravity of the turret with contents is 3 inches out of perpendicular, while the centre of gravity of the vessel and machinery, deviates from the perpendicular line $1\frac{1}{4}$ inch in the opposite direction. The weight of turret being less than one-third of that of the vessel and machinery, it follows that the latter over-balances the former, the effect of which is to put the vessel on even beam. The force required to heel the vessel over as represented on the plan, you will thus perceive, receives no aid from the leaning of the turret.

The exact amount of stability we can ascertain by calculating how much more water is displaced on the low than on the high side of the vessel. At the heeling over assumed, one foot, that quantity will be half the area of the vessel at water-line, or $\frac{174 \times 41}{2} = 2,913$ cubic feet, which divided by 35 (cubic feet per ton) gives 83 tons of water displaced on one side more than on the other. Now, the centre of gravity of the water thus displaced is $11\frac{1}{4}$ feet from the centre line, and hence at that point it would require a weight of 83 tons to heel the vessel as shown. Were the weight applied at the extreme beam, 46 tons only would be required —46 tons is the weight of 690 men (at 15 men to the ton, the usual aver-age)—and hence to heel my battery over a single foot, 690 men must stand at the very extreme of the deck. It will be safe to assert that there is not now in the service of the United States any vessel of equal size that can compare in stability to the vessel under consideration.

Commodore Smith's reliance upon Ericsson's ability was not sufficient, however, to dispel his fears. "Excuse me for being so troublesome," he wrote October 15th, "but my great anxiety must plead my excuse. I have been urging the Ordnance De-partment to furnish the guns for your vessel, but the knowing ones say that the guns will never be used on her." "In a heavy sea," he wrote again, October 17th, "one side of the bat-tery will rise out of the water or the sea recede from it, and the wooden vessel underneath will strike the water with such force when it comes down or rolls back, as to knock the people on board off their feet." Unconvinced by Ericsson's demonstra-tions, the Commodore ended the discussion of this branch of the question by a letter dated October 19, 1861, in which he said oracularly : "We shall see, I have nothing more to say on the subject but that the Government will fall back on the con-tract in case of failure."

But even this comfortable assurance was not sufficient to

stay his criticism. Returning to the subject October 21st he said: "The more I reflect upon your battery, the more I am fearful of her efficiency." The "overhang" especially was full of gloomy suggestions, and he was confident that the iron plating of the battery would settle the sides of the wooden vessel beneath "so that her deck would after a time become much curved and finally break."

The prospect of asphyxia for the dwellers on the battery also disquieted the Bureau Chief. "Your plan of ventilation appears plausible," he wrote, " but sailors do not fancy living under water without breathing in sunshine occasionally. I propose a temporary house be constructed on deck which will not increase the weight of the vessel more than eight or ten tons." In answer to similar complaints of neglect of ventilation the answer was made that " more attention was paid to the ventilation of the first *Monitor* than to its fighting qualities." Commodore Smith's letters are quoted, not to reflect upon their author, but to show the *encouragement* under which Ericsson labored during this crisis of his life. Not a single word of good cheer appears in the series of letters sent to him from Washington, but he was kept constantly in mind that his fortune and his reputation would be the forfeit if he failed to fulfil the utmost letter of his contract. December 5, 1861, came a letter from the anxious Commodore saying:

"I saw Mr. Everett to-day, who says your turret will not be ready to leave his shop short of *thirty days*. I beg of you to push up the work. I shall demand heavy forfeiture for delay over the stipulated time of completion. You have only *thirty-nine days left*."

The time stipulated in the contract was exceeded a few days, for Ericsson was not able to telegraph until January 23d that the vessel was ready for launching. Meanwhile came a letter, dated January 14, 1862, saying, " the time for the completion of the shot-proof battery, according to the stipulations of your contract, expired on the 12th instant."

If the completion of the *Monitor* was delayed a few days beyond the date stipulated in the contract this fact would seem to be sufficiently accounted for by this communication addressed to Commodore Smith by Ericsson January 4, 1862 : " I beg most respectfully to observe that while the principal outlay has now been incurred in building the battery, only $37,-500 have as yet been paid by the navy agent, and that amount was not obtained until five weeks after the presentation of your order. In view of the large amount of funds thus called for from private sources, my contemplated organization and operation by what is called night gangs has been to some extent frustrated."

The total contract price for the vessel was $275,000, and this was to be paid in five instalments of $50,000 each and one of $25,000, twenty-five per cent. being reserved from each payment as security for the completion of the vessel. The warrants for the first of these payments of $37,500 ($50,000 less twenty-five per cent.) was drawn by the Navy Department November 25, 1861, and the others followed one another on the following dates, viz.: second payment, December 3d; third, December 17th; fourth, January 3, 1862 ; fifth, February 6th. Finally, March 3d, six days before the fight at Hampton Roads, a warrant for the sixth and last payment of $25,000 was drawn. But the dates drawing the warrants and of the actual receipt of the money were so widely separated that the fourth payment was due before the money for the first had actually been received. This necessitated advances which Mr. Winslow, one of the associates, was able to make through his official connection with a bank in Troy.

An estimate in Ericsson's handwriting, dated December 26, 1861, shows that on that date, and thus before the actual receipt of the first money on Government account, $158,043.42 had been expended on the battery. A portion of this was represented by bills not yet paid. This amount had increased on February 11, to $180,168, and there was owing, according to estimate, $14,832, making the total cost, as estimated at that date, $195,000. The actual figures were $195,142.60, leaving a net profit of $79,857.40. Of this Ericsson received as his one-fourth $19,964.35, besides $1,000 for engineering services. This result was due to the fact that he was not only a skilful engineer but an experienced constructor and contractor. With the price of everything changing with the fluctuations of gold, and Government credit in doubt, it was a hazardous business to estimate upon Government work.

The Bureau of Yards and Docks showed so strong a disposition to hold the associates in the building of the *Monitor* to the strictest letter of their contract that Mr. Griswold, who was the banker of the concern, naturally became uneasy, and on February 1, 1862, wrote to Ericsson from Troy, as follows:

> I think we should take decided ground with the Navy Department that before we place our battery in their hands (before it passes from our possession) we must have the amount due us less the twenty-five per cent. reservation. Unless we do this there is no predicting when we shall get our pay. They want the battery at once, and if they take it the least they can do is to pay what is our due. On *all considerations* this should *certainly be done.*

On February 8th the ever-vigilant Commodore Smith wrote from Washington an official letter, saying:

> I shall submit to the Secretary of the Navy whether or not further payments shall be approved and drawn for before a test of the vessel shall have been made, as the contract in regard to time has been forfeited. I trust the test will soon warrant the payment in full, but the Secretary must decide. I am aware that you have used your best exertions to forward the completion of the vessel.

Fortunately the Secretary was liberal in his view of the case, and on March 5th, four days before the contest in Hampton Roads, Commodore Smith wrote: "I enclose your bill for the sixth and last instalment approved for $18,750 ($25,000 less twenty-five per cent.), and have this day drawn in favor of the navy agent at New York for that amount.

The amount reserved was $68,750, and this was not paid, even by warrant, until March 14, 1862, or nearly a week after the *Monitor* had proved her quality in one of the most striking naval engagements the world has ever known, and the fame of Ericsson was sounded the world over.

On October 26, 1861, Commodore Smith had written:

> You are the last man I desire to contest engineering questions with. I am fully aware of your scientific knowledge, skill, and experience. In the matter of the success of the iron-clad vessels, my anxiety is very

great. I make suggestions, offer objections which are only intended for your consideration, but in nowise to control your action. The responsibility rests with you, and I would not change it if I could. Excuse my interference thus far, if I have annoyed you, and I will be silent in future.

The anxiety here expressed was shared by the entire Government, and at Washington every stage in the progress of the vessel toward completion was watched with the keenest interest. The story of the progress of the Confederate ram *Virginia* had come through the lines, and if faith in the *Monitor* was not abounding she was *all* the country had to depend upon in the coming contest with the Southern iron-clad. It was with a sigh of relief no doubt that Ericsson's censor wrote from the Bureau of Yards and Docks on January 29th, just as the *Monitor* was completed :

The *Merrimac* is out of dock and ready for her trial trip. I think the wrought-iron shot of the Ericsson battery will smash in her 2½-inch plates, provided she can get near enough to her, while the 9-inch shot and shells of the *Merrimac* will not upset your turret. Let us have the test as *soon as possible*, for that ship will be a troublesome customer to our vessels in Hampton Roads.

The criticisms of Commodore Smith, though always well meant, were sufficiently annoying. In spite of them the highest praise is to be given to this gallant sailor for the measure of faith he had in the *Monitor*, and his name will be associated with Ericsson's as that of one who helped him to his opportunity. The character of the man is illustrated by a story told of him in the account given by Gideon Welles of his experience as Secretary of the Navy.

On Sunday March 9, 1862, after the despatch had been received at Washington to the effect that the *Merrimac* had come out of Norfolk and destroyed the *Cumberland* and the *Congress* lying off Fort Monroe, Secretary Welles returned from the Department to his home, and stopping at St. John's Church, in front of the White House, called out Commodore Smith who was attending service there. He briefly related what had taken place and finally said that the *Congress*, commanded by Smith's son, Joseph, had surrendered. " What ! "

exclaimed the veteran," the *Congress* surrendered ; then Joe is dead." The Secretary tried to calm his deep emotion, and told him that perhaps his son was saved. " Oh, no," he exclaimed, " you don't know Joe as I do—he never would surrender his ship." And he did not. He was killed early in the action and his flag was struck by other hands. To such a father of such a son much more might well be forgiven.

CHAPTER XVII.

BATTLE BETWEEN THE MONITOR AND MERRIMAC.

Professional Ignorance on the Subject of Armored Vessels.—Ericsson's Mastery of the Subject.—The *Monitor* Intended for Farragut's Fleet before New Orleans.—Ordered to Washington.—Stopped en route at Fort Monroe.—Timely Arrival and Encounter with the *Merrimac.*—Turns the Tide of Battle.

WHILE the Confederate Government at Richmond was paying from its lean treasury the expense of completing an armor-clad, designed to break the blockade and secure the much-needed recognition of foreign governments, the Navy Department at Washington was trying to save a portion of its appropriation of a million and a half by throwing upon an association of private gentlemen the responsibility for the success or failure of the attempt which it had expressly sanctioned to meet the impending danger. Our beneficent Government assumed toward the man who had already rendered the country such essential service the attitude of the Oriental despot, who sends his soldiers to the field with the headsman following after as an admonition to zealous service.

It is all very well for Ericsson to commend the promptness with which the Navy Department acted in accepting his services. It took good care, through its faithful servant Commodore Smith, to constantly remind him that the risk was his, and not the Nation's. "The Government requires ninety days in which to test the vessel," wrote the Commodore, September 30, 1861. "So soon as the vessel is ready for service the Government will send her on the coast and put her before the enemy's batteries in the service for which you intend her. No other test can be made to prove the vessel and her appointments than that to which both parties agreed to expose her; in fact, it is the gist of the intentions of the contracting parties. The plan is novel, and because it is so, the Government requires the designer to warrant its success. Placing the vessel before an enemy's battery will test its capacity to resist shot and shell—that is the least of the difficulties I apprehend in the success of the vessel, but it is one of the properties of the vessel which you set forth as of great merit. The Government cannot consent to receive the vessel until she shall have been tested in the manner proposed." ·

In their report, dated September 16, 1861, the Board presided over by Commodore Smith had made frank avowal of ignorance of the subject they were selected to consider, a confession only creditable to them because of its perfect ingenuousness. No such ignorance prevailed in the Confederate Navy Department, and if the facts were not known at Washington it was only because our officials there refused to be enlightened. In a letter to Commodore Smith's Board, dated September 3, 1861, Ericsson, speaking from his large experience, had said :

In laying before you the accompanying plans and specifications of an impregnable battery for naval purposes I feel called upon to make the following remarks :

The wrought-iron ordnance of twelve inches calibre, planned by the writer already in 1840, practically established the fact that iron plates of four and one-half inches thickness could not resist projectiles from such heavy guns. Previous to the experiments at Sandy Hook, which you will remember were made in 1841 with the ordnance alluded to, I had determined theoretically that six inches thickness would be required to protect ships against the same, and that iron-plates without wooden support, unless made even thicker, could not withstand continued firing. Accordingly, the revolving turret of my proposed battery is made eight inches thick, in addition to which the outward curvature of the turret will on dynamic considerations materially assist the resisting capability of the iron. Apart from the great strength of the turret, it should be borne in mind that but few balls will strike so accurately in the centre of the turret as not to glance off by angular contact. The United States may justly claim to have been far ahead of the naval powers of Europe, who have just found out what we demonstrated twenty years ago.

"In respect to the impregnable nature of the battery proposed I will not enter on a demonstration before one so experienced as yourself. It will be all-sufficient merely to ask you to look carefully at the plan. It will, however, be proper for me to advert to the fact that the iron-clad vessels of France and England are utterly unable to resist elongated shot fired from the 12-inch guns of the battery. The 4½-inch plates of *La Gloire* or the *Warrior* would crumble like brown paper under the force of such projectiles, and at close quarters every shot would crush in the enemy's sides at the water-line. The opposing broadsides would be nothing more than the rattling of pebbles on our cylindrical iron turret, which, by the way, we can make twelve inches thick, as we have some three hundred tons buoyancy to spare. A small number of these batteries will make our great Atlantic cities absolutely safe against attack from steel-clad friends on the other side. As for the rebel fleet, protected by the stolen guns at Norfolk, we can split it into matches in half an hour ; and as for the rebels at New Orleans, we can go and take a look at their cotton-bags whenever we please if they had a thousand guns mounted on the shore of their great river.

So far as concerns the statements relating to the respective powers of armor and of guns, this was not speculation but the sober rehearsal of facts, and of facts which should have been understood at Washington. The Emperor Napoleon had already made his experiments, and the results of the trials of armor and guns at Vincennes, and of those to which Ericsson called attention, were part of the naval record. The destructive effect of shell firing against wooden ships had been demonstrated at Sinope in 1853, and even a quarter of a century earlier than this by the Russians during the Greek war of independence. The naval attack upon Sebastopol had failed, and the proposed attack upon Cronstadt had been abandoned, because of the inability of unarmored vessels to stand fire ; while even the imperfect batteries employed by the French at Kinburn, October 17, 1855, had given a foretaste of the quality of iron-clads.

The necessity for adopting some new form of meeting the changed conditions of naval warfare was obvious to every instructed observer ; and yet a proposition, coming from an engineer of approved ability in naval construction, and demonstrated by the strictest application of mathematical formulas, was objected to because it was " novel." There should have been ability somewhere in our Naval Administration to determine the prospective value of Ericsson's plans, and they should have been either accepted or rejected ; and if accepted, the inventor should have been held but to one condition, which was the fulfilment of the stipulations of his contract as to the char-

acter of the vessel he was to present for acceptance. The risk
of the result was for the Government to undertake, and especially at such a crisis.

It is marvellous that Ericsson should have accepted such
conditions after the experience he had had of Washington
methods. Nothing but the spirit to put "life itself" at the
disposal of the Government could have prompted the venture.
Commodore Smith proposed that he should turn his vessel over
to men prejudiced in advance against it, and anxious, not to
demonstrate its value, but to exaggerate to its discredit the accidents and miscarriages attending the trial of a new and novel
piece of machinery.

It was Providence that decreed the success of the *Monitor*,
and not the navy. During the period of peace preceding the
war, our navy "was always grasping at the shadow and leaving
the substance. The commodore of the period was an august
personage who went to sea in a great flag-ship, surrounded by a
conventional grandeur which was calculated to inspire a becoming respect and awe. As the years of peace rolled on, this
figure became more and more august, more and more conventional. The fatal defects of the system were not noticed until
1861, when the crisis came, and the Service was unprepared to
meet it; and to this cause was largely due the feebleness of
naval operations during the first year of the war. There seems
to have been a total want of information at the central office of
administration in reference to the existing demands of naval
war, and the measures necessary to put the machine into efficient operation." *

What a stirring up of dry bones there would have been
could Ericsson have been given absolute control of naval administration! But it was not to be. In spite of all the draw-
backs, perhaps his services were quite as efficient in the sphere
to which he was confined. Thanks to the success attending
him in Hampton Roads, on March 9, 1862, he was able to secure for the United States the unprecedented experience of
producing an entire fleet of war vessels, built on a new system,
and successful for the purpose intended, without expending a

* Professor J. R. Soley, now Assistant-Secretary of the Navy, in Battles
and Leaders of the Civil War, vol. i., p. 623.

single dollar on preliminary experiments. This, too, while England and France were wasting millions in unsuccessful efforts to adapt their navy to modern conditions. From the storehouse of his own fertile invention, his own prolific experience, Ericsson was able to produce, without hesitation or delay, every requirement for modern naval warfare. This record of his experiences has shown how complete was his equipment for the work in hand—so far exceeding that of any living man. His difficulties, as we shall see, were not so much in himself as in the inability of others to understand and apply his far-reaching conceptions.

Fortunately for the country, as well as for Ericsson, there was in the Navy Department, as assistant secretary, a gentleman, Gustavus Vasa Fox, whose experience as a naval officer on coast survey duty, in command of mail steamers, and in the war with Mexico, had given him a knowledge of nautical matters, and whose five years of civil life had dissevered him from the traditions and prejudices of the naval profession. It would appear that Mr. Fox was at first indisposed to accept Ericsson's ideas on the subject of armored vessels, or at least was more favorably inclined to those originating in the Navy Department.

Reporting the results of a visit to Washington, on behalf of Ericsson's battery, Mr. John F. Winslow wrote from Troy, January 10, 1862:

While I cannot say that I found Mr. F. unfriendly, still there was at first a loftiness of manner toward us, and a confidence in the bureau plan, that was to me amusing ; yet, finding him to be a really able man, and of controlling influence in matters relating to his bureau, I was determined he should either convert me to the bureau plan, or I would him to our plan, and therefore devoted all the time I could get him to appropriate to this object, and after more than five hours' consecutive discussion of all the points involved, I left him with an admission that he was only familiar with *sailing* and *defending* a ship ; that, as to the mechanics and architecture incident to a ship or steamer building, he professed to know but little, and so far as the mechanical and other arrangements of the Ericsson battery were concerned, he would concede to me that it appeared to embody all the features of success, and if on trial this was demonstrated, ours would be the plan to be adopted. This was the substance and meaning of his parting assurances to me, and though it cost me hours of animated and earnest colloquial effort, yet I made a convert of him, as I think, and felt abundantly compensated.

This conversion appears to have been complete, for Mr. Fox soon became Ericsson's earnest champion, and when the success of his battery was demonstrated, he gave him his unvarying support, until the termination of his connection with the Department, in 1866.

Of Mr. Fox, a member of Lincoln's cabinet said:

Fox was really the able man of the administration. He planned the capture of New Orleans, the opening of the Mississippi, and in general the operations of the Navy. He had all the responsibility of removing the superannuated and inefficient men he found in charge, had the honor of selecting Farragut, and was often consulted by General Grant. He performed all his duties with an eye only to the requirements of the hour, and with no view to the advancement of any interest of his own. Mr. ——————— entered the service a poor man, and retired with a fortune ; Mr. Fox abandoned a profitable position to assist the Government, and retired from office without a dollar in the world he could call his own.

It seems to have been the intention at first to send the *Monitor* when completed to join the expedition against New Orleans. For this expedition Farragut received his orders on January 20, 1862, ten days before the launching of the *Monitor*, arriving off the mouth of the Mississippi in his flag-ship *Hartford* a month later, or after the completion of the battery, February 6, 1862. Ten days before the battery was finished Mr. Fox wrote to Ericsson a hasty note, asking :

" Can your *Monitor* sail (steam) for the Gulf of Mexico by the 12th inst. ? "

The alarming news of the approaching completion of the *Virginia* at Norfolk soon changed this purpose, for on Wednesday, February 13th, Mr. Winslow wrote from Washington : " Mr. Fox told us to-day he should be at Fort Monroe on arrival of the battery there, to witness her behavior in passing the batteries along Elizabeth River and Craney Island on her way up to Norfolk. He expects she will leave New York early next week, and that a vessel will be chartered to convey her to Hampton Roads." A week later, on February 21st, Mr. Fox telegraphed to Ericsson from Washington : " It is very important that you should say exactly the day the *Monitor* can be at Hampton Roads.   Consult with Commodore Paulding."   Lieutenant Worden had hardly left the harbor of New York when orders came to change the destination of his vessel to Washington.   It was too late ; Commodore Paulding was unable to overtake him with the tug sent in hot pursuit.   Similar orders were sent to the senior naval officer at Hampton Roads, Captain John Marston, U.S.N., but he was wise enough to disregard them, acting upon the military principle that it is justifiable to disobey an order when it is obvious that it was given in such ignorance of the facts of the actual situation, that to carry it out literally would defeat the object intended.

The *Monitor* left New York Harbor on the afternoon of March 6, 1862, in tow of a tug, and accompanied by two naval steamers, the *Currituck* and *Sachem*.   The wind was moderate and the sea smooth, but twenty-four hours later both had so increased that the waves swept the deck and forced the water in considerable quantities into the vessel through the hawse-pipes and under the turret, and broke over the smoke-pipe six feet high, and the blower pipe, rising here only four feet above the low deck.   This stopped the blowers, and the furnaces having insufficient draught, the engine-rooms were filled with gas, and the engineer, Mr. Isaac Newton, and his assistants were so nearly suffocated that they were carried into the open air to the top of the turret, apparently lifeless.

The machinery being temporarily disabled the hand-pumps were set at work and the men occupied in bailing until a smoother sea was reached, the blower-bands repaired, and the machinery once more set in motion.   These mishaps were the result partly of defects in construction easily remedied, and partly of want of experience in handling so novel a craft.   The only man on board who thoroughly understood the characteristics of the vessel was Chief Engineer Alban C. Stimers, U.S.N., the naval inspector of iron-clads, who was on board as a passenger only.   The officers were : Lieutenants John L. Worden and Samuel Dana Greene ; Masters, Louis N. Stodder and John J. N. Webber ; Assistant Surgeon, Daniel C. Logue ; Paymaster, W. F. Keeler; First Assistant Engineer, Isaac Newton; Second Assistant Engineer, Albert B. Campbell; Third Assistant Engineers, R. W. Hands, M. T. Sunstrum. The crew of forty-three men were volunteers.

The dramatic incidents attending the arrival of the *Monitor* at Hampton Roads, on the evening of March 8th, have been fully described in contemporary annals. The story was told to Ericsson in a letter from Mr. Stimers, as follows:

Iron-Clad Monitor,

Hampton Roads, March 9, 1862.

My Dear Sir: After a stormy passage which proved us to be the finest sea-boat I was ever in, we fought the *Merrimac* for more than three hours this forenoon, and sent her back to Norfolk in a sinking condition. Iron-clad against iron-clad, we manœuvred about the bay here, and went at each other with mutual fairness. I consider that both ships were well fought. We were struck twenty-two times, pilot-house twice, turret nine times, deck three times, sides eight times. The only vulnerable point was the pilot-house. One of your great logs (nine by twelve inches thick) is broken in two. The shot struck just outside of where the captain had his eye, and disabled him by destroying his left eye and temporarily blinding the other. The log is not quite in two, but is broken and pressed inward one and a half inch. She tried to run us down and sink us as she did the *Cumberland* yesterday, but she got the worst of it. Her horn passed over our deck, and our sharp, upper-edged rail cut through the light-iron shoe upon her stem and well into her oak. She will not try that again. She gave us a tremendous thump, but did not injure us in the least, we were just able to find the point of contact. The turret is a splendid structure; I don't think much of the shield, but the pendulums are fine things, though I cannot tell you how they would stand the shot, as they were not hit.

You were very correct in your estimate of the effect of shot upon the man on the inside of the turret when it was struck near him. Three men were knocked down, of whom I was one. The other two had to be carried below, but I was not disabled at all, and the others recovered before the battle was over. Captain Worden stationed himself at the pilot-house, Greene fired the guns, and I turned the turret until the Captain was disabled and was relieved by Greene, when I managed the turret myself, Master Stoddard having been one of the two stunned men.

Captain Ericsson, I congratulate you upon your great success; thousands here this day bless you. I have heard whole crews cheer you; every man feels that you have saved this place to the nation by furnishing us with the means to whip an iron-clad frigate that was, until our arrival, having it all her own way with our most powerful vessels.

I am with much esteem,

Very truly yours,

CAPTAIN J. ERICSSON,   ALBAN C. STIMERS.

95 Franklin Street, New York.

In another account Mr. Stimers states that, during part of the voyage the sea was so high that the gunboats acting as convoys rolled so much that when they careened in one direction he could see under the bilge, and when the deck was toward him he could look down the main hold. "The motion of the *Monitor* was so easy and quiet that a glass inkstand stood upon a polished mahogany case on the table in the Captain's cabin, during the entire voyage, without slipping. At the same time the sea washed over the deck in the most terrific manner. All hands were at one time driven to the top of the turret by the escaping gas from the furnace fires. During the night the wire tiller ropes came off the wheel, and all hands were occupied during most of the night in hauling on the ropes by hand and readjusting them on the wheel."

The "Greene" referred to in Mr. Stimers' letter was Lieutenant S. Dana Greene, a young officer of the Navy then in his twenty-third year. He had volunteered to go in the *Monitor*, notwithstanding the many gloomy predictions concerning her, and had been ordered to her as executive officer at the request of Lieutenant Worden. In his account of the voyage of the *Monitor* to Hampton Roads, Lieutenant Greene says:

We left New York in tow of the tug-boat Seth Low at 11 A.M. on Thursday, March 6th. On the following day, a moderate breeze was encountered, and it was at once evident that the *Monitor* was unfit as a seagoing craft. Nothing but the subsidence of the wind prevented her from being shipwrecked before she reached Hampton Roads. The berth-deck leaked in spite of all we could do, and the water came down under the turret like a waterfall. It would strike the pilot-house and go over the turret in beautiful curves, and come through the narrow eyeholes of the pilot-house with such force as to knock the helmsman completely round from the wheel. . . . The water continued to pour through the hawse-hole, and over and down the smoke-stacks and blower-pipes in such quantities that there was imminent danger that the ship would founder.*

It was evident that Lieutenant Greene did not agree with Engineer Stimers' estimate of the *Monitor* as a fine sea-boat, and in an official report to the Department, March 27, 1862, he said: "I do not consider this steamer a sea-going vessel. During her passage from New York her roll was very easy and slow, not at all deep. She pitched very little and with no strain whatever. She is buoyant, and not very lively. The inconveniences we experienced can be easily remedied. But she has not the steam power to go against a head-wind or sea. . . . For smooth water operations, such as she was engaged in on the 9th inst., I think her a most desirable vessel."

In criticising a similar discrepancy of statement between the engineer and the commander of a later Monitor, concerning the injuries received by his vessel, Ericsson said: "I should rather trust to the judgment of a skilful practical engineer as to the real damage done, than to the opinion of the gallant commanders of these vessels, most of whom know nothing of mechanical matters. It has often given me pain to think that our fighting *machines* are entrusted to officers who know nothing of mechanics, and *therefore* have no confidence in their vessels."

In replying to Lieutenant Greene's criticisms upon the *Monitor*, he explains that he intended the sight-holes in the pilot-house to be five-eighths of an inch wide, affording a vertical view eighty feet high at a distance of only two hundred yards, and this his experiments had shown him was sufficient. A subsequent alteration in the sight-holes, accounted for the entrance of water, and for the injury done to the sight of the commander of the *Monitor*, by the explosion of a shell from the muzzle of a gun not ten yards distant.

Fortunately, the impression that the sight of one eye was destroyed was incorrect, though Worden will carry the scars of this fight with him to his grave. The turret of the *Monitor* was not carried on revolving rollers, but pivoted on the centre

---

* Battles and Leaders of the Civil War, vol. i., p. 721.

and slid on the smooth surface of a flat, broad ring of bronze, let in on the deck.   Before the vessel left New York, some "expert" at the Brooklyn Navy Yard inserted a plaited hemp rope between the base of the turret and the bronze ring, to shut out the small amount of water entering there.   It was expected that water would work its way through, as it was impossible to make a water-tight joint under a revolving turret, and pumps were provided to remove what little water entered.   It was necessary to widen the space between the turret and its base in order to make room for the rope packing, and as this washed out the result was the leak around the whole circumference of the turret, sixty-three feet, referred to by Mr. Greene, through which " the water came down under the turret like a waterfall."   The entrance of water through the hawse-pipe was not due to faulty construction; it resulted, Ericsson declared, " from gross oversight on the part of the executive officer—namely, in going to sea without stopping the openings around the chain cable at the point where it passes through the side of the anchor-well." *   During the passage from New York, the working gear of the turret was permitted to rust for want of proper cleaning and oiling, and it worked with so much difficulty during the engagement with the *Merrimac* that, but for the energy and determination of Engineer Stimers, it might not have revolved at all.

These are Ericsson's explanations, and such were some of the difficulties with which he contended in proving the value of his invention at the outset.   Again, the timid ordnance officers at Washington insisted on limiting to fifteen pounds the charge with the eleven-inch guns which was subsequently increased to fifty pounds.   The wrought-iron shot intended for the vessel were not used.   But for these departures from the design of Ericsson, Worden could have accomplished the expected result of splitting "the rebel fleet into matches in half an hour."

The veteran officer in command of the *Merrimac*, Admiral Buchanan, C.S.N., had been badly wounded by a rifle ball from the shore, during the fight of the day before with the

* See Ericsson's article on "The Building of the *Monitor*," in Battles and Leaders of the Civil War, vol. i., p. 730.

wooden vessels in Hampton Roads. His successor in command, Lieutenant Catesby Ap R. Jones, says of the *Monitor:* "She and her turret appeared to be under perfect control. Her light draught enabled her to move about us at pleasure. She once took a position for a short time where we could not bring a gun to bear upon her. Another of her movements caused us great anxiety; she made for our rudder and propeller, both of which could have been easily disabled. We could only see her guns when discharged; immediately afterward the turret revolved rapidly, and the guns were not again seen until they were fired. We wondered how proper aim could be taken in the very short time the guns were in sight. It did not appear that our shell had any effect on the *Monitor.* Musketry was fired at the look-out holes. She fired forty-one shots." * No serious damage was done to his vessel, he reports.

"A Confederate soldier, who from a safe position saw the fight," describing his experience, says:

And now we are at Newport News. The frigate *Cumberland* is struck below the starboard forechains; she reels, rolls, and goes down. And the flag of the *Congress* comes down by the run; soon she will make a brilliant bonfire to illuminate the Roads. And now for the *Minnesota.* But just here the pilots insist upon bringing to anchor while yet the daylight lasts. Our anchor is down under Sewell's Point, our ship unscratched by a pin. The fire of the *Cumberland* had killed two men and wounded five, and had also carried away the muzzles of two guns, but we never ceased firing them and the damage was wholly immaterial.

In the early morning, Jones gets under way to finish the *Minnesota.* We soon descry a strange-looking iron tower, sliding over the waters toward us, and we dash at it. It is the *Monitor,* which during the previous night had come in from sea, and which by the light of the burning *Congress* had been seen and reported by one of our pilots.

Nearly two hours have passed, and many a shot and shell have been exchanged at close quarters with no perceptible damage to either. The *Virginia* is discouragingly cumbrous and unwieldy. To wind her for each broadside fire, fifteen minutes are lost; while during all this time, the *Monitor* is whirling around and about like a top, and by the easy working of her turret, and her precise and rapid movement, elicits the wondering admiration of all. She is evidently invulnerable to our shell.

Our next movement is to run her down. We ram her with all our

* Southern Historical Society Papers, vol. xi., p. 21.

force.   But she is so flat and broad that she merely *slides* away from under our stern, as a floating door would slip away from under the cut-water of a barge ; all that we could do was to *push* her.   Jones now determines to board her ; to choke her turret in some way and lash her to the *Virginia.*   The blood is rushing through our veins while the shrill pipes and hoarse roar of the boatswains call "Boarders away ! " But lo ! our enemy has hauled off into shoal water, where she is as safe from our ship as if she were on the topmost peak of the Blue Ridge.   Ten feet of water against twenty-two.   The smoke from our gun was yet floating lazily away when Catesby Jones remarked to the writer : "The destruction of those wooden vessels was a matter of course, but in not capturing that iron-clad, I feel as if we had done nothing ; " and yet, he added, "give me that vessel and I would sink this one in twenty minutes." Every watch officer in our squadron would engage, under the forfeiture of his head, with a monitor to sink a *Virginia* every thirty minutes from dawn to dewy eve.   And this is said in no spirit of boasting.   A Nelson or a Collingwood, finding the enemy's upper works invulnerable, might have tried the lower ones ; they certainly would have done something with the divine inspiration of genius to make the best ship win.   But then, Nelsons and Collingwoods only appear every century or two.

The *Monitor* was fought with plenty of spirit.   She was also fought with a plentiful lack of judgment and common-sense, and ordnance-sense.   The great radical blunder was in failing to concentrate her fire. In two instances a second shot, striking near the first, weakened our shield and caused the backing to bulge inward, and made it very manifest that a third or fourth shot would have gone through.   In these cases the shot were delivered upon the strongest part of our roof ; and if they had struck her at water-line, where there was no protection whatever for the hull (for be it remembered that she had no knuckle), they would have gone through her as if she had been of paper.   A fighting, wide-awake seaman makes the enemy's water-line his first target, and that proving invulnerable, the guns and the guns' crew the second.   Now, the enormous weight of her shield and battery kept the *Virginia* all the time just hovering between floating and sinking ; a very few tons of water through the hole made by two, or even one, well-aimed shot from the splendid eleven-inch gun of the *Monitor*, and the *Virginia* would have gone to the bottom in five minutes.

With such a gun, and at such short range, it would be no great feat for an intelligent side-boy to plant his shot every time in the space covered by an ordinary straw hat.   The *Virginia* was so large a mark that almost every shot struck her somewhere ; but they were scattered over the whole shield on both sides, and were therefore harmless.   To point her gun in our direction and fire on the instant, without aim or motive, appeared to be the object.   The turret revolving rapidly, the gun disappears only to repeat in five or six minutes the same hurried and necessarily aimless, unmeaning fire.   She could assume and keep whatever position she pleased, for with her short keel and fine engines she could play around us like a rabbit around a sloth. Once during the fight she took such a position that we could not bring a single gun to bear on her. Why did she not with common-sense keep it, and with perfect security, deliberately plant her shot where she pleased, almost to an inch?

She fired, all told, during the fight forty-one shots (taking her time, about one fire in six minutes), and any three of them properly aimed would have sunk us, and yet the nearest shot to the water-line was over four feet. Our rudder and propeller were wholly unprotected, and a slight blow from her stem would have disabled both and ended the fight. Every time the *Virginia* went to cruise in the Roads under Tatnall we bade her an affectionate good-by, we never expected to see her again. In short, considering that at noon on March 8, 1862, the *Monitor* was by immense odds the most formidable vessel of war on this planet, and that our ship was comparatively a ship of glass, and that, doing us no harm and wholly unharmed herself after four mortal hours of battle, she runs away and gives us the fight, it is impossible to conceive in what manner she could have been more inefficiently fought.*

"If that splendid invention, as we freely admit she was for smooth water, had been fought as she ought to have been," this writer concludes, "it might have saved them 50,000 men. Engaging our handful with a few brigades, McClellan might have walked past us to Richmond with the rest of his army almost any morning before breakfast."

In justice to the officers commanding the *Monitor*, First Lieutenant Worden and then Lieutenant Greene, it should be remembered that they were forced into a fight immediately upon their arrival in Hampton Roads, after a fatiguing sea voyage, under singularly trying circumstances, and with a vessel whose peculiarities they had no time to investigate. "All the men," wrote Isaac Newton, the engineer of the vessel, "were nearly exhausted. I, for one, was sick on my back, with but little hopes of being up in a week, but a short time before the action." "The *Merrimac*," he further says, "was entirely in our power when she hauled off, but orders were imperative to act on the defensive." The commander of the *Merrimac*, Catesby Jones, testified before a naval court that the *Monitor* ought to have sunk his vessel in fifteen minutes. Mr. Alban

* Wm. Norris in Southern Magazine, Baltimore, November, 1874, pp. 181, 182.

C. Stimers, speaks of meeting Mr. Jones many times after the war, and talking over the engagement. On the last occasion, said Mr. Stimers (1872), he remarked: "The war has been over a good while now, and I think there can be no harm in my saying to you that, if you had hit us twice more as well as you did the last two shots you fired, you would have sunk us." *

John S. Porter, naval constructor of the Confederate States, reported that after the engagements of March 8 and 9, 1862, he put the *Virginia* on the dry dock, and found she had ninety-seven indentations on her armor from shot, twenty of which were from the 11-inch guns of the *Monitor*. Six of her top layers of plates were broken by the *Monitor's* shot, and none by those of the wooden vessels. None of the lower layer of plates were injured.

Mr. Newton's statement concerning the defensive rôle of the *Monitor* is fully confirmed by Assistant Secretary Fox. In a letter to Captain Ericsson, he says: "I wrote the order forbidding the *Monitor* going into the upper roads to meet the *Merrimac*. Why? Because I had pledged McClellan that the *Merrimac* should not disturb his military manœuvres, and to that obligation all naval operations were subordinate. We fulfilled our duty, and kept her in until she committed 'hari kari.'" President Lincoln had also given orders that the *Monitor* should take no risks that could be avoided.

While the contest in Hampton Roads served to direct the attention of all the world to the necessity for making a complete change in naval armaments, it did not fully illustrate the possibilities of the monitor system. When his vessel had passed from the hands of Ericsson, it was beyond his control. He had done his part in furnishing an impregnable floating battery, carrying guns that were equal to the task of destroying the enemy's vessel; he could do no more. The wave of rejoicing which swept over the North was due not so much to the achievement of the *Monitor*, fought as she was, as to the sense of relief at the discovery that the Government had under its control at least one vessel that could not be destroyed by

* Letter of Alban C. Stimers to Isaac Newton, dated New York, December 15, 1876.

the *Merrimac*. The timid counsels prevailing at Washington, prevented the contest from being brought to the issue which Ericsson intended. Though the necessities of the times may have required this, the result was not less disappointing to him.

"The *Monitor* only appears upon the scene," says the Confederate writer here quoted, "after we have been on the rampage for a whole day; have cleared out everything in the Roads—men-of-war, transports, traders, and have done the enemy all possible injury, material and moral. Stocks fall ten per cent. in an hour, gold rises faster, and such a panic prevails as was never known before or since."

Secretary Welles, describing a cabinet meeting called by Mr. Lincoln on receipt of the news of the first day's disaster, says: "Mr. Stanton said: * 'The *Merrimac* will change the whole character of the war; she will destroy, *seriatim*, every naval vessel; she will lay all the cities on the seaboard under contribution. I shall immediately recall Burnside; Port Royal must be abandoned. I will notify the governors and municipal authorities in the North to take instant measures to protect their harbors. I have no doubt that the monster is at this minute on her way to Washington, and '—looking out of the window which commanded a view of the Potomac for many miles— 'not unlikely we shall have a shell or a cannon-ball from one of her guns in the White House before we leave the room!' Mr. Seward, usually buoyant and self-reliant, overwhelmed with the intelligence, listened in responsive sympathy to Stanton, and was greatly depressed, as indeed were all the members."

It is true that the Confederate writer claims the victory for the *Virginia* in this battle: a battle described by him as "revolutionizing in an instant the whole science of naval warfare; more memorable than any sea-fight of history, more pregnant of consequences," and one to be "remembered to the latest posterity as the prominent naval event of our times." This is not worth disputing over. The prestige of victory was with the *Monitor*, and it is that vessel, and not the *Merrimac*, that revolutionized naval ideas and influenced naval construction. The one was a rude machine hastily improvised to

* Welles's Lincoln and Seward.

Battle between the Monitor and Merrimac: Hampton Roads, Va., March 9, 1862.

meet an emergency ; the other the expression of the carefully
matured plans of the ablest and most experienced worker in
the field of naval construction.   The *Virginia*,* a few weeks
later, and without doing further damage, sank beneath the
waters of Chesapeake Bay, to be thenceforth remembered only
as the antagonist of the *Monitor ;* Ericsson's Battery established a type whose influence upon naval construction has not
yet passed away.

"The *Monitor*," said Admiral Luce, in a paper read before
the Naval Institute, April 20, 1876, "was the crystallization of
forty centuries of thought on attack and defence, and exhibited
in a singular manner the old Norse element of the American
Navy ; Ericsson (Swedish, *son of Eric*) built her ; Dahlgren
(Swedish, *branch of a valley*) armed her ; and Worden (Swedish, *wordig, worthy*) fought her.   How the ancient skalds
would have struck their wild harps in hearing such names in
heroic verse !   How they would have written them in 'immortal runes ! ' "

"So of the *Monitor*, Minotaur old Mr. Quincy said to me
it should have been, in its appearance in part of the great meg-
alosaurus or deinotherium, which came out in scaly armor that
no one could pierce, breathing fire and smoke from its nostrils ;
is it not the age of fable and of heroes and demigods over
again ? " †

* This vessel is indifferently known as the *Merrimac* or *Virginia*.   She
was the U.S. screw steamer *Merrimac* of 3,200 tons, 40 guns, built in 1855,
and captured with Norfolk, Va., 1861.   When she was razeed and converted
into an armored vessel, she was rechristened *Virginia*.

† See Letter of Oliver Wendell Holmes, in The Correspondence of John
Lothrop Motley.

CHAPTER XVIII.

THE SUCCESS OF THE MONITOR.

FOLLOWING the success of the *Monitor*, there swept in
upon Ericsson a great tide of congratulation and applause.
All of the "loyal" papers were filled with praises of him and
glorification of his *Monitor*, and of her officers and crew.
"The joyous news was flashed through the North, and now
from Congress and State Legislatures, now from Chambers of
Commerce and Boards of Trade, now from public meetings
and societies convened for the purpose, thanks and laudations
were poured upon the *Monitor*—Ericsson, her inventor, Worden, her commander, Greene, her executive officer, Newton,
her chief engineer, Stimers, the engineer detailed to accompany
and report upon her, and who worked the turret. All the
officers, in short, and the crew shared the honors. The President, members of his cabinet, many of the diplomatic corps,
officers of both services, and ladies too, crowded to see the new
engine of warfare and to view with their own eyes the place of
the conflict of Hampton Roads."

Stimers wrote from on board the *Monitor* in Hampton
Roads, March 13, 1862: "You can form no idea of how very
grateful the thousands of people here are to you for having
produced this vessel. General Wool" (then commanding the
Department of Virginia, with headquarters at Fort Monroe)
"told me he considered you the greatest man living. General
Mansfield said to me that our battle was of more importance
than if the whole army of the Potomac had moved success-

fully against the enemy. We are remarkably popular on shore here, and I confess it made me very proud when such men as General Wool and General Mansfield grasped me by the hand with both their own, and told me they were very proud to make my acquaintance."

Ericsson's personal friends were naturally delighted at finding all the world joining with them in proclaiming his masterly ability, already shown in so many ways but so imperfectly recognized. "God bless you, Captain," wrote Professor Mapes, on the day after the fight; "you have long deserved the gratitude of mankind, and now you have been able to appeal to the keenest nerve of human susceptibility and they can no longer withhold the full measure of praise so long and so justly due to your genius and assiduity."

From Rome, John O. Sargent wrote, March 31, 1862:

Private letters received here state that both Washington and New York were in a state of great consternation when it was known that the *Cumberland* and *Congress* had been sunk, and that the relief when the achievement of the *Monitor* was known was indescribable. Your triumph has been complete. The opinion is generally entertained here that you were on board. I hope not. It is an awful pill for John Bull. The *Times* is sneaking about it as usual, and gives the world to understand that the *Merrimac* was only disabled by "another iron-clad frigate" —not wishing it to appear that this little gunboat would handle the *Warrior* or *La Gloire* as well as the *Merrimac*. Epes wrote me on March 11th, that the one name on everybody's lips for the last two days has been Ericsson's. Ericsson is hailed as the great deliverer. The old fogies who have opposed him are humbled and silenced. Hurrah! The salvation of fleets was never carried in so small a compass before. What would not the *Merrimac* have done but for the timely appearance of the *Monitor*?

Two years later Mr. Sargent wrote from Paris that no other event of the war had created more excitement and interest in Europe.

From Ericsson's native land came numerous congratulations, and these he valued most highly. The Consul of the United States at Stockholm wrote to the Department of State at Washington, saying:

I have the honor to inform you that the delight of the Swedes in regard to the success of the *Monitor* in her combat with the *Merrimac* is manifesting itself to-day on 'Change, by the raising of a subscription for a large and splendid gold medal which is intended to be transmitted to America and presented to Mr. Ericsson, the constructor of the *Monitor*. The Swedish Government has had for some time the intention of enlarging her navy, and for this purpose has had in existence a committee of scientific gentlemen, whose duty it was to examine and report upon the best and most practical character of ships for construction; but the result of the action between the *Monitor* and the *Merrimac* has suddenly brought the labors of the committee to a stand, and they have determined to make no report until the result of further trials with Ericsson's invention are made known. The contest above alluded to has proved most fortunate for Sweden, as it has undoubtedly saved her an immense outlay in a comparatively useless direction; hence the Swedes and the Swedish Government have good reason to be truly thankful to Mr. Ericsson and the American Government, for having inaugurated a principle which will in the end save them so much money.

Among Ericsson's English friends was Sir Charles Fox, to whom he had given his first employment as a civil engineer, who was subsequently knighted for his work in connection with the Great Exhibition in Hyde Park, 1851, and whose name is connected with many extensive railroads and other engineering works. From London Sir Charles sent his greetings to his old friend, saying:

SPRING GARDEN, LONDON, June 6, 1862.

MY DEAR SIR: I have been wishing to write to you for some time past, to offer you my congratulations on the success of the *Monitor*, which I assure you afforded me much satisfaction, as in fact anything would do which tended to advance the welfare of one whose friendship I shall always look back upon with much satisfaction as having been manifested at a period when it was of the greatest value to me and in so disinterested a manner. Not long since I went to post a letter at Charing Cross, when at the same moment a lady also dropped a letter into the box. We accidentally looked at each other, when I saw that I was recognized, and upon looking more closely I found myself face to face with Mrs. Ericsson, whom I had not seen for many years. I at once received the kindest invitation to call upon her at her residence at Kensington, of which I was not long in availing myself, and was pleased to find your wife in a small, but very comfortable and nicely furnished cottage. We spoke much of you, and I was not a little pleased with the kind expressions with regard to you which I listened to as they fell from her lips. Mrs. Ericsson is delighted at your success and reads every account of the *Monitor* with the deepest interest, and is still venturing to hope that you will one day return to England, and afford her the opportunity of again proving the affection which she has ever cherished for you.

If you can, without trouble, occasionally forward me a paper containing anything of interest respecting yourself, by doing so you will confer a favor on   Your faithful friend,

CHARLES FOX.

Mrs. Ericsson sent her own congratulations as follows:

No. 2, CANNING PLACE, GLOUCESTER ROAD,
KENSINGTON GATE, April 2, 1862.

I duly received the illustrated paper announcing the most surprising intelligence of the result of your genius, which I think has startled all Europe. Your triumph has at length arrived, at a crisis which must make your heart palpitate with a pride and joy almost too exquisite to endure. You are now on an eminence from which you can survey with *scorn* those in Europe who never gave you a fair field for your talents. The *Times'* leading article is fraught with the subject of your success, and it has come like a thunderbolt upon all nations and I think has truly verified what you stated in your last letter, "that England would shortly tremble" at the revolution which would take place in warfare.

Probably you doubt my assurance when I tell you that my gratification at your triumph over all the world makes my nights sleepless with excitement, and though in *reality* I am not *tangibly* identified with it, I am in heart and soul made happy. The word of praise from *me* would fall listlessly on your ear when all are proclaiming your achievements, so good taste dictates I should be silent; yet, notwithstanding, my sympathies are fully enlisted. My prayer for your success has been granted by Providence for this proud climax of your reputation, and I feel sure soon in the midst of the tumultuous roar of praise and idolatry by which you are surrounded a stray *thought* of yours will waft its way to my home.

You are by this time in possession of mine of March 19th, to which I trust soon to have an answer. With earnest wishes that your health may be preserved and that every happiness may attend you, I am as ever,   AMELIA.

P. S.—A thousand thanks for your kindness in sending me the paper.

This letter is interesting, not only as a part of Ericsson's history at this period but because of the light it throws upon his relations to his wife. The correspondence between them had reference chiefly to his remittances for her support, but it was constant, and occasionally illuminated by flashes of the old affection which seems never to have died out from the heart of either. All the letters from Mrs. Ericsson found among her husband's files are endorsed in his handwriting " Duck," the familiar name by which she was known to him and to her family. She was a woman of great kindness of heart but wayward in disposition. They parted with mutual consent, and as she would not come to the United States, and he could not return to England, they never met again.

March 28, 1862, the 37th Congress, during its second session, passed this joint resolution :

Resolved by the Senate and House of Representatives of the United States of America in Congress assembled,

That it is fit and proper that a public acknowledgment be made to Captain John Ericsson, for his enterprise, skill, energy, and forecast, displayed by him in the construction of his iron-clad boat the *Monitor*, which, under gallant and able management, came so opportunely to the rescue of our fleet in Hampton Roads, and perchance, of all our coast defences near, and arrested the work of destruction then being successfully prosecuted by the enemy with their iron-clad steamers, seemingly irresistible by any other power at our command—and that the thanks of Congress are hereby presented to him for the great service which he has thus rendered to the country.

The Legislature of New York also passed resolutions thanking Ericsson for his great services to the country. These were handsomely engrossed on parchment, set in a fine gilt frame on which were depicted the *Monitor* and its construction, and presented by a committee of six members of the Legislature. They ever after hung in a place of honor in Ericsson's house. Some of the leading engineering establishments and shipbuilding firms also presented a magnificent model of the *Monitor* made of gold, weighing upward of fourteen pounds and costing $7,000. The entire detail of the turret, the machinery, etc., was represented in this model. It proved a white elephant, however, as its presentation established a " claim " upon the part of the artist, and after expending $4,000 in answering these demands, and in keeping this valuable piece of plate insured, Captain Ericsson finally sent it to the goldsmith's to be melted up. It yielded $600 for its metal and the proceeds were devoted to charity.

Immediately upon the receipt of the news from Hampton Roads a special meeting of the Chamber of Commerce of the City of New York was called for March 12, 1862. Ericsson was invited to attend, and he received the warmest possible greeting when he entered the Chamber under the escort of one of the members, Mr. Prosper W. Wetmore, on whose motion he was unanimously chosen an honorary member. The Chamber then adopted with great enthusiasm these resolutions offered by Mr. Charles Gould :

Resolved, That the Chamber of Commerce of the State of New York gratefully recognize, and desire to place on record, their profound sense of the obligations under which Captain Ericsson has placed the people of the United States. To his genius and activity is due their salvation from a national disgrace, and disasters for which otherwise there could have been no remedy.

Resolved, That the floating battery *Monitor* deserves to, and will be forever mentioned with gratitude and admiration.

Resolved, That the Chamber of Commerce expect that the Government of the United States will make to Captain Ericsson such suitable return for his inestimable services as will evince the gratitude of a great nation.

Resolved, That a copy of these resolutions, duly certified, be forwarded to Captain Ericsson and to the President of the United States.

Captain Ericsson was called upon and delivered a speech— the only one by him found upon record. A report of this is entered in the Minutes of the Chamber of Commerce as follows :

Captain Ericsson, during his remarks, alluding to the voyage of the *Monitor* to Fortress Monroe, said:

I cannot permit this opportunity to pass without saying that I look upon the success of that as being entirely owing to the presence of a master-mind [Mr. Stimers]. The men were new; their passage had been very rough, and the master had to put his vessel right under the heaviest guns that were ever worked on shipboard. It is evident that but for the presence of a master-mind on board of that vessel, that success could not have been achieved. Captain Worden, no doubt, acquitted himself in the most masterly manner. But everything was quite new. He felt quite nervous before he went on board. The fact that the bulwark of the vessel was but one foot above the water-line was enough to make him so. When I was before the Naval Committee the grand objection was that in sea-way the vessel would not work. I gave it as my opinion that it would prove the most easy-working in sea-way, and it is an excellent sea boat. The men are supplied with fresh air, though there is no opening except through the turret, by means of blowers worked by the engines, and they are perfectly comfortable. They can remain in the top of the turret in the sea-way; it is sixty feet in circumference—quite a promenade. Though the deck is but a foot above the water-line, the top of the turret is nine feet above; and here is the important point, that this vessel is in the sea-way perhaps the safest vessel ever built. It takes six hundred and seventy thousand pounds to bring her down. There can be no danger of her swamping. It is very much like a bottle with a cork in it.

In relation to the point whether the *Monitor* is capable of taking care of the *Merrimac*, let me say that she would have sunk the *Merrimac* but for the fact of her having fired too high. If they had kept off at a distance of two hundred yards, and held the gun exactly level, the shot would have gone clear through. But Mr. Stimers had the guns elevated a little, and the roof of the *Merrimac* is so strong that the balls rebounded. Next time they encounter the *Merrimac* they will have the guns level, and they won't mind if the ball strikes the water, because the ricochet will take it where they want it. The next time they go out I predict the third round will sink the *Merrimac*.

There is another great point. They had fifty wrought-iron shot which were not used. Captain Dahlgren issued peremptory orders that they should not be used, and they obeyed those orders. Now, a wrought-iron shot is one thing, and a cast-iron shot is another. A wrought-iron shot cannot break. The side-armor of the *Merrimac* is insufficient to resist it. The channel is very narrow, and the *Merrimac* must follow it. But the *Monitor* can go anywhere and take the very best position.

The merchants of New York might well do honor to the constructor of the *Monitor*, for through his instrumentality their anxious dreams of the destruction of their wealth had been set at rest, and their hope of final victory over the rebellious States revived. The news of the repulse of the *Merrimac* had followed hard upon a despatch of General Wool to the authorities at Washington, announcing that probably both the *Minnesota* and *St. Lawrence* would be captured, and saying: "It was thought that the *Merrimac* and *Jamestown* and *Yorktown* would pass the fort to-night [Sunday, March 8th]. It was also admitted that if the *Merrimac* prepared to attack the fort it would be only a question of a few days when it must be abandoned." As the Comte de Paris says in his history of our war:

"All the previsions of the Federals, founded upon the superiority of their magnificent fleet of wooden vessels, would have disappeared with the *Cumberland* and the *Congress*. The war would have changed front, and the Confederate flag, opening a new era in marine warfare, would easily have raised the blockade which prevented the Slave States from freely procuring supplies in Europe."

A member of the New York Chamber of Commerce, familiar with the circumstances of that time, afterward wrote to Ericsson, saying:

I recall the situation in which this city was placed in the opening weeks of the war growing out of the Rebellion, and when on several occasions the Mayor of New York (Mr. George Opdyke) called together in council some of its trusted citizens, eminent in various callings, to devise means for defending its approaches. The best plan that could be suggested was to form "rafts" or "floats" of timber which should occupy the channels and be held in place by anchorage and chains. For this purpose and to this end considerable sums of money were unofficially expended. It was not then made known to them that you were engaged on your first monitor—and even had it come to their knowledge, it is doubtful whether, with their lack of scientific information, their fears would have been allayed.

When the final hour of trial came, and the best efforts of the navy had been uselessly expended against the *Merrimac* (the source of all our anxiety), then it was that the *Monitor*, almost unknown, with its magic presence appeared to give victory to our arms and forever make secure our harbors from a foreign attack. The controlling power of other vessels, soon after constructed on the *Monitor* plan, redeemed our navy from the inefficiency and contempt with which it was regarded by our enemies, as well as the naval powers of the world.

"Great was the joy in the North," says another chronicle of the times, "when news came that the *Monitor* had turned the current of affairs, but greater yet was it in Washington where boats were laden with stone to be sunk in the channel, in case the *Merrimac* destroyed her adversaries."

Lieutenant (afterward Admiral) Worden, who commanded the *Monitor*, was much disturbed by Ericsson's speech at the Chamber of Commerce. Two years after the fight, Ericsson's associate, John A. Griswold, said, in a letter dated from the national House of Representatives: "I have just had a call from

Captain Worden. He thinks you did him injustice in your Chamber of Commerce remarks for the sake of complimenting Stimers, and says the 'master spirit' had nothing at all to do with the affair of the *Merrimac*, was not consulted, and was in no special way tributary to the result of that combat."

With this opinion Ericsson did not agree. In the only official report concerning the action of the *Monitor* on the 9th of March, which was in the shape of a telegram from the Assistant Secretary of the Navy, of that date, to the Department, Mr. Fox says: "Lieutenant Worden, who commanded the *Monitor*, handled her with great skill, and was assisted by Chief Engineer Stimers."

Mr. Stimers won upon Ericsson by his absolute faith in the *Monitor*, which went much beyond that displayed by those in control of her. March 24, 1862, he wrote:

I told the Flag (Flag-Officer Goldsborough) my idea of what should be done as follows: We get under way between two and three o'clock in the morning, and at five, as daylight commences to break, we would be alongside of the *Merrimac* in Norfolk, throwing in our heavy shot. After demolishing her we would come back, and if they placed any obstructions in our way we would tell them to remove them or we would razee their town with shells. The old gentleman and his Fleet Captain looked at each other in mutual astonishment and pleasure; they appeared to think that it was almost too much of a madcap scheme to be practicable, but I do not despair of being permitted to put it into practice just as soon as the embargo upon us is let up, which will be the case as soon as the one hundred and thirty thousand troops, now arriving, can come and go again in safety.

Confederate accounts indicate that this plan would have succeeded, if carried out with energy and skill. The "Committee on the Conduct of the War," in their report (vol. i., p. 62) say: "Had Norfolk been captured during the winter of 1861–62, and the *Merrimac* taken possession of or destroyed, the way to Richmond would have been opened and the fatal delays of the Peninsula avoided." The failure to accomplish all that was expected and intended was one of the bitter disappointments of Ericsson's life. When he first heard of the engagement he exclaimed: "The *Monitor* ought to have sunk her in fifteen minutes."

The Chief Engineer of the *Monitor*, First Assistant Engineer Newton, questioned afterwards by the War Committee of Congress why the battle was not more promptly decided against the *Virginia* or *Merrimac*, answered: "It was due to the fact that the power and endurance of the 11-inch Dahlgren guns, with which the *Monitor* was armed, were not known at the time of the battle; hence the commander would scarcely have been justified in increasing the charge of powder above that authorized in the 'Ordnance Manual.' Subsequent experiments developed the important fact that these guns could be fired with thirty pounds of cannon powder, with solid shot. If this had been known at the time of the action, I am clearly of opinion that, from the close quarters at which Lieutenant Worden fought his vessel, the enemy would have been forced to surrender. . . . But for the injury received by Lieutenant Worden, that vigorous officer would very likely have badgered the *Merrimac* to a surrender."

This want of faith in the 11-inch Dahlgrens was not shared by Ericsson, and at that period his opinion on a question of guns was worth more than that of anyone else, and it was justified by the event. His experience had been large and his studies exhaustive. Commencing with his training as an artillerist in the Swedish army, they extended through the period of his labors in connection with the *Princeton* and so down to the date of the completion of the *Monitor*. His mastery of this subject was shown a little later on in his complete victory over united ordnance opinion in England, in a controversy which he conducted through the columns of the New York *Army and Navy Journal*.

But the *Virginia* had created at Washington, and throughout the North, an exaggerated fear of her prowess. Hence the peremptory orders to take no risks, and in war all is risk. So the help McClellan counted on receiving from the navy on the opening of his campaign against Richmond, by way of the Yorktown peninsula, was denied to him, that the *Merrimac* might be watched, instead of destroyed.

As to operating in the James, the Confederate authority before quoted says: "Possibly we might have taken the *Virginia* as far as Harrison's Bar, but such action would have

been absurd from every point of view. As the enemy occupied
both sides of the river above, we could neither coal nor provision
her, and would have been compelled to destroy her in a few
days, if she remained so long uncaptured." He says further:
" The truth was that the ship was not weatherly enough to move
in Hampton Roads at all times with safety, and she never could
have been moved more than three hours' sail from a machine
shop. A shell or two amidships, between wind and water (she
had no knuckle) and her career was closed. She drew twenty-
two feet of water, was in every respect ill-proportioned and
top-heavy ; and what with her immense length and wretched
engines (than which a more ill-contrived, spindling, and unreli-
able pair were never made ; failing on one occasion while the
ship was under fire) she was little more navigable than a tim-
ber-raft. Her quarters for the crew were close, damp, ill-ventilated, and unhealthy ; one-third of the men were always on the
sick list and were most always transferred to the hospital,
where they would convalesce immediately. She steered very
badly and both her rudder and screw were wholly unprotected.
Every man and officer well understood the utter feebleness of
the ship, and the terrible efficiency of the enemy's magnificent
fleet. Most of the men had taken, as they supposed, a last
farewell of wives, children, friends, and had set in order their
worldly affairs. All the lieutenants (Catesby Jones excepted)
had several weeks previously partaken publicly of the holy sac-
rament."

Yet throughout the South expectation as to the performance of the Confederate vessel ran high, and they were as confident as were the Philistines when " they were gathered together at Shochoh " and sent forth their champion, Goliath of
Gath, " armed with a coat of mail." In correspondence with
these hopes were the exaggerated alarms that spread throughout the North, having Washington for their centre. In the
imagination of the excitable Stanton hot shot were already setting fire to the White House. The *Merrimac* was first to take
the Capitol, following the British precedent of 1812. Next
she was to levy tribute on New York, and, after raising the
blockade of the Southern ports, she was to rival the splendid
career of the *Alabama*. She was to secure the possession of

Hampton Roads, which would have made McClellan's peninsula campaign impossible, and all other campaigns requiring the control of the York, the James, and the Appomattox. Fort Monroe was to be captured and the way opened for foreign vessels to the very gates of Richmond. The foreign friends of the Confederacy were to have their hands so strengthened that they could secure the great prize of recognition.

What might have followed had the destruction of the *Virginia* coincided more nearly with McClellan's advent on the Peninsula is suggested by what Pollard in his "Secret History of the Confederacy" (p. 224) tells us of the effect of her self-destruction when, a few months later, on May 10, 1862, she was blown up by her commander "within sight of the *Cumberland's* top-gallant-masts all awash." According to Pollard this catastrophe nearly resulted in the surrender of Richmond and created a public grief so wild and bitter that at one time it was feared the building in which were collected the departments of the Confederate Government might be stormed by a mob. The vessel had been fondly named the "iron diadem of the South," and it was counted the equivalent of an army of fifty thousand men in defence of the Confederate capital.

These expectations and fears may seem exaggerated in the light of to-day, but, in the Spring of 1862, they were very real to those who were watching with hope or with dread the career of the Confederate iron-clad *Merrimac*. They contributed their part to the estimation in which the services of Ericsson were held, and to the confidence in him which placed the building of an iron-clad navy for the United States at his disposal, securing for him the control in the important concerns of a great nation such as has rarely been accorded to a private citizen, however eminent his ability. "The immediate results of the conflict between the *Monitor* and the *Merrimac*," says Swinton in his "Twelve Decisive Battles," "was obviously the overthrow of the great projects conceived by the latter vessel, the salvation of the Union squadron, and the preservation of the blockade and of Fort Monroe. Its wider result was to furnish to the Union a new engine of warfare, which, rapidly and cheaply constructed, proved impregnable in defence and irresistible in attack.

"The 15-inch gun in the impregnable *Monitor* turret, mutters with its deep voice, 'Hands off!' to whatever transatlantic nation might before have meditated an interference in the American war. Before the rapidity of the achievement was comprehended a squadron of monitors patrolled the Atlantic seaboard, capable of destroying any fleet that might challenge entrance to its harbors. The lesson was not lost upon foreign ministers, who inclined to think twice before encountering this new and terrible engine of defence.

"The story of the battle of Hampton Roads created the profoundest sensation in the court of every maritime nation. For months, not only the scientific, but the popular journals were filled with the discussion of its merits and its meaning; the professional naval world was profoundly agitated; admiralty boards and ministers of marine conned its details; in fine, Russia and Sweden promptly accepted the *Monitor* as the solution of the naval problem of the age, and followed the lead of America in reconstructing their navies on that system. France and England had, unfortunately for themselves, been committed to the broadside iron-clad before the introduction of the *Monitor*, and the enormous sums already laid out—enough to build many squadrons of monitors—joined to some national pride, and, in the case of England at least, reinforced by a wondrous obstinacy of depreciation only to be understood when one reads such histories as that of the screw-propeller—these causes prevented the renunciation in France and England of their iron-clad navies already built, and the substitution of the turreted *Monitor*.

"However, in both countries the combat of March 9th was received with the profoundest study, and was regarded as the death-stroke to wooden war vessels. In England, on hearing the news of the battle, the House of Commons, in obedience to general sentiment, stopped at once the great military project of building forts at Spithead for the defence of Portland. The Defence Commission, too, was hastily reassembled for the special purpose of considering the effect of the 'recent engagement that has taken place in the Chesapeake between the naval forces of the United States and the Confederates' on the erection of these forts. The Royal Commission found 'the expression of opinion which followed the action of the *Merrimac* and *Monitor*,' and the doubts that took possession of the public mind 'thereupon to be not unreasonable.' But when, notwithstanding these doubts, the Commission had the hardihood to recommend the construction of the forts, the Government, again menaced by the House of Commons, was forced to abandon this position, and the proposed Spithead forts were given up, reliance being had for defence, in the future, upon ironclad vessels."

The world had begun to accept the judgment pronounced upon the *Monitor* and her creator by the officer commanding her antagonist in the Hampton Roads, Catesby Jones, when he said: "I am one of the admirers of the *Monitor* and of Ericsson. He is a great genius."